To Cui

Henreitta Alten Yest

Preserve Your Memories

HENRIETTA ALTEN WEST

*This book is dedicated to the boys of Camp Shoemaker
and those of us who love them.*

CONTENTS

Cast of Characters, VII

Preface, IX

Prologue, XI

Chapter 1, 1

Chapter 2, 9

Chapter 3, 17

Chapter 4, 23

Chapter 5, 32

Chapter 6, 38

Chapter 7, 47

Chapter 8, 53

Chapter 9, 63

Chapter 10, 69

Chapter 11, 77

Chapter 12, 82

Chapter 13, 95

Chapter 14, 99

Chapter 15, 108

Chapter 16, 118

Chapter 17, 128

Chapter 18, 135

Chapter 19, 145

Chapter 20, 153
Chapter 21, 162
Chapter 22, 174
Chapter 23, 183
Chapter 24, 195
Chapter 25, 203
Chapter 26, 216
Chapter 27, 226
Chapter 28, 237
Chapter 29, 248
Chapter 30, 254
Chapter 31, 262
Chapter 32, 274
Chapter 33, 284
Chapter 34, 289
Chapter 35, 298
Chapter 36, 305
Chapter 37, 309
Chapter 38, 318
Chapter 39, 326
Chapter 40, 330

Epilogue, 337
When Did I Grow Old?, 340
Acknowledgments, 343
About the Author, 345

CAST OF CHARACTERS

Elizabeth and Richard Carpenter
Elizabeth and Richard live in a small town on the Eastern Shore of Maryland. Richard is a retired pathologist who did some work for the Philadelphia Medical Examiner's office many years ago. Elizabeth is a former college professor and CIA analyst.

Gretchen and Bailey MacDermott
Gretchen and Bailey live in Dallas, Texas. Bailey is a former IBM salesman, oil company executive, and Department of Defense intelligence agent. He currently is making another fortune selling commercial real estate. Gretchen works in the corporate world as the head of an HR department. Because she is so competent at everything she does, she actually runs the company she works for.

Tyler Merriman and Lilleth DuBois
Tyler and Lilleth live in southern Colorado. Everyone suspects that Tyler flew the SR-71 Blackbird for the U.S. Air Force during his younger years. After he retired from the military, he made millions in commercial real estate. He flew his own plane around the country. Lilleth is a psychologist who works on a reservation counseling Native Americans. She is a superb athlete and a beautiful younger woman.

CAST OF CHARACTERS

Sidney and Cameron Richardson
Sidney and Cameron have several homes and their own private plane. Cameron is a former IBM wunderkind who went out on his own to start several globally-known computer companies. Sidney is a retired profiling consultant who owned an innovative, successful, and fast-growing business before she married Cameron.

Isabelle and Matthew Ritter
Isabelle and Matthew live in Palm Springs, California. Matthew is a retired urologist, an avid quail hunter, and a movie buff. Isabelle has retired from her career as a clinical psychologist and now owns a popular high-end interior furnishings store and design business.

Olivia and J.D. Steele
Olivia and J.D. live in Saint Louis. J.D. is a lawyer who gave up his job as a prosecuting attorney to found his own extremely profitable trucking company. He is a logistics expert. Olivia is a former homecoming queen, a brilliant woman who worked as a mathematician and cypher specialist for the NSA.

Preface

SOME OF THE MOST POIGNANT MUSICAL LYRICS, FOR ME, have always been the lines at the end of the Simon and Garfunkle song "Old Friends/Bookends Theme." The music and words resonate with people of all ages. When I first heard this song as a young person, my heart was touched. Many years later, when I hear it as an old person, I am moved to tears. This book is written about old friends. *Preserve Your Memories* is a sequel to *I Have a Photograph*. The mysteries in this story center around events and memories from the past.

Prologue

THIS YEAR THEY FOUND THEIR WAY FROM ALL CORNERS OF the USA to Colorado. One of the couples in the group lived in Colorado, and they thought driving to the resort and driving back home would be easy. Everyone else had to fly to the yearly reunion.

After their adventures in Maine the previous year, the Camp Shoemaker boys and their significant others had requested that a really nice hotel was priority number one. Of course the food always had to be outstanding. The windows of the hotel rooms had to be tightly fitted into the walls. There could be no air leaks around the casings, and the windows were not allowed to rattle. The bathrooms had to have been updated recently, that is, renovated sometime in the last twenty years. There had to be an elevator that guests were allowed to use. The one handicapped person in the group was hoping there would be an accessible room for her in the same building where all of her friends were staying.

They had chosen the extraordinary Penmoor Resort in Colorado Springs, which would more than meet these criteria. The Penmoor went way beyond being comfortable in every possible way. The group of dear friends, who had been celebrating their lives with a reunion trip for the past ten years, also wanted this year's event, their eleventh get-together, to be reasonably relaxing. They were an energetic group, and a few of them craved arduous physical activity. There were two world-class golf courses at the Penmoor. There were an infinite number of hiking trails, from beginner's easy walks to expert's challenging steep mountain courses. There was a lake at the resort, but it was small and decorative, not intended for serious water sports. There would be no kayaking accidents and no water rescues on the agenda in Colorado Springs. The men were in their seventies, and the previous reunion had been way too exciting for them as well as for their younger wives and girlfriends.

Most hoped no one would bring up the subject of Bar Harbor or the man who had tried to destroy them the previous year. He had hurt some of them, but he had met his own demise in the mud flats off the coast of Maine, when he'd stumbled his way into the Atlantic Ocean. Murder and mayhem, snakes in their beds, kidnappings, and dead Russians were among the items they hoped they would not have to confront on the Colorado trip. These subjects would inevitably come up for discussion, but this year, the group was opting for luxury and low-key excitement. Would their week at the Penmoor be able to deliver the drama-free experience they were all looking forward to?

The men in the group had been friends since they were little boys. They'd met when they were eight years old and had all been assigned to Cabin #1 at Camp Shoemaker in the Ozark Mountains. They'd created countless memories during the many summers they'd spent together. They had drifted apart as they'd grown older, but more than a decade ago, Matthew Ritter had organized a reunion for the group of former campers. The boys from Camp Shoemaker, then in their sixties, had spent a long weekend in Palm Springs, with their current partners, and they'd all had the time of their lives. They'd been meeting for a fun-filled long weekend together every year since.

The former campers treasured their friendships, and the women in their lives had formed their own bond. It was a congenial and interesting group, and everyone looked forward to these special reunion trips. They chose to visit places that had stimulating things to do and great food. What they most wanted was to spend time together, talking about the past and hoping for the future. They cherished the memories from their younger years, and they were having an extraordinarily good time making new memories as older people.

Chapter 1

EVERYONE WAS LOOKING FORWARD TO THEIR STAY at the famous Penmoor Resort. Olivia and J.D. Steele were in charge of organizing the trip this year, and they'd done an exceptional job. Olivia was a genius when it came to hospitality, and she had thought of everything. Olivia and J.D. had even flown from St. Louis to stay at the Penmoor a few months before the scheduled reunion — to look at the rooms, get to know the resort's concierge, and generally check out everything to be sure it was going to be top-notch for their friends.

Because Olivia was scheduled for an upcoming hip replacement, she'd occasionally used a wheelchair when she and J.D. had made their pre-reunion visit to Colorado Springs. She made sure that everything was handicap accessible and handicap friendly. This was an extraordinary level of research into the venue that went above and beyond. All of these efforts would pay remarkable dividends.

Expectations were high. Everyone had stories to tell. During the months since they'd seen each other in Bar Harbor, they'd all traveled extensively. The Richardsons had been to Dubai and had made several trips to Panama for stem cell injections.

The Steeles had traveled to Italy, Croatia, and the Dalmatian Coast. Gretchen MacDermott was one of the younger wives, and she constantly traveled for work. Her husband Bailey was still active in commercial real estate, and he and Gretchen had enjoyed a ten-day cruise in the Baltic Sea. Most of the group were retired, but Gretchen was not anywhere close to being ready to give up the job she loved. The Ritters had spent the Christmas holidays traveling in Europe, visiting their son's in-laws in Germany. Matthew Ritter and Richard Carpenter, accompanied by their wives, had spent a week in New Orleans attending their fiftieth reunion from Tulane Medical School. The time spent with former classmates in the Big Easy had been a truly auspicious occasion. The best news of all was that Tyler Merriman had recovered from the injuries he had incurred in Maine the previous fall. Both he and Lilleth had been able to take full advantage of the ski slopes at Telluride that winter.

In spite of this vigorous and extensive travel report, there had also been some momentous changes and a few down sides in their lives since they'd last been together. Two couples had sold their large homes where they had lived for many years and raised their children. They'd moved to smaller, more manageable, and low-maintenance houses and condominiums. In addition to minor illnesses and the usual annoying vicissitudes of life, there had been: five stem cell injections, four joint replacements, three cases of pneumonia, two bouts with gout, and one idiot who fell out of her office chair. (The previous to be sung to the tune of the "Twelve Days of Christmas.") The office chair incident, the partridge in a pear tree, was not as minor as it might sound. Elizabeth's office chair had wheels. She had leaned forward, and the chair had scooted backwards — out from under her. She was unable to keep herself from landing hard on her tailbone on a hard tile floor. Thankfully, nothing was broken, but it was weeks before she could get in and out of bed or even roll over in bed without pain. Such is life when one is in the eighth decade of life, and all were delighted to still be around to tell the tales.

Olivia had given a great deal of thought to the schedule for the event. The group had decided to stay a full week this year. Travel was becoming more difficult as the years went by, and quick trips were not as popular as they once had been. Because the Penmoor is a much-loved destination, and because it is difficult to co-ordinate the schedules of six busy couples, the reunion had to be pushed into October. Usually the group met in late September, but this year they would get together during the third week of October. Colorado Springs normally doesn't get much significant snow until November, so when plans were finalized in the early spring, bad weather was the last thing on anyone's mind.

Olivia was always tuned in to everybody's needs. She had undergone two hip replacements, so she was fully aware of how difficult it was, for someone who couldn't walk very well or very far, to get around. She reserved a luxurious handicap accessible room for Elizabeth and Richard Carpenter, and she made sure every tour bus she scheduled had a wheelchair lift. This would enable Elizabeth to participate in all the activities. The foresighted Olivia was also a thoughtful friend.

The Steeles knew their group well. Olivia and J.D. had planned tours to see interesting places in the area. They'd made reservations at several of the resort's excellent restaurants, including the elaborate Sunday brunch. Good food was important to these people. And, they had included plenty of time for what was becoming something of a cultural salon for the members of the group. Because they had reserved so many rooms and because Olivia and J.D. had become friends with the concierge, the couple was upgraded to a four-room suite in the Penmoor West.

The room was large and electronically up-to-date. It would be ideal for the movie montage videos Matthew Ritter would show, the presentation on "Climate Change" Cameron Richardson wanted to give, and the documentary about the alleged dangers of cell phone use that Tyler Merriman was eager to share. Richard Carpenter had prepared a talk, based on the book he was writing about his great-great-great grandfather who had fought in several key battles during the Revolutionary War. Elizabeth Carpenter had published two books since the group's last meeting, and her friends had questions. The Steele's suite was the perfect spot for all of these activities to take place. And it was a comfortable spot for drinking wine together ... another pastime this crowd enjoyed.

Fewer physical activities were planned this year, but the resort offered everything. Those who were so inclined could hike to their heart's content. There was bowling in addition to golf. There were bikes to use, free of charge, and a number of extensive gyms and fitness centers, pools, and tennis courts. Even zip lines were available, should anyone feel especially energetic. There were plenty of offerings for the athletes, as well as for those who wanted to indulge in more sedentary and intellectual pursuits.

All participants had checked the weather and knew early on that warm clothes and coats would be necessary. Colorado Springs was in the mountains, and it was late October. No one had yet thought it would be necessary to pack snow boots. But these were savvy old folks. They had lived a long time and had frequently been faced with the unexpected. Weather almost always produces the unexpected. Even so, it wasn't until a week before they traveled to Colorado that the weather channel began to report that snow might be a factor they would have to contend with.

There was a brief but exciting snow storm in Denver and in southern Colorado the day before they were scheduled to arrive at the Penmoor. Tyler and Lilleth were driving from Bayfield in southern Colorado. Some of the group were flying directly into Colorado Springs, and two couples were flying into Denver. Those flying into the mile high city had hired sedan services to drive them from the Denver Airport to the resort. Thankfully, the weather turned out to be a non-issue for the travelers on their way to the reunion. All runways and roads were cleared and dry and functioning normally by the time they arrived. The snow was still on the ground and on the trees, and there was a winter wonderland quality to the crisp, cold air that greeted the reunion goers.

Having just endured one of the hottest summers in recorded history, everyone found the snow to be a delightful surprise. The Carpenters had been at their Atlantic Coast beach house the previous weekend, watching three of their grandchildren play in the sand and swim in the surf. The Ritters had been downright hot in the Palm Springs sunshine. Dallas and St. Louis had just lived through a frightening series of tornadoes. The quiet serenity of the snow-covered landscape refreshed these older souls.

The Penmoor's main hotel, known as the Penmoor Main, is one of the most beautiful buildings in the United States. All of the resort's hotel rooms are spacious and well-appointed. Anything and everything you could possibly hope for from a hotel, the Penmoor delivers. Probably the best part about staying at the Penmoor is the friendliness of their staff. Every one of them has a smile and a kind word. Guests feel welcomed and at home and know immediately that they will have a more than pleasant experience.

Elle, the lovely and competent concierge, was in the lobby to greet each couple as they arrived. She was gracious and eager to accommodate any special requests the group had. Their luxurious accommodations were in the Penmoor West. There was a tiered tray of fresh fruit and cheeses in each room. There was also a bottle of each couple's favorite wine and a box of special chocolates. Wow! The reunion could not have been off to a better start.

The terrors of the previous year's reunion in Maine were put aside, if not entirely forgotten. The attempted murders and the actual murders had occurred at a different time and in another place. Injuries that had been sustained had healed. The memories would never entirely go away, but this was a resilient bunch. They were ready to make new memories.

Olivia had sent each couple a packet of brochures that included a useful map of the resort, information about everything guests could do at the Penmoor, and flyers about what to see in Colorado Springs. One week would not be enough to take it all in. A schedule of events the Steeles had planned for the reunion group was included. No one wanted to miss anything. The first scheduled item on the agenda was to meet that evening for cocktails at the Penmoor Main's bar.

Olivia, always on the alert and anticipating the unforeseen, determined that the bar in the main building of the Penmoor, the evening's original destination, was full. She organized a table in the bar at the Italian restaurant, La Firenze, located in the Penmoor West where they were all staying. Everyone had been warned about the altitude. Some of the group were coming from zero altitude places, that is, sea level, and they would have to accommodate to being several thousand feet up in the mountains. Sidney ordered hot tea, and Elizabeth ordered a non-alcoholic vanilla Italian cream soda. White wine, in all of its many varieties, was always a favorite. Chardonnay, Pinot Grigio, and Sauvignon Blanc were consumed with gusto. Someone ordered three enormous platters of deep-fried calamari for the group to share. The seafood came with two dipping sauces — marinara and homemade ranch dressing. Those who had flown to Colorado and not had lunch on the plane were starving. They dug in. The calamari was consumed almost before the second glass of wine was ordered.

They were delighted to be together again. Stories were told, and there were many more to tell. Gretchen and Bailey had *another* new grandchild … a boy this time! This beautiful baby had been born just a little more than twelve months after their granddaughter had made her appearance the year before. Cameron had published a new book. Sidney and Cameron were building a river house, an elegant and rustic getaway on a beautiful piece of property in the woods. It sounded like heaven. The Ritters had sold the house they'd lived in for forty years and moved to an elegant condo. They loved their new place. It was within walking distance of many of their favorite restaurants.

Richard's beloved hunting dog, Daisy, had died in March, and he still got tears in his eyes when he reported this sad news. Elizabeth had finally recovered from her fall and from the bad case of pneumonia she'd struggled with all winter. She was thrilled to feel better and to be able to make the trip to see her good friends. Olivia and J.D. had traveled to Italy and the former Yugoslavia, arriving home just two weeks before coming to Colorado Springs. Olivia's hip replacement had scarcely had time to heal. She had hobbled all over Europe, and she continued to use a cane. They were still excited about the beauty of the Dalmatian Coast and the private art tours they had arranged at the Uffizi. Gretchen had just flown in from a conference in Los Angeles. She was always up to something exciting. Bailey reported that the recent tornadoes which had hit the Dallas area had missed their house by one mile. They were thankful to have been spared. Tyler and Lilleth arrived after having driven for six hours, and they were more than ready for a glass of wine.

One member of the reunion group, Teddy Sullivan, and his actor friend Conrad Watson were in Los Angeles, working on a full-length movie. They were way too busy to even think about coming to Colorado Springs. Teddy reported that he'd been either promoted or demoted from being a technical advisor to having an acting role in the film. According to Elizabeth, who stayed in touch with Teddy, he sounded happier than he'd ever been. Maybe the silver screen had been his true calling all along. Elizabeth was thrilled for him, but she was sorry he couldn't attend the reunion this year. She missed Teddy.

Someone asked how another member of the group, Darryl Harcomb, was doing. He had suffered a stroke the previous year in Bar Harbor when his wife had died right in front of his eyes, a victim of poisoning. He had never known the beautiful Elena was a Russia spy. Her secret life, as well as her violent death, had been such a shock to him, his blood pressure had gone sky high, and a stroke had threatened his life.

Tyler had learned that Darryl was doing better and was happy to report that Darryl's mind was completely intact. But the physical effects of the stroke still haunted him. He had been released from the rehabilitation hospital and was going every day for outpatient physical therapy. The scuttlebutt was that Darryl had fallen for his physical therapist and she had also fallen for him. He was enjoying his physical therapy sessions, more than he'd ever expected he would. Those in the know said his physical therapist made house calls ... at night ... for her one special patient. Darryl was recovering from his wife's death. The younger and very pretty physical therapist apparently was also an effective grief counselor. Darryl's luck was changing for the better.

Chapter 2

DINNER THE FIRST NIGHT WAS AT THE SALOON, the famous steak house restaurant located on the ground floor of the Penmoor Main, the original building of the historic resort. The Penmoor Main was across the lake from the Penmoor West, the hotel where the reunion group's rooms were located. The temperature was close to freezing that night, and they all had to put on warm coats and gloves. They crossed the lake on the walkway and the footbridge to get to The Saloon. The ambience at the restaurant was Western ... rustic with lots of wood.

The seafood from the raw bar and the steaks were the best. Prime rib is not found on many restaurant menus these days, but it has a prominent spot on the menu at The Saloon. It was a favorite that night — served with au jus, horseradish sauce, and a baked potato loaded with everything. Onion soup, steaks of all sizes and cuts, and Colorado lamb chops were other delicious choices. The bottles of Malbec that Cameron ordered went with everything, including the pistachio-encrusted halibut.

Seated together at a table for twelve, they were completely engaged with their own group of friends and oblivious to the other diners. They wanted to continue to catch up on what had happened in each other's lives since the last time they'd been together. They weren't paying attention to other tables or other patrons who were dining at The Saloon. Their table was a little loud and boisterous at times, as the laughter could not be contained, but no one else in the restaurant seemed to care.

Olivia, who always noticed things, had seen someone interesting at a table nearby. She wasn't able to interrupt the lively and ongoing discussion about basketball and the tumultuous events in Hong Kong that held the undivided attention of the guys at her end of the table. She finally was able to catch Isabelle's eye and ask her about the woman who was seated at the table on the other side of the pillar from their group of twelve.

"Is that who I think it is? I know a lot of famous people come here, including a lot of movie stars. Turn around if you can, and see what you think." Olivia's curiosity had the better of her.

"I can't turn around without being obvious. I don't want to stare … even if it is somebody famous. Who do you think it is?" Isabelle had her back to the table where the person, who perhaps was famous, was seated. Isabelle would have to turn completely around in her chair to see who Olivia was talking about.

Famous people had often stayed at the Penmoor Resort during its long history as a world-class hostelry. Several hallways in the Penmoor West were lined with hundreds of framed photographs of the rich and famous, politicians, movie and television stars, world leaders, journalists, and others. It was fun to walk along and see who had visited this delightful place in years past. It was not a stretch to believe that a celebrity was having dinner at the next table.

Elizabeth overheard a bit of what Olivia was saying, and she had a good view of the blonde woman on the other side of the pillar. Sure enough, she agreed that the famous movie actress was sitting there ... cracking the claws of a bright red lobster. For a moment, Elizabeth had a flashback to the last reunion, the trip to Bar Harbor where they had all indulged frequently and outrageously in the mighty crustaceans. Pulling herself back into the present, Elizabeth confirmed that indeed it was Withers Singleton, the star of multiple motion pictures and a two-time Oscar winner. She had an uncanny resemblance to Gretchen MacDermott. Gretchen didn't think they looked that much alike, but people occasionally stopped Gretchen on the street and in other public places to ask her for an autograph, thinking she was Withers.

"You should go over and introduce yourself to her. See if *she* thinks you are her clone." Olivia wanted to meet the famous star and thought Singleton might find it amusing to meet her Doppelganger, aka Gretchen.

"Don't be silly. I would never do something like that. Most famous people don't like to be outed. They have a right be left in peace to enjoy a meal." Gretchen went back to her Caesar salad topped with slices of medium-rare filet mignon. But she did keep glancing at Withers. Gretchen had been compared to Withers Singleton for many years, but she'd never seen the star in person. She'd seen lots of photographs, but this was the first time she'd been able to have an up-close look at the real human being. She had to admit to herself that she was intrigued, but there was no way she was going to approach the woman she so closely resembled.

Olivia continued to watch Singleton's table. The star and her small entourage got up to leave. They had to pass the reunion group on their way out of the restaurant. Olivia could not resist giving a quiet shout out as they walked by. "Love your movies, Withers. I'm a big fan."

The petite blonde turned and smiled and waved at Olivia. "Thanks!" She'd responded, and she seemed pleased to be recognized. She moved on out the door. There was no haughty arrogance, just a polite acknowledgement that someone liked her. Olivia beamed.

"You see, it pays to be assertive." Olivia directed her comment at Gretchen. Gretchen laughed.

Monday had been a full day, and the traveling, the altitude, and the excitement of seeing good friends again and catching up had left them all ready for bed. Plans were made to meet for breakfast. Olivia reminded everyone that they needed to be in the lobby at 9:00 a.m. to get the bus that would take them on a tour of the Garden of the Gods and the United States Air Force Academy. Everyone toasted and thanked Olivia and J.D. for their excellent choice of the Penmoor and their meticulous planning. It had been a great evening.

It was bitterly cold on the walk back to the Penmoor West from the Saloon. Richard Carpenter, who was coming from sea level and was not yet acclimated to the altitude in Colorado Springs, was struggling to push Elizabeth's wheelchair along the walkway across the lake that divided the two hotels. He almost lost control as he began to push his wife over the steep footbridge. Lillleth, noticing that Richard was having a hard time, came to the rescue. She effortlessly pushed Elizabeth's wheelchair the rest of the way to the Penmoor West and down the long hallways to the elevator. Richard was running to keep up with the strong, fit younger woman who had stepped in to help him. He was effusive with his thanks. The modest Lilleth murmured something about living at 6,500 feet and already being used to the altitude. Elizabeth thanked Lilleth for "saving both their lives."

The next morning, Richard brought pastries and coffee to Elizabeth in their room. Sidney joined the men for breakfast in the beautiful sunroom that overlooked the mountains and pine trees, now arrayed in white. They gathered in the lobby to wait for their tour bus to arrive. There was a fire in the fireplace and comfortable couches and chairs where they could sit together and talk. Gretchen wanted to say something important to the group, and everyone gave her their full attention.

"I hate to have to tell you this, but I am being stalked. And I think you all need to know about it. The reason I was able to take an entire week off for this trip is because my company wanted me out of harm's way. I am not exactly hiding out here at the Penmoor, but I want you to know what my situation is. I don't think there's any real danger," she paused, "but I've been threatened."

Several members of the group had noticed that Gretchen hadn't been herself the night before. She'd looked tired and had been preoccupied. Revelations about the stalking explained a lot. Sidney asked, "Can you tell us any more about who's threatening you? Do you know who it is? Do you know what he looks like? More importantly, does he know what you look like?"

"Oh, yes, I know quite well who is stalking me. The situation has little to do with me directly, but because I am the boss of the boss of the person who is involved, I have been drawn into the circle of danger, so to speak. I have a picture of the man, and I will show it to you all this afternoon." Gretchen decided to tell her friends more of the story. "My company had to fire an employee at our Chicago headquarters. The man who was fired threatened to come after his boss who is the head of HR there. I am that HR director's vice president, and she appealed to me. She told me everything that had happened, and I supported her decision to terminate the man's employment. She had done all the right things … absolutely, no question about it. The details about why the guy was let go aren't important to the story, but the employee somehow found out that I had agreed with his boss that he should be fired. So both the head of HR at the Chicago office and I are on the man's hate list. He is an angry and dangerous fellow. He went to his former boss's home and shot at her through her front door. He knocked on the door, and when she came to answer it, he opened fire. She was seriously wounded. She was taken to the hospital for surgery, but she's going to make it."

"This is a terrible story, like something on the nightly news. How unfortunate that you've become involved with this troubled individual." Richard Carpenter was worried. As a retired pathologist, he had done too many autopsies on victims of workplace shootings.

"It is a pretty terrible story, and it gets worse. The former employee escaped after he shot his boss at her house. He's at large, and the FBI is searching for him. They don't believe he's in the Chicago area any longer. He's never actually seen me in person, but he knows who I am. He sent a barrage of threatening faxes to our Dallas headquarters, all with my name on them." Gretchen sighed and her shoulders sagged. She loved her work so much, and having this black cloud over her office was getting her down.

She continued. "Our company's promotional pamphlets and brochures show photos of the vice presidents of various divisions. My photograph appears in much of this company literature. So he may have seen my photo, or he might not know what I look like at all. We just don't know. My photo in the corporate literature was taken several years ago. I look a little older now." Gretchen tried to smile when she said all of this. "But still. He announced, when he left the company, that he was going after his immediate boss and after me because I agreed with her that he should be fired. In light of the crimes he has already committed, the company and I have had to take his threats seriously. The hospital room of my colleague in Chicago is being guarded 24/7 in case the shooter returns to finish the job."

"My boss asked me to take some time off. This nut job threatened to come to Dallas and find me. It's safer for me and for others in the company if I don't go into my office until the man is caught. Although taking time off right now throws my work schedule into utter chaos, this trip to Colorado Springs came along at the perfect time." Gretchen was trying to make lemonade out of her lemons.

Gretchen's friends were all quite concerned. No wonder Gretchen had been preoccupied last night. No wonder she had not been herself. Everyone had hoped this year's reunion would be free of danger, but it looked as if danger had been stalking one of their own even before she'd arrived at the Penmoor.

"How can we help make this easier for you?" Cameron was asking. He was a fixer, always trying to make things better, in big ways and small ways.

"My boss told me to get out of Dallas, go to a nice place, and have a good time. He said to think of it as a paid vacation. He likes me and doesn't want anything to happen to me. He paid for my plane fare to Colorado Springs. He's paying for my room and for my meals while I'm here. I am trying to relax and enjoy myself, but I can't help but be tense. Please forgive me if I'm grumpy or if I snap at you. I don't mean it."

"Does the FBI have any idea where this guy is now? Are they telling you anything?" J.D. was a former prosecutor and knew how badly something like this could turn out. He was worried, too.

"The FBI is keeping my boss informed, and when they tell him something important that he thinks I ought to know, he sends me a text. Nobody knows I'm here, except you guys. Nobody at work knows where I am. My boss doesn't even know. He didn't want me to tell him where I was going. I'm not going to wear a disguise or anything like that." Gretchen gave Bailey a small grin, remembering that Bailey had tried to disguise himself as a woman at a restaurant in Maine the year before. Bailey grimaced at her joke. "Mr. and Mrs. Bailey MacDermott are registered to a vacant room. The room Bailey and I are actually staying in is registered under my maiden name. I talked to Elle, the concierge. She understands my situation. Many people who require extra security, come to the Penmoor. She's used to things like this, more used to it than I am."

Olivia signaled that their bus had arrived, and they all headed for the porte-cochère in front of the hotel's main entrance to get on board for the tour. Several people in the group gave Gretchen hugs as they left the lobby's warmth and comfort. Gretchen looked more relaxed, now that she had shared the burden of her predicament with the others. Bailey looked hugely relieved that somebody besides himself knew what Gretchen was facing. They were all sobered by what they'd heard. They would not leave Gretchen by herself. She would be protected, by anonymity and by her friends.

Chapter 3

BAILEY MACDERMOTT GRADUATED WITH AN engineering degree from the University of Arkansas. He was hired by IBM directly out of college, and because of his outgoing personality and gift for gab, he quickly became one of Big Blue's best salesmen in his region. But Bailey was an independent guy, and he felt as if he was being smothered in the corporate world. He'd been selling computer systems to the oil industry, to help them with payroll and inventory and to keep track of where their oil was coming from and where it was going. Bailey let a couple of his clients know he was interested in making a change, and within a few weeks he had a job offer from a major oil company. He submitted his resignation at IBM and left his job in Chicago. Houston was calling, and Bailey was ready to conquer the oil business and earn some big money. Soon he was flying back and forth from Houston to the oil-rich kingdoms in the Middle East. Before long, he knew the countries and who the movers and shakers were in the world's wealthiest oil-producing nations.

When the Shah of Iran fell, the world, and especially the Middle East, was turned upside down. Previously ignored actors on the world's political and economic scene were on the march, and a few days after the hostages in Iran were taken, the U.S. Department of Defense was knocking on Bailey's door. He was a patriot and agreed to work with the DIA, one of the pentagon's spy agencies.

At first, he just met with other Americans in Riyadh and other Arab capitals. He carried the packages and papers these agents asked him to take back with him when he flew home to the U.S. Then he was asked to meet with foreign nationals and accompany them to safe houses. Once, in Lebanon, he had to rescue an American who was in desperate shape, running from Hezbollah, and suffering from serious gunshot wounds in his leg and thigh. Bailey drove the man to the airport in his rental car and slipped him aboard the oil company's plane. Bailey's assignments became more and more complex and more and more dangerous. He told himself he was doing all of this because he was helping to fight terrorism, but he also loved the rush he got from taking risks.

After a particularly harrowing mission, Bailey had to take some time off from his regular job with the oil company and from his special work for the DIA. He spent a month recuperating in Paris. He slept late and ate well. He also met and fell in love with an American woman he met at the Rodin Museum. Bailey had gone there to learn more about the sculpture. Marianna Archer was at the museum posing for magazine photographs. She was a gorgeous redhead who earned her living as a highly-paid fashion model. She was doing a photoshoot for an American fashion magazine and was dressed in tight stretch stirrup pants, enormous earrings, and a sexy faux suede off-the-shoulder top. Bailey stumbled into the room where Marianna had her arms draped around "The Thinker." That day Bailey completely missed seeing Rodin's most famous work of art, but he couldn't take his eyes off Marianna as she pranced and posed around the naked man made out of bronze.

It was the 1980s and Bailey MacDermott decided he had been a bachelor long enough. Marianna was a lonely ex-pat living in France, and she quickly succumbed to Bailey's warm and friendly personality. They spent a lot of time at her apartment getting acquainted, and before Bailey's month of vacation was over, the two were married. It was probably a mistake for them to marry, even under the best of circumstances. The complexity of their work lives and the travel both of their jobs required meant they spent a lot of time apart. Their time together was frenetic, and they never had a chance to really get to know each other.

What Bailey didn't know about Marianna was that she was manic-depressive, a mental illness that has since been renamed "bipolar 1 disorder." If she stayed on her meds, Marianna was mostly fine and a lot of fun. When she went off her meds, all bets were off. When they returned to the U.S., she realized she was pregnant. Bailey and Marianna's son was born in Houston, and Bailey was beside himself with joy. Marianna, on the other hand, lapsed into post-partum depression and a serious depressive phase of her mental illness. She reached the point where she didn't want to get out of bed at all.

Bailey and Marianna eventually divorced. She ceded custody of their son to Bailey, but Bailey was juggling too many things. He told the DoD he wasn't able to work for them anymore, and he quit his job working for the oil company because he didn't want to travel all the time. He began dealing in oil futures and was incredibly successful in this field. He made a lot of money, but the best part of his life at this time was that once he settled down in Dallas, he was able to make a home for himself and his son.

Before he met Gretchen, rumors flew that he had married again in haste twice and then quickly divorced twice! He didn't like to talk about what had happened in his love life during this period, and no one wanted to ask. It was clearly a painful subject for Bailey.

Gretchen Johanssen technically worked in human resources, but she was one of those people who was so competent that, wherever she worked, she eventually took over running much more than the HR department. She was petite and fit, and her good looks and style attracted attention. Once you got to know Gretchen and once you had worked with her for a while, because of her extraordinary competence, you forgot how small she was. Her abilities and her organizational skills belied her size, and she took on a significant presence in any room where she worked or spoke.

Gretchen had married twice and had two wonderful sons. She adopted and raised a foster daughter. When her sons were launched, one into the military and the other to college, and her daughter was in graduate school, Gretchen decided to take a job with an international financial group. She had always wanted to travel and was excited to be sent to run the HR department at her company's office in Zurich.

As always happened when Gretchen arrived on the scene, her ability to get things accomplished was immediately recognized, and she took on more and more responsibilities, above and beyond her HR duties. She always attracted attention at a board meetings. When she made an outstanding presentation to a group of international businessmen, the head of one of Switzerland's wealthiest and most secretive banks noticed her. He wanted to date her and wanted to hire her to work for him. He offered her a salary three times what she was earning in her current job. She agreed to take the lucrative position as his special advisor, but she never mixed business and romance.

The Swiss banker was smart enough to agree to her terms, and Gretchen spent several years making top-level decisions in the arcane world of Swiss banking and international finance.

She became fluent in German. She met arms dealers, heads of state, assassins, movie stars, Russians and Saudis, and people she was sure were mafia figures or drug dealers or both. She helped her employers invest their clients' riches. She knew the identities of many who had secret money and needed to conceal it.

When one of her ex-husbands was murdered, Gretchen returned to the United States. Her son, who was a Navy Seal, was involved in an almost-fatal car accident, and Gretchen wanted to spend time with him, helping him heal and boosting his spirits as he recovered. She was an accomplished corporate operator, but she was first and foremost a mother. It was while her son was recovering the use of his legs at a rehabilitation center in Texas that Gretchen met Bailey.

Bailey volunteered at the VA hospital where Gretchen's son was going for physical therapy. Bailey still made deals of all kinds. He had branched out from oil futures into commercial real estate, and it seemed that whatever he touched turned to gold. Volunteering to work with military personnel who were trying to get back on their feet was Bailey's way of giving back. He loved his work, but he loved working with the disabled vets even more. He spent time with Gretchen's son on an almost daily basis, and it was the young Navy Seal who introduced Bailey MacDermott to his mother.

Bailey and Gretchen had both been burned in the marriage department. Neither one was looking for a spouse. Each of them was happy living alone, but as they spent more and more time in each other's company, they realized how much they loved each other and wanted to spend the rest of their lives together.

Gretchen had taken a job with a company in Dallas, and in no time, she had, as she always did, made herself indispensable to her new company. She was the kind of employee who quickly became critical to the organization. When she mentioned the possibility of retirement, she was offered a large bonus to stay on for two more years. At the end of those two years, when the subject of retirement came up again, she was offered an even larger bonus, if she would just stay on a little longer. She might never retire because she was making too much money just by mentioning the word "retirement."

Bailey had moved into doing deals in international real estate, and this new clientele sometimes presented challenges. There were language barriers, although most people involved in the upper echelons of the business world spoke English. There were cultural differences, especially when it came to determining what was legal and ethical and what was not. Most of his clients were legitimate buyers who actually wanted to own a warehouse in Hong Kong or Mexico or an apartment building in Singapore. But a few clients who contacted Bailey were interested in buying real estate for the purposes of laundering money.

The schemes the money-launderers devised were complicated and slick. Bailey found himself involved in a couple of these transactions before he caught on to what was happening. When he realized what these faux buyers were up to, he had to say no. He refused to participate in any money laundering intrigue. More than once, a disappointed money launderer had threatened Bailey's life. Bailey loved the rush and the risk of doing high-flying business transactions, but he definitely did not enjoy having a loaded gun pressed against his head. When one of these crooks tracked him to his home and threatened him, Bailey and Gretchen had to move to a different house. Bailey learned to be more discreet, but it was impossible for him to give up the thrill of making a deal. Now he was always wary when he took on a new client. In his early seventies, he was a vital and busy wheeler-dealer in the financial world.

Chapter 4

Boarding the tour bus was more exciting than usual because Elizabeth was being loaded by means of a wheelchair lift. It was difficult for her to climb up the steps to get on the bus, and impossible for her to climb down the steps to get off the bus. She thought she might need her wheelchair during the tour, so she put herself in the hands of the bus driver. She had never boarded a bus on a wheelchair lift before. Everyone had their fingers crossed that the driver had a lot of experience using the lift and loading wheelchairs. Elizabeth held her breath, as she was easily maneuvered up and into the bus. The contraption worked perfectly. She sighed with relief. Locking the chair's wheels onto the floor of the bus took more time and was more trouble than actually lifting the wheelchair onto the bus. Elizabeth got out of the wheelchair and sat in one of the more comfortable bus seats next to Richard. The driver took his place behind the wheel, and the tour was underway.

The Garden of the Gods is a popular Colorado Springs tourist destination of breathtaking vistas and natural sandstone formations. Their driver gave a good history of the place and told them how it had acquired its name. He stopped the bus, and most of the group chose to get out and walk around to look at the sights. Elizabeth stayed on board. Next they were on their way to the United States Air Force Academy. One of their group had attended the USAF Academy, but many years had passed since Tyler Merriman had been a cadet. Much about the campus had changed.

J.D. Steele had also been in the United States Air Force. He had not attended the Air Force Academy, but he had served his country as a member of the USAF JAG Corps. Both U.S. Army and U.S. Air Force military personnel were stationed at Ft. Bliss in El Paso, Texas in the 1970s. J.D. was there as part of the USAF legal team. After his active duty service, he'd remained in the Air Force Reserves and had attained the rank of colonel. He still carried his military ID that identified him as a retired U.S. Air Force Colonel. The ID would come in handy when they tried to get through the security checkpoint to drive onto the USAF Academy grounds.

The bus driver had a special ID and was well-known to the security people at the academy's gate. What was unexpected was that the guard said he would be coming on board to check the ID of each person on the bus. The men had their wallets, but several of the women had not brought their IDs. They hadn't known IDs would be necessary. J.D. pulled rank before the security guard stepped onto the bus. He handed his well-worn military ID to the guard through the bus window. The guard looked carefully at J.D.'s military ID and then looked closely at J.D.'s face.

"The photo is a little out of date. I was younger then." J.D. stated the obvious.

The guard was impressed to have an Air Force colonel in his presence, even a retired one. He snapped to attention and saluted J.D. "We were all younger then, Sir." he said. Then he asked, "Is everyone on the bus known to you, Colonel Steele? Can you vouch for each of them?"

J.D. laughed. "Yes, I can vouch for each of them. I have known every one of these jokers for a very long time."

The guard handed back J.D.'s identification and nodded to the driver that it was all right for him to continue through the checkpoint. The guard stood at attention beside the security kiosk, saluting Colonel J.D. Steele, until the bus was out of sight. A cheer for J.D. went up. He had saved them time and probably considerable embarrassment. Some of the group might not have been allowed to enter without an ID.

The most interesting sights were the planes displayed outside at various locations around the academy grounds. The B-52 bomber was so impressive, and J.D. knew more than the driver did about what this plane had done in past wars and what it continued to do today. J.D. had a captive audience for his stories. The "Warthog," the Fairchild Republic A-10 Thunderbolt, was on display, as well as the jet that was similar to the planes used for stunts by the Blue Angels in their airshows. The group gawked and oohed and aahed as they viewed these mighty machines.

The next stop was at the Academy's visitors' center. There was a short movie that several people wanted to see, and there was a bathroom that even more of the group wanted to see. Everybody except Elizabeth got off the bus to check out the visitors' center. Even the driver got off. He excused himself to Elizabeth, who was the only passenger still on board, and said he was going to take a smoke. Elizabeth frowned and was silent. She didn't like smoking.

Elizabeth had a rich interior life and was good at entertaining herself. She never minded being left alone with her imagination. She looked out the window and thought about the Rocky Mountains. She loved having this magnificent view of Pike's Peak, and "Purple Mountains' Majesty" became very real for her. She was glad she was old enough that no one expected her to hike anywhere in those beautiful Rockies.

Being at the Air Force Academy brought back a long-forgotten memory for Elizabeth. The event had occurred many years ago, when she was just eighteen. As a senior in high school, Elizabeth had won first prize in a state essay contest sponsored by the American Legion. The prize was a trip to Washington D.C. with several other essay contest winners. While they were visiting the District of Columbia, the group attended a concert at the Washington National Cathedral. The concert was given by the United States Air Force Academy's choir. It might have been called the glee club or the chapel choir at the time. Elizabeth couldn't remember exactly. The concert had been almost sixty years earlier. At the time, the USAF Academy was all male, so the choir had consisted entirely of young men. The concert had been excellent. Elizabeth was musical and had sung in several singing groups. She'd had the leading role in her high school's recent musical production. She had a special appreciation for the music the singing group from the Air Force had just performed.

After the concert, Elizabeth was standing in the vestibule of the Cathedral, waiting for the group of essay contest winners and their American Legion chaperones to get themselves organized to leave. As she stood there, a tall, good-looking Air Force cadet in his dress uniform approached her. Obviously a member of the group that had just finished singing, he introduced himself to Elizabeth and said, "I would be delighted if you would be my guest at the reception that's being held for members of the Air Force choir and their dates."

Taken by surprise, Elizabeth smiled at the handsome young man. "Oh, I would love to go. I'm Elizabeth Emerson." Elizabeth had been "a looker" at age eighteen, and she had put on her best outfit to attend the concert. She was going to the Washington National Cathedral after all. She wore a yellow silk sheath dress with a wide matching cummerbund-style belt. She was slim and shapely and looked terrific in the snugly-fitted silk. It was April, and she wore a brimmed straw hat that had a yellow silk ribbon hanging down the back. The ribbon matched the fabric of her dress. A blue cashmere cardigan, that was the exact color of her eyes, was over her arm. She knew she looked good. The cadet looked directly into those blue eyes when he spoke, and at that moment Elizabeth wanted nothing more than to take the arm of this young man and accompany him to the reception.

Because she was the oldest in the group of essayists, the American Legion chaperones were somewhat leery of Elizabeth. Elizabeth was legally an adult and would be off to college in a few months. It was 1962, and the chaperones were strict. They wanted to know if Elizabeth had been introduced to the cadet by a mutual friend. They wanted to know if Elizabeth's parents knew the cadet. They wanted to know a great many other ridiculous things. Elizabeth introduced the young man to the chaperones. He was a student at the United States Air Force Academy, and he sang in the choir, for heaven's sake! There was nothing the least bit suspicious about the clean-cut youth in uniform. But her chaperones had suspicions. They looked at him as if he were a sex fiend who wanted to ravage one of their own. In the end, they said Elizabeth could not attend the reception. It would not be proper. The cadet offered to include all the members of the group in his invitation. The chaperones still said no.

With regret on both their faces, they realized that Elizabeth was not going to be allowed to accompany him to the reception. They shook hands and said goodbye. Elizabeth watched his back, as the young man with perfect posture, dressed in his military uniform, walked away and out of her life. She was left standing there, wondering what might have been. Now, being at the USAF Academy for the first time in her life, she wondered what had happened to that nice, polite, and lovely fellow who had been dismissed so gratuitously by her American Legion chaperones. She hoped he hadn't died in Viet Nam or one of the nation's other terrible wars.

Day dreaming and remembering that time from long ago, Elizabeth was brought back to the present when she heard shouting outside the bus. No one else was anywhere in sight, but two men were wrestling and pummeling each other on the ground underneath her window. They were throwing each other up against the side of the bus. The sound of their bodies slamming into the metal was horrific, and they were both screaming.

Elizabeth wondered what she ought to do. Should she call 911? Was it a crime for two people to engage in a wrestling match? Was a public fist fight something 911 needed to know about? She had never before been presented with a situation like this, so she didn't know. When she peered out the window to see how the fight was going and saw blood splattered on the ground, she decided she needed to call the authorities. But her call to 911 would not go through. She wondered if being inside the bus was the reason she didn't have cell phone service. Maybe it was a security thing because they were on Air Force Academy grounds. Maybe cell phone calls were blocked on military installations. Was the service academy considered a military installation? Elizabeth didn't know for sure. She did know her cell phone wasn't working. She watched with alarm as one of the men seemed to gain an advantage over the other. The older man of the two was taking a terrible beating. Elizabeth caught a glimpse of a knife. Somebody could die here today.

She knew it was not possible for her to intervene in any way, and she knew better than to get involved. Elizabeth stayed silent and sank down lower in her bus seat so only the top of her head could be seen from the outside. No one knew there was anybody on the bus to witness the fight. She looked out the window from time to time. Suddenly, one of the men gave up the fight and ran away, leaving the older man in a heap on the ground. The man in the heap wasn't moving, and he looked like he was in pretty bad shape. Elizabeth was panicked that he was dead or dying. She desperately wished that the bus driver or one of her friends would return to the bus. Somebody had to do something.

As she tried to stand up and get to the front of the bus, she saw Matthew Ritter exit the visitors' center and walk towards the bus. He was several hundred yards away, but Elizabeth pushed the window down and yelled to Matthew. "Matthew, get over here! There's a badly injured man lying on the ground beside the bus. He needs a doctor, and he needs 911." Elizabeth didn't know if Matthew had understood anything she'd said, but when he saw her leaning out of the bus window, waving and shouting at him, he began to run in her direction.

While Elizabeth was shouting and before Matthew Ritter could reach the bus, the man lying on the ground had grabbed hold of the side of the bus and pulled himself to his feet. He struggled towards the doors of the bus and pounded on them, wanting someone to open up and let him inside. Elizabeth didn't know what to do. She didn't know how to open the doors of the bus, and even if she'd known how, she had serious reservations about doing that. The man was desperate to get onto the bus and managed to claw the doors open with the brute strength of his hands. He stumbled up the steps. He was covered with blood and had slash wounds on his face and neck. He looked scary. His eyes sought Elizabeth's, and he pleaded, "Please, please. I need help. Don't be frightened. You must let me stay on your bus. You must hide me. I have been betrayed. I have to get to the hotel, to the Penmoor. I will be killed unless you help me." He collapsed across one of the seats, unconscious, bleeding onto the floor.

Elizabeth stood up in the aisle of the bus and began to make her way towards the injured man. Thankfully, Matthew boarded the bus at that moment. He was taken aback by the scene that greeted him. Because he was a physician, when he saw all the blood, he rushed to see what he could do for the victim.

Elizabeth tried to explain. "This guy and another man got into a fight in the parking lot, on the pavement right here beside the bus. I saw them, and it was a pretty serious fight. The other man ran away. This one forced his way onto the bus. He mumbled something about being in danger, that we needed to hide him on the bus. He said he'd been betrayed, that he would be killed unless I helped him. I think he's an American. He sounded like an American, before he lost consciousness."

"Did you call 911? This is a situation for 911. The guy needs an ambulance."

"I tried but the call wouldn't go through."

Matthew took his cell phone from his pocket and dialed 911. His call wouldn't go through either. "I need to go back to the visitors' center and use a land line to get an ambulance here." While he was speaking, Matthew had his handkerchief out of his pocket and was searching for paper towels or something to wipe the blood from the unknown man's face. Elizabeth handed him her bottle of water and a small package of Kleenex.

As he wiped the blood away, Matthew suddenly stopped. The bottle of water he was holding in his hand rolled onto the floor. Elizabeth could see shock in Matthew's eyes as he stared at the face of the man who lay on the seat of the bus. "Oh, no. I don't believe it. I just cannot believe this. How can it possibly be?" He paused in disbelief. "Elizabeth, I know this man."

"You know him? How can you? Is he from the hotel? He said something about wanting to get to the Penmoor."

Matthew was quiet, and Elizabeth could tell he was trying hard to remember something. "Holy Moly! This is unreal. This is just too strange. It's been thirty years ago, at least ... even longer. I knew I'd seen this person before, but I couldn't place him right away. I couldn't remember where I knew him from. Now I've remembered it all. His name is Afif. He isn't an American. He's a Russian. I met him in Afghanistan in the 1980s."

"Afghanistan ... in the 1980s? What are you talking about? The United States wasn't in Afghanistan in the 1980s. What were you doing in Afghanistan in the 1980s? The U.S. didn't get involved in Afghanistan until after 9/11. That was in 2001. We were looking for Osama Bin Laden." Elizabeth knew her Twentieth Century history and remembered quite well who had been causing trouble in Afghanistan in the 1980s. She knew it could not have been her friend Matthew Ritter.

Chapter 5

WHEN ELIZABETH EMERSON WAS A SENIOR AT Smith College in Northampton, Massachusetts, the CIA was actively recruiting from the Ivy League men's schools and from the Seven Sisters women's colleges. The spy agency had decided women had good brains after all and made good analysts. The CIA was especially interested in hiring economics majors because they'd found that people who understood economics had analytical minds, were able to process information in a systematic way, and could reach conclusions and solve problems. The CIA was not looking for covert operatives when they interviewed the college seniors. They were not hiring women to wear the classic fedora and trench coat spy outfit, lean against a lamppost in rainy, post-war Vienna, and wait for a rendezvous with a Russian double agent. The CIA wanted desk jockeys.

Elizabeth, an economics major, was of the duck-and-cover generation and had lived in the shadow of the Cold War all her life. She was intrigued by the pitch from the CIA and decided to look into what would be required for her to pursue a career with The Agency. She went to the initial meeting on the Smith campus and then made the trip to Boston with three other women from her college class. In Boston, the four were given a battery of tests, designed to evaluate their abilities to do the work the CIA would require of them. This was the first step in the application process. Those who passed the initial tests would be given more tests, some interviews, and then perhaps the offer of a job in Washington, D.C.

Elizabeth scored "off the charts" in the inductive reasoning part of the testing. Only one other person in CIA recruitment history had ever scored higher than she did in this one very important area, critical to the kind of work the CIA needed doing. Although she had never realized it before, Elizabeth was told she could read and evaluate vast amounts of material in an incredibly short period of time and come up with an accurate analysis and conclusion. The testing people made a big deal over her, and this embarrassed the somewhat introverted Elizabeth. They singled her out, and she didn't like it. Since she'd never known she had this special skill, she wasn't that impressed with herself. She wondered what all the fuss was about.

Elizabeth had been seriously dating a graduate of Princeton who was now a first-year medical student at Tulane. Elizabeth was in love, and she thought Richard Carpenter was, too. It was 1966, and women married young. It was early in the women's liberation movement. Not all women, even well-educated ones, had careers. Many became housewives and mothers. Elizabeth had always been remarkably independent, but she couldn't imagine her life without Richard. Richard was not enthusiastic about her pursuing a career with the CIA. He didn't really understand that she wouldn't be in any danger, sitting in an office in Langley, Virginia, reading newspapers and looking at data sets. He wanted her with him in New Orleans, although he'd not yet asked her to marry him.

When he did pop the question, Elizabeth said yes. They would be married that summer. The CIA was disappointed when Elizabeth turned down their offer of a position as an analyst. They pulled out all the stops and harassed her mercilessly for the remainder of her senior year. They played the "serving your country" card and everything else they could think of. Elizabeth did not waiver, and she and Richard were married in August. She got a job teaching in the New Orleans public schools, and the CIA became a distant memory. But the CIA kept its eyes on her, and years later when she decided to change careers, they welcomed her with open arms.

After she left New Orleans, Elizabeth went to graduate school. After spending two years on the faculty at the University of Texas at El Paso, she took a position teaching economics and economic history at a small college in Maryland. She was pressured to change a grade so that a failing student could become a "C" student. The student, who had not put forth any effort whatsoever in her class, had to have a "C" in order to maintain his eligibility to play basketball for the college team. The academic dean leaned on and threatened Elizabeth. Because she was only a part-time professor, the dean told her she could easily be fired from her position, if she didn't do as she was told and change the grade. Elizabeth refused to knuckle under to the threats and gave the student a "D." He had barely made the "D" and had just escaped failing her class by the skin of his teeth. After she'd turned in her grades, someone went to the registrar's office and changed the student's grade to a "C." The young man never missed a step or a dribble on the basketball court because of his failing academic work. Learning and getting an education had proven to be an afterthought, or given no thought at all, when it came to qualifying for a sports team.

Elizabeth thought she could hang on to her job, but she decided she did not want to be a part of the rotten system any more. She'd always known academia was fraught with politics, corrupted by competition to get ahead of one's colleagues, and filled with bloated and narcissistic egos. She decided life was short, and she didn't have to play the stupid games required to succeed in the university arena. She didn't want to be around the grasping and ambitious meanies any more.

She made some phone calls and began the difficult task of hiring babysitters, drivers, and a housekeeper. She made complicated arrangements for her duties at home to be taken care of when she was gone. She began to build her cover story, that she was taking a research position at the Wharton School in Philadelphia. It was a three hour commute one-way to her new job, and she would be away from home a couple of nights a week, sometimes more. It was a big commitment, but her new boss was willing to work with her to maintain the illusion of the imaginary job she supposedly had at the University of Pennsylvania. She was a valuable commodity, and the CIA helped her manage her home duties and her cover position in Philadelphia, as she committed to the more dangerous job she'd really been hired to do.

Most of her work was in Virginia, using the skills she'd demonstrated when the CIA had wanted to hire her years earlier. Occasionally she had to make trips overseas. None of her family or friends ever doubted for a minute that she was working at the Wharton School. They thought it was odd that she was gone from home so much, but by now, two of her children were away at boarding school in New England. Only one daughter was still at home. No one, not even Richard Carpenter, was allowed to know what Elizabeth did when she was out of town.

It was a rocky period in the Carpenters' marriage. Richard was consumed with his work as head of the Pathology

Department and the clinical laboratory at the local hospital. He participated in the children's activities whenever he could, but he was pretty much oblivious to Elizabeth's needs at this time in their lives. He was angry that she wasn't around all the time, as she had always been before, but he was so preoccupied with his own career, he only noticed she wasn't there when something went wrong.

Richard Carpenter had risen to the top of his career and was the main partner in his pathology group, Richard Carpenter, M.D., P.A. He had done his internship and residency at the University of Pennsylvania, and during those years he'd had the opportunity to work with Philadelphia's medical examiner. In addition to spending his days accompanying the Chief Medical Examiner on his rounds, Richard had done moonlighting for the medical examiner's office to earn extra money. The young doctor became a skilled and convincing expert witness. He was a favorite with prosecutors because juries loved his boyish looks and earnest, honest voice. When he was on the witness stand, members of the jury believed everything Richard Carpenter, M.D. had to say. If he gave evidence against someone in a murder trial, that person was always convicted. Vance Stillinger, M.D. was the Philadelphia Medical Examiner, and Richard Carpenter M.D. became his golden boy.

Carpenter's testimony had sent a number of bad guys to prison. The child molesters, murderers, drug dealers, and drivers who had committed serial DUIs all should have known it was their own behavior that had caused them to be convicted. But bad boys and girls always want to find someone other than themselves to blame. Carpenter became a lightning rod for their anger, and some wanted to blame the blonde, cherub-faced scientist who had so convincingly swayed the juries that had convicted them. Occasionally, a defendant would shake his fist at Carpenter when he was on the witness stand.

Once a man stood up and shouted threats at Carpenter after he'd given his expert witness testimony. The defendant, who had been resoundingly drunk when he'd crossed the highway's median strip and run headlong into a van full of children, said Carpenter had misrepresented his blood alcohol level. The driver of the van and four of the children had died, and the defendant was sent to prison. The drunk vowed that when he got out of jail, he would hunt down Carpenter and kill him and his family.

Elizabeth Carpenter had just come home from the hospital after giving birth to the Carpenters' second child. Law enforcement took the threats against Carpenter and his family seriously, and until the convicted criminal was sentenced and safely locked away, the police kept a guard on Carpenter's rented house in the Philadelphia suburbs. Elizabeth wondered who would be there in a few years to watch out for her family when the man was released from prison.

Stillinger tried to convince his protégé to stay in Philadelphia and become a forensic pathologist, but Carpenter owed Uncle Sam two years of his life, serving in the U.S. Army. Furthermore, Carpenter had educational debts and needed and wanted to earn some money. He wanted more income than the salary of an urban medical examiner would pay him, and he didn't want to live in a city. The Army sent Carpenter to William Beaumont Army Medical Center in Texas for two years, and from there, Carpenter took a position at a hospital in a small town in Maryland where he built a successful pathology practice. He still testified as an expert witness, but the threats that had come his way when he was at the Philadelphia Medical Examiner's Office were long-forgotten. The question was, had the men he'd helped send to prison forgotten him?

Chapter 6

"I WAS IN AFGHANISTAN IN THE 1980s. I WAS THERE for two weeks. It's a long story. I was never supposed to tell anybody about what I did during those two weeks, but all of that now seems as if it was another lifetime ago. I don't think it matters any more if I talk about what happened to me over there. There isn't time to explain right now. This man, Afif, was a Soviet soldier in 1983, but he was also an agent for the CIA." Matthew cringed as he listened to what he was saying. "I know; it sounds preposterous. It was preposterous. Things got complicated back then, over there in the Hindu Kush."

"How can you possibly be sure this is the same man, the man you knew? People change in thirty years."

"Most people do, but this guy looks almost exactly the same as he did more than three decades ago. He's hardly aged at all. Trust me. This is one of the good guys, or at least he used to be." Matthew could see the skepticism all over Elizabeth's face. As he talked, Dr. Ritter was unconsciously putting pressure on the bleeding man's wounds. "He saved my life in Afghanistan. I owe him. Please. We have to hide him, if that's what he said we had to do. Tell me exactly what he said to you when he first got on the bus."

"He said he'd been betrayed and that I had to hide him. He said he had to get to our hotel, to the Penmoor. I wondered how he knew we were from the Penmoor, because this isn't one of their buses. This a private hire. Then I realized that the lighted sign in the front says 'Penmoor.' That's how he knew where the bus was from. Maybe that's why he came here. He said someone would kill him if I didn't help him. He never said his name or anything about Afghanistan. But, Matt, he sounded totally American, not at all like a Russian. He didn't have any accent." Elizabeth thought her friend Matthew Ritter was behaving strangely. He was usually a person who played by the rules and lived a life free of drama. She was shocked to hear him mention thirty-year-old intrigue, and was stunned that he'd said he knew this injured man. What were the chances? Elizabeth couldn't believe her ears when Matthew asked for her help to save the guy, to hide him.

Elizabeth wanted to help Matthew, but she had serious misgivings about what was happening. "I personally think this is a 911 situation. Or maybe a call to the campus police is the right move. They must have campus police here. 911 may not even be allowed to come here." Elizabeth looked Matthew in the eyes, trying to make a decision. "If we don't call 911, what the heck are we going to do with him?"

"I don't think he's that badly hurt. I think I can take care of his injuries. What worries me most is that he's unconscious. He must have sustained some kind of blow to the head. Did you see if the person who attacked him had a weapon, other than his hands?"

"I'm sure I saw a knife, but they were really going at it. His neck and face look like they've been slashed. He could have hit his head on the parking lot pavement or on the side of the bus. I know they bumped into the bus quite a few times, and they hit it hard. They were both fighting fiercely, to-the-death kind of fighting. I don't know why the other one just ran off all of a sudden. Maybe he saw you coming out of the visitors' center and didn't want to be caught."

"Now the question is, how are we going to get him back to the hotel and get him into my room without anybody seeing him?"

"Wait ... we're taking him back to the hotel? Why wouldn't we take him to the ER at a local hospital?"

"If Afif says he is on the run and needs to hide, I have to believe him. We can't take him to a hospital."

"Matt, this is crazy. This isn't like you. What is going on?"

"I know it isn't like me. This man saved my life, and now I have to do everything I can to save his. If he says someone is after him and wants to kill him, then that's the truth. Please, Elizabeth. We have to do something. The bus driver will return any minute. The movie they're watching is almost over, and the others will be back at the bus."

Thinking she was probably agreeing to participate in Loony Tunes, Elizabeth decided to trust her friend of more than fifty years. Matthew had been a groomsman in the Carpenter's wedding. He needed her help. "I have an idea. For now, let's hide him in the back ... behind my wheelchair. There's a little space back there where you can conceal him. You'll have to cover him up with a jacket or something, so no one notices him. Can you move him by yourself?" While Matthew struggled to drag the dead weight of the unconscious man to the back of the bus, behind the wheelchair, Elizabeth explained what her plan was for getting the Russian off the bus. "It isn't a perfect plan, and we will probably end up getting busted. But, it's the best I can come up with on the spur of the moment. What do you think?"

"I think it's brilliant. If we can just get him into your coat, I think it might work. I can probably get Cameron or J.D. to help me distract the driver or get rid of him for a few minutes. I don't think we ought to say anything to Richard. His mind doesn't work this way."

"I agree with you. We shouldn't tell him anything about what is going on until later when you can give him the entire story. The problem is, he always wants to supervise my wheelchair and everything that's going on with it. You will have to get Isabelle or Sidney or maybe both of them, to occupy Richard's attention while you get the wheelchair off the bus. You'll have to be sure my husband is someplace other than close to me. You'll have to make sure he's looking at something else while the driver is lowering the wheelchair. He will notice that something's wrong, and he will speak up about it."

"I know what needs to be done. We're going to have to stop at a pharmacy on the way back to the hotel. The Penmoor has a good little shop, but they don't have the heavy duty bandages and other medical supplies I'm going to need. I'll have to talk the driver into making a stop. If I give him some money, I bet he'll do it. I know everybody is hungry and anxious to get to lunch. They can just be mad at me for delaying the bus and stopping at the drug store. This is important."

"I'm taking my coat off now. I will manage to get myself off the bus, but it will take me some time. I can't move fast, and I don't want to fall. You'll have to figure out how to get both the driver and my husband out of the way, if you want this goofy plan to work."

"I'm going to get J.D. to sit next to me while we're on our way back to the hotel. I can tell him what's going on. Then I'll talk to Cameron. He's a risk taker, so I can probably count on his help, too. I don't know about Sidney, though. She doesn't like for Cameron to get out there too far. If I can get Cameron to engage the driver and get him talking about the bus, or something, I'll send J.D. back to help you get off the bus."

"You don't have to do that. I can get off by myself. But I don't want the bus driver to see me, and I especially don't want Richard Carpenter to see me struggling to get down the steps. He would immediately begin screaming about where in the world is my wheelchair and why am I not in it."

Matthew had settled his patient into a not-very-comfortable spot on the floor at the rear of the bus. "Here they come. I don't see the driver. Maybe I'll have time to explain to the group a little bit about what's happened before the driver gets back. He should be here by now, but maybe we're lucky he's taking a long break." Matthew looked around frantically for something to wipe the blood off the seats and the floor.

"He's a smoker. He's taking a smoke break." Elizabeth let her disgust show in her voice. She thought the bus should be a smoke-free zone, and she had to admit to herself that technically, it was. The driver got off the bus to smoke.

Bailey was the first person back on the bus, followed by Olivia and Gretchen. "I learned some things from the movie, but I'm really disappointed that we can't visit the chapel. That was the one thing I really wanted to see." Bailey loved beautiful architecture, and he had been looking forward to seeing the famous USAF Academy chapel. Everyone was sorry the chapel was undergoing renovations. Elizabeth had intended to disembark from the bus to go into the chapel, if it had been open to visitors.

Cameron remarked, "I saw our pilot watching the film. He has a friend who's an instructor here. He was surprised to see me, too. I told him he'd better already know everything there is to know about flying a plane. He laughed and said he was thinking about having his daughter apply to the academy. That's why he's here and watching the film. He's checking out the place." Sidney and Cameron had their own plane, and their pilot always stayed in town, wherever they were. They wanted him ready to leave at a moment's notice.

Olivia wanted to make sure everyone was happy. "We don't have a reservation anywhere for lunch today. I thought everybody could be on their own. Those of us who want to eat together can meet at the Golf Club. They have really good lunches. J.D. and I have eaten there several times. Elizabeth, were you terribly bored here in the bus, all alone for hours?" The Steeles had paid for the bus tour today, and Olivia had arranged for the bus to have a wheelchair lift so Elizabeth could come along. "You could have come in with us. There was a ramp at the side of the visitors' center, although I have to say, I don't think they have many handicapped cadets at the Air Force Academy."

"What about handicapped vets who teach on the faculty and others who work here? They have to be accommodated." Tyler remembered a couple of World War II amputees who had been on the faculty when he'd been a cadet in the 1960s.

"That's why they have the ramps, I guess. You could have made it, Elizabeth. But you probably know most of what that movie had to say. I think it's for prospective candidates, high school kids who think they might want to come here. You didn't miss much, really. So were you bored?"

"Was I bored, waiting on the bus?" Elizabeth might have laughed out loud, if she hadn't been so nervous about what had to happen in the next half hour. "No, Olivia, I was anything but bored while you were all inside watching the film." Elizabeth smiled to herself.

"Oh, you, and your rich imagination. You are always talking about how you are never bored and how being an only child forced you to learn to develop your interior life." Olivia had everybody's number. She knew what made them all tick.

"What's an interior life?" Bailey was joking. He knew what an interior life was. He had one.

"Men don't have interior lives. They are unidimensional." Olivia was brutal, and she was mostly joking.

"I need your attention." Matthew Ritter stood up and addressed the others who were getting seated. "If you see something odd happening in the next half hour or if I say some things that surprise you or are out of character for me, just go along with it, please. If you notice something that's not quite right, like blood, don't say anything about it out loud. I will explain everything later. Please, just act as if everything is normal."

The driver was about to get on the bus, and Matthew had run out of time to say anything more to the group. Everyone but Elizabeth looked puzzled and stared at Matthew, but they seemed to accept what he was trying to get across to them. "Isabelle, can you move and let J.D. sit by me for a few minutes? I need to talk to him." Isabelle gave her husband a strange look.

They settled down for the return trip to the Penmoor. Matthew went to the front of the bus and leaned over to speak to the driver. He had a one-hundred dollar bill in his hand and explained that he needed to stop at a pharmacy on the way back to the hotel. The driver said something about sticking to his schedule, but when Mathew surreptitiously slipped him the money, he agreed to extend the tour beyond its time limit. If they were a few minutes late, he said he would tell his supervisor there had been road work or a traffic tie-up. He didn't drive for the Penmoor anyway.

When they stopped at the pharmacy, Matthew got off the bus and went to make his purchases. Sidney and Lilleth decided to go inside to look for some things they needed that the Penmoor didn't have at their store. Richard Carpenter had forgotten to pack his toothpaste and wanted to buy a certain brand the gift shop at the hotel didn't carry. Isabelle wanted to ask her husband what in the world he was up to, but he was avoiding her. The stop took more than a few minutes, but everyone seemed to be okay with that.

Matthew hoped he hadn't forgotten anything. He had two large shopping bags full. His wife gave him another odd look when he climbed back onto the bus with all his purchases. He had bandages, antiseptics, and other medical supplies he needed. He had a box of trash bags for the injured man's bloody jacket and clothes. He would need the trash bags to get rid of used bandages and the bloody paper towels and other things he would have to use to clean up the Russian's wounds. The retired doctor had purchased two inexpensive blankets, plastic sheeting, and some clothes he thought would fit his patient. The ones the man was currently wearing were soaked with blood and would have to be thrown away.

It would not be a good thing for the cleaning staff at the Penmoor to find bloody clothes and blood-soaked gauze and tissues in the trash in the Ritters' hotel room. That would certainly raise an alarm at the exceptionally well-run hotel. Matt had also found a cheap, disposable plastic raincoat, the kind serial killers in the movies wear so blood doesn't splatter on their clothes. He'd looked for a surgical staple gun to close Afif's wounds, but that was too much to expect from Walgreens. He would have to make do with Steri-Strips and a primitive suture kit. He had been lucky to find the suture kit, even though he was dismayed at the price the drugstore charged for it. A blood pressure cuff and the cheapest stethoscope he could find completed his shopping. Matthew thought he'd remembered all of what was on his mental list. He would find a way to get antibiotics, if that became necessary. Drug stores have everything these days, even medications.

Mathew had explained to J.D. what he wanted him to do. J.D. was understandably curious about what Matthew said to him, but he intended to follow his orders with enthusiasm. When they got back on the bus after the stop at the drug store, Matthew asked Cameron to sit beside him. He also needed Cameron's help to pull off his plan.

If he could just get the former CIA operative off the bus and through the lobby of the Penmoor without raising any eyebrows …. Matthew knew it would be touch and go. Was this only the second day of their reunion? Had they just arrived late yesterday afternoon? That was less than twenty-four hours ago. How could all this have happened in such a short period of time? What were the chances a man he had not seen in thirty years, a man he'd thought he would never see again, would turn up bleeding on the tour bus he was riding.

Chapter 7

CAMERON RICHARDSON HAD ALWAYS LOVED TO build things. From the time he was a child, he'd been taking things apart and putting them back together again. He loved to tinker. He loved to invent. He liked to change something, even just a little bit, to make it work better. That was the way his mind worked. There were stories of the rockets he and a friend had constructed and tried to launch; they were just in junior high school at the time. There were stories of gunpowder explosions in the woods and the resulting craters in the ground. Of course he would study science when he entered Sewanee. He transferred to a university with an engineering program for his last two years, and upon graduation, he was immediately recruited by IBM.

Mastering the technology of computers opened up a whole new world to Cameron, and it wasn't long before he was out on his own, inventing and tinkering and making things better. He built an innovative and tremendously successful computer empire. Then he built a second revolutionary electronics enterprise. The man lived to challenge the status quo, and his head was always in the future.

Cameron's businesses dealt with enormous amounts of

data, and thanks to computers, this data could be accessed relatively easily. It made him millions. It was inevitable that the U.S. federal government would, from time to time, come asking for help with something. Cameron was a straight shooter, a good guy. He was an entrepreneur of the first order, but he was also honest, through and through his character and soul. He would not knowingly do something that was illegal or wrong. Sometimes he helped out the feds, and sometimes he didn't. He knew how to say no, even to Uncle Sam. When he said yes, it was never for his own gain but because he felt a patriotic duty to lend his expertise. He helped crack the cell phones that led to the arrests of terrorists. He helped out whenever he felt it was the right thing to do. He didn't want his part in any of these operations to become public, but there were some people who knew he had been instrumental in tracking down and gathering evidence on the bad guys. The question was, did any of the bad guys know that Cameron Richardson had helped to finger them and put them away?

There was no question about it. Cameron had information on everybody and everything. He didn't use it for nefarious purposes, but he did have it. Anybody who knew what his companies were all about knew he had the goods, and the bads. Anyone who has achieved the level of success that Cameron had, and anyone who has made the hard decisions about everything, including personnel, has acquired some enemies along the way. Because Cameron was a fair and benevolent boss, he'd made fewer enemies than most, but he had appropriately fired the dead wood that unfortunately but inevitably turned up, from time to time, among his employees. He'd made some people angry. He was cavalier about his own security, but his second wife Sidney worried about him.

Cameron had married for the first time when he was just out of college, and he'd married a woman several years older than himself. His friends had been puzzled about the union that, to those on the outside, seemed unusual. Were these two well-matched? Did they have anything at all in common? The guys loved their buddy and accepted his marital decision. Sometimes, love is strange. The marriage produced two children but eventually came to an end. The failure of the marriage wasn't anybody's fault.

After being a bachelor for a few years, Cameron met the love of his life. He had made his fortune and his reputation, and he finally had the time to invest in a relationship. Sidney Putnam insisted on it. She let Cameron know that, to make their marriage work, he needed to listen to what was important to her and spend time with her. He was wildly in love with Sidney, but she refused to marry him until he learned that she would be an equal partner in their marriage. She was not a back seat kind of woman.

Sidney's first marriage had also ended in divorce. She had one son, to whom she was devoted, and she'd been able to remain friends with her first husband, her son's father. Most people can't achieve this almost impossible feat, but Sidney had people skills that most people don't. Sidney had been the runner-up in her state's beauty pageant for the Miss America contest. She'd always had the looks, but more importantly, she had the smarts — of all kinds.

Sidney's most exceptional way of being smart was her gift for reading people. Her uncanny ability to know when someone was lying was an asset when she worked as a consultant for the Texas Department of Criminal Justice. She was the prosecutor's secret weapon. She consulted on jury selections and sat in on law enforcement interviews with suspects and witnesses. She was never wrong in her assessments. She didn't necessarily tell the authorities what they wanted to hear. She told the truth. And sometimes, nobody wanted to hear the truth. Sidney demanded that her assistance in criminal cases remain confidential, but she was almost too good to be true. Eventually, what she could do leaked out beyond the walls of the justice department, and she knew being exposed could put her in danger.

Her ability to vet people was invaluable to Sidney when she started her own business. As a single parent, she needed to support herself and her son. With her business, You Are Home, she identified a need that existed and built a business that responded to that need. Her first clients were corporations that frequently moved their employees from place to place. Corporations arranged to move their employee's household goods and paid for the packing and moving and unpacking. The gap in these employee benefits came when the wife, and it usually was the wife back in the day, had to put it all away and set up the new household. The husband, and it usually was the husband back in the day, was off doing his corporate thing, and the wife was at home with the kids, trying to find a place to put their stuff in the new kitchen and the unfamiliar closets.

Sidney's company was hired to come in and put their household goods away where they belonged. Her well-trained employees would organize the kitchen, at the housewife's direction, but with suggestions from the experts about the best kitchen logistics to make it fully functional. They put shelf paper in the drawers and on the shelves. They put away everybody's clothes — organizing, folding, and hanging everything in the most efficient and easy-to-access way. You Are Home would arrange for a room to be painted and would bring in other professionals to position furniture to its best advantage and hang art work. Sidney was good at this, and she taught her carefully-selected employees to be good at it, too. She charged high prices for her services, but there was a huge demand for what she was selling. Her company grew rapidly. She was a very successful entrepreneur in her own right when she literally ran into Cameron Richardson in a restaurant.

It was an expensive steak house in Fort Worth, and Sidney was there having lunch and closing a deal with a corporate client. It was summer, and she was dressed in a stunning white designer linen dress. She had a white cashmere cardigan sweater over her shoulders because the air conditioning was turned up so high in the steak house, to counter the July Texas heat. She got up to go to the ladies' room, and a tall, good-looking man didn't see her making her way through the tables in the dark, wood-paneled restaurant. The man pushed back his chair and stood up from his table with a large glass of iced tea in his hand. He ran straight into Sidney and spilled the entire glass of tea all over her dress, cashmere sweater, and expensive white high-heeled shoes. They were both stunned. He looked into the bright and beautiful eyes of the woman whose clothes he'd just ruined and couldn't turn away. To say it was love at first sight on his part would probably be the truth. She was angry that her outfit had been spoiled, but Cameron Richardson was so gracious about sending a car to drive her home to change her clothes. He insisted on paying for dry cleaning and replaced the clothes that could not be saved. Sidney had to soften her annoyance.

She had no idea who Cameron Richardson was, and they'd had several dates before Sidney fully grasped the extent of Cameron's wealth and success. Sidney was not looking for a relationship of any kind at this point in her life. She had a business to run and a child to raise. She was incredibly busy. But Cameron always went after what he wanted, and he usually got it. He went after Sidney like nothing he'd ever gone after in his life. Cameron pulled out all the stops to court the independent and strong-willed Sidney Putnam. The more she got to know him, the more she realized that Cameron was not only a success. He was also a kind and caring human being. She finally had to admit to herself that she'd fallen in love with the man.

Chapter 8

THOSE WHO DIDN'T UNDERSTAND WHAT WAS GOING on were confused and annoyed. Those who did know what was happening and what was going to happen, were nervous. Cameron took the seat directly behind the bus driver and started to chat with him.

"Jim, I watched you operate that wheelchair lift when we were getting on the bus this morning, and I'm real curious about how it works. You got Elizabeth on here without any problems. It was smooth as silk, the way the whole thing functioned. Have you done this a lot, or is it pretty easy to operate that lift? I'm an engineer, and stuff like this fascinates me."

"I've been running this bus with the wheelchair lift for my company for several years, but to tell you the truth, it's really pretty easy to use. It's a simple mechanism, and it is well-designed. The lift operates on a rechargeable battery. The bus's engine recharges it." Jim, the bus driver, was happy to talk with Cameron about the lift and how skilled he was at operating it.

Cameron interrupted him. "Do you think I could operate it? I mean, like if there was an emergency, would one of us be able to operate it to get a handicapped person off the bus?

Without your help, I mean? If you were incapacitated for some reason?"

"Oh, sure. It really isn't difficult. I'll show you, when we get to the hotel, how easy it is."

They were almost back at the Penmoor. Cameron was going to push his luck with Jim. "I know you probably aren't supposed to do it, but would you let me push the buttons? I was watching what you did when you got her on this morning."

"Oh, I don't think so. I could get in trouble for that. I'm the only one who's allowed to operate the lift."

"I'd want you standing there, right beside me, watching everything I do, you know, to be sure I get it right." Cameron discretely flashed two one hundred dollar bills and stuffed them into the driver's jacket pocket.

"Well, maybe. We'll see how it goes." Jim was hooked. Cameron knew he had him.

They arrived at the entrance to their hotel. There was the inevitable confusion as everyone gathered coats and scarves and purses and bags and things they'd purchased at the gift shops and the pharmacy. During the confusion, Mathew and J.D. removed the Russian's bloody jacket and stuffed it into an empty plastic bag Matthew had procured from the drug store cashier. They wrestled their man into the newly-purchased plastic raincoat and then into Elizabeth's leather coat. It had to be done quickly, and it wasn't easy. The coat was a tight fit, but they made it work. Elizabeth's coat was oversized and had a hood. A distinctive and much-loved piece of clothing, the coat had been a part of Elizabeth's wardrobe for decades. It was out of style, with the dated leather ruching around the neck and sleeves and the voluminous leather hood. But the coat was warm, and it was waterproof. It was the perfect thing to wear if one was outside during a snowstorm. Elizabeth didn't often use the hood, but today the hood would be up and in place as part of the disguise for Matthew's patient.

Mathew wrapped a scarf he'd commandeered from Lilleth around the Russian's head and face and struggled to put the gloves he'd borrowed from Bailey on the man's hands. It was cold outside, so bundling the guy up in scarves and pulling up the hood of the coat did not seem like an unreasonable thing to do. The occupant of the wheelchair was ostensibly an elderly woman in frail health. Everyone was trying to keep her warm. J.D. and Matthew got the Russian into the wheelchair and tucked one of the new, thin Walgreens blankets around his legs. They draped the other blanket over his head and neck.

The wheelchair was secured to the floor of the bus with special heavy-duty clamps. The driver would have to unclamp each wheel, and this would be one of the moments of truth for their deception. Cameron was keeping the driver distracted with his constant chatter about how the lift worked. Cameron really was an engineer and did understand these things. He could talk ad infinitum about gears and pulleys and battery-powered technology. The driver was so distracted, he didn't bother to look at who was actually sitting in the wheelchair. He was looking at the floor, focused on unclamping the wheelchair and trying to answer Cameron's non-stop questions.

J.D. jumped in to be a further distraction while the driver unlocked the wheelchair's wheels from the bus floor. "I'm in the transportation business, and I am particularly interested in how these locks work. I run a trucking company, and sometimes we have special cargo that absolutely cannot be allowed to shift in transit. This locking system looks like an excellent way to keep something perfectly stable. I'd like to watch you while you unlock those wheels." J.D. and Cameron closed in on the driver and successfully blocked his view of the person in the wheelchair. They fired questions at him and kept his mind on every possible subject except the identity of the person he was putting on the wheelchair lift.

Sidney had insisted that Richard sit with her at the front of the bus. Elizabeth was trying to stay hidden, lying down in her bus seat, out of view of the driver. He was supposed to think she was the person in the wheelchair, so he couldn't be allowed to see her. Elizabeth was amazed at how her friends had completely bamboozled the driver. It had been a masterful performance.

The driver opened the doors to the lift and pushed the wheelchair out onto the platform. To keep the wheelchair from moving, J.D. and Matthew locked the wheels. One of Matthew's shopping bags from Walgreens sat in the lap of the person sitting in the wheelchair, further obscuring that person's face. Matthew carried the other shopping bag in his hand.

Cameron hustled the driver out the door of the bus and around to the side where the controls for the lift were located and where the lift would come down. Cameron kept up his steady stream of conversation about what a slick apparatus the whole wheelchair lift thing was and how neatly it had been tucked into the bus, with its own side doors, and on and on. The driver took hold of the remote control device that powered the lift. Cameron reached out to take the remote control from the driver who hesitated for a minute before turning it over. Cameron would be the one to lower the platform to ground level and allow the wheelchair to roll off the platform onto the blacktop of the hotel driveway.

This would be another critical moment, when the driver would be able to look directly into the face of the person in the wheelchair, as it rolled off the platform at the end of its journey down from the bus. Cameron's skills at distracting the driver would be put to the test. As the platform lowered itself slowly, Matt raced off the bus to take charge of the wheelchair once it reached ground level. Cameron would not only have to keep the driver from looking at who was riding in the wheelchair, he would have to keep the driver from looking at the door of the bus where J.D. would be helping Elizabeth negotiate the stairs. She would have to disappear into the hotel without being noticed by the driver or by her husband.

Fortunately there were lots of people, lots of cars, and other tour buses jockeying for position under the porte-cochère. Cameron was able to push the buttons to lower the platform of the lift, while the driver looked down at the buttons on the remote control, watching Cameron's fingers like a hawk. The driver wasn't looking at the wheelchair. This is what they had hoped would happen. Matthew had made it off the bus and unlocked the wheelchair's wheels before the driver knew what was happening. Cameron kept the driver's attention focused on the remote control device, barraging him with another set of technical questions about how it all worked so smoothly.

Matthew unlocked the wheelchair, pulled his patient off the lift's platform, and easily stepped behind the wheelchair. Keeping his head down, he proceeded directly away from the bus and across the driveway to the hotel door. It was cold and windy, so everyone who was outside was bundled up. Once on its way inside the hotel, the figure in the wheelchair did not attract undue attention. Matthew was playing the part of the good spouse, pushing his handicapped wife quickly out of the cold and into the warm lobby. The hotel's doormen opened the door for him, and Matthew pushed through and did not stop. He kept going and wended his way through the lounge and down many hallways. Finally, he was on the elevator.

Another couple was on the elevator, and they were a talkative pair. They tried to engage Matthew's wheelchair occupant in conversation, asking if she had enjoyed her outing. On the verge of panic, Matt was hoping his patient would remain unconscious and that the friendly couple would get off on the next floor. Matthew put his finger to his lips and said in a whisper, "She's fallen asleep. It's been a long morning." The two talkers nodded their heads in understanding and blessedly got off at the next stop.

He was almost home free. He fumbled with the room's key card. As he bumped the wheelchair across the threshold of the room, he began to rehearse the explanation he was going to give to his wife, Isabelle, the one who might be waiting in their room when he arrived with his Russian patient. He also began to think about what he was going to do to care for the man who was still unconscious and bloody. He unloaded his shopping bags. He had to get Elizabeth's coat back to her somehow. He hoped it wasn't stained with blood. He wondered if Elizabeth had been able to get off the bus without help and if J.D. had been able to give her any assistance. Matthew Ritter had a lot on his mind.

Elizabeth moved as quickly as she had in years. She didn't have her heavy coat to contend with, so getting herself off the bus was easier than it might have been. It was bitterly cold outside, and she would miss her coat. She maneuvered herself to the front of the bus. The door was open. She turned around and crawled backwards down the steps, holding on to anything she could find to hold onto. She had crawled backwards down the steps of a couple of airplanes in the past. One time was in her own hometown when the airport crew couldn't find the ramp, and the other time was at the airport in Barbados when there *was no ramp* to be found anywhere at all. So, it was not her first test in terms of being able to climb down difficult steps ... backwards. She was so relieved to see J.D. at the bottom of the steps, ready to help. Elizabeth held her cane in one hand and put her other hand through J.D.'s arm.

They looked to see if the driver had noticed Elizabeth's departure from the bus, but he was nowhere in sight. Cameron's assignment had been to keep the driver occupied as soon as the wheelchair had rolled off the lift platform. He was to distract the driver so Elizabeth could get safely off and away from the bus. If the driver saw Elizabeth stumbling off the bus, he might wonder who in the world had been in the wheelchair they'd just lowered to the ground.

As they walked away, J.D. noticed that Cameron and Jim, the bus driver, were underneath the lift, looking at something. Their driver was deep into a complicated explanation about how the lift was put together. He was pointing out every part to Cameron, the engineer and a man with the gift of gab par excellence. Cameron had carried his role in the charade to an extraordinary level.

It seemed that, miracle of miracles, they were all home free. With Elizabeth hanging onto his arm, J.D. was inside the hotel in no time. He knew Elizabeth had to rest. She couldn't walk a long way at one time, and it had already been a stretch for her to get safely off the bus. They sat down in the lounge by the fire for a couple of minutes.

While they were sitting there, Richard Carpenter descended on them, angry as a hornet and worried about what had happened to Elizabeth. "Where have you been and what is going on? Where is your coat? Where is your wheelchair?"

"Don't get your blood pressure up, Richard. I am right here, and I'm fine. My coat and my wheelchair are on a secret mission, without me. Don't fret. You can go to the concierge and get me another wheelchair. Ask for a newer one. That other one made a funny noise and was kind of falling apart. The stuffing was coming out of one of the arms." Elizabeth wanted Richard to have something to do to occupy his mind and body while she caught her breath and figured out what to tell him.

"I'm going to get the wheelchair for you, but I want to know what the heck is going on around here. Everyone is acting weird, including Sidney and Olivia." Richard left to find the concierge and another wheelchair.

Olivia and Sidney had followed Richard into the lounge, and both women began to talk at once. "We don't know what is happening, either, but I will tell you, getting Richard Carpenter away from Elizabeth and her wheelchair was more than a notion. He just would not give it up." Sidney looked drained from her assignment of trying to distract Richard.

"I hope Matthew has a good explanation for us, and I hope he gives it to us soon. I thought I was going to have to knock Richard over the head and incapacitate him to keep him away from that lift. He thinks he is the only person who can lock and unlock the wheels of her wheelchair, and he thinks he has to supervise everything the driver does. Whatever you all were doing in the back of the bus with the wheelchair, it was way easier than what we were doing." Olivia was worn out, too. She wanted to know what all the commotion was about.

"I told Richard to let Matthew push her onto the platform and into the hotel. I told him the rest of us like to give him a break and take our turns pushing the wheelchair. I said it wasn't fair that he had to do it all the time." Sidney sighed. "Rationality was not going to win the day with that man. He was like a bulldog. It took both of us, pulling on his arms and dragging him, to keep him from bolting and running back to the lift. We managed to get him off the bus, but then he wouldn't budge."

"To get him to move away from the bus, we finally had to tell him Elizabeth wasn't in the wheelchair and to 'cool it.' That opened up a whole new can of worms, and he tried to go back to the bus. He said he needed to help her get down the steps, if she wasn't using the wheelchair and the lift. I told him J.D. was helping her. That seemed to calm him down a little bit. He trusts J.D. with Elizabeth." Olivia had been able to convince Richard to let J.D. help, but that small victory had lasted for only a minute or two.

"We got him into the hotel, but he was stomping around, snorting like a bull with a red cape flying. The man has a one-track mind. Wow! I won't be coming between him and that wheelchair again any time soon. Poor Elizabeth." Sidney was hungry. They all were. "Matthew Ritter had better have a pretty good story for us. I thought this year we were going to have a relaxing and drama-free time. When is the relaxing part going to start, I'd like to know? This craziness is not at all in character for Matthew. I think I like him better when he is showing us a thousand movie montages. Things have gone sideways, and I think it's Matthew's fault. I may go to the spa this afternoon. Too much testosterone is on the loose around here."

J.D. could see that Sidney and Olivia were stressed and upset. "I have to say, Sidney, Cameron was beyond brilliant the way he wrapped our driver, Jim, around his little finger. I didn't know he could throw the bull like that. He was amazing."

"The thing is, I suspect it wasn't entirely acting. He probably wanted to know every detail about how the contraption worked. He can get into something like that and not be able to let it go until he has figured out where the last nut and bolt are supposed to be. Here he is now, grinning like a fool. He loved every minute of the whole thing. I can see it from the look on his face. And he can't wait to tell us about it."

Cameron couldn't wait to tell them everything. "I can build the thing myself, from the ground up. Now I know it all, inside and out … down to the last detail. I know where every part belongs and how it all goes together." Cameron was having fun. "It really is kind of a work of art, very well designed." He was honestly taken with the way the wheelchair lift was constructed. "I hadn't planned to learn all of that, but James was such an avid teacher. And I was such an enthusiastic student." Cameron roared with laughter. "Did it work? Did Matthew get his patient off the bus and to his room without anyone being the wiser? Did we all give good performances?" He laughed again.

J.D. assured everyone. "I just got a text from Matthew that he has his patient safely in the room. Other than the fact that he has an injured and unconscious guy on his hands who is on the run and hiding from something, his main concern now is what he's going to say to Isabelle. I'm not getting involved in that one … no way. Matthew Ritter is totally on his own as far as that performance goes."

Chapter 9

THEY MET IN NEW ORLEANS WHEN HE WAS A FOURTH-year medical student at Tulane and she was a freshman at Newcomb College. They both had roots in Tennessee, albeit at different ends of that very long state. Their first few dates had long-term relationship written all over them. Isabelle Blackstone was considerably younger than Matthew Ritter, but he was committed to being eternally young and worked out every day to stay that way. They made a handsome couple. Isabelle was blonde and beautiful, and Matthew knew she was the one. He was in love, but he wasn't ready to settle down. He had places to go and people to see. He had an internship and a residency to do, and he had signed up to fulfill his obligations to his country by spending two years working for the United States Public Health Service. She had just finished her freshman year in college. Matthew was moving on to California for his internship, the next chapter in the long quest to become a urologist. Would Isabelle go with him or would she stay in New Orleans?

In the end, she decided he was worth it. She would transfer to UCLA and complete her undergraduate studies there. Her parents were not happy when their nineteen-year-old daughter told them she wanted to leave Newcomb College and move to California to complete her degree. But they trusted her and agreed to pay her tuition in California. She was an excellent student and worked hard to graduate with a dual degree in psychology and sociology. Isabelle and Matthew married after Isabelle finished her undergraduate studies, and they moved to the Phoenix area where Matthew served his two years in the U.S. Public Health Service, working on what was then called an Indian Reservation. While they lived near Phoenix, Isabelle earned a master's degree in clinical psychology at Arizona State University, and she later opened her own counseling practice in Palm Springs, the same year Matthew joined a thriving urology group in that California city.

The professional corporation Matthew Ritter joined was the leading group of urologists in Southern California. Movie actors and other famous people from Los Angeles drove to Palm Springs for medical care, especially when they had an embarrassing problem they didn't want anyone in L.A. to know about. Matthew was bound by the Hippocratic Oath and the covenant of professional confidentiality not to talk about his patients. And he never did. He kept many confidences about highly-placed people in all walks of life. As well as the Hollywood crowd, he treated wealthy businessmen and politicians, including two governors of Western states, several United States Senators, and assorted Congressmen and judges. His group was known for its medical expertise as well as for its discretion. Matthew knew scandalous things, secrets quite a few famous people hoped he would carry to his grave. He would, but did they all trust that he would always abide by his commitment to confidentiality?

Isabelle likewise knew her clients' secrets. She was an effective therapist and a warm and caring human being. Her patients loved her. She had a successful practice within a year of hanging out her shingle and had to begin hiring additional counselors to join her. There was a lot of money in Palm Springs. There were also some large egos in residence, a not unexpected circumstance, as the financially successful wanted to live, vacation, and retire in this golf course mecca that was reputed to have more sunny days than any other place in the United States. There was a great deal of infidelity, and many people came to her with problems that were associated with their addictions to drugs and alcohol. There was domestic abuse, and women, who did not want to be seen in public with a black eye or a broken arm, left Beverly Hills to hide out and seek counseling in Palm Springs. Isabelle listened and dispensed advice to the rich and famous.

Isabelle was sometimes called to testify in court, something she hated to do. She didn't like to break a confidence, but sometimes, she was legally bound to respond to a subpoena to appear in court and to testify honestly when questioned under oath. She had almost been called to testify in the extraordinarily high-profile murder trial that involved a famous football player and his second wife. Everyone knew the athlete had been beating up his wife on a regular basis. He'd finally killed her and was on trial for murder. Isabelle thankfully hadn't had to testify in that case. But there were other cases where her testimony had resulted in an unstable parent being denied custody of their child or children in a divorce. She had received direct and personal threats as a result of some of these court cases.

She had struggled to work, at least part-time, while she raised the couple's two children. Isabelle had household and babysitting help, and she spent as much time in her office as she could. She knew she needed the stimulation of doing her own thing while dealing with diaper changes, wiping down counters, making endless peanut butter and jelly sandwiches, and driving her children to their after-school activities and numerous sports events. When her children graduated from high school, Isabelle realized she was burned out being a clinical psychologist, and she began to look for a new and less stressful career.

She found her next identity as an interior designer and owner of an elegant high-end shop that sold European antiques, lamps, and other delightful and expensive accessories for the home. Isabelle's store, *Blackstone White*, immediately became everybody's favorite place to find the perfect piece to make a room both interesting and classy.

What Isabelle had not expected was the extent to which being an interior designer and a store owner would call on her skills as a therapist. People came into the store to talk and sometimes to cry. Her clients had a great deal of money, but they did not always have much happiness or contentment. Isabelle was a good listener. She was patient and kind. People she barely knew poured out their hearts to her. If a husband was laundering money, his wife might express her disgust or her fear about his activities to Isabelle. If a boyfriend was involved in the drug trade, the girlfriend would confide in Isabelle. There were plenty of Mafiosi living in Palm Springs.

Isabelle sometimes helped a client disappear. It started with a woman who was a prolific shopper and regular customer of Isabelle's. The woman came into the store one day, terrified that her husband had sent his henchmen to kill her. She begged Isabelle to allow her to hide in the storage room at the back of *Blackstone White*. Isabell trusted her gut and helped the woman lie down, well-concealed, behind a pallet of oriental rugs. Sure enough, two greasy looking tough guys with tattoos all over their arms, arrived at the store, and without asking, searched high and low for the gangster's wife. Isabelle was frightened, but she was also angry. The mobsters were unable to find Isabelle's client, and as soon as they'd left, Isabelle called the police and reported the two for bursting into her store, turning everything topsy-turvy, and searching her property without her permission. She knew nothing would come of the police report she'd filed, but felt she had done the right thing.

Isabelle hid the frightened woman in her own home for several days and then drove her to Mexico. The woman had a secret bank account in L.A. and hoped to start a new life south of the border. The incident had been terrifying, but Isabelle had found a new calling. She was now an interior designer, store owner, and rescuer of the abused. It was a lot to take on, and Isabelle often asked herself if she had merely traded one stressful job for another even more stressful job.

The interior design part of her business was booming. Isabelle had excellent taste. Everybody wanted her to design the addition to their house; consult with them about the space planning in their new kitchen; and do the paint, curtains, and new furniture in the family room renovation. She had more business than she could handle. She spent a lot of time in clients' homes and often drew on her counseling skills to settle disputes within their families. The husband, who was paying the bill for the redecorating project, didn't like white walls. The wife, who would be spending most of her waking hours in the room, wanted only white walls. He dug in his heels. She refused to talk about it. The interior designer/marriage counselor came to the rescue and brought a compromise and reconciliation. Isabelle often wondered how interior designers without experience in clinical counseling were ever able to accomplish anything.

Isabelle saw and heard many things she never wanted to see or hear. She kept her secrets, but she sometimes wondered if an angry father, who had been denied access to his children because of his mental illness, would remember her court testimony and come after her. She worried that the women she'd helped disappear would be found. Would the assistance Isabelle had given to rescue and hide these victims be exposed? Would an angry abuser come after her?

Chapter 10

THANKFULLY, ISABELLE WASN'T IN THEIR ROOM when Matthew arrived with his patient. She'd gone to lunch at the Golf Club with the others. But Matthew knew his reprieve would be short-lived. Isabelle deserved to know the whole story, and he was going to have to tell it to her.

Matthew had been told, back in 1983, that he wasn't to share any of the details of his trip to Afghanistan with Isabelle. She'd believed he was at some kind of medical meeting. Their children were small, and she didn't want to go with him anyway. She had thought it was odd that he would be gone for two weeks, but he'd come up with a reason for that. Matthew remembered that he'd told Isabelle he was going to Washington University in St. Louis for special training. He was going to take a course to learn how to operate a new piece of medical equipment, essential to his practice of urology. He'd told her it was a complex device, and it would take several days for him to become familiar with how it worked. Now he was going to have to tell her the truth. He would have to tell her he had lied to her back then ... more than thirty-five years ago. They had promised never to lie to each other.

As he was thinking about all of this, he continued to tend to his patient. Matthew needed help, and he sent a text to J.D. and asked him to come to the room. He knew J.D. was probably eating lunch by now, but Matthew couldn't move this man by himself. He was still unconscious in the wheelchair. Could it possibly have been just two hours since they had left the U.S. Air Force Academy grounds? So much had happened; time had twisted and collapsed in on itself for Matthew. It was 1:30 p.m. He had discovered his comrade-in-arms from the Soviet-Afghan War on the bus at 11:25 that morning.

J.D. arrived at the door, ready as always to help his friend. "I've ordered my lunch, so this had better be quick." He looked at the man in the wheelchair and had his doubts. Matthew had removed the scarf that was wrapped around his patient's face, and he'd been able to ease his injured arms out of Elizabeth's leather coat and the cheap plastic raincoat. He'd cut away his bloody shirt and undershirt. The ruined clothes were in a heap on the floor.

"Can you grab a trash bag out of that shopping bag from Walgreens? I don't want the clothes to leave blood stains on the carpet in here. That would make for a whole new set of explanations I'm not prepared to give. Thanks. There's also a package of vinyl gloves in the bag. Put a pair on before you gather up the bloody clothes." J.D. followed orders and cleaned up the debris. Matthew was cutting away the guy's pants and underwear. "I need your help transferring him from the wheelchair to the bed. I wish I had a gurney in here, but this bed is going to have to do. The room with two double beds was large enough to maneuver the wheelchair into position. Matthew had prepared one of the beds for his patient. He had pulled back the bedspread and top sheet and arranged a large piece of plastic over the bottom sheet.

It isn't easy to move an unconscious person. They are dead weight. Matthew and J.D. were both strong and in excellent shape, but they were seventy-six years old. Heavy lifting was something they did in a gym, not in a hotel room. With effort, they managed to get the man out of the wheelchair and onto the bed. Matthew had a basin with surgical soap and warm water and some throw-away wipes. He began to clean the man's wounds.

"Thanks, J.D. You've been a tremendous help. Obviously, I could never have moved him on my own. Can you ask Richard to come by the room? I'd like to talk with him about this case." Matthew smiled a weak smile.

"When are you going to tell us what this is all about, Matt? We have gone along with your plan and followed your instructions, but I think you owe us more in terms of why we are doing this. I know Richard Carpenter isn't going to come down here and consult with you unless you give him a convincing reason for doing so. The women are more than curious. Cameron had a blast keeping the bus driver dancing around and explaining stuff to him, but the rest of us need to understand the situation. Who is this man? We all trust you and know you would not have done anything like this without a very good reason. You just need to let us in on what that very good reason is." J.D. was a loyal and patient friend, but he and the others insisted on being told what was happening, and soon.

"I have to explain it all to Isabelle first. She deserves that. She is going to be furious with me. Imagine finding an unknown man, who is bleeding from multiple places, unconscious in your bed. I know she will eventually understand, but it is going to be a tough, if not impossible, sell."

"Maybe if you told some of the rest of us, we could help with Isabelle." J.D. had noticed that the Ritter's room adjoined another room. There was a connecting door beside the walk-in closet. "Do you want me to find out if that adjoining room is vacant. If it is, you should call the concierge and to ask her to book it in your name. Isabelle won't want to share a room with this guy, trust me. You know that as well as I do. No matter how good a sport she is, she's not going to sleep here. And she shouldn't. He's not just an unknown man in the bed in her hotel room. He's a *naked,* unknown man in the bed in her room. It would be better if she never saw this scene ... the guy on the bed and all the blood. If the room next door is available, I hope it's at least as nice as this one. Then you need to move your things and Isabelle's things over to the other room. I may have lost a few wives along the way, but I have also learned a few things. Get another room, and move your stuff. Tell her it's an upgrade. Tell her something."

"Can you call down to the concierge for me and arrange it. Try to get Elle on the phone and ask if the room is vacant. I'll talk to her. I don't want anyone to suspect that anything fishy is going on up here. My reason for wanting an additional room has to sound plausible. I'm already freaking out about what to do when housekeeping wants to come into the room. I'm also worried about what the bus company is going to do when they find blood all over their seats and smeared on the floor. They will probably get in touch with you or Olivia to find out what the heck happened on that bus this morning. I hope you don't get in trouble or have to pay some big fine."

"Don't worry about it. You have enough other things to think about right now. We paid a damage deposit, or something. I'll make up a story. I just hope they don't think a crime was committed and notify the police or the FBI." J.D. called Elle, their concierge, and she said she would check her computer to see if the room next to Matthew's and Isabelle's room was available. J.D. handed the phone to Matthew.

"Elle, I'd really like to have that room next door. No, I want to keep the room we have, too, but it would be great to have the adjoining room as well." Matthew listened to the concierge explain what the additional charges would be.

"The room next to yours is larger than your room, and it's more expensive. It's a suite with a separate living room. Since you are taking two rooms, I'm not going to charge you a higher rate for the larger room."

"Thank you so much. That's all great news. You see, I snore, and we have separate bedrooms at home. It's difficult when we go to a hotel and have to share a room. Sometimes we tough it out, but since we are staying here for a week, I would really like to have that extra bedroom."

"Of course, Dr. Ritter. Don't think a thing about it. Many couples, young and old, have separate bedrooms. It will be arranged." Elle was quiet for a few seconds, as she worked her magic. "I now have you booked into both rooms, #504 and #505. I have unlocked the door between the two rooms for you. The room next door is made up and ready for you to move in."

"You can do all that from where you are? You unlocked the door from your office?"

"Isn't technology grand? Yes, everything is taken care of. You can access both rooms with the room key cards you and your wife are currently holding. The keys will open both doors from the hall as well as the door that joins the two rooms. Is there anything else I can do for you?"

"Thank you, Elle. I think you have just saved my marriage." Elle laughed at Mathew's little joke.

J.D. was in the transportation business. He knew how to move things, and he began to move clothes from the closet in the "sick room" to the closet in the new suite. Within a few minutes, he and Matthew had moved suitcases, shoes, electronics, and toiletries from one room to the other. "Isabelle is going to like the new room. I think you may get away with only minor injuries, Matt."

"Go back to your lunch. I will text Isabelle that we have moved to a suite. I will tell her to go to room #505, next door, and not to come back here. Where is she, by the way?"

J.D. was eager to leave. He was hungry. Breakfast had been a long time ago, and there had been much intervening excitement since his last meal. "She's at the Golf Club. Cameron wanted to take a shower after climbing around under the bus, so Sidney said they would order room service for lunch. I think Elizabeth and Richard also went to their room. Elizabeth was tired, and Richard was upset. You know how he gets when things don't go as he expects them to. The rest of us are at the Golf Club. You should order something sent to the room for yourself. You need to keep up your strength so you can take care of this guy."

Matthew knew J.D. was right about his need to eat and keep up his strength. He'd been working constantly to clean and assess the wounds on his patient's body. He thought two rather nasty cuts needed stitches, and several other places would probably heal with sturdy butterfly bandages. It appeared to him that something other than bare hands had been used in the assault. He was not an expert on fist fights or weapons used by thugs, but he was putting his money on brass knuckles. A knife had definitely been used on the man's face and neck. Because of the cold, the injured man had been dressed in a down ski jacket and other layers of warm clothing. These had protected him during the fight, from the brass knuckles as well as from the knife, except for his face. He was lucky not to have deeper lacerations. Because Afif winced whenever Mathew pressed on his abdomen, he worried that his patient might have a ruptured spleen. And he was still concerned about a head wound. He also wondered if his patient could have been poisoned or drugged with something. He should have been awake by now.

Matthew knew what he had to do, but he took a few minutes to order soup and a sandwich from room service. He went back to work, and when his lunch arrived he scrubbed his hands with antiseptic soap and quickly devoured his meal. It had been years since he'd had to put stitches in a patient. It took more time than he had planned to put the man's badly beaten body back together.

He finished what he could do for the moment. He pulled the sheet over Afif and put one of the drugstore blankets over him to keep him warm. When he heard his wife opening the door to their new room with her key card, he slipped into the adjoining suite and closed the connecting door. Matthew knew he had a lot of explaining to do … to his wife and to his friends. He was exhausted with the stress and the effort of practicing medicine again, something he hadn't done in a long time. He'd remembered how to do wound care and stitch up a gaping cut, but it had taken a toll on the retired physician. He was ready for a nap, not for a lengthy discussion with his confused and angry wife. Sometimes, life gets complicated.

As it turned out, Isabelle was thrilled with the new room. Matthew explained to her that he had an unexpected patient recovering in the hotel room next door. He began the long and involved explanation about what had happened at the Air Force Academy this morning and what had happened in Afghanistan in 1983. Isabelle had many questions. She was hurt and disappointed that her husband had lied to her years ago. His admission made her wonder what else he might have lied to her about. She understood that he had been under orders from the United States government to lie to her, but she and Matthew had promised never to lie to each other.

This was a fundamental premise of their relationship and their long marriage. Why did orders from the CIA take precedence over that vow? Isabelle was an understanding and forgiving woman, but she hated lying. Matthew pled his case with all the conviction he could muster. He hoped it would be enough.

Matthew would have to tell this story all over again to their group of friends. He had to rest before he took on that task. If Isabelle asked fifty questions, he knew his friends would have five hundred questions. He fell asleep on top of the bedspread on one of the two queen-size beds in their newly-acquired suite.

Meanwhile, Elizabeth had explained to Richard what was happening; at least she told him as much as she knew. She let him know that smuggling the injured man out of the bus and into the hotel had been her idea and that she had freely given up her leather coat and her wheelchair to the cause. Her explanation hadn't done much to calm Richard's confusion. Surprisingly, he'd agreed that it had been a good decision not to involve him in the subterfuge. Even before J.D. told Richard that Matthew wanted him to come to the room to see his patient, Elizabeth had suggested to Richard that Matthew might need some help, or at least the advice of another physician.

Richard and Elizabeth ordered turkey club sandwiches from room service. Richard ate a bowl of the navy bean soup, and Elizabeth ordered beef barley soup with mushrooms. It was a soup kind of day, and they were both hungry. After lunch, Elizabeth lay down to take a nap, and Richard left the room to find his friend Matthew.

Chapter 11

J.D. STEELE HAD BEEN AN ATHLETE AND A SCHOLAR in high school before he matriculated at the University of Oklahoma. He was handsome and outgoing as well as smart. He joined a fraternity and dated many women, but he also managed to make good grades, at least good enough for him to be admitted to the University of Oklahoma College of Law after he finished his four undergraduate years. After law school, J.D. fulfilled his obligation to Uncle Sam and was stationed in El Paso, Texas with the JAG Corps. J.D. had always wanted to be a prosecutor. He had a strong sense of right and wrong and wanted to help make sure the bad guys were found guilty and put in jail. He would devote twenty-five years of his life to this cause, and he became a legend in Tulsa legal circles. His specialty was trying the most complex and difficult criminal cases, including murder, rape, and drug cases. He was a relentless defender of justice and a dispenser of appropriate punishment. He was always prepared and performed brilliantly in front of the jury. J.D. seemed to thrive on convicting the worst of the worst, and he could count the cases he'd ever lost on one hand!

J.D. and his first wife were married just after they'd finished college. They were both too young, and neither of them was ready for marriage. The two had almost nothing in common, and after less than a year, they realized their union had been a mistake. They had no children and few assets, so their divorce was relatively amicable. They remained friends.

After his divorce, J.D. became one of Tulsa's most eligible bachelors and was quite the man-about-town for a few years until he met Signa Karlsson. It was a love match, and they married and had two children, twins, a boy and a girl. Signa had her pilot's license and loved to fly. Both of their children had graduated from college when Signa was killed in a plane crash. She was a passenger in a friend's private plane. J.D. was devastated and terribly angry. He was convinced that if Signa had been flying the plane, there would not have been an accident. He didn't handle his enormous grief well and vowed never to marry again. He resigned abruptly from his job as an assistant district attorney, abandoned his beautiful Art Deco mansion without even cleaning out the refrigerator, told no one except his grown children goodbye, and left the country for French Polynesia.

This was where J.D.'s life and marital history became murky. Some say he married again on the rebound … two times! But no one is really sure whether he ever married again at all, or if he did, whether it was once, twice, three or even four times. Rumors flew, and J.D. wasn't talking about it. It didn't matter. J.D. never went back to Tulsa, and his house was sold. He eventually returned to the United States, and with the money he had saved, combined with an inheritance from his now-deceased, well-to-do parents, he bought a trucking company. The company's headquarters were in Missouri, and J.D. bought a condo in St. Louis.

He'd never thought he would enjoy anything as much as he'd enjoyed being a prosecuting attorney, but he found he loved running his own transportation empire. He was good at logistics and good with people, and RRD Trucking made him ten times more money than he'd ever dreamed he would make in his lifetime. He bought a cattle ranch. J.D. liked to travel to Washington, D.C. to lobby his legislators in person about transportation issues. It was on one of these trips to the nation's capital that he met Olivia Barrow Simmons.

Olivia Barrow had been a cheerleader and her high school's homecoming queen. She was beautiful and outgoing. She was the prettiest and the most popular girl in her school, and she was also smart. After graduating from the University of North Carolina with a degree in mathematics, Olivia moved to Washington, D.C. where she shared an apartment with three other young women. Olivia had landed a job as a cypher specialist at the National Security Agency, so she wasn't able to talk to anybody about what she did at work.

Because Olivia was so attractive and had such a winsome personality, the NSA quickly identified her as a person who could represent the agency at Congressional hearings and other official public events. She always had all the answers, and although she would rather have been spending her time working on the complicated puzzles, mathematical constructs, and computer coding she loved, she was happy to be the pretty face of the No Such Agency. It was during one of her appearances before the Senate Select Committee on Intelligence that she was introduced to Bradford Simmons, the youngest man ever to be elected to the United States Senate. He was from Colorado, and he had a reputation as a womanizer.

Once he'd laid eyes on Olivia, he had to have her. She was young and vulnerable and flattered that a United States Senator wanted to date her. The women with whom she shared her apartment were envious and urged her to continue going out with Bradford. Olivia was eventually persuaded by the young senator's attentions, and within eighteen months, they were married. Olivia was devoted to her work and insisted on keeping her job at the NSA. Olivia and Bradford had three children, and Olivia chose to stay married to the senator until all three had graduated from college. Then she divorced him and took him for everything she could get in the divorce. Simmons had continued his womanizing behavior all during their miserable marriage, and Olivia had finally had all she could stand of the ridiculously handsome and adulterous cad.

Olivia vowed she would never marry again, and she focused her life on her children, her grandchildren, and the career she loved. Olivia had an exceptionally high security clearance and was a valuable employee at the NSA. Nobody could ever know exactly what she did, but whatever it was, she was extraordinarily good at it. She knew lots of secrets about everything and everybody, but she was a person of the highest integrity. No one ever worried that she would suffer from "loose lips."

Many eligible bachelors in the nation's capital wanted to date her, but she was done with men ... or so she said. Even in her late fifties, she was a beauty. She was a fascinating conversationalist, and everyone, men and women, wanted to sit next to her at dinner. It was at one such dinner party, hosted by her best friend, that Olivia was seated next to J.D. Steele. The two hit it off immediately and were roaring with laughter before the main course was served. The hostess, who had known Olivia for decades, had thought J.D. and Olivia would appreciate each other's company, but she'd greatly underestimated the enormous amount of fun they would have together. For Olivia and for J.D., there was nobody else at the party.

They were inseparable from that night on. J.D. bought a townhouse in Georgetown and courted the woman who had swept him off his feet. He had never expected to fall in love like this so late in life, but he adored Olivia and didn't want to be away from her. Olivia was just as shocked to find herself head over heels in love with J.D. She liked men, but after her disastrous marriage, she wanted nothing more to do with romance. But these two were a match that was destined to be. They had such a good time in one another's company. Each of them had a wonderful sense of humor, and they could always make the other one laugh. Even their skeptical grown children had to admit it was a beautiful thing to behold.

It was Olivia's idea to move closer to where J.D.'s business had its headquarters. The couple bought a house in St. Louis. She hated to leave her job at the NSA, but it was time to retire. Because Olivia insisted on spending one week out of every month near her children and grandchildren, who all lived in the Northern Virginia, Maryland, D.C. area, they kept the townhouse in the District. This was fine with J.D., and he usually came East with her. They traveled and enjoyed their lives. In spite of love and compatibility, Olivia was skeptical about marriage for many years. She didn't see why it was necessary. J.D. finally convinced Olivia that being married would not be the kiss of death, and they ended up tying the knot when they were both in their late 60s.

Chapter 12

THE GROUP GATHERED IN OLIVIA AND J.D.'S SUITE at 4:00 that afternoon. This pre-dinner confab had originally been scheduled for the cocktail hour so that Matthew could show several video montages, movie clips he had put together on assorted topics. His montages always inspired spirited discussion, even controversy. Other members of the group had presentations to make. With several authors, a poet, an expert on climate change, and an historian who was searching for his ancestors' grave stones, the gathering of friends had serendipitously taken on a kind of salon quality. Quite a few of them had things to share, and everybody learned from the presentations. It was fun and interesting and a good excuse for drinking wine together ... as if any excuse for that were needed.

Matthew told the group he was going to forego his movie presentations this afternoon, a decision his friends found downright shocking. They knew how he loved his montages. They loved them, too. Today, Matthew had his own personal true story to tell, and what he had to say would be more compelling and intriguing than almost any plot that had been conceived in Tinsel Town.

"I served my country as a member of the U.S. Public Health Service, the USPHS. Carpenter likes to tease me by referring to my service as the 'Yellow Berets,' but I don't feel any need to apologize for the work I did during the two years I spent at the USPHS Phoenix Indian Medical Center. I was assigned to an Indian Services facility. It was an honor to serve in this way, and I felt fortunate to have the chance to take care of those in the Native American community who needed my expertise. Even in the 1970s, we were aware of how our government had, in the past, mistreated indigenous populations. The Native American culture has had and continues to have many problems, and it can be argued that some of these, at least in part, are a result of their mistreatment by the white man. But I digress. This is not about indigenous populations or about my years in the U.S. Public Health Service. This is about what happened because the United States government had me in their sights and on their payroll in the 1970s. They came knocking on my door again in the 1980s.

"I'd already begun my private practice in Palm Springs, and Isabelle and I had two young children. She was juggling her counseling practice and taking care of our home and family. We were busy, but we were young. My USPHS commitment was behind me. You can imagine my surprise when two people, who said they were from the U.S. Department of Defense, came to my office one day after hours and insisted on talking to me in private. I could not imagine what in the world they wanted from me. What I realized later was that these two guys were almost certainly from the CIA. They wanted me back in government service, but only for a few weeks. They wanted to send me to Afghanistan. I quickly let them know that my going to Afghanistan was completely out of the question.

"The Soviet Union had marched into Afghanistan on December 25, 1979. To be exact, the Soviet Army began to

Christmas Eve of that year with 30,000 troops. This ...i was an attempt to prop up the faltering Communist government of Afghanistan that had taken power in 1978 as the result of a left-wing military coup. The leftist government, which was closely aligned with the Soviet Union, had little popular support. Draconian purges of their domestic opposition and their radical land and social reforms had been bitterly opposed by the overwhelmingly Muslim population. Anti-government guerilla groups, who of course were mostly followers of Islam, mobilized against the Soviet-backed puppet government, and chaos reigned. The Soviet Army entered the country, they said, to bring order. But that was a sham of gigantic proportions. They were really there to solidify Afghanistan as an additional piece of the Soviet Empire. It didn't work."

Tyler interrupted Matthew's discourse. "What does any of this have to do with the guy you smuggled into the hotel today?" Tyler wanted Matthew to get to the point.

"I'm getting to that. I wanted to explain what was happening in the wider world at the time this happened. You need to have some idea about the circumstances surrounding the man whose life is currently in my hands."

Matthew continued. "The ill-conceived Soviet foray into Afghanistan was a disaster. Even the Soviets had to admit it. The Mujahedeen, a Muslim coalition that formed to fight the Soviet Army, was backed by the United States. Through the CIA, we supplied this guerilla group with arms, funding, and intelligence. Significantly, we supplied them with shoulder-held surface-to-air missiles. These SAMs were a decisive factor in neutralizing Soviet air power in the Afghanistan war. The United States was in reality fighting a proxy war against our long-time nemesis and enemy, the USSR, and we used the Mujahedeen to fight that war for us.

"You will all remember that, in protest over the Soviet invasion of Afghanistan, Jimmy Carter, who was the U.S. President in 1979, decided to withdraw the United States from participation in the 1980 Summer Olympic Games that were held in Moscow.

"Having committed 100,000 troops to the fight and suffered 15,000 military fatalities, the Soviet Union withdrew its troops from Afghanistan in February of 1989 after investing almost ten years in the futile conflict. Two million Afghan civilians died during the war with the USSR. Just to give you a little bit of perspective, in terms of world events, the Berlin Wall fell in November of that same year. The Soviet Union collapsed two years later on December 26, 1991."

"The CIA was heavily involved in Afghanistan, and when one of the important leaders of the Mujahedeen had a urological problem, the CIA recruited me to be his specialist. The CIA agents who came to see me played several varieties of the 'duty to your country' card. After vehement protests on my part, I finally acquiesced and agreed to see the patient. The men from the DOD did not exactly threaten me, but they weren't going to take 'no' for an answer, no matter how many good excuses I had for turning them down. I accepted that I'd been beaten and within three days, I was on a private jet, no doubt owned by the CIA, headed for Pakistan.

"Americans were not welcome in Afghanistan at the time, so I was smuggled into the country as an Australian physician, a member of Doctors Without Borders. I was told by my handlers, the whole time I was in Afghanistan, that I would constantly be at risk of being kidnapped. This is a detail they'd failed to mention until after I was already in country. I was assigned two armed body guards. The Soviets would kill me on the spot, or they would capture me to trade for one of their spies or other valuable assets. It would be a public relations nightmare. Or, some Mujahedeen, who was not thrilled that the Americans were messing in their country, would take me hostage and hold me for a big bucks ransom. Of course, the CIA would have had to pay them to get me back, and I might have been lucky enough to live to celebrate my release. Kidnapping would not have been a good thing for me or for the CIA.

"I was not given any time to rest after the long flight that had taken me half-way around the world. This was an emergency, and there was no time to waste. It was an extremely rough trip into the mountains where I had to travel to examine the Mujahedeen leader. One of my CIA handlers told me that I'd been chosen, not only because of my abilities as a urologist, but because I was young and in good shape. Being as fit as I was had put me at the top of the list. No matter how brilliant a urologist he might have been, the overweight fifty-year-old doc with an irregular heart beat who taught at the university would never have been able to make the journey into the Hindu Kush. The terrain was too rugged and demanding. I wasn't sure I was going to make it, and I was in my 30s at the time. I traveled by donkey, by mule, and by foot, and the trip took three days. Lucky me! So much for the rewards of staying in shape.

"PSA testing was being used back then as it is now, and my patient's PSA had been tested at a lab in Pakistan. It had taken a long time for the blood sample to reach the lab, and it had taken almost as long for the results to get back to the patient's internist. It was difficult for the patient to pee, and his discomfort had reached a critically painful level. His PSA was elevated, but it was not in the range that would lead me to believe it was an aggressive cancer.

"I was never allowed to know my patent's real name. All of the Mujahedeen back then called themselves Mohammed. Of course they did! Mohammed's primary care physician, a

Pakistani internist who had been trained in England, did not think he had prostate cancer, but he wanted a urology consult. He wanted the opinion of a well-trained urologist, and he wanted treatment for whatever was causing the Mujahedeen leader to have so much trouble urinating. All of my communications with Mohammed occurred through an interpreter. Mohammed spoke no English, and I didn't know either Pashto or Dari which was sometimes called Afghan Persian. Even if I'd spoken one of these Afghan languages, I probably wouldn't have been able to understand him. Mohammed spoke a dialect.

"After I'd examined him, I suspected that my patient had a benign enlargement of the prostate, not prostate cancer. The difficulties of making a medical diagnosis in primitive conditions are obvious, but benign prostatic hyperplasia was my best guess. As challenging as it was to make the diagnosis, it was even more problematic to figure out how to fix his problem. He needed surgical treatment, an operation called a transurethral resection of the prostate, TURP, but we were in the middle of nowhere. And that was a staggering understatement.

"I gave Mohammed some medications that made it easier for him to empty his bladder. He was incredibly grateful for this, and he formed an instant attachment to me, I think, because of the relief the meds had afforded him. I was more than ready to get out of the mountains of Afghanistan and return to Palm Springs, but Mohammed insisted that I perform the surgery he needed. He refused to let anyone else touch him. He wanted the surgery done in the Kush, where he was living. I explained that it was impossible for me to perform the TURP, the procedure he had to have, without a sterile operating room and an anesthesiologist. I could not operate on him in these crude mountain conditions.

"He refused to be airlifted to Pakistan and go to a Western-style hospital. The options were limited. We finally decided that the easiest thing to do, to satisfy all parties, was for us to make the trek overland to Kabul. The CIA would arrange for a rudimentary operating suite there, probably in a tent. I would, reluctantly, do the surgery on Mohammed's enlarged prostate. He continued to insist on it and would not be dissuaded. I knew that all of this was easier to contemplate and talk about than it would be to accomplish.

"It had taken three days for me to reach the isolated compound in the mountains where Mohammed lived and ruled. We had been traveling light and fast, or so my body guards and the guides had told me. Making the journey with Mohammed Mujahedeen who was in his mid-fifties and suffering from severe BPH, we would not be moving as fast. Mohammed traveled with an extensive entourage. Our caravan would be larger, with more people and more animals. This made us a bigger and better target for the Soviet helicopters that were omnipresent and always eager to take out a gaggle of Muslim rebels. Mohammed's men carried SAMs, but we would be in a great deal of danger as we made our way slowly through mountain passes and attempted to reach the environs of Kabul.

"The people of Afghanistan are tough. They have been invaded many times during the last thousand years, by many different interlopers, and still they have prevailed. Mohammed did not seem to be frightened by the thought of the long and hazardous journey ahead, and he was not at all worried about the impending surgery. I, on the other hand, was terrified and sick to my stomach just thinking about what I was being asked to do. I'm not exactly sure how many days our trip was supposed to take to reach the make-shift field hospital near Kabul and a tent where I would operate on my patient. It seemed as if it took forever. We were fired on by Soviet helicopters at least three times, but the tough guerilla fighters, who led our party through the mountains, knew our route, a road that they and their ancestors had traveled for centuries. They always knew where there was a cave, a place to hide, around every corner. When they heard the helicopters approaching, they hurried us into the caves, out of sight and out of gun range. They'd done this many times.

"One day a man appeared, seemingly out of nowhere, in the traditional dress of an Afghan Muslim. Mohammed and my two CIA body guards knew him and greeted him with much enthusiasm. He was introduced to me as Afif. He looked me up and down with skepticism, but when he heard that I was Mohammed's physician, he seemed to accept my presence. He spoke at great length with Mohammed in private. It wouldn't have mattered if I'd overheard them because I had no idea what they were saying to each other. I learned that Afif was an accomplished linguist and spoke English as well as several other languages and multiple dialects. He stayed with us for a meal that evening. Afterwards, he sat around the campfire and talked and sang some songs in a language I didn't understand. He had a beautiful and haunting singing voice."

"I asked him what the name Afif meant. He seemed to be quite intelligent and well-educated. I'd not heard the name before."

"He told me that Afif meant 'pure, chaste, modest and virtuous.' After he'd said this, he burst out laughing. When he'd stopped laughing, he continued in his excellent, if heavily-accented, English, 'But I have many names. Not all of them make me sound as wonderful as Afif makes me sound.' He roared with laughter again. His laughter was contagious.

"I asked him why he had many names. He looked at me for a long time, and I could see he'd come to a decision of some kind. He'd decided to trust me. He said, 'I have many lives, and each life requires its own name. I am from Uzbekistan, so I have an Uzbek name. I am also a member of the army of the USSR.' He lifted his long white Pashtun robe and showed me that underneath the traditional Afghan dress, he wore a Soviet army uniform. I was stunned. 'So I also have to have a Soviet name.' He smiled at my shock on seeing the Soviet uniform. 'I am a friend of Mohammed, so I have an Afghan name. That name is Afif. I am also an asset of your CIA, so I have a CIA code name. That name is Delilah. You can call me Afif.' He smiled again. By this time, I was totally speechless and couldn't think of anything more to say."

"Afif continued. 'You are right to be confused. This is a confusing time in a confusing world. You are an American, I think. You have come a long way to help Mohammed, and I am grateful to you for that. Mohammed is my friend.'"

"I agreed with Afif that it was a very confusing world. I admitted that I was completely out of my element. I told him, 'I live in California, although I don't think I'm supposed to tell you that. I'm supposed to tell you that I am an Australian who works for *Doctors Without Borders*.'"

"Afif already knew that my CIA cover name was Fleming and remarked, 'Not too clever, are they?'"

"I had to laugh, too. Fleming was such an obviously British name. 'The least they could have done was give me an Australian-sounding cover name. Kookaburra or Koala would have done nicely.'"

"Afif went on to tell me more about his life. 'I was born in Tashkent. That's the capital city of Uzbekistan. You have probably never heard of my country. The USSR, as part of their empire building, took over Uzbekistan in 1924. We have been a part of the Soviet Union since that time. Most of the people in Uzbekistan are Muslims. The Soviet military has conscripted soldiers from all the countries over which it has taken control — from Estonia, Latvia, Ukraine, Lithuania,

Uzbekistan, and all the rest. The Soviets are a blunt instrument, and they are idiots. They draft Uzbeks, who are Muslims, to fight in the Soviet Army in a war that they have begun against another Muslim country. Is it any wonder that some of us, who hate the Soviets to begin with and do not want to be part of their empire, let alone a part of their empire's army, have gone over to the other side? I have gone over to the side, and I am now with the Afghan guerillas. They are Muslims. They are members of my own Islamic faith. Why would I fight against these people on behalf of an atheistic regime based in Moscow? I have never been to Moscow. I have never been to Russia. I fight with Mohammed.'"

"Afif's English was eloquent as he spoke about his rejection of the Soviet Union and his embrace of the Mujahedeen, his Muslim brothers in Afghanistan. He hated the Soviet invaders with a passion it would have been difficult for the Afghans themselves to match."

"He told me, 'I have an important job in the Soviet Army. My position is not so important to the Soviets, but it is extremely important to the Afghan rebels. I am a major in charge of supply. I know where all the Soviet Army's supplies are stockpiled. I know where the ammunition and the machine guns are secured. I know where the gasoline for the tanks is kept and where the fuel for the helicopters is stored. I know it all. I know where everything that is important can be found at this exact moment.'"

"Afif could see on my face that I fully grasped how important a Soviet supply officer would be to the Mujahedeen in this particular war. Not only could munitions be stolen; they could also be sabotaged. I imagined contaminated fuel in helicopters that fell out of the sky. I imagined tanks that blew up because of booby traps that had been planted underneath. I contemplated the ammunition duds and the thousands of AK-47s that might be missing firing pins. In my mind's eye, I could see the explosion in the Soviet ammunition dump. Afif was a walking gold mine.

"Later that night, as we slept, our camp was attacked by a company of Soviet foot soldiers. They arrived in a helicopter and descended to the ground on ropes, assaulting our small band with machine guns blazing. Their helicopter never landed on the side of the mountain. It hovered in the air and kept firing its guns at our campsite. We'd been caught unawares. Someone had betrayed us. I was certain that we were all going to die.

"Afif was not much taller than I was, but he was incredibly strong. When the shooting began, he lifted me out of my sleeping bag and carried me to a space between the rocks. The bullets were coming from every direction and going in every direction. Afif lay on top of me, a human barrier protecting me from the gunfire and certain death.

"When the Soviets thought they had killed us all, they climbed back up their ropes and into their Mil Mi-24 helicopter, leaving their carnage behind. We had been taken completely by surprise, and only a few defensive shots had been fired by Mohammed's body guards. My CIA bodyguards had not had time to get off a single round. Mohammed was dead. All of Mohammed's bodyguards were dead. One of my bodyguards was dead, and one was injured. Most of our pack animals had been shot. Afif and I were safe, without a scratch. I had survived only because of Afif's quick thinking and his willingness to cover my body with his own.

"We'd started out with two communications radios. They'd both been destroyed in the attack. Afif had a backup radio in his pack, and he quickly called for help. The U.S. did not officially send helicopters into Afghanistan. If they presumed to fly over a Soviet-controlled country, they would be taking a terrible risk of starting World War III. And the Mujahedeen did not check carefully when they shot down a helicopter. All whirly birds looked like Soviet aircraft to them. The CIA was taking a tremendous chance, sending a helicopter in from Pakistan to pick me up.

"I tended to my bodyguard's wounds and was confident he would live. Although we were close to the Pakistan border, it was hours before help arrived. They had to wait until dark before they could send a helicopter to rescue me from my mountain perch. When it arrived, it couldn't land. It stayed suspended in the air above us and lowered a harness. Afif shook my hand and slapped me on the back. I was still in shock. He helped me into the harness and watched as I was lifted into the small aircraft that would take me to safety in Islamabad. Afif and my wounded bodyguard wouldn't come to Pakistan in the helicopter with me. Afif's mission was to remain in the Kush. He raised his hand and made the V for victory sign with his fingers. I made the V sign in return. With a big smile on his face, he screamed at the top of his lungs, loud enough to make his voice heard above the helicopter's rotors, 'Fuck the Russians.'"

"Afif gave me a very American thumbs up as the black helicopter without any markings on it, turned and flew away from the mountainside. I waved goodbye, thinking I would never see Afif again.

"Less than twenty-four hours later, I arrived at Fort Bragg in North Carolina for debriefing. The mission had not been successfully accomplished. My patient had died, not from his disease, but due to enemy fire. It was a war, but it was not our war. So I could not talk about it, not with anyone, not even my own wife. I hated that, and protested vehemently. I was not exactly threatened, but my CIA handlers let me know, in no uncertain terms, that the United States had no presence in

Afghanistan. The CIA had no presence in Afghanistan, and I had never been to Afghanistan. I was back in Palm Springs twelve hours after my debriefing ended. I was expected to resume my civilian life and my medical practice as though none of this had ever happened. I was so happy to be back in the USA and reunited with my wife and children, I put everything that had happened in that far-away land behind me. After all, I had never been to Afghanistan."

Matthew took a deep breath. "Then this morning, at age seventy-six, almost forty years later and thousands of miles from our last encounter, I got on a tour bus at the United States Air Force Academy and found Afif, the man who had saved my life so many years ago, soaked in blood and lying on one of the bus seats. He had begged Elizabeth to hide him. He'd said his life was in danger. I did the only thing I could possibly do. I had to save him. I had to protect him. What would you have done?"

Chapter 13

TYLER MERRIMAN WAS A HIGH SCHOOL FOOTBALL star. The Air Force Academy recruited Tyler to play football, and he played for one year before he was sidelined by a shoulder injury. Tyler stayed on and graduated. He subsequently earned an MBA from Stanford. He became a pilot for the United States Air Force and spent ten years flying military missions for the USA. He never talked about the years he'd spent in the USAF, but his closest friends speculated that he was flying the Lockheed SR-71, "the Blackbird" spy plane that supposedly had the capability to see the numbers and letters on the license plate of a car parked in Red Square. When anyone came right out and asked him if he'd flown the Blackbird, Tyler would hum a few bars of the Beatles' song of the same name and smile his enigmatic smile. If he had flown the Blackbird, he would have been able to see everything and everybody from way up there. But he would never tell.

Tyler had married, briefly, when he was in the military, but his wife was young and somewhat spoiled. She resented the time Tyler spent away from home, and they divorced when they'd been married for less than two years. Tyler moved to Northern California after he left the Air Force. He built a commercial real estate empire and became a wealthy man. Tyler dated well-known and glamorous women — movie actresses, anchorwomen who appeared on national television, and female politicos. He was a good-looking and much sought-after bachelor, but he successfully avoided the altar for decades after his first marriage ended.

Tyler Merriman had been smart and lucky in his business dealings, and he was an outstanding athlete. He bought a condominium in Telluride, Colorado so he could ski for several months in the winter. Because he was such a skilled and outstanding performer on the slopes, it wasn't long before he was hired as a ski instructor. His time was his own, and he arranged his schedule so he could spend most of the winter in Telluride. He found he loved teaching others to ski. Tyler had his own plane and flew around the country to check on his commercial real estate holdings. He hiked and biked and ran, and he even sometimes played squash, when he couldn't be outdoors. Tyler was an active sportsman. He decided he wanted to be closer to his condominium in Telluride and eventually relocated from California to Colorado.

He was in his early seventies when he met the stunning Lilleth Dubois. He first saw her on the ski slopes. Lilleth was skiing The Plunge, the most demanding run on the mountain, with confidence and ease. She was a beautiful and aggressive skier, and her grace and athleticism caught Tyler's attention. He skied close to her and watched her as she turned and handled the difficult moguls and made her way down the slopes. He knew he had to meet her. At the end of the day, he followed her into the ski lodge and wasted no time introducing himself. She did not appear to be with a date, and Tyler moved in to get to know this lovely woman who was at least his equal in the snow.

Lilleth lived in Farmington, New Mexico, and was on vacation in Telluride. Every year, she spent a week of her vacation at a nearby ski resort with demanding runs. She loved the challenge. Lilleth had been married before, but she never talked about her ex-husband. She was not at all interested in a new relationship, but she dated occasionally. When Tyler approached her in the ski lodge, there was something about him that she found intriguing and appealing. She decided to give him a few minutes of her time. As they talked, it became apparent that she and Tyler had much in common in terms of their love of physical activity. She accepted his invitation to dinner, and they drank a bottle of wine and talked late into the night.

Lilleth was a psychotherapist, and her practice consisted primarily of counseling Native Americans who lived on the Navajo reservations in Northwestern New Mexico. Her job was another challenge she enjoyed. A significant percentage of Native Americans have problems with addictions, and Lilleth spent many client hours dealing with these. Her clients spilled the beans to her about who was embezzling money from the casinos, who was cooking meth on the reservation, who was running the bootleg alcohol business, and other confidences. All psychologists hear people's secrets, but because of the particular circumstances of Lilleth's practice, her clients had more secrets to tell.

Lilleth's patients liked her, and most were grateful for her help. Occasionally, one would fall off the wagon, and his or her dark side would take over. He might beat up his wife and children or rob a bank. A client who was polite and meek when sober could turn into a deranged lunatic if he or she indulged in too much alcohol.

Once a client had attacked Lilleth when she was getting into her car. The man had been drinking excessively and was wandering around the parking lot of the community center where Lilleth met with her patients. The man had been in trouble before, and that night he pushed Lilleth down when she tried to open her car door. She hit her head, and the resulting gash required several stitches in her jaw. But Lilleth was tough, and she was able to call 911 on her cell phone while she tried to talk the inebriated man down from his anger and confusion. He was threatening her with a knife when the reservation's law enforcement officers showed up to take him into custody.

Lilleth hadn't wanted to testify against him at his trial, but because, on several previous occasions, he had assaulted other people when he'd been drunk, he was sent to prison. LIlleth visited him while he was incarcerated. She was sorry she'd had to participate in sending him to jail. She had forgiven the man for hurting her. Trying to keep her clients away from the bottle was one of the toughest challenges she faced. She wouldn't allow herself to live in constant fear, but she never knew when someone she was treating would go over the edge.

Lilleth and Tyler dated long-distance for many months. Tyler was in love like he had never been in his younger years. Lilleth was even more wary of commitment than he was, but she had grown fond of Tyler. It was a big step for her when she accepted his invitation to move in with him and live at his house in Bayfield, Colorado.

Tyler had been attending the reunions for years and looked forward to seeing his old friends and their wives and girlfriends. He'd never brought a date or a partner to one of the events. Last year, he'd finally convinced Lilleth to accompany him. She was anxious to see Maine, and Tyler had assured her that the group was friendly and would welcome her as if they had known her all their lives. Lilleth was skeptical, but she agreed to go to Bar Harbor. Tyler had planned extra days of hiking, biking, kayaking, and other activities. Lilleth knew he liked to show off his own vigor to his friends. She suspected he also was proud of how strong she was and that she had the stamina to keep up with the men in the group.

Chapter 14

MATTHEW RITTER'S FRIENDS SAT IN STUNNED silence. Even Isabelle, who had heard most of the account earlier that afternoon, had not heard all the gory details of what had happened on her husband's long-ago trip to Afghanistan, a trip that officially had not happened at all. Her face was ashen. No one said anything. Matthew was worn out from talking, from finally revealing the secrets he had kept to himself for far too long. It was cathartic for him to tell his story, but he was spent from the effort.

Richard was the first to speak. "I had no idea. I can't imagine going through all of that, and then not being able to talk about it. I'm surprised you're able to sleep at night, that you don't have nightmares. I'm sorry I ever gave you a hard time about ordering those frozen daiquiris. They are not a sissy drink … really. From now on, I'll buy you a frozen daiquiri every time we go to a restaurant. In fact, I'll buy you two. How is it that you haven't suffered from PTSD?" Richard and Matthew hunted quail together in the Arizona desert. They had been best friends for decades. Richard was feeling guilty for having ridiculed his friend for ordering frozen daiquiris when they went out for dinner together.

"So, is the guy you found in the bus Afif, the one who saved your life? And you haven't seen him or heard anything about him since 1983? Are you certain this is the same man?" Bailey asked the questions everyone wanted to have answered.

"He is Afif. I am certain he's the same man. He looks remarkably unchanged, and even if I hadn't recognized him when I saw his face, he has a distinctive tattoo of a bird on his ankle. It's Afif, without question. I suspect he has another name now, an American name. Elizabeth said that when Afif spoke to her, he didn't have a foreign accent of any kind, that he sounded like an American. I haven't heard him speak at all, not one word. He's still unconscious, and I'm pretty worried about that."

Tyler attempted to bring some common sense to the discussion. "You need to take him to a hospital. What if he's been poisoned or something? He might need tests. If he's been drugged or given something toxic, maybe there's some kind of antidote. You said he worked against the Soviets back in the day, so he could be in big trouble. Everybody knows what happens to those who've crossed the former KGB thugs who run that country now. Putin is tying up loose ends and cleaning up all over the world. He murders his enemies — former enemies as well as current enemies." A long time in the past, Tyler had done secret work for the U.S. Air Force, and he didn't talk about it. But he knew a lot about the Russians and the KGB, and he kept up with world events.

"I probably should take him to a hospital, but from the things he said to Elizabeth, it's obvious that, for whatever reason, he's afraid for his life. He believes someone is trying to kill him. He specifically said he wanted her to hide him. He also said he wanted to get to the Penmoor. That was puzzling. Does he have a friend here, someone he thinks can help him? Well, he's here now, and he doesn't even know it." Matthew

Ritter was going to protect his patient. He felt it was more important to keep him hidden than to subject him to lab tests and imaging studies. "If he doesn't regain consciousness soon, I will reconsider taking him to the hospital."

"I'd really be surprised if Putin and his gang of bad boys would go that far back. The Soviet-Afghan war was a long time ago. There's no doubt that somebody has him in their sights, but you don't really know who's after him. You don't know that it's the Russians. Maybe it's just an angry husband." Bailey paused. "Is he going to make it … if he hasn't been given a Polonium cocktail or something like that? Will he recover from the beating he took?" Bailey had done secret work for the Department of Defense. It had been decades since he'd been involved in that kind of intrigue, but he also knew the Soviets and the Russians. He knew they played hard ball. They killed the people who had betrayed them in the past as well as those who would not do their bidding in the present day.

"None of his wounds are life-threatening. If he hasn't been given a lethal dose of something or if he doesn't have a brain injury or if he doesn't have a ruptured spleen, he should recover."

"That's a lot of ifs." Lilleth was the reality tester for the group. She brought them back from their speculating and their hypothesizing. "Did he have a wallet in his pocket or any kind of identification on him?"

"Good question, and the answer is 'no.' He didn't have anything on him, not a scrap of paper, not even a receipt from the Quick Mart."

"What if he wakes up while you're here telling us this long, involved saga about who he is and how you know him? Won't he panic, if you aren't there to tell him what's going on?" Sidney wanted to be sure the man they'd gone to so much trouble to smuggle into the hotel wasn't going to make a break for it.

"Of course, I've thought of that. I left a long note, addressed to Afif, on the bed beside him. In the note, I explained where he was and what we'd done to get him to the hotel. I reminded him of how I'd met him and what had transpired in Afghanistan in 1983. He will not have forgotten that. I left my cell phone with him and asked him to call Isabelle's phone if he wakes up. I told him I'd come right back to the room as soon as he called. He's just down the next hall, on this same floor."

Everyone looked at Isabelle. She rolled her eyes, shrugged her shoulders, and held up her phone. "I've been married to him for a long time. I try to help. At least we now have a suite." She smiled a half-hearted smile, a woman resigned to her spouse's schemes.

Olivia had a question about the time Matthew had traveled in the Hindu Kush. "You obviously spent quite a few days wandering around the mountains and caves of Afghanistan. How did you stay in touch with Isabelle while you were away? It's not like you could pick up the phone and call her every night. But you had to have called her a couple of times during the time you were gone."

Matthew looked at Isabelle and sighed a deep sigh. "That was a huge sticking point with my CIA handlers. I told them I had to be able to call Isabelle while I was in Afghanistan. She thought I was in Saint Louis, Missouri at a conference, learning how to use a new piece of medical equipment. She would have been very hurt, angry, and suspicious if I hadn't called her." Matthew hated the lies he'd told his wife, but he decided to confess the full extent of his deception.

"The CIA had satellite phones or radio phones or some kind of phones that they used in the mountains to communicate with the rest of the world. They let me use the phone to call Palm Springs a few times. I told Isabelle I was incredibly busy with my classes, that the days were long, and that I was exhausted when I got back to my hotel room. I told her I couldn't call her often. She wasn't really happy about that. Remember, I was half-way around the world, and with the time-zone differences, I had to get up in the middle of the night to make these calls to her. Communicating with my family was a definite weak spot in the lie the government had forced me into." It was obvious that Matthew was still full of regret about this part of his Afghanistan adventure.

Matthew was eager to change the subject. "Because Elizabeth said he spoke English without an accent, I am assuming Afif has been in this country for a number of years. I also assume he can read English as well as speak it. I know he's a smart guy. If he's been anywhere out from under a rock for five minutes, he knows how to use a cell phone. Even if he wakes up and wants to try to get away, I don't think he's well enough or strong enough to go anywhere. I'm continuing to palpate his abdomen and monitor his blood pressure. I'm more worried about a nick in his spleen than I am about his having ingested Polonium. Richard has examined him and doesn't think he has any internal bleeding. Of course, Richard is used to palpating dead people's abdomens." Matthew had to get in a friendly dig at his pathologist friend.

"So what was he doing at the Air Force Academy?" Cameron had been quiet until now. He was always looking ahead, to what was going to happen next. He wanted to know what Matthew was going to do about Afif in the next hours and days. "Do you really think we can protect somebody who is in the sights of a Russian hit squad? We're a bunch of old people. We don't even have a gun ... at least I don't think we do. This is more than a little bit crazy."

Of course Cameron was exactly right. But there was more to this than rationality, and it was clear that Matthew was not going to give up his patient to the authorities, to any Russian hit men, or to anyone. Matthew didn't have to say a word for his friends to understand how important it was that Afif, or whatever his name was now, be kept safe.

"Whatever happened to our relaxing, drama-free week at the Penmoor?" Elizabeth said wistfully. A few of the group laughed. A few cringed, remembering the troubles they'd encountered in Bar Harbor the previous year.

Olivia knew it was important to keep everyone's blood sugar and spirits up. "Our dinner reservation tonight is here at the Penmoor West. We don't have to cross the lake. We don't even have to go outside to get to the restaurant. We just have to ride the elevator down to the main floor. It's Italian tonight, actually it's Northern Italian … La Firenze. We have our own table in an alcove at the end of the rear dining room. We can continue our discussions there."

Matthew left to check on his patient and said he would meet the group at the table. Not a single bottle of wine had been consumed during Matthew's monologue. They had not been able to pry themselves away from his fascinating story long enough to open a bottle or find a wine glass. On their way to dinner, trying to shake their memories of wars, long-past and present, they decided they would to try to talk about other things the rest of the evening. Even though everyone's thoughts were still in the Hindu Kush, they tried to lighten the mood.

"I'm going to order two bottles of Prosecco. I think we need to have some fun tonight." Gretchen had a son who was a Navy seal, and she did not want to think about how much danger he put himself in every day. She wanted to do a bit of partying.

"Are you going to drink both bottles yourself, or are you going to share them with the rest of us?" Tyler liked to tease Gretchen. He and Gretchen both had things in their pasts that were confidential, even this many years after the fact.

A certain comradery had formed between the two of them. "Maybe I'll order two bottles of Prosecco for myself." Tyler smiled at her.

"Silly."

"I'm going to order two bottles of Chianti. What I really want is two bottles of the wine that come in those bottles that are in a basket, the straw thing, you know." Cameron liked to order wine.

"That's the cheap stuff, the wine that comes in those basket bottles, the bottles covered in straw. I bought that rot gut for a dollar a bottle when I was in college. I always got Ruffino, I think. You don't want that." J.D. knew all about the bottles of basket wine. He'd drunk more than a few of those in the past, but he'd moved on.

"They don't put it in those straw bottles any more. Now Chianti is enormously expensive, and it's called Super Tuscan. You want to order Brunello." Bailey had also downed his share of cheap Chianti during his youth. He was hoping the bad wine in the basket bottles was no longer available.

"I know all that. I have also given up Chianti for Super Tuscan. I was just saying that … about the basket wine. Those bottles bring back memories. I like the way they looked. We used to keep the bottle and put a candle in it. Very romantic. Very collegiate." Cameron motioned for the waiter. "Three bottles of your best Brunello, please."

The waiter blanched. "Are you sure, sir? We have some Brunellos that cost $900 a bottle and more."

"Well, maybe I don't need anything that good. Give me the wine list. I can find something that's pretty good for less than that, can't I?" Cameron had a lot of money, but he didn't go crazy spending it.

The Tuscan potato soup with sausage and kale was a popular choice on this cold night. The bakery at the Penmoor was world class, so the Italian bread was devoured quickly, and more was ordered. They ordered the pasta course to be served family style, and passed around the bowls of spaghetti in marinara sauce topped with fresh basil and grated Locatelli Pecorino Romano and the bowls of linguine fini with clams and breadcrumbs.

There was a discussion about the Italian word for the French word chiffonade. The fresh basil on top of the spaghetti marinara had been cut into tiny, thin ribbons. Someone Googled it, and everyone learned that what they were tasting on top of their spaghetti was called 'basilico striscioline.' Then they began talking about the Pecorino Romano. Elizabeth knew without a doubt that the sharp and tangy cheese was made from sheep's milk. But Tyler said he knew for a fact that it was made from goat's milk. More discussions ensued. Where had the clams come from? They tasted fresh, and the dish was perfect. But who ordered anything with clams in Colorado, and why was linguine fini better for this dish than regular linguine?

The restaurant was Northern Italian, so a few of the men had to have Bistecca alla Fiorentina. The veal chop was pricey, but several in the group ordered it. It came with roasted rosemary potatoes and spinach sautéed in garlic and olive oil. They sighed with pleasure. Olivia ordered a second bowl of soup for her main course. Everybody loves Italian. The Italian cream cake was a popular dessert, but most were too full and settled for gelato in a variety of flavors. No matter how full one was, one could always eat some gelato.

They sat around the table for a long time after dinner, finishing the wine, drinking decaf espresso drinks, and eating biscotti. There was much laughter and much remembering. The guys spoke fondly of their days at Camp Shoemaker and who had won the prizes there. They remembered a particularly adventurous scavenger hunt when J.D. had carried three poisonous toads in his pocket. They'd always wanted to win every contest.

During dinner, Matthew had made two trips back to his room to check on Afif who was still not awake. Matthew was beginning to panic because his patient had not regained consciousness. Dr. Ritter was giving some thought to calling an ambulance to take the man to the hospital. Matthew knew he could call on his friends for help if he needed them. They knew his story now, and without exception, every one of them was on board to help him try to save Afif, or whatever the man's American name was.

Olivia reminded everyone that they had an art tour scheduled for the next day. The current owner of the Penmoor Resort was an enthusiastic and prolific art collector. His Western art was on display everywhere, in all the halls and lounges and conference rooms. A special docent, an expert on the Penmoor's collection, had been hired for a "Behind the Scenes" tour of the art in all the Penmoor buildings. Everyone in the group was interested in art, and they were looking forward to their special tour.

Chapter 15

On Wednesday morning, everyone except Matthew arrived to have breakfast together in the Penmoor West's sun-filled restaurant. The wind had died down, and the sky was gloriously blue and without a cloud. The group welcomed another beautiful day, and they would walk together to the Penmoor Main to begin their tour of the famous collection of art work, architecture, and decorative interior design.

The resort housed an enormous number of the owner's personal Western Art collection. Priceless works were on public display in all the main floor hallways and in the many meeting rooms. Everywhere one looked on the main floor, there was a valuable and interesting work by a famous Western artist. The paintings by Frederic Remington and Charles Marion Russell and others provided a feast for the eyes at every turn. The display of so many high quality works of art begged to be studied and was almost too rich to be believed. How generous that the owner of the Penmoor was willing to share his remarkable collection with those who stayed at the resort. It was worth a trip to this wonderful spot, just to look at the artwork that hung on the walls.

In addition to the tour that any visitor to the Penmoor could sign up for, Olivia had wanted to do something special for the group, who all had an interest in art. When Olivia and J.D. had made their preview trip to the Penmoor, she had talked to the docent and convinced her to schedule a special "Behind the Scenes" tour for their group. This would include a look at the underground rooms where the resort owner's art collection was cleaned. Repairs to the art work itself as well as to the frames were taken care of in these subterranean workrooms. The lights that showed the paintings off to their best advantage were repaired and replaced here.

There were too many paintings in the collection for all of them to be on display at one time, so the art was rotated, from building to building and in and out of storage. The paintings that were not being displayed at any one time were carefully stored in climate-controlled storage rooms below the public floors of the main hotel.

One of the things this group of friends was particularly curious about was how security was provided for the massive art collection. It was so openly displayed to the public in the hallways and other heavily-trafficked rooms of the hotel, everyone wondered how it was protected – from theft and vandalism. Were there security cameras pointed at every work of art? Were security cameras pointed at everyone who looked at each work of art? Did anyone monitor these cameras, if indeed there were cameras? Were they monitored by human security guards, or were the recordings viewed only if something went wrong? If the monitoring was done by humans, was it constant? The art enthusiasts had many questions, and quite a few of these could not be answered. Some of the answers, as they'd expected, were confidential and part of the security protocols.

Matthew Ritter loved art history, and he had been especially excited about this art lecture and tour. He was torn between staying with Afif and not wanting to miss a word the docent had to say. Matthew decided it wouldn't hurt to take a break from caring for his patient. It helped that Richard had volunteered to leave the lecture periodically to return to the Ritters' rooms to check on Afif. To try to keep housekeeping out, Matthew had put a "DO NOT DISTURB" sign on the door of the room where Afif was recovering, and he'd locked the door between Afif's room and the suite. Matthew knew he couldn't keep housekeeping out of the room indefinitely, and he thought he had an idea about how to handle that. Things were getting complicated.

Their tour guide and art docent's name was Dolly Madison Wilder, and she was a treasure. An older woman with a delightful sense of humor, her audience was captivated when she uttered her first sentence. She knew the Penmoor's architecture and art collections backwards and forwards, and she had family history on the owners and anecdotes that kept the group mesmerized. The main building of the resort was the original hotel built on the grounds. It exhibited the best of Italianate architecture and displayed the incredible handiwork of the Italian artisans who had been brought in to do the decorative ceilings when the resort was being built. The intricate and priceless embellishment of the hotel, especially the ceilings of its public rooms, was awesome to behold. Combined with Dolly's running commentary, as they moved from room to room, their tour was nothing short of magical.

Dolly explained that her father had been a history buff and had been thrilled when his daughter had been born so he could name her Dolly Madison. She also confided that indeed she was a distant cousin, quite far removed to be sure, of Laura Ingalls Wilder. She laughed that she was old, but not quite old enough to have rescued the famous Gilbert Stuart painting of George Washington from the burning White House during the

War of 1812. What Dolly did not tell her tour group was that she had graduated from college with a dual degree in psychology and criminal justice and had been a private investigator for forty years before retiring. She admitted that she'd initially become interested in art history and architecture as a hobby ... because of her name.

When they'd completed the standard tour that most visitors enjoyed, the group took the elevator to a floor that was at least one level below the ground floor of the main building. Once she had them all inside the elevator and the doors had closed, Dolly inserted a special key into the panel where one pushed the buttons for the floors. The tour group didn't know how many floors below the main floor they traveled. Dolly led them down a long hall, through a couple of doors she unlocked with a master key, through storage rooms where extra chairs and tables were piled high, and finally through a set of double doors.

They arrived at the nerve center of the art collection. This was where the paintings were stored that were not on display. This was where the artwork was cleaned and reframed. This was where the inventory of the Penmoor Resort's hundreds of valuable paintings was catalogued. Members of the reunion group were amazed and surprised they'd been allowed to see this well-secured and important part of the Penmoor's art collection.

"I'm surprised you were willing to bring us down here and show us all of this. I know it must be off-limits to most people. I think I'd be afraid to let anybody know this was here. Thank you for trusting us and bringing us to see where the work is done." Isabelle knew they were being allowed to observe something quite special, something most of the public would never see.

Dolly Wilder laughed. "We do trust you, of course, but if you had not all passed a strict vetting process with flying colors, you would never have been allowed to come down into the crypt and see the inner workings of the collection." She smiled at the surprise in the wide eyes that stared back at her.

"You vetted us so we could come down here and look at this secret art storage facility?" Gretchen knew there probably was some kind of federal law that prohibited the vetting the hotel had done. As an HR person, she had to know in detail about privacy rights and every other kind of individual rights. There were so many laws now about everything, it was difficult to keep up with all of it. As part of her job, she directed an entire legal team that made sure her company didn't violate any of the laws or step on any toes.

"No, of course not. Let me explain. I knew you would be surprised, even shocked, when I told you that you'd all been vetted. It was my little joke … to tell you about it. I hope I didn't give anyone palpitations." Dolly was surprised to see how shaken her group of senior citizens had been to hear what she'd just confessed to them. "Don't worry. As I said, you all passed without a hiccup. Mr. Merriman had a few top-secret years that we weren't able to access, but it was the U.S. government that had done the redacting of that part of his life. So we knew he'd probably had some kind of spy job going on during that period. Between the military service and the alphabet soup jobs that both the men and the women in your group have held, there was a lot to sort through. Or so I was told. I don't know any details, really. That's all confidential. I was told that you are quite an upright bunch of citizens. But let me tell you why we had to vet you in the first place."

Cameron knew he had a public persona, and most of his secrets were already known. He'd written two books and put it all out there himself. "Yes, I'd love to know why we are that important. We're just a bunch of old friends who get together once a year to talk about ourselves, try to count the number of wives we've had, and remember how good looking we were when we were younger. We're not that interesting anymore, but we are having a hell of a good time in our old age. So why would anybody want to know anything about us or go to the effort to find it out?"

"As you know, many famous and wealthy people visit this resort. Some, in fact, think they are much more important than they really are. But you didn't hear that from me." Dolly chuckled to herself. She'd been doing this docent's job for more than two decades. "It happens that we have an unusually high-profile individual staying here this week. This person's stay coincides exactly with the days your group made their reservations for. It was somewhat unusual to have your group book so many rooms for a Monday through until the following Monday. Elle, our concierge, made a point of getting to know J.D. and Olivia when they were here a few months ago. That was another thing that was somewhat out of the ordinary .... that the Steeles came for a dry-run of your weekend, to check things out." Dolly looked at the Steeles. "We realized right away that you are exactly who you say you are, but several of you have, in the past, worked at some highly-classified government jobs. This was also somewhat unusual, that there would be so many of you 'classified' people in one group."

"But now we're just old folks, mostly retired and having fun." Elizabeth still did not understand.

"We know that, but our V.I.P. special guest, who is also staying with us this week, insisted on doing his own background checks, just to reassure his security people. If it makes you feel any better, there were several other guests this man's security team vetted as well. And, as I have said, you all passed. No problems. There was nothing at all sketchy about any of you. That was also a bit surprising. None of you have ever been in jail, not even for disorderly conduct." Dolly was trying to make light of what her art enthusiasts had taken much too seriously. "And, that is why you were allowed to have this special 'inside tour' of the Art Department. The vetting wasn't really our idea, and we didn't do it. Our staff had nothing to do with vetting you. The Penmoor doesn't vet its guests. It was all done legally and confidentially and by somebody who has no official connection with the Penmoor. Please don't be angry. Nevertheless, I have to tell you that, if the security checks hadn't been done, I would not have been allowed to show you around down here and tell you *our* secrets. You were already cleared. We knew there was no risk, bringing you here."

No one in the group had anything to hide anymore, if they ever had, so after the initial surprise and discomfort of knowing their lives had been under the microscope, most of them decided to let it go. At least they pretended to let it go. None of them liked it that they'd been investigated, but what could they do about it now? They loved Dolly Madison Wilder. She hadn't done the investigating, and if she said it was all good, they believed her.

She continued with the tour and told them some fascinating stories about the Penmoor collection that most guests never heard. There had been thefts in the past and breeches of security. She told them all about it. They hung on every word.

A few people were working in the art compound that day. Some personnel were working at computers. Others were sorting and organizing the works of art and placing them carefully into numbered bins that were specially sized and cushioned to protect the frames as well as the paintings. All of these people wore gloves and smocks. A few even wore masks. Some of the personnel were cleaning and repairing the paintings. They also wore protective clothing. Attempting to look as if they were cleaning the floor, there were a few housekeeping types down here, but everything in this basement room was already spotless. Dolly told her tour group to feel free to walk around and look at anything that interested them. They just could not touch anything. And she did mean *anything*. She was available to answer their questions.

The group was fascinated with what they saw. They still had no idea about how the security of the collection was maintained. That would forever remain off-limits to visiting eyes, even well-vetted visiting eyes. Any misgivings they might have had about the security checks and the vetting had been mostly forgotten or at least forgiven. Dolly had to pry them away and round them up when it was time to leave. Three hours had flown by.

They felt like Dolly was an old friend by now and insisted she join them for lunch. She agreed. They had a table reserved for their group at the Golf Club. A few of them had eaten there the day before, and they'd raved about the food. Everyone was going to eat there together today. It was a gloriously sunny day, and they hoped to eat outside on the patio, overlooking one of the Penmoor's famous golf courses. As they were about to leave the resort's main building to walk to lunch, someone came up to Dolly and asked to speak to her urgently. She excused herself and stepped away from the group to have a conversation.

Tyler was standing nearby and could see the concern, even the flashes of what he thought might be fear, that crossed Dolly's face as she listened to what her colleague was saying. Tyler wore hearing aids, and he could turn them up so that he was able to clearly hear conversations that were taking place at the next table in a restaurant. Although it was not his nature to eavesdrop on a regular basis, he was curious about what was upsetting their calm, cool, and collected docent, Dolly Madison Wilder. He stepped as close to her as he thought he could get away with and turned the volume on his hearing aids up to maximum. What he managed to overhear, upset him and worried him.

Dolly came back to the group that was waiting for her to go with them to the Golf Club. She was obviously disappointed. "I'm so sorry," she said. "Something has come up, and I'm not going to be able to have lunch with you today. Maybe another time? I've enjoyed you all so much. You're all knowledgeable about art, and it has been my pleasure to get to know you. Sorry to throw you a curve with the revelations about vetting you, and all of that. I hope you've forgiven me." Dolly was rambling. "Really, I had nothing to do with it."

She tried to smile, but she was obviously preoccupied about something. She wasn't really thinking about what she was saying as she bid the group goodbye. She would receive a generous tip for the tour she had given, but they were concerned, as they made their way to their lunch on the patio of the Golf Club, about what was troubling their friendly docent. Several in the group verbalized their concerns, wondering out loud what had happened at the last minute, that Dolly had not been able to come to lunch with them.

Tyler knew, because he had overheard Dolly's conversation. What he had learned was not good news. Of course he would be sharing what he'd discovered with the others. He was debating with himself about when would be the best time to tell them what he knew. He decided that for now, they'd had enough about art and intrigue and needed food. He would wait to share with them what he knew about the art theft at the Penmoor.

J.D. had ordered the smoked turkey club sandwich the day before. It had been served with a basil-flavored mayonnaise and tiny, French fried shoe string potatoes. It had been so good, he was tempted to order it again. But he also loved shrimp salad, so today, he was going to have that. Cameron also ordered the shrimp salad, served in a Louis-style dressing and heaped into a ripe avocado. It didn't get any better than that for lunch. Elizabeth was torn but finally ordered the club sandwich. Several in the group chose from the variety of Mexican food options. A few had a glass of wine. Most ordered iced tea or soft drinks.

All enjoyed the view. It was a glorious fall day, and the sun was so warm. They were sitting outside and had to move the huge table umbrellas closer to their tables to provide shade and keep themselves from getting sunburned. There were two deer fawns on the golf course, making friends with a group of golfers. The grass was brilliantly green. It sloped up and down the fairways at the foot of the rugged rises of the Sangre de Cristo Mountain Range. Some of the golfers in the reunion group discussed renting clubs and taking a day to enjoy one of the Penmoor's courses.

A women's spa day was planned for Thursday. On Friday, the group was scheduled to spend the morning at Seven Falls and have lunch there. The Cheyenne Mountain Zoo was not to be missed, and at the Penrose Heritage Museum, there was an antique vehicle collection that had been amassed by the original owner of the resort. All of the guys and some of the women wanted to see the assemblage of unique horse-drawn carriages, race cars, and exotic automobiles.

Tyler was preoccupied during lunch, and Lilleth was concerned. He wasn't himself. Everyone else was talking so much, they didn't seem to notice how quiet Tyler was. They'd almost forgotten about the injured man who was in the Ritter's hotel room, except that Matthew was not having lunch at the Golf Club with them today. After the art tour, he'd gone back to the Penmoor West to see his patient. He felt guilty about having been away from his room for the three-hour art tour. He left the group when they headed for the Golf Club and hurried back to check on Afif.

Chapter 16

IT HAD BEEN A WISE DECISION FOR MATTHEW TO skip lunch with the others and return to his room. When he unlocked the door that adjoined his suite, Matthew heard mumbling and groaning coming from the bed. Afif was making sounds for the first time and might even be awake. Matthew hadn't worried too much about giving him any pain killers, because until now he'd been unconscious. Matthew didn't have a narcotics license in the state of Colorado, so writing a prescription for any kind of powerful drugs would not be possible. Matthew had purchased some OTC pain medicines at the drugstore the day before, but he hadn't wanted to give Afif anything until he was certain he had no internal bleeding.

Matthew had been monitoring Afif's heart rate and blood pressure with the stethoscope and BP cuff he'd purchased at the pharmacy. He continued to be reassured that his patient did not have any internal injuries because his blood pressure and pulse remained relatively normal. If and when Afif woke up, he could answer Matthew's questions about pain and weakness and other symptoms. The answers to these questions could go a long way towards keeping the injured man out of an ambulance and out of the ER.

"Afif, Afif, can you hear me?" Matthew had allowed his patient to rest for twenty-four hours. It was time he began to communicate.

Afif opened his eyes a little bit, and tried to look around the room. "Who are you and where am I?" He attempted to focus his gaze on Matthew. "Nobody has called me that name in many, many years. How can you possibly know that name?"

"You look almost the same as you did in 1983. I look much older. My hair has mostly disappeared, and the little I have left on my head is white. It isn't any wonder you don't recognize me. In 1983, you saved my life in the Hindu Kush. I was not allowed to tell you my real name at the time, but I remember I told you I was from California. The CIA was trying to pass me off as an Australian who worked for Doctors Without Borders. My cover name was …."

"Fleming!" Afif said it before Matthew could get it out of his mouth. "You are the doctor who came to try to help Mohammed. I remember you."

"Yes, my CIA cover name was Fleming. I always wondered if they were thinking about Ian Fleming, the novelist, or if they wanted me to pretend to be Sir Alexander Fleming, the Scottish biologist who discovered penicillin. My real name is Matthew Ritter. You are in my hotel room at the Penmoor Resort."

"And now I am an American citizen, and my name is Geoffrey McNulty. How did you ever get me here? The last thing I remember was jogging on the Air Force Academy grounds and being attacked by a member of the Russian mafia. We were duking it out in a parking lot. He was getting the better of me, and he had a knife. I am older, too, even if I don't look it. I have become soft, a desk warrior. I'm not as much of a fighter as I used to be. And, my adversary had a hypodermic needle full of something. Of course, I don't know what was in the needle, but I figured he intended to either kill me on the spot or knock me out so he could take me someplace and torture me before he killed me. Either way, I knew I was a dead man."

"Your American English is perfect, by the way. I know languages were your thing, even back then, in '83. To hear you speak today, I would never have known you were not a native speaker. Elizabeth said you spoke like an American, without any trace of an accent."

"Who is Elizabeth?"

"I have so much to tell you, but first I need to examine you and ask you some questions." Matthew did a physical exam on his patient and determined that he was fine. He could tell that Afif's or Geoffrey's mind was fully intact. There was no brain damage. He seemed surprisingly well, considering the beating he'd taken. He didn't appear to have a serious head injury or any internal injuries.

Based on the information about the hypodermic needle, doctor and patient determined that the contents of the needle must have been some kind of a heavy-duty tranquilizer. The attacker had jabbed Afif's arm with the needle, but Afif had been able to almost immediately swat the needle out of the man's hand. The syringe had ended up smashed on the ground beside the bus, just before the Russian had run away. In spite of his quick response and his deflection of the attack, enough of the tranquilizing agent had reached Afif's blood stream to keep him knocked out cold for more than twenty-four hours. It had been a potent brew, but it hadn't been Polonium. Whatever it was, it hadn't killed him. Matthew proceeded to tell Afif about how he'd stumbled onto the bus, bleeding all over the place, and how Matthew and his friends had smuggled him off the bus and into the Penmoor.

"How did you know I wanted to get to the Penmoor?"

"You said so … to Elizabeth. She's the woman who was on

the bus when you forced the doors open and climbed aboard. You begged her for help. You told her that you'd been betrayed and asked her to hide you. By the time I reached the bus, you had lapsed into unconsciousness. Now you know everything that happened after you made your way onto our tour bus. No one, except friends of mine, know you are here."

"No wonder the CIA picked you to bring to the Kush. I have to say, you were resourceful and quick ... to think of such a clever way to smuggle me into the hotel."

"Actually it was Elizabeth's idea. Some of us suspect she might have actually been in the CIA a long time ago. But no one asks her about that."

"I look forward to meeting this Elizabeth."

"How did you make it all the way from Afghanistan and being in the Soviet Army to fighting in a parking lot at the USAF Academy?"

"It's not as difficult to understand that journey as you might think. I was a CIA asset, and I continued playing my multiple roles for a few more years after Mohammed was killed. After a while, my secret work was about to be discovered. My Soviet superiors were becoming suspicious. Because I'd helped them successfully for such a long time, the CIA promised to relocate me. They kept their promise. I knew many languages, so I had options. I asked to be relocated to the United States. My handlers even brought me to a place with mountains. I have always lived in the mountains, and I am comfortable in the mountains. They gave me a new identity, an American passport in my new name, and a job at the Air Force Academy ... doing, guess what? Being in charge of supplies." Afif smiled. "I also had duties as a translator, but back then, not many people at the Air Force Academy spoke Dari or Pashto.

"I remember. You were invaluable to the guerillas because you knew where all the Soviet military equipment and ammunition was stored. You knew where the fuel depots were ... you knew everything."

"Yes, I am very good at being in charge of supplies. I can keep it in my head, but now, of course it is all on the computer. I loved my job at the academy. My title changed over the years, and I think my last one was something like "Materials Management Specialist." I worked my way up and eventually was in charge of handling all the non-lethal supplies the academy needed. I made sure it all arrived when it was scheduled to arrive and got to where it was supposed to go. By the time I retired, I was in charge of it all. I'm not good at being relaxed and idle, and I missed my job terribly. They took me back part-time as an independent contractor."

"It sounds as if you were safe here in the United States for a long time. What happened, all of a sudden and after all these years, that the Russian mafia came after you?"

"I don't know exactly how I was outed, but I have some strong suspicions. The Russians once again have become the nemesis of the United States. After the last Presidential election, the Russians have been blamed for absolutely everything. If your toilet is broken, it is the Russians. If there are pot holes in your street, it is the Russians." Geoffrey laughed out loud at his Russian jokes. "No one hates the Russians more than I do, and no one would love it more than I would, to blame them for everything. But really .... Ha!" He laughed again. "All joking aside, there is also no doubt that Vladimir Putin is on the march and wants to put Humpty Dumpty back together again. He thinks the fall of the Soviet Union was a tragedy of the highest order, the supreme catastrophic event of the Twentieth Century. He wants his empire back. He's a terrible KGB thug. Of course, you and everyone else in the world know all of this."

"What I want to know is who betrayed you. Did someone find out that you'd been a CIA asset in the Soviet-Afghan war?" Matthew found it hard to believe that Geoffrey's attackers could have targeted him because of what had happened decades ago. It didn't seem possible.

Afif, now Geoffrey, continued to tell his story in his own way. "Now the Russians supposedly fix our elections. If you believe what is on the news, Putin's agents sneaked into our voting booths, pulled the levers and marked the ballots, and every one of them voted for Trump. I don't know about that, but I do know it's a fact that the Russians are hacking us all the time. So are the Chinese and everybody else. They're all inside our electronic data bases, stealing our secrets. Sometime I will tell you how I know so much about that. For now, with regard to my own case, I am only hypothesizing. I know nothing with absolute certainty. I have no proof. But, I think Russian hacking, perhaps randomly, uncovered my history as a CIA asset. I think the Russians somehow found a link to my American name. They must have rediscovered that I'd deserted from the Soviet Army during the Afghanistan war, and they decided to come after me. Old-line KGB people like Putin are tying up loose ends and making an example of all those they feel betrayed the Soviet cause. Vlad is a Soviet. He still believes in the Soviet Union and breathes the Soviet air. He cannot let it go. The whole truth is probably a lot more complicated than that, but I think the attempt to kill me is part of a clean-up effort from the old days."

"But you said the person who tried to kill you or kidnap you is a member of the Russian mob. How would you be in the sights of the Russian mafia?"

"Putin uses the Russian mafia around the world to do his dirty work. He says publicly that he is 'wiping out the Russian mob' and all of that BS, but in reality, they are his cadre of enforcers. They do his bidding and kill his enemies. They are doing this in almost every country in the world, and they are certainly an enormous presence here in the United States." Geoff looked at me and shook his head. "You Americans are still so naïve. And now I am one of you. Putin pays them, and I am certain he pays them enormous amounts. These people are his personal hit squad."

"I believe you. We are so tied up with special prosecutors and worrying about Ukrainian quid pro quo here, we sometimes lose sight of the big picture."

"I don't know how the Russians found out about me, but they have. I need to disappear again, but I am too old for this now. Some of our past presidents and other politicos have chosen to be AHB's with Putin. Somebody in the Air Force might have given me up, but only a few people here knew anything at all about my past. I don't think anybody at the academy knew the whole story, that I had been in the Soviet Army and was a CIA asset. It is a mystery to me how it happened, but I suspect it was Russian hacking that uncovered my secrets. I am sure my life is now in grave danger."

"Do you have a family? If you have to assume a new identity and relocate, what happens to them?"

"That's another whole story. I did have a wife and two sons. But I was not a good husband. I admit to this. I have never been good with relationships, and my wife divorced me. She had every reason to leave me. Although I ought to hate her, I am not angry with her for taking my kids with her. She eventually remarried, and her new husband adopted both my sons. They have his name now, and they are adults. They live in Florida, and I see them only once a year. I love my boys, but I was never cut out to be a family man. So, no I don't really have a family anymore."

"Let's get you well, and then we will figure out what to do about the future."

"I have a friend who works here at the hotel. That's why I said I had to get to the Penmoor. He's a landscape person here. I share a house with him, and I know I can trust him. He may be the only person left in the world, except for you, that I can trust with one-hundred-percent certainty. Somebody betrayed me, and until I can figure out how that happened, I trust no one ... except you and Baktash."

"Baktash is your friend, the one you trust and the one you share a house with? He works here?"

"Baktash is from Afghanistan. He is a linguist, and he worked for the Air Force for a while. Now he works as a landscaper at the Penmoor. He loves to work outside. He owns a small house in Colorado Springs, a house he can't afford on his own. When my wife left me, I needed a place to live. Baktash and I had become friends through our jobs at the academy, and I moved into his house. He is a bachelor, and he loves women. He always has a girlfriend, and he doesn't spend much time at his house. I mostly have the place to myself. I pay him rent, and my rent money allows him to pay the mortgage on his home that he doesn't live in. It's a bit convoluted, but it works for both of us. I have known him for years, and I trust him."

"We have to talk about housekeeping here at the hotel. They want to come in and change the beds, clean the bathrooms, vacuum, and all of that. I am going to have to move you to my other room, to the suite, while the housekeeping staff does their thing. I don't want them suspecting that I am keeping an injured man here, in this room. If I keep them out for another day, I'm afraid they'll become suspicious."

"I get it. They have to get in to clean the room, and they can't find any trace of me."

Matthew could see that his patient was becoming tired. He'd been badly injured and unconscious for an entire day.

Immediately after he'd regained consciousness, he'd had a prolonged and intense discussion with Matthew. All that talking had sapped whatever energy he'd been able to muster.

"You must be hungry, and you have to stay hydrated. I tried to get you to drink some water, but it mostly rolled out the sides of your mouth. I gave some thought to starting an IV, but I didn't have the equipment to do that. I'll get you a bottle of water from the mini-fridge and order food for you. After you've eaten, I'll help you get into the wheelchair. I'm going to wheel you into the other room. You can watch TV or rest next door until housekeeping has finished with this room. I don't want you to try to walk around yet. You haven't eaten anything in a couple of days, and you are weaker than you realize. Humor me on this. I know you are tough, but I want you to use the wheelchair, just for today."

Matthew let Geoffrey know he was going to be in charge of things for now. His patient's eyelids were closing. Matthew wanted to keep him awake until he was hydrated and until he'd eaten something. "Here's the room service menu. I haven't eaten lunch either. Tell me what you think you can eat, and I'll call down and place the order. I'll wheel you into the other room when room service arrives to set up their table. Then I'll bring you back in here, and we can eat our lunch." Matthew unscrewed the tops from two bottles of cold water and handed them to his patient. "Drink!"

"I am hungry, now that you've brought it to my attention. I know the food is good here." With some help, Geoffrey was able to get into the wheelchair so Matthew could move him to the room next door. Geoffrey admitted he was surprised at how weak he had become in just one day. He was thankful to have wheels and someone to push him from room to room.

Within an hour, Matthew had fed himself, and he'd fed and rehydrated his patient. He called housekeeping. By allowing the Penmoor staff to clean the room as well as the suite, he hoped he'd allayed any suspicions they might have had. There had been a lot of back and forth from room to room for Afif, aka Geoffrey McNulty. After housekeeping left, Matthew had wheeled Geoffrey back to his room. He'd fallen asleep sitting in the wheelchair, and Matthew had fallen asleep on top of the room's other double bed.

Chapter 17

THE PENMOOR RESORT HAS GREAT SHOPPING. IT has many high-end chain stores, one-of-a kind specialty retailers, and first-class art galleries. It even has a store called the Unique Boutique. Sidney, Gretchen, and Olivia were eager to explore some of these expensive and interesting shops. Isabelle wanted to see the shops, too, but first she headed back to the Penmoor's main hotel to make some sketches. She hired artisans to make things for her home furnishings store in Palm Springs, and the examples of decorative arts at the Penmoor were unparalleled. Isabelle never missed an opportunity to appreciate something beautiful.

Richard decided he would check on Matthew's patient. He was taking Cameron and Bailey with him to room #504. J.D. wanted to check the hours for the Penrose Heritage Museum that contained antique cars and a variety of old-fashioned horse-drawn carriages. He hoped to visit there the next day. Then J.D. was opting for an afternoon nap. Elizabeth was tired after the intense art tour, and she needed some down time. Tyler was anxious to discuss with Lilleth what he had overheard that morning between Dolly, their docent and guide, and her colleague. Everyone was doing their own thing after lunch, and they would meet in the Steele's suite at four that afternoon for cocktails.

Gretchen tried on a Dolce and Gabbana silk shirt. It was way too expensive to actually buy, but it was so beautifully made and had just the right shades of navy and light blue for her skin tones. It was tempting, but she decided to put it back on the hanger and back on the rack. She sighed with some regret, but it was always fun to look. She needed a pick-me-up and wondered if her two shopping companions wanted to get a cup of coffee or tea. Just then her phone chirped to let her know she had a text. She wondered if it was her boss. Maybe he had good news that her stalker had been apprehended.

She left the store and spotted a coffee shop across the plaza. She checked the incoming text as she navigated the cobblestones in the direction of her coffee fix. The text was longer than she'd expected, so she bought her vanilla latte and found a seat close to the door.

Before she'd joined the major corporation in Dallas where she was now employed, Gretchen had worked at a private bank in Zurich. Eventually, the bank's clientele had become too much for the American woman who had been raised in the Midwest with solid middle class values. She had known she needed to go home. She gave up a lucrative position with the Swiss bank and moved back to the United States. Her banker boss in Zurich had not been happy to see her leave. They had stayed in touch, emailing and texting from time to time, and Gretchen knew he had retired eighteen months earlier. He was bored in retirement but had been trying valiantly to make a life for himself with his rather severe French wife. They had planned to travel, but he'd decided, out of desperation, he wanted to go back with the bank part-time. Retirement had not agreed with Arnold Sprungli. He was related to the chocolate family that, together with the Lindt family, made fabulous candy.

Gretchen was stunned when she read the text from her boss in Dallas. Arnold Sprungli was dead. He'd been in his late sixties, but he had not died of natural causes. He had been shot while driving his Mercedes sedan on the road between Zurich and Lucerne. The results of the autopsy allowed the police to determine that a sniper rifle had been the weapon. Sprungli had been targeted. His death had been an assassination. Things like that did not happen in Switzerland. It was unheard of, but the facts were indisputable.

All Swiss citizens have firearms in their homes, and they know how to use them. Because each Swiss household is required to be part of the nation's volunteer militia, Switzerland's military defense, everyone is careful, in the extreme, with their weapons and responsible for them. The police, who were investigating the assassination, had tried to keep the shocking incident quiet. They'd put out the word that Arnold Sprungli had died in a car crash, which technically was not a lie. After his head had been blown to bits, his car had run off the road and careened down the side of the mountain. If he'd still been alive when his car left the pavement, he would have died because the car fell five hundred feet from the road down into the valley below.

The banking community of Zurich, all of whom knew the true cause of death in less than twelve hours of Sprungli's demise, was in shock. They knew that Herr Sprungli sometimes did business with less-than-desirable groups and individuals. But they all did. There was distress among Sprungli's colleagues, but there was also fear. The sniper who had fired the shot that had taken Sprungli's life had disappeared into thin air. He'd left no clues, and the Swiss authorities were completely at a loss as to who had perpetrated the disturbing and unthinkable crime. This sort of thing happened frequently in the United States, in places like Chicago and Los Angeles and Washington, D.C. Assassinations were not expected and were not welcomed in Switzerland.

Gretchen was completely speechless after she'd read the long message from her current boss. Someone from the Swiss bank where Gretchen had worked for Sprungli had called Gretchen's Dallas office with the news, and Gretchen's current boss had taken the phone call. That was how he happened to have all the details — details which had not been made public or reported on the news. Gretchen was beside herself. She was as shaken as she knew her Swiss banker colleagues had to be. If her former boss had died from poisoning, Gretchen would have immediately suspected Sprungli's wife, but the MO on this murder was definitely not her style.

Arnold had been a smart and shrewd businessman, and he was a genius with numbers. But he had been mild-mannered, even introverted, in his personal life. Gretchen had known him well. She'd felt he was considerably henpecked by his domineering spouse, who was definitely the boss at home. His wife's personality was probably one reason Arnold's retirement had not worked out well for him. The couple had never had any children. Arnold had not had many friends, and Gretchen did not think he could possibly have had any enemies. He was not that kind of person. But now he was dead, and he had been deliberately and brutally murdered.

The assassination had occurred ten days earlier. Shivers ran up and down her arms as she held the phone that had brought her this terrible news. As she reread the text, she realized Arnold's memorial service and burial were being held today. She wouldn't have attended anyway, but she would have sent some flowers. She sat and stared at her latte as it grew cold in front of her.

Gretchen was sitting there, deep in thought and still staring at her almost-full cup, when Sidney and Olivia found her in the coffee shop. "What's wrong with you?" Olivia wanted to know. She was joking when she said, "Who died and didn't leave you any money?"

Gretchen stared back at Olivia. Rather than explain it all, she handed her friend the phone. After Olivia had read the text, she handed the phone to Sidney so Sidney could read it.

Olivia went to the counter and ordered three hot coffee drinks. She brought six large chocolate chip cookies to the table. Olivia believed that food could almost always help, to celebrate in times of triumph and to comfort in times of tragedy.

"You said he was into deals with some sketchy people. You always said there were some dangerous guys who brought money to your bank. Isn't that one of the reasons you left your job over there? You told me one time that some of them made your skin crawl." Olivia worried about Gretchen and the fact that she'd once had a job where she'd hobnobbed with a criminal element who traveled to Zurich to secure and hide their money.

"All banks in Switzerland do business with an occasional international criminal as well as some wealthy people who are rough around the edges. One of the rules of the banking business in that country is … no one asks you where you got your money. They just keep it safe for you. Or, if you want, they will invest it and make more of it. But no Swiss banker ever wants to know how you made your millions or your billions. Arms trafficking, drug dealing, government corruption, money laundering, and everything else you can think of, are sources of huge windfalls of cash and diamonds and bitcoin and bearer bonds and on and on. These are the secrets that nobody talks about."

"You don't think this has anything to do with you, do you?" Sidney was concerned. She had once worked for law enforcement as a jury and witness profiler, and she was always putting things together and figuring things out. "I mean, somebody went after your former boss in an extreme and serious way. There was no mistake made. Whoever took out the contract on him wanted him stone cold dead, not just frightened or intimidated. It's been more than ten years since you quit your job in Zurich and came back to the states, right? Would there be any reason why you might be a target, too?"

That same thought had been niggling at the back of Gretchen's mind as she'd read the news about Arnold's death. Sidney had put her finger on exactly what was bothering Gretchen. Gretchen had been Sprungli's assistant. Had anyone they'd done business with even known her last name? Occasionally, Gretchen had accompanied Arnold when he had entertained clients at lunch or dinner or for drinks. Gretchen was the arm candy that her boss liked to show off, although all of their clients understood that Gretchen was not just a pretty face. Everyone knew she had the smarts to more than match her good looks. Had she ever mentioned her last name at these social events outside the bank? Swiss banks were discreet, and she didn't think many clients had ever known her full name. And, she had a new name now. She had taken Bailey's last name, MacDermott, when they'd married. If anyone had tried to track her down, it wouldn't have been difficult to figure out that she had remarried and what her married name was.

Gretchen was upset about Arnold, and she was concerned about whether or not there were implications for her as a result of the way he had died. Her friends tried to reassure her and told her not to worry. "I'm sure there isn't anything to worry about. This all happened in Europe and has nothing to do with you." Olivia wanted it all to be over and for there to be a happy ending. "You've got enough to think about already, with the stalker ...." Olivia clamped her mouth shut quickly, but not before she'd contributed to Gretchen's inevitable angst. "It's a good thing you're hiding out here at the Penmoor. I mean, you're not really hiding out exactly, but it's a good thing you're here and not at your office. Nobody knows you're here, right?" Olivia realized she probably ought to keep her mouth shut before she dug herself any deeper into a hole.

"I hope nobody except our group knows where I am. My boss doesn't know I'm here. My kids don't even know. I guess somebody could track my cell phone, if they really wanted to get to me. Maybe I should get rid of this phone and buy a new one."

Sidney wasn't as certain as Olivia was that Arnold Sprungli's assassination in Switzerland had been an isolated and far-away event. She wasn't as convinced as Olivia was that Gretchen's former boss's death had nothing to do with Gretchen. She didn't want to alarm Gretchen any more than she already had, but she felt that Gretchen ought to be on the alert and especially careful about everything she did. Sidney had a sixth sense about things like this, and she was worried about Gretchen's safety.

"It will soon be time to meet for drinks before dinner. We'd better get back to the hotel. I need to close my eyes for fifteen minutes before we watch Matthew's movie montages. Of course, he may be tied up with mystery man Afif and not have his film clips ready to show. I loved the art tour this morning, but my brain is tired after trying to take it all in." Sidney had decided not to say anything more to Gretchen about the danger she might be facing.

Chapter 18

Richard, Bailey, and Cameron were in Room #504 with Matthew, talking to Geoffrey McNulty. Richard asked their patient several medical questions, and he agreed with Matthew that there was nothing physically wrong with the man that would not be cured by the tincture of time. The two doctors both were of the opinion that Geoffrey's mental faculties were functioning perfectly.

Bailey and Cameron, who'd previously seen him only in a wheelchair disguised as Elizabeth, were delighted that Afif, former Soviet supply officer and CIA asset, had regained consciousness and had turned into Geoffrey McNulty, American citizen. They'd been brought up to speed on Geoffrey's story since he'd left Afghanistan and were trying to figure out what to do going forward. Geoffrey was convinced that he was marked for murder. The other men in the room believed him and would make plans accordingly. Geoffrey didn't know which of his colleagues at the Air Force Academy he could trust, so he refused to contact anyone there for help.

Although he had some suspicions, he didn't really know how anyone could have found out about his past. He only knew for sure that the Russian mafia had come after him and wanted to kill him. The man who had attacked him in the academy parking lot had called him a "traitor to the Soviet Union," as if that entity existed anywhere anymore, except maybe in Vladimir Putin's imagination. As the Russian had pummeled him and tried to chop him up with a knife, he had called McNulty "a CIA snitch." Whoever had tracked him down had known too much about his history. From now on, Geoffrey was completely on his own. He had to disappear. He had to give up the life he'd loved in Colorado Springs.

Cameron and Bailey both had resources. They each knew a great many people. Cameron was very skilled at placing his employees in jobs within his company. He felt it was critical that people like the work they do. The great lengths he went to, to be sure the people he hired were in the right positions, was one of the many factors that drove his tremendous success in business. He asked each potential member of his organization many questions before he hired them to come to work for him. He made sure they were a good fit with his company and with the other people they would be working with. Because he was so careful about the hiring and placement of his employees, he had scarcely any turnover in personnel. Because he had a reputation for hiring high-quality people, his friends in the business world came to him for help with their employment needs. Cameron wanted Geoffrey to be happy in his new life, and he used his considerable expertise to question the former CIA asset.

Bailey worked with veterans on a daily basis, and he understood the mind set of those who had fought in wars and been in combat. He was sensitive to their particular kinds of fears. Bailey immediately knew that Geoffrey really believed he was in mortal danger, and Bailey believed him. Bailey grasped what the others in the room might have doubted, why Geoffrey refused to trust anyone he'd known or worked with at the Air Force

Academy. Although he knew Geoffrey did not really believe that any of his former colleagues there had betrayed him, it was the not-knowing that made him leery. Bailey realized that no one from the Air Force Academy could ever know anything about what might happen in the future to Geoffrey McNulty.

Because Matthew trusted them, Geoffrey trusted Matthew's friends. Because of the way they had questioned him and had made an effort to understand him, he knew they were sincere and wanted to help him. Because of their obvious concern for him as a person, they had earned his trust on their own. Geoffrey was reassured that these people were on his side, and he was in awe that they were willing to extend themselves and go to a great deal of effort on his behalf.

This new friend, who had fought for the Mujahedeen against the Soviet Union in Afghanistan, had become important to their group who had never met the man until two days ago. Because he had serendipitously fallen into their laps and they had helped to smuggle him off the tour bus and into the hotel, they'd become invested in his safety and well-being.

Going forward, the once-upon-a-time Uzbek had to have a place to live. He had to have some kind of income. The guy was obviously smart and had many talents. He hated to leave the Colorado Springs area, but realized he had to. He would not be happy in a busy urban area. He loved the mountains and being out of doors.

Bailey knew someone who was looking for a person with Geoffrey's skill sets. He hoped he could convince the former CIA asset to take the position he had in mind. There were details to be worked out. Cameron knew he could deliver on several pieces of the puzzle. Bailey could deliver on a few others. They knew they would not be able to do it all on their own and would need help from others. But they had the beginnings of a plan.

"What's the name of your friend, the one who works here at the Penmoor? We need to contact him and get his input about what to do with you. How do you know you can trust this man, if you are so sure you can't trust anybody else?" Bailey thought they needed to include Geoffrey's one trusted friend in their planning process.

"I explained it all to Matthew. I've rented a room in my friend's house for many years. I can read people well, and I know I can trust Baktash. He works here at the Penmoor, in the landscaping department. It's fine for you to talk to him, but please, do not involve anyone else from the resort. Baktash loves his work here, and I would not want to be the cause of his losing the job or his supervisor becoming suspicious of him for any reason."

Cameron reassured him. "We know how to be discreet, but we're going to need some help from Baktash. What does he know about any of this? Does he know about your background? Does he know your life has been threatened?"

"As I told Matthew, I don't see Baktash very often. He lives with his girlfriend and isn't at the house most nights. He knows nothing for sure about my background. I have never spoken of it with him. If he knew what I had done in the past, I'm afraid it would put him at risk. I think he suspects some things, but he knows nothing for sure. He does not know I have been targeted by the Russian mafia. He doesn't know I've been injured or that I'm here at the Penmoor, hoping to find him."

Bailey sought to reassure Geoffrey. "We will say nothing to him about the details of your past. We will tell him only that you are in trouble and have to leave Colorado Springs. We will tell him you are preparing to leave the country to begin a new life. In case he is ever questioned by anyone about you, that's what we want him to think is going to happen, even though you will not really be leaving the country. Do you think he will believe us? Will he help us, knowing as little as we intend to tell him about what's going on?"

"He will help you. Bring him here when it is time to include him in the planning. I will explain that you are helping me, and he will do whatever you ask of him."

Bailey described the job and location he had in mind for Geoffrey's future. The proposed new site, in another Western state, was quite similar to Colorado, but it was hundreds of miles away from Colorado Springs. Geoffrey liked the sound of the place that might become his new home. He said he thought he would enjoy the work he would be doing there. He was willing to put his life in the hands of these new friends and work with them to help transport him out of danger.

Bailey told Geoffrey and the others in the room what he wanted to do. There were holes in his plan, and he needed suggestions about how to plug those holes. Cameron could help with some, but not all of them. They thought they would need J.D. and his trucking company at some point.

They were stumped on two important issues, and they didn't think anyone in their group of friends could come up with either of the missing things that they felt were vital to their plan's success. Geoffrey needed new identity papers, and they had to be the real thing. Geoffrey would have to have a new birth certificate, a driver's license, and a U.S. passport. He would need a genuine social security number and other convincing documentation and credit cards to allow him to live a normal life in a new location.

The planning team also desperately needed a dead body. The body would be discovered as evidence of Geoffrey's death. Whenever a dead body was mentioned, everyone looked to Richard, a retired pathologist who had, in the distant past, worked for the Philadelphia Medical Examiner's Office.

"Don't look at me. I only cut them open and determine how they died. I don't provide them. They are provided to me."

Bailey insisted they had to have a body. Once they had it, he knew what to do with it; he just didn't know how to get hold of a corpse. "I am not in any way suggesting that we make a live body into a dead one. We need a body that is already dead. This part of the plan is not essential for moving Geoffrey to his new life, but I feel it is critical in terms of convincing the Russians that he's dead. If they don't believe he's dead, they will keep looking for him until they find him. And they will find him. We have to convince them, beyond a shadow of a doubt, that he has died. It has to be fool-proof, authenticated, verified, and signed, sealed and delivered."

"I don't know how we're going to do it, but I agree with Bailey. It has to be done." Cameron didn't like it, but he faced up to the hard reality of the situation. "We will have to keep moving you over and over again, out of harm's way, unless we can convince the people who are trying to kill you that you are already dead."

"They beat you up and left you on the ground in the parking lot. It is not a stretch to believe that you wandered away, maybe got help from somebody or maybe not, and died. You were badly injured, but your attackers don't know exactly how badly. They might believe you died within a few hours of the fight. You might have been able to make your way to someplace where you rested and tried to heal. The man who shot you with the hypodermic needle doesn't know how much of the tranquilizer, or whatever it was, he put into your bloodstream. For all he knows, he might have actually finished you off himself." Richard was looking at what would be believable from a medical point of view. Richard knew about death.

"We can use the fact that they attacked you and tried to kill you to our advantage. We can weave a story around the actual facts that will make them believe they succeeded in killing you themselves." Cameron was already thinking ahead. "But there has to be a body, and it has to be found in such a way that there is no question about who is dead. Everyone will have to be convinced that you are the corpse. The death and the identity have to be substantiated by the authorities and reported on the news. Making all that happen in the next day or two is going to be tricky, if not impossible."

Bailey was more positive. "Talking about it in a hotel room is theoretical, but I think we can actually pull this off in the real world. I know a few shady people who might be able to help me get some fake papers for Afif here. I just don't know about the quality of those papers. I have my doubts. If this were WITSEC or some other witness protection program, he would have the real thing, but we are not going that route." Bailey was trying to figure his way out of a number of various dilemmas, and they were all still wondering who would do the dirty work for them.

Geoffrey McNulty spoke up. "Call Baktash. Bring him here today, if you can. I will tell him to get you what you need. He has friends who can get the documents. Baktash does this for illegal and undocumented immigrants who come to Colorado to work. For a price, he can get you a convincing fake birth certificate and a real driver's license. He can get the social security number, too. The passport is another story. He doesn't do passports. If the birth certificate is good enough, you can get your own passport. Also, Baktash volunteers at a local soup kitchen. He remembers the days when he was starving and had nothing to eat. It is his way of giving back. Because of this volunteer work, he has some friends among the homeless. He might be able to help you."

"Is he working today?"

"I don't know his schedule, and I can't call him. My phone

and my wallet are at the house. I went out for a run and left everything behind. The Russian guy attacked me while I was jogging on the academy grounds. If I call Baktash from one of your phones, he won't recognize the number, and he might not pick up. But I can leave him a voice mail. He will call me back right away."

"We need to talk to him today. We're going to have to put our plans in motion immediately." Bailey was insistent.

"I'll try to reach him. One thing ...." Geoffrey hesitated to rain on the parade of his new friends who were trying so hard to help him. "I think Baktash should meet with me and with only one of you. As much as I trust him, I am afraid he might be caught and forced to talk, either by the authorities or by the Russians. I don't want him to be able to name any of you or to describe what you look like. I am going to ask that only one of you stay with me when Baktash arrives, and I would like for whoever that person is, to wear some kind of a disguise and use a false name. There is no point in taking unnecessary risks."

Cameron agreed with Geoffrey. "I can see why the CIA loved you. I am willing to be the go-between with Baktash. I would love it, but I am afraid he might recognize me from somewhere. My photograph is on the back of my books, and I've been interviewed quite a few times on national television shows. It will have to be one of the others. I will do all I can from behind the scenes. Whatever Baktash has to pay to get the fake documents and whatever other costs are incurred, I'm your banker."

"I volunteer to be the go-between. This is basically my plan, and I need to be the one to co-ordinate things with Baktash." Bailey was stepping up to take care of business. "I don't think we ought to meet with him here in this hotel room. I don't want him to later be able to say he was in room

#504. This room can be traced directly back to Matthew and Isabelle. Because of the disgruntled employee that's threatened her, Gretchen has another hotel room on the third floor that the concierge assigned to Mr. and Mrs. Bailey MacDermott. Having our name on that room is to throw off her stalker. Nobody is using the room, and the room adjoining it is also vacant. I checked it out when we first got here. I have the key card to the hall door and the door that connects the two rooms. We can take Geoffrey down there in the wheelchair, and I will bring Baktash to the room on the third floor. I'll try to keep him from seeing the number of the room we're going into. That way, he won't be able to bring anyone back here and tell them where he met with the conspirators, that is, us. Of course, I'm hoping he won't ever be suspected of anything, and all of these precautions will have been taken for no reason."

"I'll put some duct tape over the number of Gretchen's unoccupied room and the room next door. He will never see the room numbers beside the doors." This kind of thinking was not like Richard. His friends stared at him. Richard shot back. "What? I love duct tape and am always thinking about new ways to use it. I saw that Matthew bought some duct tape at the drug store. It's right over there."

"Wonders never cease." Matthew laughed at his friend the pathologist. He knew Richard Carpenter wanted nothing at all to do with this plan or any kind of intrigue, but gave him points for coming up with the idea about the duct tape.

"So what is Bailey's disguise going to be this time?" Cameron liked to tease him. On the previous year's reunion trip, Bailey had shown up at a seafood restaurant in Maine, dressed as a woman and wearing a wig.

"Don't go there, Cameron. I have an idea for a disguise, and I won't be dressed as a woman this time."

"Gretchen will be happy to know that."

Bailey was adamant. "Gretchen is not to know anything about the meeting with Baktash or me in a disguise. For starters, she has enough on her mind, worrying about the stalker. Also, she never approves of the things I get myself into. And, she would not be happy to learn that we are using her 'secret' hotel room for possibly nefarious purposes. The less she knows, the better. She is to know nothing, and I mean absolutely nothing. Understood?"

They all agreed and had a good laugh before Geoffrey started calling Baktash. He got him on the first try, and they made a plan to meet.

Chapter 19

Baktash was working that day and was on the Penmoor grounds. Geoffrey briefly explained over the phone that he'd been attacked, that someone was trying to kill him, and that he had to leave the country. He didn't go into details or make any references to the Russian mafia. He told Baktash not to ask him any questions and not to talk to anyone about his situation. The less Baktash knew, the better it would be for Baktash and for everybody else. Baktash finished his shift at 4:00 p.m. Geoffrey arranged for Bailey, aka Christopher Hamilton, and Baktash to meet in the lobby of the Penmoor West at 4:15 p.m.

Christopher Hamilton would be dressed in ski clothes and carrying a pair of skis. Since the weather was sunny, and no snow was predicted for several days, chances were good that no one else in the lobby would be dressed to ski or have skis in hand. Geoffrey told Baktash that Mr. Hamilton had dark curly hair. Baktash might realize that Bailey's hair was actually a wig, but it was quite different from Bailey's own real hair which was blonde and straight and slowly turning white. Christopher Hamilton would take Baktash to the room where Geoffrey McNulty was waiting.

Intrigued by the conversation they'd overheard, Matthew, Richard and Cameron looked at each other. "Where does he get these disguises? Does he really have skis and ski clothes?" Richard was more than curious about Bailey's ability to come up with a disguise so quickly.

"He can rent all the ski equipment and the clothes right here, but where does he get the wigs? He would have to buy those." Cameron, too, was astonished at his friend Bailey. This was a side of their friend they hadn't known about. They'd thought Bailey's disguise in Maine had been a one-time thing. They'd had no idea that Bailey had a whole repertoire of disguises and wigs.

"Do you think he travels with them, in case he thinks he might need one? Or does he buy one when he needs it? I wouldn't have any idea where to get a wig at a moment's notice. I've never bought a wig." Matthew was almost completely bald. He would never consider wearing a wig of any kind, even if his life depended on it.

Bailey could tell from the expressions he saw on his friends' faces that they had listened in on Geoffrey's phone conversation with Baktash. "Don't ask, okay? Many years ago, I did some work that required me to wear a disguise every now and then. I know where to buy wigs, and I know how to find disguises and costumes. It comes in handy. Remember, don't tell Gretchen anything, and I mean anything, about this. She hates my disguises." Bailey's friends realized he had talents they'd never dreamed he had.

"Our lips are sealed." Cameron spoke for himself and the others. They continued to stare at Bailey in amazement and amusement.

"I have to go and pick up some packages I had delivered to the concierge. Gretchen's other room is #327. I have the key card, and as you know, that key card also opens the door to the adjoining room which I'm pretty sure is #326. Richard, you are going to put duct tape over the room number beside the door to #327 and over the room number beside the door to #326. Wait until the last minute to put on the duct tape. We don't want duct tape over the room numbers to attract attention from housekeeping or from anybody else."

Bailey continued. "I will let you all in to #327 before I go down to meet Baktash. You will leave Geoffrey there in the wheelchair. The rest of you will stay in #326. The door between the two rooms will of course be closed, and you will have to be quiet. You won't be able to hear what we are saying. Geoffrey will be waiting in #327 for me to bring Baktash there. I'll meet Baktash in the hotel lobby and bring him up to the third floor. Baktash and I will enter through the main door of #327. When the meeting is over, I'll leave Geoffrey in #327 and accompany Baktash back down to the lobby. After we've left, you'll bring Geoffrey back here." Bailey was definitely in charge now, giving orders and telling everybody exactly when and where they were supposed to be and what they were to do.

"So, we will meet you outside room #327 at 4:00 p.m. Don't be late. We don't want to be standing out in the hall with Geoffrey in the wheelchair waiting for you. Housekeeping might be lurking, and we don't want anybody to see us."

"Why don't I go early and unlock the door to room #327? That way I won't have to wait around outside the room to let you in. I'll fix the door so it doesn't close all the way. Just push the door to #327 open and go in. Be sure to be there with Baktash by 4:00 p.m. and get yourselves into the room next door. I'll see you there in #326 for just a few seconds to be sure you're all in place where you are supposed to be." Bailey was on a mission, and he was quickly out the door and on his way.

"He had his wig and the ski stuff sent to the concierge. Those are the packages he's going down to pick up. You know,

I think he loves the intrigue. This subterfuge and the secretiveness scares the you-know-what out of me, but Bailey is having the time of his life with all of it." Cameron wondered what Bailey would look like with dark, curly hair and hoped he wouldn't laugh.

"I'm going to cancel the montage showings for this afternoon. I don't have time to get things set up to show them, and my mind is in a hundred other places right now." Matthew's voice revealed how disappointed he was to have to cancel showing his movie montages.

"Yes, there's plenty to think about in the next hour without worrying about presentations for cocktail hour. You won't even be there. How can you show a montage? None of us will be there either. Bailey's busy. It would mostly be J.D. and the women there to watch anyway. Tyler doesn't like your montages much, so he probably wouldn't show up."

"Do you think Baktash will be in the lobby on time?" Richard asked Geoffrey.

"He'll be there on time."

"Will he be able to come through for us … with what we need for him to do?"

"He will come through, if he possibly can."

"We have fifteen minutes. Are you ready for this, Geoffrey?" Matthew was always solicitous of his patient. "When I bring you back to the room after we meet with Baktash, I'm going to have to leave you and spend some time with Isabelle. She says I've been neglecting her, and I have. I suggest you wait until Isabelle and I have left to go to dinner and then order from room service. I will knock twice on the adjoining door to let you know when we leave."

Geoffrey picked up when Matthew paused. "After I order from room service, I will take a shower and put on the terry cloth robe that has a hood. When room service arrives, I will come out of the bathroom to open the door. I will sign your name on the bill, give the waiter a big cash tip, and immediately disappear back into the steamy bathroom while he sets up his table. He will remember the big tip rather than the face of the man in the hotel robe." Geoffrey looked at Matthew and laughed. "I've done this before, you know."

"Of course you have. Not your first rodeo."

It was time for the show to begin. They decided to have Matthew push Geoff in the wheelchair on the elevator. Cameron and Richard would leave a few minutes later and use the stairs to go down to the third floor. They thought two people together would be less remarkable than four men riding on the elevator.

When Cameron and Richard reached room #327, the door was unlocked as Bailey had said it would be. Matthew and Geoffrey were already inside, and Bailey came through from the adjoining room. His friends were dumbfounded. He looked nothing like Bailey MacDermott, the man they'd known since he was a boy. Bailey appeared to be much younger, taller, and slimmer in the smart ski outfit and the dark, curly-haired wig.

"Nobody will know me, will they?" Bailey grinned. "Just remember, Gretchen must not know anything about this. She is already mad at me about something, and I don't have any idea why. I usually don't know, although I probably should."

Richard put duct tape over the two room numbers in the hall. Housekeeping was nowhere in sight. The men went over one more time what everybody was supposed to do. Cameron, Richard, and Matthew went into the next room and closed the door. Bailey left to become Christopher Hamilton and meet Baktash in the lobby.

It seemed like a long time before he returned with Baktash. The three men in room #326 stayed quiet and tried to listen through the door. They could hear a word now and then, but for the most part, they were in the dark about what Bailey and Geoffrey were saying to Baktash.

Geoffrey spent some time filling in his long-time friend about how he had been attacked and how he felt his life was in danger. That he was in a wheelchair added gravitas to Geoff's account about the severity of his injuries. He told Baktash he had to leave the country and needed his friend's help to accomplish that.

"Why do you think you need to leave the country? That's an awfully extreme thing to do. I can't imagine that anyone really wants to kill you. What did you ever do, that someone would want you dead?"

"I can't talk about that. It's for the best. I don't want to tell you anything more because I don't want to risk putting you in danger. I hope you understand. I'm going to ask you to help me with some things that I know you can provide."

"Whatever you need. I will do my best for you."

Geoff explained about the documents he needed. He would leave it up to Baktash to choose his new name and identity. Baktash had done this before, and he assured Geoff that, for a price, obtaining the papers would not be a problem. He could have them by the next evening. Christopher Hamilton made arrangements to meet Baktash to pick up the documents. Geoffrey asked Baktash to bring his laptop and some other important things from his desk, when he brought the documents to Hamilton the next afternoon. He told Baktash exactly where to find the files he needed. He told Baktash to bring his wallet and his cell phone from the house. These were essential to the plan, to prove that Geoffrey was dead.

"This is the part I'm not sure you can help me with,

Baktash. It's the most dangerous part of our plan, the illegal part. We need a body." Geoffrey paused to see how Baktash would react to hearing this unusual request. Baktash looked directly into his friend's eyes and knew he was serious. This was not a joke of any kind. Geoffrey really did need a body. "I don't want to kill anybody to provide the body. I was thinking that, because of your work with the homeless population, you might be able to come up with a body from someplace." Geoffrey sounded hopeful.

"Why do you need a body?" Baktash was not judging his friend or refusing to help. He just wanted more information.

"I have to convince the people who want to kill me, that I am already dead. We have a plan. But our plan depends entirely on having a dead body. Christopher and his friends will discover the body. The corpse will be dressed in my clothes and have my wallet in the pants' pocket. My cell phone will be on the body. The authorities will be called. A note in my wallet will designate you as my emergency contact and 'next of kin.' You will be called to go to the morgue to identify the body. You will identify the body as mine. You will be shocked. You will cry or act sad or be convincing in some way. Do you think you can do that?"

Baktash nodded his head. "You must be very frightened, to go to all of this trouble to make someone believe you are dead."

"You will arrange for my burial. It should be a simple thing. I will give you money to cover the cost of everything, including the new identity papers and all of my funeral expenses. Also, I am making arrangements to pay off the mortgage on your house. You have less than three years' worth of payments remaining before you would own it anyway. As of tomorrow or the next day, you will own the house free and clear. You have to pay the property taxes every year, and you will be responsible for paying for utilities and repairs, as always. But there will be no more mortgage to pay. This is my gift to you, for your years of friendship and for taking on this one last favor for me."

If Baktash had considered telling Geoffrey he wasn't going to be able to find a body, hearing that he no longer would have a mortgage payment won him over completely. Baktash would find a body, no matter what. Baktash, Geoffrey, and Hamilton discussed the details of the plan, at least the parts of the plan that Baktash needed to know about. Baktash would contact Christopher Hamilton as soon as he'd acquired the body. Christopher had a new prepaid phone that he'd purchased to communicate only with Baktash. Christopher gave Baktash that cell phone number. He would give Baktash further instructions once they had a body.

Baktash and Geoffrey said their goodbyes. They tried not to think about the possibility that they might never see one another again. Christopher Hamilton left the room with Baktash. Baktash had never even glanced at the room numbers beside the doors. Christopher Hamilton again made sure Baktash had his cell phone number. They reconfirmed the time and place of their meeting the next day when he would hand over Geoffrey's new identity papers. Hamilton accompanied Baktash to the lobby and showed him to the door of the hotel. He briefly watched the Afghan walk away and then raced back upstairs to shed his wig and ski getup. He needed to smooth the waters with his wife. Gretchen was upset about something, and Bailey was sure it was because of something he had done. It usually was.

Matthew pushed Geoffrey down the third floor hall and onto the elevator. Cameron and Richard quietly slipped out of room #326. As they left to head back to their own rooms, Richard stripped the pieces of duct tape from the room numbers outside the doors.

Chapter 20

Matthew had sent an earlier text to Olivia to tell her he wasn't going to be able to show his movie montages at 4:00 that afternoon. He said he would meet the group at the bus that was scheduled to be in front of the hotel at 5:45 to take them to dinner. This was so out of character for Matthew. His montages were the most important thing he had going on in his life right now. It was unheard of for him to cancel showings for a second time.

Sidney sent Oliva a text that she was tired and was going to rest until it was time for dinner. She would meet the group at the bus. Within a few minutes, Olivia also received texts from Cameron and Bailey that they wouldn't be meeting the others for cocktails at 4:00. After reading all these texts, Olivia and J.D. realized that something must be going on with Afif. If Sidney was tired, others in the group must be tired, too. Olivia sent out a text that the cocktail hour and salon in the Steele's suite was cancelled for Wednesday night. Everyone was to meet in the lobby to board the bus at 5:45. The bus would drive them to the restaurant for their six o'clock reservation.

That night, they were having dinner at The Peak, the resort's trendy farm to table style restaurant. Several wild game choices were on the menu, as well as trout from a local lake or river. Quite a few vegan and vegetarian dishes were available. The Peak was far enough away from their hotel that they rode the resort shuttlebus to get there. The bus driver, oddly enough, recommended the pork chop with mashed potatoes. She said the pork was from a local farm. Of course it was; it had to be, didn't it?

The heirloom tomato salad was one of the best Elizabeth had ever eaten. She ordered the pork chop as suggested, and it was as delicious as the bus driver had said it would be. It was perfectly cooked. Too many places these days served pork that was pink. Elizabeth's aunt had once been quite ill with trichinosis, and Elizabeth had never been fond of underdone pork.

Several in the group chose the grilled trout with pureed celeriac, broccoli rabe, and roasted beets. Others opted for shrimp and grits. Luscious and very "in," the entree was on everybody's menu these days. Grits were ubiquitous, but Sidney couldn't help but wonder what mountain stream the Colorado shrimp had come from.

The high point was the profiteroles that almost everyone ordered for dessert. They were beautiful, and they were scrumptious. The chocolate sauce was plentiful. Those who had chosen a different dessert were crying in their bread pudding, which was also quite wonderful.

They arrived back at the Penmoor West early, and the group decided to walk across the lake to the bar in the Penmoor's main building to have an after-dinner nightcap. Hot tea and decaf would be popular choices for this crowd. The bar served a warm spiced cider to which rum could be added. Any hot drink was appealing on this cold night.

As the group prepared to leave the bar, Richard looked around to see if Lilleth was available to help him push Elizabeth's wheelchair. He didn't see her. He thought he was more acclimated to the altitude than he had been on their first night in Colorado, when he'd needed help to push his wife across the lake after dinner at the Saloon. He thought he had the lung power to push her by himself tonight. The temperature had dropped considerably since lunch time.

Elizabeth's white hair shone in the lights that lined the lake. She and Richard had become separated from the rest of their group, but there were lots of other people around who could help Richard push the wheelchair, if he needed help. Richard was taking his time. They were in no hurry, and he was conserving his breath for the long trip back to the room. They were more than half-way across the lake when the unthinkable happened.

The man came out of nowhere and attacked Richard from behind. He hit Richard hard, pushing him down. Richard was unable to keep control of Elizabeth's wheelchair, and as he fell forward on the pavement, he pushed the wheelchair hard ahead of him. It flew out of his hands, and Richard collapsed on the ground. The wheelchair kept going. It rolled faster and faster, downhill to the edge of the lake where large rocks lined the bank. Elizabeth frantically tried to stop the wheelchair by putting on the brake, but she couldn't. She attempted to throw herself out of the wheelchair before it hit the water, but that didn't work either. The wheelchair gained momentum on its downward trajectory. When it hit the rocks at the edge of the lake, Elizabeth was still in the chair. Both the old woman and the chair soared into the air. They almost appeared to be supernaturally propelled as they flew out over the lake and sank into the water, at a considerable distance from the bank.

Several bystanders looked on in horror. Two began to dial 911 on their cell phones. One woman ran into the Penmoor West lobby for help. But nobody went into the water to try to rescue the woman in the wheelchair. Richard was down and unable to get up. Because he was on the ground, he didn't even know that his wife and her wheelchair had ended up in the lake.

Elizabeth was an excellent swimmer. She had a pool in the back yard of her house in Arizona, and she swam laps in the pool for an hour every evening before dinner. She had always loved the water. The difference was that the water in her Arizona pool was heated. The water in the lake at the Penmoor was freezing, literally. That night, the air was so cold that ice had begun to form around the rocks at the edges of the man-made lake.

Elizabeth had been catapulted out of the wheelchair just before it hit the water. She knew she had to get out of the water quickly, before her arms and legs became so numb with cold she couldn't move them. She was wearing the leather coat that had been returned to her after it had served its purpose as a disguise for Afif. The coat was terribly heavy, and she knew she couldn't swim to the shore of the lake while she was wearing it. It would weigh her down. As much as she hated to do it, she got her arms out of the coat sleeves and allowed the coat to fall away from her shoulders to the bottom of the lake. She couldn't reach her shoes to take them off. She felt lucky she hadn't hit her head and been knocked unconscious when she'd crashed into the water.

After dropping her coat, she swam toward the voices that were yelling at her from the shore. Her waterlogged clothes slowed her progress. Her frozen arms were not moving nearly fast enough. She'd almost reached the edge of the lake and was within a few yards of safety, when her limbs began to cramp with the cold. All of a sudden, no matter how hard she tried, she couldn't move her arms or her legs. She went under and didn't come up again.

Lilleth and Tyler were just beginning to walk across the lake when they saw the wheelchair, with someone in it, fly up into the air and go down into the water. Tyler knew immediately that it was Elizabeth. He took off his down-filled jacket and prepared to jump into the lake. Then he saw Elizabeth was making good progress, swimming towards the land, and he began screaming words of encouragement in her direction. Suddenly, just as she was almost close enough that he could reach out and grab her arm, she sank below the surface.

Tyler jumped into the frigid water and dove down to try to find Elizabeth. The water wasn't too deep, but Elizabeth had lost her strength and wasn't able to swim any more. Her clothes were soaked with freezing water. Tyler was finally able to find and grab one of her arms, but he wasn't sure he could drag her out of the lake. He struggled to hang on to her as he tried to climb back onto the rocks. People rushed to help. Tyler had hold of Elizabeth, and someone grabbed hold of Tyler. A third person grabbed hold of the second person, and together they pulled Tyler and Elizabeth to shore. One bystander was wearing a long wool coat, and she took it off and put it over Elizabeth who was shaking violently.

Tyler was also shivering uncontrollably. He had no body fat at all, nothing to insulate him from the freezing temperatures. Lilleth put his dry jacket around his shoulders and pushed him towards the hotel. She wanted to get him into a hot shower. There were many people gathered around Elizabeth, and Lilleth knew an ambulance would arrive shortly. Elizabeth would be taken care of. Lilleth had to take care of Tyler. A crowd was also gathering around Richard. He had sprained or broken his wrist when he'd fallen.

A pair of EMTs arrived to treat Elizabeth. Getting her out of the cold air was imperative. They moved her at once into the warm ambulance. They stripped off her wet clothing and wrapped her in warm blankets. After covering her body with a foil space blanket, they started an IV of a warm electrolyte solution. The patient's pulse was weak and slow. She was not conscious, and her breathing was shallow. Even though she had not been in the cold water for long and even though she had considerable body fat to protect her, she was well into the advanced stages of hypothermia. She did not appear to have any injuries, but she was elderly. Her blood pressure was dropping.

A Good Samaritan, who had seen the whole thing, told the EMTs that Elizabeth had been in a wheelchair and that she had been pushed into the water. It had not been an accident. The EMTs immediately called the sheriff and asked the Good Samaritan to stay on site and give his story to the authorities. Within a few minutes of its arrival, the ambulance left with lights flashing and siren blaring. It was on its way to the Penrose Hospital Emergency Room, the hospital closest to the resort. Because she was unconscious, the emergency responders were not able to ask her anything — her name, her age, or about any existing medical conditions.

Of the reunion group, only Lilleth and Tyler knew what had happened to Elizabeth. Even Richard hadn't actually seen her wheelchair go into the water. Through the crowd that had gathered, Richard caught a glimpse of his wife being loaded into an ambulance. There were so many people clustered around her, blocking his view, he couldn't actually see her. He was desperate to get to her, but he was also hurt. Because of his injured wrist, he couldn't get back on his feet without help. He wasn't able to reach Elizabeth before the ambulance sped away.

Several members of the hotel staff had run outside when they'd heard screaming coming from the direction of the lake. Eventually, one of them realized that Richard was the husband of the woman who had ended up in the water. Richard was frantic to find out where Elizabeth had been taken in the ambulance. Reliable information was in short supply. Richard was cold, and his hands were bleeding. He rudely rebuffed offers of help from the hotel staff, but finally one of the bellman from the hotel was able to convince him to go inside the building to get warm.

As he made his way towards the hotel entrance, Richard turned around and looked back at the lake. A man in a small boat was dragging Elizabeth's wheelchair out of the water. Her leather coat was caught in the chair, and it trailed behind as the wheelchair was lifted into the boat. When Richard saw the empty wheelchair and the empty coat, he grabbed one of the hotel security guards. Richard demanded to know if the woman who had been in the wheelchair had been alive when she'd been rescued from the water. The security guard had arrived late to the scene and didn't know the answer to Richard's question.

Richard was inconsolable, but he allowed the night concierge, who did not yet really understand what was going on, to lead him into the hotel's lounge and sit him down in front of the fire. The concierge asked Richard if he needed help or if he wanted anything. He ignored her questions, but she decided to bring him a hot drink anyway.

Lilleth found Richard in the lounge with a cup of hot tea and honey in front of him. Before she'd left their hotel room, Lilleth had made sure Tyler took a hot shower and was resting under a pile of blankets. She did not want another hypothermia victim that had to go to the hospital. Lilleth apologized to Richard for leaving the scene. She hadn't seen what caused "the accident" and didn't know how Elizabeth and her wheelchair had ended up in the lake. She told Richard that Tyler had gone in after her and helped drag her out of the water. Lilleth knew 911 had been called, and that was why she had felt free to turn her attention to taking care of Tyler.

Richard wanted to set the record straight. It had not been an accident. "I was pushed. Somebody came up behind me and pushed me. Because of my momentum, I couldn't stop the wheelchair. I fell forward and pushed the wheelchair forward. I ended up face down on the pavement, but the wheelchair kept on going. I saw it hit the rocks and fly up in the air. At that point, I was down myself and didn't actually see it hit the water. I know she got out of the lake." He was almost afraid to ask. "Do you know if she was alive when they pulled her out?"

"She swam most of the way to shore on her own. She couldn't have been badly hurt when she fell into the lake or she wouldn't have been able to swim as well as she did. We thought she was going to make it to the shore, and Tyler was standing at the edge, ready to pull her out. Just before she got to us, she sank down into the water. She might have had a muscle cramp. Something happened that kept her from making those final few swimming strokes to bring her close enough so that Tyler could grab hold of her. When she disappeared below the surface of the lake, he went in to try to get to her. It took two people to pull Tyler and Elizabeth out of the water."

"Did you see her? I was too far away and couldn't see what was happening. There were too many people milling around and in the way, standing between me and the ambulance. They were blocking my view. I couldn't stand up, and I couldn't see her or get to her." Richard was desolate.

"She was unconscious and shaking badly. I won't tell you she wasn't in bad shape. It looked pretty serious. I'm sorry."

"And you left her there?"

"Tyler was in bad shape, too. I wanted to be sure he took care of himself. I knew 911 was on its way to help Elizabeth. There was nothing I could do for her. I knew she would be cared for."

"Do you know what hospital they took her to?"

"No, but we can ask the concierge to find out for us. She will know where we can find Elizabeth."

"Is Tyler okay?"

"He's still shivering, but he's had a hot shower. I've put him to bed with lots of warm blankets. I'm going to talk to the concierge and have room service send up warm liquids for him to drink. He needs chicken broth, hot tea, and warm sugar water."

"Where is everybody else? Didn't any of them see what happened?"

"I don't know. They may have stayed later in the bar or they may have taken a different route back. Somebody said something about going for a walk. I'm not sure where they went." Lilleth shrugged her shoulders.

"Thanks for telling me what you know. I'm going to call Matthew and let him know about Elizabeth. I hope he's still awake and will take my call this late."

Lilleth looked at Richard's wrist which was swollen to twice its normal size. He had scrapes and cuts on the palms of his hands from where he had fallen on the rough walkway. "You need to have someone take a look at your wrist. It might be broken. If it isn't broken, it's badly sprained." Richard was so distraught about Elizabeth, he wasn't listening, and he wasn't thinking straight. His wrist had to be terribly painful, but he seemed oblivious to it and to almost everything that was happening around him.

Chapter 21

Richard called Matthew and tried to explain over the phone what had happened to Elizabeth, but Richard didn't really know much of anything. He didn't know what hospital she'd been taken to, and he didn't know what condition she was in. He wasn't even sure whether or not she had survived her rescue from the lake. Matthew realized he had another crisis on his hands. After spending the day dealing with Afif/Geoffrey, Matthew was relieved that his patient's condition was stable. There was a plan going forward, and the doctor had been thinking longingly of his bed and a good night's sleep.

But now, Elizabeth had ended up in the lake, and she might even be dead. As exhausted as he was, Matthew knew that Richard needed his support. He had to go to his friend and do whatever he could to help. He hated to drag Isabelle into any of this. The trip to the Penmoor was supposed to have been her vacation, but Matthew needed her.

Isabelle and Matthew found Richard alone in the hotel lounge. He looked terrible. His hands were bleeding and his wrist was horribly swollen. His face was gray, and he scarcely registered that they had arrived and were sitting on either side of him on the couch. His account of what had happened was garbled. Matthew went to find the concierge, thinking she might have more information.

Isabelle sat with Richard and tried to get him to talk to her. Even though she knew he had to be in pain, he was in another world and didn't seem aware of his wrist at all. As they sat there, a hotel guest came up and introduced himself to Isabelle. He said he recognized Richard as the man whose wife's wheelchair had gone into the lake. He had seen the entire incident and had just given a statement to the police. He described to Isabelle everything he'd witnessed in detail. He told her he thought Elizabeth had been taken to Penrose Hospital's ER. The man knew it was the closest ER to the resort, and he said emergency responders usually took people to the closest hospital.

Isabelle was horrified to hear that the supposed accident had not been an accident at all. Richard had been intentionally pushed, and Elizabeth had ended up in the freezing water. Isabelle questioned the witness about Elizabeth's condition when she'd been pulled from the lake. The news was not good. The man said he didn't know whether or not the elderly woman had been alive when she was taken away in the ambulance. Isabelle was heartsick to hear that Elizabeth was in such bad shape and possibly dead. Isabelle began sending texts on her phone. Most of the group would be in their rooms by now, but she was certain they would want to know what she had just learned.

Isabelle was not having any luck talking to Richard. He was incommunicado. She tried asking him about his wrist. He needed to have it x-rayed, but she doubted he would agree to do anything to take care of himself until someone had found out where Elizabeth was and what condition she was in. Even if it was terrible news, not knowing was worse. Where was Matthew? Isabelle didn't need him often, but he always managed to disappear when she did.

J.D. was the first to make it to the lounge. "Tell me everything. How is it possible that we don't know where she is? Have you made any phone calls?" One look at Richard, and J.D. shook his head. "Somebody needs to get him to the hospital. He's had a terrible shock, and he's bleeding. His hand is double its normal size, and his arm is swollen up to his elbow." J.D. was a man of action. He was quite fond of Elizabeth and was terribly worried about her. When Isabelle told him about Richard's fall and Elizabeth's wheelchair racing downhill into the water, he was angry. When he grasped that none of it had been an accident, he was furious.

J.D. was a former prosecutor, and he had seen and put away a lot of very bad guys. But even he was shocked that someone would stoop so low as to push a disabled woman in a wheelchair into the lake. Isabelle could almost see the steam coming out of J.D.'s ears as she told him what she knew.

J.D. texted Olivia and told her to get dressed and come to the lobby immediately. Then he called her on his phone and told her not to take the time to put on her makeup. "We need you down here now, please. Nobody cares if you have eyeliner on your eyes. You are beautiful enough without all that goop on your face. Elizabeth might be dead." J.D. knew his superbly competent wife could get things done. She would find out exactly where Elizabeth was.

Olivia arrived in minutes. J.D. was giving orders. "Go find out what's holding up Matthew. Somebody needs to take Richard to the hospital, and it ought to be Matthew. He's a doctor and knows Richard better than any of the rest of us do. Get him out here." J.D. was in CEO mode.

"Isabelle, stay here with Richard. I'm going to have one of the bellmen call us a cab or a hotel car, whichever is quicker.

Tyler and Lilleth have a car, but it's a tiny little thing. You can't even get into the back seat, if there even is a back seat. We need a real car to get Richard and Matthew to the hospital." J.D. drove a Chevy Suburban so he thought almost everybody's car was a "tiny little thing." "I won't call 911 for a broken wrist, but he's in shock and needs treatment for that, too. I'm not a doctor, but I know that much." J.D. had a hotel employee buttonholed in seconds.

Olivia returned with Matthew following behind, trying to keep up with her. Olivia had news. "We've confirmed that the ambulance took her to the Penrose Hospital ER. It's the closest hospital. That's probably where you ought to take Richard, too."

J.D. came back to the lounge. "A hotel car will be here in two minutes to drive us to the hospital. Matthew, you have to go with Richard, to be sure he gets the x-rays, treatment, and whatever else he needs. You can expedite all of that at the ER. I'm going with you. While you're taking care of Richard, I'm going to find out what's happened to Elizabeth. Don't you think they would have called the hotel or something by now … if she hadn't made it?" J.D. was a realist, but he definitely did not want to get the news that Elizabeth had died.

"She might not have had any ID with her, and if she was unconscious when they pulled her out of the lake, they might not have any idea who she is." Olivia hated to have to say this, but it was one explanation for why no one had been able to get any news about what had happened to Elizabeth. "They might not have been able to figure out yet what her name is. I guess I'll stay here and let the others know when we get some news. J.D., promise you will keep me informed, no matter what the news is, even if it's the worst possible news. Don't forget to text or call me with updates. You know what it's like to be left behind and not know anything."

The hotel SUV had arrived. It took Matthew on one side and J.D. on the other side to get Richard up and moving towards the door of the hotel. It was going to be a long night. J.D. was upset, and when he was upset, he rambled. He was rambling now, about the term "sedan service."

"Why do they continue to call it a 'sedan service'? I have yet to see a single sedan here at the Penmoor. All of their sedans are in fact SUVs. Why don't they just call it an SUV service? Who even drives a sedan anymore? Do any of the automobile companies even still manufacture sedans?" J.D. was in the transportation business, and he had lots of opinions on the subject. "I don't know anybody who has a sedan. Everybody I know drives a pickup or an SUV. Of course, if I lived in California, everybody I would know would be driving a hybrid, or a Prius, or an electric car, or a Tesla." J.D. paused and looked at Matthew. "Don't say anything. I know that Prius makes a hybrid and Tesla makes an electric car. I know all of that. I just needed to sound off about it all right now. And I'm right about at least one thing. Those cars are so small you can't carry anything in them." J.D. owned a trucking company, and his trucks were large and could carry a lot of stuff in them.

When the men had left, Isabelle and Olivia collapsed on the couch in front of the fire. "Do we order a glass of wine, or do we order hot tea?" Olivia was thinking that, considering the circumstances, maybe a stiff shot of whisky was in order, but she didn't drink whisky.

Isabelle just wanted a bottle of water. "I won't be able to go to sleep now anyway, until I hear something from Mathew about Elizabeth's condition. She's the oldest one of the wives in the group, you know. This whole thing isn't anywhere close to being natural causes; this is a violent attack. But the older you are, the more difficult it is to recover from any kind of illness or injury. Considering that Elizabeth was in a wheelchair and that she's elderly, this could be viewed as attempted murder. I can't even imagine what will happen to Richard if she doesn't make it. They've been married for more than fifty-three years."

"She's not that much older than I am. She just seems older." Olivia went to find Isabelle's water and her own glass of white wine. Olivia wasn't going to be able to sleep either. They settled in for the long vigil.

Cameron was asleep and hadn't seen Isabelle's texts. J.D. called Cameron's cell phone from the SUV on the way to the hospital. J.D. explained what was going on and told Cameron he wanted him to try to find out who had pushed Richard. J.D. the prosecutor was on the job and wanted Cameron to begin the investigation right away. There had to have been quite a few people on the walkway that went across the lake, and somebody had to have seen something.

J.D. knew how slowly the police sometimes worked. Because of his background, he knew that law enforcement resources were scarce. If Elizabeth died, homicide would be all over the case. If she didn't die, and J.D. had to believe she wouldn't, a case of assault would not receive priority. No matter how egregious the assault was, even an attack on a disabled person in a wheelchair, there would not be enough manpower to devote to a thorough investigation. J.D. was upset. He told Cameron he wanted to hire a private investigator to take over the case because he knew the police would not be able to do anything.

"Calm down, J.D. Is Elizabeth going to be okay? Why doesn't anybody know anything about her condition?" Cameron was groggy, and it took him a while to get his brain in gear and realize the gravity of the situation. "Why don't we wait to see how badly Elizabeth's been hurt before we go off half-cocked with private investigators and all of that? I'll get on it, but can't the investigation wait until morning?"

"All the witnesses will have disappeared by morning. They've probably already disappeared. An eyewitness sat down in the lounge and told Isabelle the whole story. He'd seen everything, but she didn't get his name. He actually saw the person who pushed Richard. The attacker was dressed in all black, of course, and had a windbreaker with a hood over his head ... of course. No one will ever be able to identify that guy."

"Why would anybody want to attack Richard or Elizabeth? They don't really have anything at all to do with the Afif situation. Maybe it was just a random act of violence, a bad person looking to hurt somebody for no reason." Cameron was trying to be rational and hoped he could convince J.D. to let it go until the next day.

"I hope you're right, about it being a random hit. Because, if they weren't attacked by chance, whoever is after them will be back to cause more trouble. If it really was an attempt to kill Elizabeth, whoever is after her didn't succeed. My fear is that they will try again and again until they finish the job. I know we don't need more drama going on right now, but this is for real. Elizabeth really is in the hospital, and we still don't know if she's alive or dead. Richard is a mess, as you might imagine."

"I'll get dressed and go down to the lounge. At least I can keep Oliva and Isabelle company until you get back from the hospital. I can't promise I will last the night, though. We have big plans in the works for Afif. His name is Geoffrey McNulty now, by the way. I have a lot to talk to you about. We're going to need your help to get Afif out of this mess. I know you are a man of the law, but we need you anyway. What happened to the nice, relaxing vacation we'd all been looking forward to? Sidney may not come with me next year. She's tired of people dying and being hurt. We're all tired of that." Cameron tried to wake himself up.

"Olivia is fond of Elizabeth, and she's really worried …." The SUV pulled up to the hospital's emergency room entrance. "Okay, I've gotta go. We're just arriving at the hospital now. I'll call you as soon as I know anything." J.D. hung up the phone.

The hotel driver dropped them at the door to the ER. Matthew knew he had to find out something definite about Elizabeth before Richard would agree to have his wrist examined. The doctor decided to pull rank. He approached the ER intake desk. "Hello, Gladys." He read the name on the lanyard that hung around the nurse's neck. "I'm Dr. Matthew Ritter, and I'm meeting one of my patients here. Her name is Elizabeth Carpenter, and she was brought in by ambulance from the Penmoor resort. Can you tell me where she is now?"

Gladys shuffled through some papers and looked at Matthew with a blank look on her face. "You need to go to the hospital information desk in the main lobby. My computer is down, so I can't tell you anything."

"How do I get to the main information desk?"

Gladys pulled a map from somewhere and began marking on it with a Sharpie pen. "It's complicated to get there from here. This is an old hospital that's been added onto over the years. Elevators are not exactly where we want them to be." She gave complicated directions about hallways and following the blue line on the floor. They had to go up one floor, and the elevator they had to take wouldn't let them off anywhere close to the main entrance of the hospital. Matthew was a good-humored man and slow to anger. His frustration with the directions Gladys was giving him was pushing him over the edge.

The three set out with the map to try to make their way to the fountain of all knowledge, the main information desk. Richard walked like a zombie and didn't say anything. He went where his two friends led him.

After being lost only three times, they finally reached the hospital's main lobby. The woman who sat behind the information desk had spiky black hair with green highlights. She had a stud in her tongue, and the lanyard around her neck said her name was "Tammy." Matthew went to work again. "Hello, Tammy …."

The woman behind the desk interrupted him before he could say anything more. "Actually, I'm Tanya. Tammy is my sister, my twin sister. We aren't identicals, and we really don't look anything alike. But some people think we do. My mother thinks we do. Anyway, Tammy wasn't feeling well tonight, so I volunteered to take her shift. This is her ID badge. Don't tell anybody. But I'm not really Tammy."

"Okay, Tanya." Matthew gritted his teeth but kept his cool. "We are looking for a patient of mine who arrived a while ago by ambulance. I'm Mathew Ritter, M.D. My patient is Elizabeth Carpenter, and I'd like to know her condition and where I can find her. The nurse in the ER sent us here. Their computers are down."

Tanya consulted her computer, and then she shuffled through a stack of papers. "Yep, mine was down, too, for a while." She went back to the computer. "Oh, I am so sorry to tell you this. Elizabeth …, did you say Carpenter? Yes, Carpenter. She arrived DOA earlier this evening. Her body is in the morgue in the basement."

Richard grabbed his chest and began to collapse. If his friends hadn't caught him and guided him to a chair, he would have ended up on the floor. Matthew and J.D. were stunned and devastated. Tanya, the hospital employee who had obviously never heard of HIPAA, had more to tell them. "There's an alert marker here beside Elizabeth's name. Her boyfriend, the one who beat her to death with the baseball bat, is still at large. We are asking everyone to be on the lookout for him.

There's a description here telling what he looks like. Do you want me to read it to you?"

Richard wasn't hearing any of this, but Matthew and J.D. stared at the green- haired Tanya. They were dumbstruck. J.D. finally found his voice. He was so upset, he could barely speak, but he looked Tanya in the eyes and spoke to her with exaggerated patience. "Check your computer again." He grabbed a piece of paper and a pen from Tanya's desk and wrote Elizabeth's first and last names out in block letters. He shoved the paper under Tanya's nose. "This is the way our Elizabeth Carpenter spells her name. Are you sure you have the right person, the one who came in DOA? Our Elizabeth was not attacked with a baseball bat. She almost drowned in the lake at the Penmoor resort."

Tanya looked at J.D. as if he had three heads. She smirked at him, but she picked up the piece of paper and reentered Elizabeth's name. "Here it is, look for yourself. It says, "Elizabeth Carlisle, age thirty-two, arrived DOA at 8:45 p.m."

"That is *not* the name I wrote on the piece of paper I just gave to you. Our Elizabeth is CARPENTER, NOT CARLISLE." J.D.'s voice grew louder as his anger overwhelmed him. He was shouting now. The few people who were sitting in the hospital lobby were all looking at him.

"Oh, well. Carpenter, Carlisle, whatever. Okay, here she is. Elizabeth Carpenter, age seventy-five, admitted at 11:17 p.m. to intensive care. Condition is critical. Is there anything else …?"

They were already making it towards the elevator, practically carrying Richard with them, before Tanya finished her spiel. They knew where intensive care was. They had seen it on the map, and they were on their way.

Intensive Care had its own waiting room. There were other people there, family members of ICU patients who were keeping watch during the long hours of the night. Some were sleeping. Some were crying. Some were speaking quietly into their cell phones. Matthew had regained his equilibrium, and he had his voice back. He played the doctor card again. He spoke to the ICU nurse, the gatekeeper who decided who would be allowed in to see her critically ill patients.

"I'm Dr. Matthew Ritter. I've been told that my patient Elizabeth Carpenter is in ICU. She was hurt in an accident. Her husband has been really worried about her. I have him here with me. He needs medical care himself, but he refuses to go to the ER until he has seen his wife. Please work with me. They've been married more than fifty-three years. He's my patient, too, but he won't cooperate until he's certain his wife's alive. We've had a terrible time finding out anything about her."

"We just found out what her name was fifteen minutes ago. She came in without a purse or identification of any kind. She was unconscious and is still unconscious. She wasn't able to tell us her name. We knew she'd come from the Penmoor, and that she had fallen or was pushed into the lake there. She's suffering from hypothermia. If we have room, we bring hypothermia patients to the ICU. The concierge at the Penmoor is the one who finally called to let us know what her name is."

"I know we can't see her for long, but I want to take her husband, Richard, in for just a couple of minutes. I need to get him to the ER. Look at his wrist, and you'll see what I'm talking about. He's unsteady on his feet, so I've got to help him." The nurse nodded, and Matthew took hold of Richard's arm and led him towards Elizabeth's bed.

She was so still. She had bandages wrapped around her head, so it was impossible to see her white hair. She had IV's in both arms and was hooked up to a bank of electronics that measured every possible vital sign. Matthew would not have known it was Elizabeth lying in the bed, if the nurse had not assured him it was his friend's wife. Richard stared at the woman everyone said was Elizabeth. His eyes showed grave doubt and terrible sorrow.

"It's Elizabeth. I'm sure of it. She doesn't look her best right now. But from what I can tell from this monitor, her heart is strong. She's going to recover." Matthew didn't know that with certainty, but he wanted to reassure Richard and get him headed towards the ER.

Richard reached down and took his wife's hand. He knew those hands that had been a part of his life for so many years. The hands that had washed his clothes and cooked his meals and taken care of his children were old hands now. They were crippled and bent with arthritis, but they were undeniably Elizabeth's. Richard gently squeezed the wrinkled hand and carefully placed it back on the bed at Elizabeth's side. He smiled a weak smile at Matthew and said, "Okay."

J.D. had told the ICU nurse that he was Elizabeth's brother, so she was going to allow him to sit in the ICU beside her bed for a while. Matthew and Richard, map in hand, wended their way along the convoluted path, following the blue line on the floor, back to the hospital's emergency room.

Chapter 22

They waited more than two hours while Richard had x-rays taken of his wrist and an MRI of his head. Matthew had not felt the MRI was necessary, but apparently the test was routinely ordered for older people who had fallen and were uncommunicative. Matthew tried to explain to the ER doctor that the reason Richard wasn't speaking was because he had just experienced a tremendous psychological shock in addition to his relatively minor physical injuries. The doctor put five stitches in Richard's thumb and cleaned the abrasions on his hands. He gave him a tetanus shot and put a removable cast and a sling on Richard's wrist. It wasn't broken, but it was badly sprained and had to be immobilized. They wanted to admit Richard overnight for observation, but Richard refused and stomped out of the hospital. Matthew went after him and tried to talk him into coming back inside where it was warm. Richard sat on a bench outside the entrance to the ER, and he wasn't moving. Matthew sent J.D. a text that he was calling an Uber to take them all back to the Penmoor.

It was 4:30 in the morning when the three returned to the hotel. While he'd been keeping watch by Elizabeth's bedside, J.D. communicated all his information to Olivia. Olivia cried with relief when she heard that Elizabeth was alive. She sent word to everyone in the group, and she and Isabelle and Cameron went to bed to try to get some sleep. Thursday was spa day, and all the women had appointments. The Penmoor spa was supposed to be something special, and they were looking forward to a day of being pampered. Olivia and Isabelle were so tired, they knew that, no matter how wonderful it turned out to be, they would probably sleep through the entire day.

Richard spent what was left of the night in his own hotel room, and he was more coherent the next morning when Matthew went to check on him. They'd both slept late. Matthew insisted that Richard get dressed and go to breakfast with him. Matthew had arranged for a car from the hotel to drive them, and they would leave for the hospital to visit Elizabeth after they'd eaten.

Breakfast at the Penmoor was just as delightful as all the other meals at the resort. The omelets were superb, and fried potatoes were served with every breakfast entrée. This morning, Matthew opted for a giant glass of freshly squeezed orange juice and the stone ground oatmeal, which arrived with brown sugar and a pitcher of heavy cream. You could also have raisins and walnuts with your oatmeal, if you asked for them. Matthew, who usually ate sparingly, was hungry this morning. He ate a whole English muffin slathered in butter and orange marmalade. Richard ordered fried eggs and sausage with a side of buttermilk pancakes. It looked like a heart attack on a plate to the health-conscious Matthew, but he was happy to see that his friend had an appetite.

Cameron came by their table and wanted an update on Elizabeth. He had already eaten breakfast and had news about Tyler. Tyler was on the mend, being closely watched over by his caretaker Lilleth. He had not succumbed to pneumonia or even a cold. The group of friends was lauding him for his role in rescuing Elizabeth, and he was basking in the praise from underneath the pile of blankets Lilleth insisted he needed. She had scheduled some spa appointments for today, but she was thinking about cancelling them. She didn't trust Tyler to stay in bed and take care of himself.

Cameron and J.D. planned to go to the Penrose Heritage Museum. Cameron had been a life-long car and motorcycle enthusiast, and he wanted to see the collection of vehicles and other artifacts that philanthropists, Spencer and Julie Penrose, had collected. It was an impressive assemblage of classic antique cars and old-fashioned carriages. They were planning to visit Elizabeth at the hospital later in the day. Bailey, of course, was tied up with secret matters.

When Richard and Matthew arrived at the hospital, they went immediately to the ICU. Elizabeth wasn't there, and the nurse they'd interacted with the night before was also gone. They had to explain, all over again to the new ICU nurse, who they were. After their initial surprise and concern about why Elizabeth was no longer in the ICU, they were given the good news — that she had been transferred to a regular private room. She'd regained consciousness, and her doctors had determined she no longer needed to be in intensive care. The computer was consulted, and they were given another map of the hospital. They set out to try to find Elizabeth — again.

They heard the laughter while they were still in the hallway, before they'd even reached the door to Elizabeth's new room. A young doctor in a white coat was just leaving. He'd been laughing so hard, the tears were rolling down his face. "Are you here to see Elizabeth? She's a real live wire, isn't she?" He shook his head and chuckled to himself as he continued down the hall.

Richard looked at Matthew, and Matthew looked at Richard who shrugged his shoulders. The woman they had feared might be dead, less than twelve hours earlier, had just been described to them as a "live wire." They stopped at the entrance to the hospital room. There was a cluster of doctors and nurses around the patient in the bed. The patient was indeed Elizabeth, and she looked wonderful. There was color in her cheeks and her eyes were bright. She was holding court.

"What I said was that I could not possibly have sunk into the lake because I have too much avoirdupois. You do know what that is, don't you? Look at me for a clue."

One of the doctors said something Matthew and Richard couldn't hear.

"No, no, no. Not peau de soie! Peau du soie is what shoes are made of. Avoirdupois is what I'm made of." The group laughed again.

Just then, Elizabeth looked up and saw Richard and Matthew at the door. She waved and introduced her husband and his friend, Dr. Ritter, to the gathering of medical personnel standing around her. One of them said to her, "You're doing great. We are leaving now, but we will be back for the next show ... around noon? Take care of yourself, Elizabeth." He was smiling as he started to leave the room.

Richard buttonholed this doctor who seemed to be in charge, and he and Matthew questioned the physician about Elizabeth's condition. The man in the white coat introduced himself as Dr. Franklin Pierce. He was a pulmonologist. "When she regained consciousness, we began asking her questions about current events, like who the President of the United States is and what day it is. We do that whenever anyone wakes up from being unconscious for more than a few minutes. We're trying to determine whether or not they've suffered any brain impairment. When we asked her who the

President of the United States was, she went off on a tirade … about Presidents, past and present, politics, and assorted politicians. She even remembered my name and made a comment about having a really, really old President right here, at this very moment, in her hospital room. She said the fourteenth president of the United States was masquerading as a doctor, and how old was I, really? How did she know Franklin Pierce was the 14th president? I know that, but not many other people know it. Then she segued into telling us how she had ended up in the lake at the Penmoor. She said she'd been in a wheelchair, and her husband had pushed her into the lake. There was a whole outrageously funny tale about a leather coat and Elizabeth trying to take off her clothes and speculating about how many birds had pooped in that lake. She said all that bird poop was now in her hair, and she wanted a mirror to see if her hair had turned brown. She's a live wire, isn't she? She told us she's a writer. I told her we thought she was a stand-up comedienne. She said she would be except that she has a really hard time standing up these days and can't do it for more than a few minutes at a time. She's going to be fine. She is fine. All of her vitals are normal. We want to keep her here one more day. Her chest x-ray looked a little hazy. We want to be sure she doesn't develop pneumonia. She's quite a remarkable woman, having recovered so quickly from what she's just been through. I'll be back later."

Just as Dr. Pierce was about to leave the room, he stepped back in and said to Richard, "I know you didn't push her wheelchair into the lake, and I know she doesn't think you did it on purpose. But you need to tell her exactly what did happen. As far as she knows, you pushed her, even if it was an accident.

"The truth is, I did push her into the lake. But somebody pushed me. That's why I pushed her. The police are involved. They may come here to ask you some questions." Matthew thought he should warn the hospital staff that this incident had not been an accident.

"I figured you didn't push her on purpose. I didn't know any details until Elizabeth gave us her version of what happened. Thanks for the heads up about the police."

Richard was delighted his wife was going to be all right. He already knew she was a live wire, but he was happy to hear she was back to her old self so soon. He hugged her and sat down beside the bed. She immediately asked him about his wrist and the stitches in his thumb. He was glad to have the chance to give her his side of the story about the wheelchair. He knew she didn't think he had pushed her into the lake intentionally, but he needed to let her know what had happened. Of course, she hadn't known anything about the man in the black hoodie who had been the instigator of the debacle. Richard told Elizabeth about Tyler's part in saving her life. Matthew sat in the chair on the other side of the bed. He also was impressed that Elizabeth had bounced back so quickly.

"I know all of the other women are going to the spa today. I had appointments scheduled, too, all day long. I'm disappointed to have to miss it. The Penmoor said they might be able to reschedule me for tomorrow, but I'm afraid I won't be out of here in time. Is Saturday our free day, without any activities scheduled? I might be able to go to the spa on Saturday."

Elizabeth saw Matthew was about to ask a question. She pointed. "There's a phone right there, beside the bed. It's a land line. Remember those? I called first thing this morning to cancel my appointments. They'd already heard from the concierge that I was in the hospital. They said they would do everything they could to reschedule my services when I get back to the hotel." Matthew should have known Elizabeth could read his mind. Richard had been telling him for years about her uncanny ability.

They didn't want to stay too long and thought they might like to try to make it to the Penrose Museum. They hugged Elizabeth and said goodbye. Richard was scheduled to check in at the ER before they left the hospital. The doctor who had put the brace on his wrist wanted to see if the injured hand and arm were remaining immobilized, and he wanted to check the stitches in Richard's thumb to be sure there was no infection.

Later that afternoon, Elizabeth was just dropping off to sleep when a CNA, a certified nursing assistant, came into her room, carrying two flower arrangements. One was a large multi-colored display in a silver ice bucket. It held all of Elizabeth's favorite flowers — hydrangeas, lilacs, daisies, tulips, hyacinth, roses, and iris. Even the bells of Ireland and a touch of Scottish heather were in there. Someone had given a lot of thought to ordering this gorgeous bouquet. The other arrangement was a beautifully woven wicker basket full of pink roses and pink tulips. The CNA had a lot to say about the flowers. "These are real nice. You must have some rich friends. You just got here last night, and here you already have all these flowers. Some people come in here and never get a single flower. And these two … definitely not FTD."

Elizabeth was thrilled and somewhat surprised. Hardly anybody knew she was here. She'd called her children to let them know that she was okay, in case there was anything on the news. She'd not told them any details — just a quick call. She didn't think she'd even told them the name of the hospital. She'd called a couple of friends on the East Coast and her next-door-neighbor in Tucson. Who would have had time to send her flowers already? The ice bucket was sterling silver. Definitely not FTD.

"Will you open the cards for me? My hands don't work like they used to. Thanks."

The basket of pink roses and tulips was from the Penmoor Resort. Elle, their concierge had signed the card. It read: "Hope to see you back with us soon." Elizabeth was impressed with the thoughtfulness of the hotel and its management staff. Good PR. Very sweet.

The card that had arrived with the large arrangement in the silver ice bucket read: "Much love from a secret admirer." This gave Elizabeth pause. The CNA who had been reading over her shoulder said, "Wow! Look at you. You are so old, and you still have a secret admirer. This is so impressive." Elizabeth was quiet. She needed to spend a little bit of time with her thoughts and her memories. She thought she knew, but she wasn't sure.

A few minutes later, the little CNA came through her door again with another arrangement. This was a small bouquet of violets in a cut crystal glass. The certified nursing assistant had more to say. "I swear, you are one popular lady. Can I open this card for you?" Elizabeth handed her the card and it read: "From your secret admirer." The CNA went nuts. "You've got two, count them T-W-O, secret admirers … in one day. I would love to have just one secret admirer, or even one non-secret admirer would be nice." She placed the glass of violets next to Elizabeth's bed. She stepped closer to Elizabeth and looked intently at her face. "Who are you anyway? Are you somebody famous?" Elizabeth laughed, but there were tears in her eyes.

Lilleth decided to cancel her spa appointments that day, but she'd rescheduled for Friday afternoon. Olivia and Isabelle had briefly given some thought to visiting Elizabeth this morning, but they had decided Elizabeth would want them to carry on with their spa day, without her. They knew how much

Elizabeth loved having a long and really intense therapeutic massage, so they were going to go ahead with their massages and other services, in her honor. They knew how disappointed she was to miss it. Gretchen and Sidney had early appointments and had skipped breakfast to get to the spa on time.

Chapter 23

The spa at the Penmoor was as good as they had anticipated it would be and better. The facility was classically luxurious and designed to encourage relaxation. Everyone who worked at the resort was helpful and nice. They'd been hired because they had pleasant personalities, and customer service was important at the Penmoor. This commitment to their guests was even more apparent at the spa. Each client was made to feel as if she or he were the only person receiving services that day. The individual attention and personal care were above and beyond what the women in the reunion group had expected.

Gretchen's spa day began with a pedicure, followed by a facial. Then she would have her massage. A manicure was next, and she would finish in the hair salon with a cut. Sidney's facial was scheduled first. Then she would have her massage, followed by a pedicure and a manicure.

The massage rooms were along both sides of one hall. Each room was numbered and had two slots beside the door. The name of the massage therapist went in one slot, and the name of the client went in the other slot. If the client left her massage room for any reason, to use the bathroom or to get something to eat or drink, having the client's name beside the door of the room was helpful. Everyone could easily find their correct massage room, and nobody accidentally wandered into the wrong one.

The pedicure and the facial had been heavenly, and Gretchen was beginning to relax. She'd been unusually tense lately because of the stalker who was threatening her. Then she'd received the news about Arnold Sprungli's death. She desperately needed the massage and the pampering the Penmoor spa promised. She'd extended her massage time from the standard fifty minutes to the deluxe eighty minutes.

Hilda, her massage therapist, met her in the spa lounge and escorted her to the hallway where the massage rooms were located. As they walked, Hilda asked Gretchen questions about what she wanted from her therapeutic massage. She wanted to know where Gretchen carried her body's tension. Most people carry their tension in their neck and shoulders. She wanted to know if Gretchen had experienced any recent injuries the therapist might need to know about. Gretchen noticed, as they walked down the hall, that the name Withers Singleton was in the name slot on the wall outside one of the massage rooms. Gretchen was surprised that the move star was still here at the Penmoor until she realized that it had only been a couple of days since they'd seen her in the Saloon restaurant.

"We're going into this one." Hilda directed her towards the room that had Withers Singleton's name beside the door. Gretchen pointed to the name and started to ask about it. "Oh, Ms. Singleton thought she felt a draft in this room and asked to have her massage in a room that was warmer. We moved her to the room you were supposed to have, and we turned up the heat a bit in this room. I don't think there really was a draft, but we try to accommodate even our most particular clients." Hilda smiled. She realized that almost everyone would recognize Withers' name, and Gretchen would understand that Hollywood stars could be picky and demanding. "If the room feels too cool for you, we'll be happy to make a switch. Please let me know."

Gretchen thought the room felt perfectly fine. She took off her robe and crawled between the sheets of the massage table. She gave herself up to the ministrations of the expert. It was pure bliss.

The man had planned far ahead for this moment. There were several male massage therapists who worked at the spa, and he had stolen his uniform from one of their lockers. He'd been hanging around the Penmoor and spying on the employees for several days. He had given a great deal of thought to how he was going to kill her. She thought she could fool him, but he was too smart for her. He had tracked her every move and knew everything she was doing. After an autopsy was performed, the authorities would know it was not an accident, but initially, it would look like she had died of a heart attack or a stroke or an aneurysm. That would give him time to get away and establish his alibi. He would silence her forever, and no one would ever know who had done it.

The man had planned carefully for this kill. He'd had a difficult time locating her, but once he'd found her, he was determined to finish her off as soon as possible. Alexi had blown it in Bar Harbor, and he'd paid the ultimate price. It had all been a terrible mistake, and now his cousin was going to finish the job and find some redemption for Alexi. The avenging cousin had been checking things out around the Penmoor for several days, and he'd decided the spa was the best place to kill her. The location offered the best chance of escape. He had everything arranged, and if everything went as planned this time, it would all proceed smoothly. His mission would be accomplished. The one thing he was worried about was his disguise. It wasn't great. The assassin would be wearing one of the terry cloth robes the clients wear, but it was very short, too short. He couldn't figure out a way to cover up his dark pants and foreign-looking boots. He'd rolled up his pants, but he couldn't take off his boots because he had to be dressed to make his escape. He wouldn't have time to put his pants and boots back on. He'd only have time to get rid of the robe, grab his coat, and leave the building. Timing was everything, and he didn't have the luxury of changing his clothes. He had to hope that nobody would notice the boots.

The man had decided the spa at the Penmoor was the best place to stage his attack. He had traced her to the resort through calls she'd had made to her daughter on her cell phone. People thought he wasn't smart, but he knew more about how to find somebody than most of the people he had worked with. He'd certainly known more than his former boss, about almost everything. The woman he was after today was one of the conspirators against him. He'd never seen her in person, but he had hacked into the Penmoor's computer. He knew she'd scheduled a massage for this morning.

Her massage therapist had been gracious about Withers' request to change rooms, but Withers could tell the masseuse wished she were in her own room. Each of them had their own oils and creams and other equipment in a particular room. They liked their own spaces, and the change Withers had requested had annoyed the therapist, even though she'd pretended it hadn't. Withers was terribly thin, and she worked hard to stay that way. Because she had no body fat, she was often cold, and there had definitely been a draft in the other room. She felt only a little bit guilty for requesting that her massage room be changed.

Hilda stepped out of the massage room for a minute, and Gretchen drifted off to sleep. Her back and neck felt so much better. She felt years younger. She wished she could always feel this stress-free. In the next instant, there was a pillow over her face, and she was fighting for her life. She knew the stalker had found her, and he intended to kill her. When one's life is threatened, a person sometimes finds superhuman reserves of strength to call on to survive. Gretchen knew she was going to have to divine a miracle to live through this attack. She gathered all of her strength and pushed the man away. She stared at him, and he stared back at her.

"You're not Diane. Where is she? I'm sorry. I didn't mean to hurt you." The attacker was apologizing? Seriously? He rushed out of the room and hurried down the hall. One minute he was trying to smother her with a pillow, and the next, he was saying he was sorry. Then he ran away. Gretchen was dazed, and her neck was quite painful. She didn't know what to do. She was afraid to leave the room. What if the man changed his mind and was waiting for her outside in the hall? There was a lock on the door. She went to the door and locked it. Then she hid underneath the massage table. She would stay there ... until somebody came to get her, until she was sure the coast was clear, until the danger had passed, until the man who had tried to kill her had been apprehended.

She had been so relaxed after the facial and the massage. Now she was a nervous wreck again. She'd left her cell phone in her locker, hoping she wouldn't be tempted to think about work, or anything at all, for a couple of hours. She was trying to wean herself from her electronic devices. Of course, the one day she really needed to have her phone with her, she didn't have it. She could have called for help. She could have called the police. Then she heard the shots. It sounded as if they were coming from the room next to hers.

Sidney had thoroughly enjoyed her facial and her massage. She was particular, and she didn't give every resort a top grade in the spa department. The Penmoor had more than measured up to her expectations. She was sitting on a bench in the hall outside the massage rooms, waiting for someone to come and take her to have her pedicure. Her massage therapist had left her on the bench with a cup of hot tea and a plate that held three triangular watercress tea sandwiches and several enormous and deliciously sweet black raspberries. This was world-class service. Sidney closed her eyes and sighed with pleasure. She was about to drift off to sleep when she heard footsteps and looked up.

A male massage therapist carrying a pillow was hurriedly leaving one of the massage therapy rooms. Sidney hadn't noticed exactly which room he'd just come out of, but she didn't think it could have been Gretchen's. Gretchen would have scheduled a woman to do her massage. Sidney knew there were male massage therapists here at the Penmoor and at many other spas. She personally preferred to have a woman, and so did Gretchen. They had discussed it. This man had looked upset, as if he were lost. He had on a maroon-colored smock, the men's version of the rose coverall that the female massage therapists wore. The man in the maroon uniform hurried down the hall, opened the door of another massage therapy room, and went inside.

Sidney began to doze again. Something startled her, and as she opened her eyes, she noticed a particularly odd individual at the end of the hall. She could swear it was a man, but he was dressed in the light pink terry cloth robe the spa gave its women clients to wear when they had massages and facials. The robe didn't fit him, and his feet were too big for the flip flops he was wearing. Why was he wearing a pink robe anyway? He was reading all the names in the slots by the doors along the hall. Was he looking for his own name? If he was a man, he was in the wrong place. He couldn't be looking for his massage therapy room; men didn't belong in this hallway.

Then a third man came and sat on the bench beside Sidney. He eyed her watercress sandwiches. She grabbed the plate in her hands before he could help himself. What was it with all these men in the women's massage area? Sidney had been led to believe that the men who came to the Penmoor spa for a massage had their own hallway that went off in an entirely different direction from the main lounge. Sidney was most suspicious of this man, the weirdest of the three. He had on one of the pink terrycloth robes, too, but he had on black shiny pants. He'd rolled them up, but she could see them peeking out below the pink robe. And he was wearing strange-looking black boots. The boots were what got Sidney's attention. They were strictly Eurotrash boots. Sidney and Cameron traveled extensively, all over the world. Sidney knew her Eurotrash boots. These boots did not belong at the Penmoor in Colorado Springs. They were more than out of place here. They screamed trouble!

The Penmoor was a first class resort, and Withers Singleton had enjoyed her stay. The spa was one of the nicest she'd ever visited. She had loved her massage and was sitting in the chair beside the door in the massage room, relaxing and waiting to be called for her facial. She had just drifted off to sleep when the door opened and a man stepped into the room. When the door swung open, Withers was in the corner of the room, behind the door, so the man who'd just entered couldn't see her. He raised a gun and looked at the massage table. The sheets and blankets were in a jumble, and the pillows were piled on top. It could look as if someone were lying on the table under the bedding.

The gunman took careful aim at what he must have thought was the head of a person lying on the table and fired six shots at the pillows. Feathers flew all over the room. The gunman turned around to leave, when the door opened again. Another man stepped into the room. The second man drew a gun from the belt of his pants and fired five shots into the body of the man who had just destroyed the pillows. The first man's gun dropped out of his hand onto the massage table. He fell across the table, and blood ran down over everything.

The second gunman took a few steps closer to the massage table. He realized there hadn't been anyone lying on the table. This unexpected man with a gun that he'd just shot, was sprawled across the table and bleeding to death. What was going on here? Who was this nearly dead man, the man he had blasted? The assassin didn't have time to worry about that. Even though he had used a silencer, the first gunman had not, and those shots had to have been heard all over this part of the spa. Where was the woman he had come to kill?

When he turned around and looked at the chair in the corner, he saw the small woman with short blonde hair sitting there. Her eyes were wide and staring. She was paralyzed with fear. She was definitely his mark. Her name was on the slot beside the door. This had to be the right woman. He hadn't seen her in person for many years, but he had a recent photo. Without question, this was the person he'd come to eliminate. He raised his gun to fire at the woman in the chair when the door to the massage room flew open. The door swung backwards and blocked his target. He moved to the side to try to get a better line of sight. He would shoot whoever was coming through the door, too.

Just as he was moving into position for the kill, he thought he heard something move behind him on the massage table. Maybe the man he'd shot wasn't dead after all. The assassin made an instantaneous and almost unconscious decision. He had not cleared the man's gun. Or maybe the gunman carried a second gun? If the man he'd shot was still alive, he could be armed. Neither the person coming through the door nor his target in the corner of the room would be armed.

He turned quickly with his gun in his hand, ready to fire again at the bleeding man draped over the massage table. It was a big mistake for him to turn around, to turn his back on the door. As he aimed his gun at the unknown man who was sprawled across the massage table in a pool of blood, he was attacked from behind.

The man coming down the hall in the pink robe and flip flops, opened the door and stepped into the massage room that had

Gretchen's name beside the door. Sidney stood up. Why was he going in there? He had no business going in there. Her friend Gretchen was in that room. Then she heard the gun shots. She was terrified to hear someone shooting a gun in a place like the Penmoor spa, and she was even more terrified that he was in the room with Gretchen. Sidney was going in. Then the man in the Eurotrash boots, who was sitting beside her and looking at her watercress sandwiches, stood up and rushed past her towards the door of the room where the shots had been fired.

Sidney didn't stop to think about how dangerous it might be for her to enter that terrible room. She was right on the heels of those ugly boots. She threw open the door and grabbed a large lamp that sat on a small table to the right of the door. It was a heavy lamp with a solid brass base. Sidney was strong, and she was tall. Just as Sidney entered the room, the gunman in the bad boots made a big mistake and turned around to look at the carnage he'd left sprawled on the massage table. Sidney swung the lamp with all her might. She smacked the man who held the gun, hard, on the side of his head with the base of the lamp. Wielding the lamp with both hands like a baseball bat, she smacked him again. The heavy base struck a second solid blow. And one more time for good measure. He went down. He was out. Sidney began to scream at the top of her lungs.

She dropped the lamp. Withers Singleton, who had been too frightened to move until that moment, jumped out of the chair in the corner of the room, threw herself into Sidney's arms and began to weep. At first Sidney thought it was Gretchen. She thought she had saved Gretchen's life. Gretchen's name had been posted in the name slot beside the door outside the room. This was supposed to be Gretchen's massage room.

Sidney looked down at the small blond who was sobbing and clinging to her for dear life. This wasn't Gretchen. It was Withers Singleton, the Hollywood star. This was worse than

Alice in Wonderland. Where the heck was Gretchen? What the heck was going on in here? Sidney was always brave and in control. She didn't faint. But, for one brief moment, she thought she might.

Blessedly, within seconds, two security guards and some other people rushed into the room. Withers had her own security team, and her bodyguard and another woman peeled the hysterical star out of Sidney's arms and took her away to someplace safe. Two polite Penmoor security guards escorted Sidney to a room that had comfortable chairs and several chaise lounges. All the rooms at the Penmoor spa were beautifully appointed, but this one had blue silk draperies and upholstery. The carpet was white. It looked to Sidney as if she was in the VIP lounge. She kept asking where Gretchen was. Finally, a woman security guard escorted Gretchen into the VIP lounge. Sidney hugged her friend who was pale and clearly in distress. "What happened to you?" Sidney asked Gretchen.

"Somebody tried to smother me with a pillow. But he didn't. He looked at me, said I was the wrong person, apologized, and left the room. I locked the door and hid under the massage table. Then I heard the gunshots. I thought there was a mass shooting going on in the spa. I stayed where I was until a security guard came to the room and talked me into coming out. It took a lot of convincing to get me to leave my hiding place. What happened to you?"

Sidney said, "I don't really know." She was quiet for a few minutes, trying to find the words to tell Gretchen what she'd just experienced. "I don't know what happened. I thought you were in that room, but it was Withers Singleton. It all happened so fast; I honestly have no idea what in the world just happened."

Before too many minutes had elapsed, there were multiple law enforcement people in the VIP lounge. Sidney didn't know if she had anything worth saying to them. She didn't know who either of the gunmen was. She didn't have any idea why they were after Gretchen, or after Withers, or whoever they were after. She didn't know anything. She didn't have a clue. She wished Cameron would show up and take charge of it all. Cameron would later say to her, in an effort to cheer her up and make her smile, "You know what they say … 'Don't take a lamp to a gunfight.' But, you know, Sidney, you did a really good job with that lamp."

Chapter 24

THE FACT WAS THAT SIDNEY HAD SAVED WITHERS Singleton's life. Sidney had believed, at the time she had performed her extraordinary act of bravery, that she was saving her friend Gretchen MacDermott. Sidney had saved a life. It just hadn't been Gretchen's life she'd saved. Gretchen hadn't needed anybody to save her life. She had been able to save her own life when she'd fought back hard enough to keep her attacker from smothering her to death with a pillow. She had seen his face clearly, but she had no idea who he was.

Both women wanted answers from the law enforcement people. What was going on in the massage rooms of the Penmoor Resort? Three unknown and violent assailants, bent on murder, had, within a period of about five minutes, invaded the calm and quiet of the resort's upscale spa. Two of the attackers had been armed with guns, and one had been armed with a pillow. One was dead, one was in custody with a number of severe wounds to the head, and one had escaped.

Sidney was a person who had seen it all and could cope with anything. She'd worked in law enforcement for years before she'd met and married Cameron Richardson. She knew very well how police investigations worked and how the process sometimes seemed mired in molasses. But, she had never been on this side of a crime or on this side of an investigation. She had never been a victim of or a witness to a crime. She was not really a victim in the attack inside Withers Singleton's massage room. She had come close to being a victim, but she hadn't been hurt. She was a witness, and she certainly was the hero. She had brought down a dangerous assassin, and she hadn't had to kill him to subdue him. She had given him a terrible headache, and she did not have a guilty conscience about that at all.

Gretchen and Sidney had retrieved their cell phones. They'd asked the officers who were questioning them if they could go to their lockers and get dressed. Their spa treatments were definitely finished for the day. A policewoman accompanied them to the dressing rooms and searched both of their lockers. She said she was looking for explosive devices. She stayed close by while Sidney and Gretchen got dressed and accompanied them back to the VIP lounge for more questions. One of the men in charge tried to confiscate their cell phones. Sidney made a deal with the man. She promised not to report any of the details about what had happened here at the spa, if he would allow her to text her husband to let him know that she was all right.

"If he hears about this, either through the hotel staff or on the news, and he doesn't know that I am fine, you will be very, very sorry that you did not allow me to send him a text. If he doesn't hear from me first and hears there was a shooting in the spa, there will be hell to pay. He will make you sorry you were ever born. You will regret for the rest of your life that you didn't allow me to communicate with him. I'm not going to give him any details about the shooting over the phone. You can read the text before I send it. However, when I finally see him in person, you can be certain that I will tell him every gruesome detail. That's my offer. Take it or leave it." They took it. They'd known, before they'd ever laid eyes on Sidney, that they were not dealing with a shrinking violet.

The hall where the women's massage rooms were located was quickly shut down and cordoned off with yellow crime scene tape. Law enforcement had made a search of the other areas in the spa but had decided, after intense lobbying from the resort staff, to allow the rest of the spa to continue normal operations. The police and the sheriff had wanted to shut down the entire spa, but they'd reached a compromise. The manager of the spa, after consulting with the resort's upper management, had agreed to allow law enforcement personnel to search the entire spa and the other floors of the building, without a search warrant, if they would allow the spa to remain open. If they did not allow the spa to continue to serve its customers, those who had in no way been affected by the violence on the massage room hallway, searching private property would be delayed by the time-consuming effort required to obtain an official search warrant signed by a judge. Law enforcement accepted the compromise. They blocked off the crime scene and did their warrantless search of the other rooms of the spa. They searched all the floors of the building and found nothing.

Sidney sent a text to Cameron, and Gretchen sent a text to Bailey. They'd heard nothing back from either one of their spouses. Sidney knew that Cameron had intended to go to the Penrose Heritage Museum with J.D. to see the antique cars and carriages. Maybe he was having such a good time there, he'd turned off his phone. He hardly ever did that, but he was on vacation this week. Sidney knew that he and J.D. had planned to go to the hospital to see Elizabeth later in the day. Maybe he was at the hospital and had turned off his phone.

Gretchen wasn't surprised that Bailey hadn't responded. She knew he was up to something. She didn't have any idea what it was that he was up to, but she realized he didn't want her to know about it. He'd promised not to do this to her anymore. He knew she was already stressed about the man who had been stalking her and about her former boss who'd been murdered in Switzerland. But she always knew when Bailey was on a mission, and he was on one now. Gretchen had confronted him about it, and he'd tried to look innocent. He denied everything, but she knew he was hiding something. He disappeared for long periods of time and refused to tell her where he'd been.

Bailey carried three cell phones, and he had recently been turning them off. This was unusual, as Bailey thought he needed to be constantly in touch with the world via his phones. Gretchen suspected he had at least one new cell phone because she'd heard another phone in their room, a phone with a ring tone that was different from Bailey's other phones. She was familiar with the ring tones of her husband's three cell phones, and this new ring tone was not one of those. She wondered how anyone kept up with three cell phones, let alone four.

She'd also found a dark brown, curly wig on the floor of the closet in their hotel room. Bailey had promised he wouldn't use his disguises on these trips with the reunion group. He had humiliated her the previous year by disguising himself as a woman and making a public appearance at a restaurant. Gretchen had been having dinner at the restaurant with their friends. She'd been furious, and Bailey had promised not to do it again. Even knowing how he loved the rush of putting on a disguise didn't keep Gretchen from being angry about it. She needed to talk to him right now. Someone had tried to kill her today. She wanted to let her husband know she hadn't been hurt. She was a strong and independent woman, but it wasn't every day that someone tried to murder her. What Sidney and Gretchen wanted more than anything, was an explanation from the investigators about what had happened. They had many questions.

But law enforcement didn't know, at this point, any more than Sidney and Gretchen knew. These two intelligent women would have to figure it out on their own. A man had tried to kill Gretchen, and then he'd apologized to her. He had clearly targeted Gretchen by mistake. When he'd seen her face, he'd said, "You're not Diane." Then he had said he was "sorry." That meant he'd been looking for a woman named Diane and intended to kill her. Gretchen had not been the target of murderer #1. Diane, whoever the unfortunate woman happened to be, was that man's target.

Did murderer #2 and murderer #3 intend to kill Withers, or did they intend to kill Gretchen? That was the question they could not answer with certainty. Everyone knew that beautiful Hollywood stars had stalkers with various motives, weirdos who wanted to get close to them. That's why movie stars employed bodyguards and hired their own security teams. Jodie Foster and John Hinckley could not help but come to mind when thinking about famous Hollywood stars and stalkers. Hinckley had gone so far as to attempt to assassinate the president of the United States. Hinckley's grossly misguided intention had been to impress the starlet that he was insanely obsessed with. It was not impossible to believe that one or both of the gunmen, who had gone into Withers' massage room, had intended to kill her, hurt her, or take her hostage.

How had either one of the murderers known that Withers was in that particular massage room? Her name was in the name slot outside an entirely different room. The name that was posted on the wall outside the room that both gunmen had entered was "Gretchen." Gretchen and Sidney could not avoid the obvious conclusion. Both gunmen had gone into that massage room with the intention of killing Gretchen. But why? And who were they?

Obviously, the shooters had not been working as a team. The first man had entered the room where he believed Gretchen was having a massage. He had fired his gun at the massage table and had killed two pillows. He had believed that Gretchen was lying on the table. In fact, no one had been lying on the table. The second gunman had also entered the room that had Gretchen's name posted beside the door. He, too, must have believed that Gretchen was in that room. The second gunman who entered the massage room had shot and killed the first gunman who'd entered the room.

Sidney had seen all three murderers moving up and down the massage room hallway. One of them had even sat down next to her ... and tried to steal her watercress tea sandwiches. She had seen the man who'd exited the massage room assigned to Withers Singleton. That was the room Gretchen had actually been in to have her massage. One might mistakenly conclude that he had been after Withers. Even though her name had been posted outside, because she had complained about the room's temperatures, she had not been in that room. Because of what the man had said to Gretchen, they knew he'd been trying to find and kill someone named Diane, not Withers or Gretchen.

Sidney had seen both gunman enter the room that had Gretchen's name posted outside. Sidney had assumed Gretchen was in the room. Wouldn't everyone assume that? Only a few people knew that Withers had complained about a draft and been taken to a different massage room, the room that had originally been assigned to Gretchen. Who could keep it all straight? No wonder the gunmen had targeted an empty massage table and the wrong petite blond woman.

Gretchen and Sidney realized that a woman named Diane was in trouble. If the man could find her, he was going to try to kill her. Gretchen thought one of the policewomen in the VIP lounge might listen to her. She approached the law enforcement official and told her story, for the tenth time, it seemed. Gretchen told her that she believed a woman named Diane was in serious danger. She recounted exactly what the man had said to her about "not being Diane." Most of the attention right now was on the dead gunman and the gunman who'd killed him and been taken into custody. The murder that had not happened, the attempt on Gretchen's life, was not receiving much attention. Gretchen had finally had enough.

"I don't want to hear on the news about a woman named Diane, who was having a spa treatment or staying at the Penmoor, being found dead in her massage treatment room or in her hotel room. I will go to the press and tell them I warned you that a woman whose name is Diane was the target of a murderer. I will tell them that this man tried to kill me. I will tell them everything. You all don't seem interested in taking me seriously, that a woman named Diane is in jeopardy. I will go to the manager of the Penmoor spa and to the CEO of this resort, if necessary, to let them know that one of their guests is in mortal danger. They had better find out who she is and do something to protect her. Don't doubt for a minute that I will do exactly what I say I'm going to do. Either you do something about this, or I will."

Lilleth had cancelled her appointments to take care of Tyler, but Olivia and Isabelle had also been scheduled to have spa services today. Olivia and Gretchen were good friends, and Gretchen wondered where they were. Gretchen hadn't made any promises to the police about sending texts, so she felt free to communicate with the others in the group.

"Where are you? Do you know what's happening at the spa? Lots to tell. Sidney and I are fine. We're in the VIP lounge, giving statements to law enforcement. We're not in trouble,

just witnesses to a few attempted murders. Two gunmen were shooting. Can you believe it? Can't reach Bailey or Cameron. Can you reach J.D. or Matthew? Tell them to come to the spa and demand to see us. Get Elle involved if you have to. GM"

Gretchen immediately had a text back from Olivia: "OMG. R U sure you R okay? Our massages have been cancelled. Women's massage area of the spa is a no go zone. No one is talking. Staff people look terrified but won't tell us anything. J.D. not answering his phone or my texts. Elle not answering my phone calls either. Should we try to find you? WTF????"

"You won't be able to find us. We are too well guarded. Keep trying to reach J.D."

Olivia and Isabelle were worried sick. Their friends said they were okay, but they were apparently being held, or sequestered, in the VIP lounge. There had been a shooting at the spa, but no one would give out any information. Some intensely serious men, who looked like they could be police or FBI, had come through the area where Oliva and Isabelle had been having their facials. The men had moved quickly and seemed to be searching for someone. Everyone's massages had been cancelled. There had been a general announcement. In her text, Gretchen had made reference to "a few attempted murders," implying that there was more than one and maybe more than two. How was that even possible? Isabelle tried to call Matthew, but he wasn't answering his phone either. He almost always took Isabelle's calls. Where was everybody? They'd all been so relieved when they'd heard the news that Elizabeth was out of ICU and apparently doing fine. And now this. Would it never end?

Chapter 25

RICHARD AND MATTHEW HAD LEFT THE HOSPITAL and were on their way back to the hotel in a taxi. Matthew decided they were going to the Grille at the Golf Club. The Grille had become everybody's favorite lunch place. It was chilly today, so they would eat inside. Just as they were about to enter the restaurant, Matthew received a text from Isabelle. She asked him to call her right away. He saw that she'd tried to call him a couple of times, but he hadn't heard his phone ring. Then he remembered he'd turned off the ringer when he'd been at the hospital and had forgotten to turn it back on. He motioned Richard to go in and get them a table. He called Isabelle from outside the entrance to the Golf Club.

Isabelle's words began spilling out, as soon as she answered her phone. "There's been a shooting at the spa. No guests were hurt, and Sidney and Gretchen are fine. But they were involved in some way. I think they were witnesses to something pretty terrible. I don't know where you are, but you might go over there and see if you can find out anything. Gretchen sent a text to Olivia and me to tell us she and Sidney are in the spa's VIP lounge answering questions. They aren't being held as suspects, or anything like that. They're witnesses, but they can't leave. The spa is still open, but the area where the shootings took place, the massage therapy section, is closed. Supposedly, it's a crime scene. I don't know what the crime is or if anybody is dead or has been injured. No one on the spa staff is talking, if they even know anything. All massages have been cancelled for the day. It's quite mysterious. How is Elizabeth doing?"

"Isn't the spa in the same building where the Grille is located, the building where the Golf Club is? It's called the Golf and Tennis Club, or something like that. I saw it on our map. I'm right there now. I'm right outside the door of the Golf Club. That's where I'm calling you from. Richard and I are just going in to the restaurant for lunch. Everything seems to be entirely normal here, but we will keep our eyes open. If law enforcement is here, they're keeping a low profile. Maybe we'll go around to the back of the building and see if there are any police cars parked there. Thank goodness Sidney and Gretchen are all right. I wish you had more information about what's going on. I'll try to reach Cameron. Bailey is incommunicado right now."

"Isn't Bailey always incommunicado? Yes, try to get Cameron over there to the spa to get some information. Sidney is incredibly independent, but trust me, she would love to have Cameron's help right now. And Gretchen would like to let Bailey know she's all right. So please, if you know where he is, let him know she's okay."

"Elizabeth is out of ICU and almost fully recovered, as far as I can tell. She's entertaining the medical staff and the nurses with her stories about how her husband pushed her into the lake at the Penmoor. She's coming home tomorrow, if her lungs are clear."

"Actually, you know, he really did push her into the lake. It was an accident, but he did push her. So that is not a joke."

"You know Elizabeth. Everything is a story for her, and she loves being able to tell everyone that Richard pushed her. She especially loves that it's true. Poor Richard. He's not doing very well. He can't use his left hand at all. Thank goodness it isn't his right hand. He hates seeing Elizabeth in a hospital bed. He hates it that he's the one who pushed her into the lake, even though she doesn't blame him at all and has made a whole comedy routine out of it. Everyone keeps telling him she's a live wire. I think he's heard enough of that. She's the one who almost died, and she's fine. I'll be glad when she's back at the hotel with Richard and can cheer him up. I'm not doing a good job of it. Right now, I'm just trying to be sure he eats. We came here to have lunch, but first, we're going to check out the back to see if we can find the coroner." Matthew was only half kidding about trying to find the coroner. He was shocked to hear there had been shootings in the resort's spa, but he was greatly relieved that Gretchen and Sidney were all right. He called Cameron, and Cameron picked up.

"Cameron, wherever you are and whatever you are doing, drop it and come to the Golf Club at the resort, where we had lunch yesterday. Come immediately. Sidney is fine, and so is Gretchen. I just talked to Isabelle, and there has been a shooting at the spa. Gretchen and Sidney were witnesses to something. Information is scarce, and details are non-existent. Law enforcement is questioning Sidney and Gretchen and won't let them leave. They're in the spa's VIP lounge. Gretchen sent texts to Olivia and Isabelle. Sidney probably tried to call or text you. We could also use J.D. He's a lawyer, or was a long time ago. He might be able to rattle some cages or at least get the women released from the VIP lounge. Richard and I are having lunch at the Grille. The spa is on an upper floor of this same building, so come here."

"Are you sure Sidney and Gretchen are all right? One hundred percent? What the hell is going on around here?" The serious concern in Cameron's voice belied his usual calm manner. "I turned off my phone when I was at the Penrose Museum. I've got a bunch of texts here. I see some are from Sidney. We'll be right there. Are you sure they're all right?" Cameron asked again.

"One hundred percent sure. They are fine. I imagine they must be pretty upset, if they witnessed a shooting, and I am saying, 'if.' I don't know anything other than what I've told you. I'm thinking they must be angry that they're not allowed to leave and have to stay there and answer questions. They are not hurt. I repeat; they are not hurt. We could use a little moral support here, though."

"We were on our way to the hospital to see Elizabeth, but I'll tell the cab to turn around and take us back to the Golf Club."

"I saw Elizabeth this morning. She's doing great. I might be wrong, but I think she may be in better shape than the rest of us are in right now. I don't think we should tell her anything about the shooting at the spa, but I have a feeling she will know all about it before any of us mentions a word to her."

"J.D. and I will be there in a few. Get a table for four, if you ever make it into the dining room. We haven't eaten lunch either."

Matthew went into the Grille and found Richard talking to the hostess. That he was talking to her was a good sign. Maybe he was beginning to come out of his funk. Matthew told the hostess, "We want a table for four at 1:30. We're expecting two more. The name is Ritter. We're going to take a walk while we wait for our friends to arrive. Their names are J.D. Steele and Cameron Richardson."

"You couldn't wait to get me in here to eat lunch, and now we're going to take a walk? What's going on?" Richard asked.

"I have a lot to tell you. Everyone in our group is okay, but there has been a shooting at the spa, directly upstairs in this building. I think the spa is on the third floor. You and I are going to walk around to the other side of the building, in case there are any law enforcement vehicles, coroner's vans, or CSIs hiding back there. I seem to remember that you were quite a bit of help to the medical examiner in Maine. And, you found out a lot of inside information for your curious friends. I'm expecting you to work your magic again. That is, if we can find anybody for you to work your magic on." Matthew was propelling Richard around the side of the building, as he told him the little he knew about what had happened and why they were looking for the coroner. If Richard could talk to the coroner, it would be the ideal way for him to get his confidence back after the Elizabeth fiasco.

There wasn't really any back door to the Golf Club building. Matthew had heard that there was a system of underground tunnels that provided delivery vehicles access to the resort. He and Richard walked around the entire building and didn't see any police cars or CSI vehicles. He figured law enforcement had entered the way the food delivery trucks and other maintenance vehicles enter, underground and unseen by guests. He'd been hoping they might accidentally run into the coroner, but Matthew had known that was a long shot. Cameron texted him that he and J.D. were pulling up in front of the Golf Club. Attempting to get information from law enforcement would have to wait.

Cameron came through the front door like the successful CEO he was. Without saying a word to anyone he headed straight for the elevator and the spa on the third floor. He was going to find Sidney and see for himself that she was all right. J.D. took the next elevator. He was going to leave Cameron to his own devices and try to find Oliva and Isabelle.

Cameron was upstairs in the spa's reception area speaking quietly but earnestly with a woman who looked like she was the spa manager. Cameron was not making a scene, but he definitely had the woman's attention. She listened to what he was saying and motioned for him to follow her. J.D. tried to follow, but they went through a doorway that closed in his face and locked behind them.

J.D. sent a text to Olivia to let her know he was at the spa, and he had a seat in the beautifully decorated lounge area to wait for his wife. The view of the mountains was magnificent, and the colors in the room were soothing and relaxing. The surroundings were so peaceful, he couldn't bring himself to associate any kind of violence with this place. He decided he might have to sign up for some spa services himself, just to be able to spend more time in this luxurious spot. Who said only women could enjoy the spa? He knew there was a world-class fitness center associated with this building and at least one magnificent indoor pool.

Olivia texted that she was in the middle of a pedicure and Isabelle was in the middle of a manicure. Neither one of them could meet him until later. Olivia told her husband she'd asked a number of the spa staff if they'd heard about a shooting in the women's massage area. She'd not been able to confirm anything. She had not heard a single word about a shooting or about anything at all out of the ordinary. She was amazed nothing had leaked out about an untoward incident in the building. If she hadn't heard about it directly from someone she knew well, someone who was a first-hand witness to the trouble, she might have begun to doubt that anything at all had happened. The Penmoor really knew how to keep a lid on things. They were masters at discretion. The waters were smooth in every direction. It was as if nothing at all had happened, let alone a murder and an attempted murder or two.

Olivia told J.D. she would meet him on the first floor when she was finished with her spa services. Cameron was still in absentia, so J.D. decided to go back down to the Grille and have lunch. The hostess guided the three men to a table for four. Richard and Matthew were disappointed that J.D. had not learned anything. They each ordered a beer, two Heinekens and one Corona with lime. Just as they were placing their orders for lunch, Cameron took his seat at the table. He did not look happy. He asked for a Corona, and all four men ordered half-pound cheeseburgers and French fries to go with their beer. There were no wives around today to suggest they chose one of the healthy salad options from the menu. It was red meat and beer from foreign countries for the men today.

Cameron didn't wait for the waiter to walk away from the table before he exploded. "I talked to Sidney. She's fine. She's under a tremendous amount of stress, and they wouldn't let her leave with me. She's made a statement, and she has to wait until it's typed up so she can sign it. They said they might let her leave after she's signed the statement. They almost wouldn't let me in to see her, and I admit I got a little hot under the collar before they let me through the door of the VIP lounge. I asked if she needed a lawyer, and they said she didn't. They said she was a hero and a bunch of other stuff, like how she could really pack a punch, how she'd 'saved the day,' and other clichés like that. I have no idea what they were talking about. Sidney said she would explain it all later. I told her not to sign anything until a lawyer could take a look at what she was signing. She gave me a look and said she wasn't going to sign anything except the statement she herself had given. She was glad to see me, but they hustled me out of there in a hurry."

"Did you see Gretchen? Was she okay?"

"I just saw her across the room. I waved to her, and she waved back. Her face was as white as a sheet. There were two policewomen sitting on either side of her, just daring anybody, including me, to come anywhere close to her. They acted as if Gretchen might somehow be in danger. It was weird. I decided I would leave her to her guard dogs and find out what was going on with her later. Gretchen has to meet with a police sketch artist. Apparently she saw the face of someone they are looking for. She saw him up close, very close. That alone is pretty frightening. That was all Sidney had a chance to say. They really didn't want her talking to me. They shuffled me out of there in no time. I don't like to be shuffled out of anywhere. I'm not used to that."

J.D. reassured Cameron. "Sidney is correct about signing her statement. She doesn't really need a lawyer for that. She will read it over after it's typed up. If it isn't right, she won't sign it until it is. She's smart, Cameron, and you know she won't be intimidated by anybody. Don't worry about Sidney. It's Gretchen I'm worried about. It sounds as if they are being extremely protective of her, almost as if they believe she really is in danger. If she has to meet with a sketch artist about someone they are searching for, it means she saw one of the bad guys. She saw him well enough that she can describe him to an artist. He's still on the loose. No wonder they are guarding her. It's possible she really is in danger. What we know for sure is that Gretchen's their eye witness and can identify someone for them. I wonder if any of this has to do with that stalker thing she was telling us about. You know, the guy who shot up his boss's house in Chicago and put the woman in the hospital. He threatened to do the same to Gretchen."

"How could that be? Nobody knows Gretchen is here at the Penmoor. Her boss doesn't even know where she is." Cameron was relieved to hear his attorney friend say Sidney didn't need a lawyer, but he was concerned about Gretchen. "They were definitely treating Gretchen differently from the way they were treating Sidney. I wonder what happened to Gretchen? She looked fine physically, except her face was terribly pale. She looked exhausted. Well, Sidney looked exhausted, too, and it wouldn't be any wonder. Why would they be saying Sidney was a hero? What did Sidney do? She doesn't know Kung Fu or anything like that. If we only could get some real information. I asked Sidney to tell me what had happened, but the FBI chased me out of there before I really had a chance to talk to her. Yep, the FBI was in there, too. What's that all about?"

Two men walked into the Grille with the hostess and were seated at the table next to the four cheeseburger-eaters. One ordered a Scotch on the rocks and the other ordered hot tea with honey. The tea-drinker had draped his windbreaker over the back of his chair. It had big letters printed on the back, and Richard was trying to see what it said.

The table of four grew silent when the man they thought might be the medical examiner began to speak to his table companion. "You know, I've played golf here so many times, and my wife and I like to go to the Saloon for dinner. I've been called a couple of times to pronounce somebody, usually a heart attack. But I never thought I'd be called here to investigate a crime, or should I say crimes, as bizarre as this one — or these two, or these three. It seems to me there were multiple crimes committed … and in a high-end spa like this. It is just too strange to get my head around. And that one woman who took out the assassin with a lamp. Wow! I hope she never gets mad at me. I am almost positive that the one who's in custody is Russian mafia, a hired gun, hired to kill somebody. His gun had a silencer. He's a professional hit job kind of guy, and that kind of a guy never talks. Somebody from his own organization, maybe even from his own family, will silence him, even if he's in jail or in prison, before he has a chance to say a word."

As they eavesdropped on the conversation at the table next to theirs, eight ears strained to hear every word. It sounded like the tea-drinker and the Scotch-drinker were connected with the investigation that was taking place upstairs at the spa.

"I will bet you anything that he's going to turn out to be Russian ... because of the gun he used. Probably Russian mafia."

"You're the firearms expert. What's special about his gun? I didn't see it. Somebody had bagged it before I had a chance to take a look."

"You can't buy that gun anywhere. It's a Kalashnikov prototype made of polymer. I've never seen one before, except in pictures and on the internet. It's a Lebedev PL-15 pistol. The ones similar to it, the guns that are available for sale to the public, are made of aluminum ... very light weight. The pistol this guy dropped when he got hammered with the lamp is made of polymer. Supposedly a prototype of polymer is currently being tested by the Russian Government for their military. It's an assassin's gun ... for close-range assassinations and for use by Special Forces. But, nobody has one of these military-style guns yet. Except somebody does, and he used it today. You would *never* see even the aluminum version of that PL-15 pistol in the hands of a run-of-the-mill criminal, your everyday street thug. And our guy is using a gun that's not available to anybody, anywhere. How did he get it? That man is definitely a high-end killer. The dead gunman, on the other hand, the one who murdered two pillows, used one of the cheapest guns around. He was carrying an LCP Luger Pocket Pistol. It has a single-action trigger and is easy to use. It's popular with beginners and costs about $250. The guns are like night and day, in terms of availability and cost. Interesting."

"The pattern of the shots the guy with the Kalashnikov fired at the guy with the Ruger was unusual, too. I won't go on the record until I've completed the autopsy, but I think I'm going to find he fired two shots to the body, one shot into the neck to sever the spinal cord, and two shots to the head. I've not seen this pattern of shots used by a professional assassin before, and I've not read about it either. He used a silencer, but he was amazingly accurate. He's quite a superb shooter. Think about it. Those massage rooms are pretty dark. There probably were feathers flying around. He may or may not have known there was another gunman in the room when he entered. The guy who is already in the room has a gun. Kalashnikov guy is firing at close range. He fired his shots quickly, in a darkish room, maybe full of feathers, and each shot was perfectly placed."

Cameron was frantically Googling for a picture of the Medical Examiner for El Paso County, Colorado. He found a photograph online and handed the phone to Richard. The man at the next table was Eliot Landers, M.D., Chief Medical Examiner for the county where Colorado Springs was located. Cameron was making head and hand gestures to try to get Richard to go over to the table and chat with the two men whose conversation they'd been listening in on.

Richard thought it would be rude to just walk up to the table. He indicated to Cameron and the others that he would try to talk to the guy when he got up to leave the restaurant. The two men at the next table had each ordered a sandwich and a second drink, and they'd eaten quickly. Richard was sure they were going back up to the spa to do more work at the crime scene. Matthew was still wondering where the coroner's van was parked. J.D. was wondering who the other guy at the table was, the firearms expert. The man knew about assassins and the latest trends in Russian pistols. The ME had consumed two cups of hot tea with his lunch. The other guy had downed two tumblers of scotch on the rocks ... for lunch. Interesting.

As the men at the next table finished eating and left the restaurant, Richard stood up from his table and followed them. He tapped the man he believed was the coroner on the shoulder. "Excuse me, are you Dr. Eliot Landers? I'm Richard Carpenter, M.D. I'm a pathologist who used to be with the Philadelphia Medical Examiner's Office. Vance Stillinger was my mentor. I couldn't help but overhear you talking shop in the Grille, at the table next to mine. You seemed puzzled by the five-shot assassination. I know a little something about that, if you want to talk with me about it sometime."

Dr. Eliot Landers had initially looked annoyed at being accosted. When he'd heard Richard list his credentials and mention the five-shot assassination, he was more cordial. Richard stuck out his hand, and the coroner shook it and smiled. "What was your name again?" Landers asked.

Richard had realized the year before, when the group had been in Maine, that he needed to have a professional card with his name and contact information on it. He'd had a hundred cards printed up, and this was the first time he'd had a chance to give one to anybody. He retrieved his wallet and gave Dr. Landers one of his business cards. "Richard Carpenter. I'm retired now, but here's my card. Give me a call on my cell phone when you have time, and we'll talk. I'm staying here at the resort. You look like you're in a rush right now. I know how the five-shot is used, if you're interested."

"Thanks, Carpenter. I know Vance Stillinger was the best in the business. If you worked with him, you must know a thing or two. You're right, I'm in a serious time crunch right now and don't have time to talk. But I will call you. I'd like to hear what you have to say about the five-shot." The medical examiner looked at the card and put it in his shirt pocket. "Thanks. I guess I should keep my voice down, shouldn't I? But maybe it's my good luck that you overheard our discussion.

If you can shed any light on the mixed-up mess I'm working on here, I need all the help I can get. I'll look forward to talking with you."

"Good luck with your mixed-up mess. Lots of them start out that way. I'm happy to help, do whatever I can." Richard nodded, and Landers stepped onto the elevator. Richard returned to his table. "I think I hooked him. I think he'll call." Richard smiled a real smile, the first one in days.

Chapter 26

THE POLICEWOMAN GRETCHEN HAD APPEALED TO about "Diane" had taken her seriously and spoken with the manager of the spa. There were two women with the name Diane who had scheduled massages that day. The Diane who had kept her massage appointment lived in Colorado Springs and had already left the spa. She was a regular customer and came in often for massages and pedicures. The police would be contacting her. The second Diane had rescheduled her massage for Saturday morning. She was a guest at the Penmoor. The police would be contacting her as well.

The spa manager had put the policewoman in touch with the assistant manager of the Penmoor resort. A computer search had found nine women guests currently staying at the resort who had a first name or middle name of Diane or Diana. That was far too many people to put under police protection. They would have to narrow down the field of potential victims before they even began to interview all the Dianes and Dianas who were staying at the Penmoor. And what if the Diane in danger was not a guest at the resort?

As it turned out, three of the women in question were young girls, under the age of twelve. They could reasonably be eliminated. That left six to be interviewed. They would begin with the Diane who had rescheduled her massage for Saturday. She was an older woman who was staying at the resort with her husband. They were celebrating their fortieth wedding anniversary. She had no enemies that she could think of. The police had some difficulty locating all of the potential victims, but they eventually were able to talk to each of them. None of them seemed to fit the profile of a possible murder victim, but you never know. One of them could be a target and have no idea that someone wanted to kill her. It was unlikely, but it was not impossible.

People sometimes register at hotels and motels under assumed names. There are several reasons they might do this. It occurred to the policewoman, after she'd struck out interviewing the Dianes and Dianas staying at the resort, that perhaps the woman they were seeking had made her reservation at the Penmoor under a name other than her own. Maybe she knew someone was trying to kill her. She might be living and/or traveling under a false identity. She could be in a witness protection program. But the person who had tried to smother Gretchen had known his victim's name, or thought he did. Otherwise, how could he have found her? He'd had to know the name she was using to find out she'd scheduled a massage.

The FBI was busy investigating the possible Russian connection, and they were pretty much ignoring Gretchen's assailant and the "Diane" he wanted to kill. It was going to be up to the local police to find the woman. Hopefully she would be found before the man who wanted to kill her tracked her down. Because the man apparently knew his victim's name, he had a head start. Neither the police nor the resort knew her as anything except "Diane." Security cameras were needed. The sketch Gretchen and the artist had come up with would be useful in recognizing her attacker. There were thousands of security cameras all over the resort. It would be a long and laborious process to go through all the security footage and look for the man who looked like the sketch of the man who was after Diane.

Gretchen told the policewoman, who had taken on the task of trying to find the woman whose life was threatened, that she had to go back to her room and lie down. Gretchen was so exhausted she felt sick to her stomach. She hadn't had any lunch, and she hadn't had any dinner. She wasn't hungry, but she knew her blood sugar was low. She was so tired she couldn't walk back to her room which was in a different building and seemed a long way from the spa. "If you can't drive me back to the Penmoor West, can you call a cab for me? I'm too tired to walk that far. I am close to collapsing. This has been a long day for me. I'm sorry, but I just cannot be of any more help to you. I've had it."

The policewoman took pity on Gretchen and drove her back to the Penmoor West. She escorted Gretchen up to her room and discussed with her the possibility of putting a guard on the room. Gretchen made a convincing argument that only one of the three killers was still at large, and he was definitely not after her. He had told her so himself. The policewoman agreed not to put a guard outside, but Gretchen suspected that somebody, probably disguised as housekeeping, would be staking out the hallway and her room ... from somewhere. Maybe they would install a miniature surveillance camera outside her door, a camera she couldn't see, to monitor who came and went or who might be lurking.

Gretchen collapsed on the bed. She had given up trying to reach Bailey. She let Olivia know that she wouldn't be coming to the cocktail hour or to dinner with the rest of the group. She was beyond worn out and wanted to be left alone to rest.

She was secretly glad that Bailey was nowhere to be found. She didn't have the energy to tell him what had happened to her that day. She really did just want to be by herself. She wanted to take a shower but didn't have the energy. She wanted to get up and find an extra blanket because she was cold, but she didn't have the energy to do that either. She stayed where she was, lying on top of the bedspread. She pulled it around her and slept.

With everything that had happened that day, the cocktail hour, movie monatages, talks about climate change and cell phones, book discussions … all were cancelled. Even Tyler's long-delayed revelation about the Penmoor art theft would have to wait. Olivia invited everyone who was up to it that night to come to the Steele's suite for dinner. Olivia was ordering food from what the Penmoor referred to as "in-room dining" which was really just another name for room service.

Sidney had taken to her bed and was too exhausted to move or eat. Cameron was staying with her and would order dinner delivered to their room. Gretchen was not answering her phone, and everyone understood that she was trying to recover from her terrible day. Lilleth was being protective of Tyler, and she insisted they stay in their room for the evening. Elizabeth was still in the hospital, but she would be released the next afternoon. Richard was lonely so he made his way to J.D. and Olivia's suite and ordered from room service with them. Matthew wanted to get out of his hotel room and think about something other than his patient. Isabelle needed to debrief herself on the overwhelming day they'd all experienced. The group was down to five, as they opened some bottles of Chardonnay and Pinot Noir and gathered around the dining room table in the Steele's suite. Olivia had ordered turkey club sandwiches, an assortment of salads, and the famous corned beef Ruben from the Silver Spur Restaurant. She also ordered the ultimate comfort foods, roast chicken and lobster mac and cheese. Brownie sundaes were delivered. Olivia knew her friends needed comfort tonight.

Richard was quiet. He was still concerned about Elizabeth, even though she was fully recovered and would be back at the hotel by afternoon the next day. Richard had been hard hit with the realization that he could lose her, and it had scared him. She was old, and so was he. He had been the one to push her into the lake, although that was the last thing in the world he would ever have done intentionally. His friends tried to cheer him up. "I'll be better once she's out of the hospital." He said it, and everyone knew it to be true.

Matthew was preoccupied with what was going to happen the next day and what was going to happen with Afif long-term. Matthew had passed the buck to Bailey and was feeling somewhat guilty about that. Bailey was always in trouble with Gretchen, and this latest project would only add to Bailey's woes. But Bailey had volunteered to be the liaison between Baktash and Afif. Matthew had heard from Bailey earlier in the evening that they had a body. Matthew hated what they were doing, and he didn't want to be told any details. He had wished a thousand times he'd not become involved in any intrigues or shenanigans. But he'd not had a choice. He'd had to save Afif.

In spite of his discomfort, he thought what they were planning was the only thing they could do. Matthew was waiting to hear from Bailey that the "Eagle had landed." It was a corny reference to NASA's landing on the moon fifty years earlier. Matthew wasn't into code words and secrets, but he had to admit the phrase exactly described what Bailey and Baktash were planning to do with the body they'd procured.

Dropping the homeless man's corpse from The Eagle's Nest at Seven Falls was an essential piece in convincing the

Russians, law enforcement, and the world that Afif, aka Geoffrey McNulty, was dead. It had to happen, as brutal and probably illegal as it was. Matthew had not confided in Richard any of the details about what was happening. If he chose to go to lunch with the group at Seven Falls the next day, he would know soon enough.

Matthew had to talk to J.D. tonight. He would tell Isabelle to go on to bed, and he would stay behind. J.D.'s help was going to be essential in relocating Afif. Cameron was going to fly the decoy out of Colorado Springs on Saturday. It would be up to Matthew and J.D. to organize the real journey that Afif would make to his new home. J.D. did not yet know that this responsibility rested on his shoulders, but Matthew was certain J.D. would want to do his part.

Matthew finally had a chance to talk to J.D. privately. Richard had gone back to his room after dinner. Isabelle had gone to the Ritter's suite, and Olivia excused herself after the waiter had removed what little remained of their in-room dining experience. Matthew had decided not to tell J.D. anything about the part of their plan that included a corpse, but J.D. would probably figure it out when the group visited Seven Falls the next day. Matthew wanted to finalize the plans for Afif's travels before they were confronted with a dead body.

"I can tell you are dying to talk to me about something." J.D. was perceptive, and Matthew was not good at concealing things. What he felt and what he wanted were right up front for everybody to see. He couldn't hide much, and he didn't try.

"Afif, who is now known as Geoffrey McNulty, has almost fully recovered from his injuries and is ready to be moved. As you know, he's been staying in the room next to Isabelle's and mine, so I could be close and keep an eye on my patient. He's healed quickly, and we are ready to take the next steps. We've obtained a new identity for him, and Bailey and Cameron have been in charge of what is going to happen going forward. Bailey's found a position for Afif that we think is a good match for his personality, his likes and dislikes, and his skills. I might as well tell you; it's in Wyoming."

Matthew continued. "We need your help to get him there. It is a big favor to ask. Cameron will be flying a decoy out of the Colorado Springs Airport early Saturday morning, but we need one of your trucks and one of your drivers to take the real Afif to Wyoming." Matthew watched J.D.'s face to see if he looked amenable or if he was going to be unwilling to participate in the scheme.

J.D. smiled. "I thought you were leaving me out of the loop on purpose. I want to participate. Of course I will help get Afif to his new home. I'll drive him to Wyoming myself. When will he be ready to leave? I can get one of my trucks here by noon tomorrow. Just tell me what I need to do."

"We need a truck, one Afif could hide in if he had to. I think the best time for him to leave will be tomorrow night, Friday night. Cameron will be flying out Saturday morning. I would like for Afif to be out of Colorado Springs and at least on his way to Wyoming before Cameron's decoy flight leaves. Can you do that?"

"I will rest up after we go to Seven Falls tomorrow, and Afif and I will leave as soon as it's dark on Friday night. There will be traffic, but depending on exactly where in Wyoming we're going, I think I can deliver him and get back here in time to show up for breakfast on Saturday morning. I suspect that what I'm participating in might be somewhat sketchy, and I'd like to keep my alibis intact. If I eat dinner here at the resort on Friday night and eat breakfast here on Saturday morning, no one will ever know I wasn't in my room sleeping all night Friday night. I will charge the meals to my room and those charges will provide me with an alibi ... if I should ever need one. I intend to pay cash for gas on the drive to Wyoming. As the head of my own company, I make up the schedules and oversee the books. I can easily make the trip from here to Wyoming and back disappear into the paperwork. It will be as if it never happened. I will be the driver, and who will I be cheating with an unauthorized trip ... myself?"

"I'm thankful you're on board. Cameron has offered to bankroll the trips and other expenses. If you want to be reimbursed, let him know."

"I am delighted to help Afif, and I can afford a few tanks of gas for the truck and a little wear and tear on my fleet." J.D. was happy to have a role to play. "We won't take any of the toll roads between here and wherever-it-is Wyoming."

"It's south of Gillette, Wyoming. Bailey will give you the exact coordinates. It really is the middle-of-nowhere, Wyoming. It's a ranch. We think Afif will love it there. Bailey has packed up all of Afif's worldly possessions. You'll need to take eight large packing boxes with you."

"Not a problem. We'll take one of my smaller trucks, but there will be plenty of room for Afif's things." J.D. was all in.

Matthew continued. "He has a new identity and a new name now. We should probably begin calling him that right away so he will get used to thinking of himself as a different person. He has had several names during his lifetime, but he's been Geoffrey McNulty longer than he's been anybody else. His friend Baktash was the one who found the new identity papers for him. Afif's got a birth certificate, a driver's license, credit cards, a social security number ... everything he needs. His new name is Gregory Robicheaux. It sounds like Louisiana to me, but that's fine. He likes it, and Greg is not that different from Geoff. That's good if he makes a slip and forgets his new name. He can fake it and pretend he said Greg. They both begin with G. He said he always wanted to be a Cajun. He says they like good food and cook good food. He always looks on the positive side of things. So, call him Gregory Robicheaux when you talk to him. I've told him he's to introduce himself that way from now on."

J.D.'s brain was working overtime now. "I need to make some phone calls. I'll have the truck here tomorrow, and I'll talk to Bailey about collecting Gregory's boxes. Maybe you don't want to tell me, but is Bailey going to masquerade as the decoy that Cameron will fly out of town on Saturday?"

"I'll never tell, but I think that's a pretty good bet. Elizabeth is out of the picture. I won't let Isabelle do it. Sidney volunteered to do it, but she and Gretchen have been through too much. Cameron doesn't want Sidney to do it now. Lilleth won't leave Tyler, and she sure as heck wouldn't let him participate in our masquerade. We really need to have a man in the wheelchair when we board the patient onto the plane. So it wouldn't work with any of the women anyway. Richard will be taking care of Elizabeth, or more likely, she will be taking care of him. Cameron was originally going to use his own plane, but I think he's decided to lease a jet for the day. He will definitely be riding on the plane. That leaves you, me, and Bailey. You are driving to Wyoming. I'm too tired to travel on the decoy flight, so guess who that leaves? Figure it out. He loves disguises anyway. We don't think anybody will be watching, but the decoy flight is just in case. They are keeping their plans close to the vest, so I don't know the exact details. I think they will fly to Little Rock, turn around, and fly immediately back here. If anybody is watching, the trail will be completely cold as soon as they leave Little Rock. End of Afif. End of Geoffrey McNulty. Gone into the wild blue yonder forever and ever."

"Sounds like a pretty good plan to me."

Gretchen had nightmares and woke up at midnight. Her clothes were soaking wet. She was still so tired she could barely move, but she knew she would feel better if she took a shower. She wanted to wash away the memories of the pillow on her face and the man standing over her. She wanted these things out of her consciousness and off of her body. She wanted to be cleansed from the horrors of somebody trying to kill her. She scrubbed her hair and soaped her skin again and again and let the hot water run down on her head for as long as she could stand up. She did feel better after the shampoo and hot water therapy. She climbed under the sheets and immediately fell asleep again. Bailey was still nowhere to be found. That was fine with Gretchen. She would deal with him whenever he showed up. She was glad to be left alone to sleep tonight. It had been a very bad day. She did not wake up when Bailey collapsed beside her in the king-size bed at 4:30 that morning.

Chapter 27

BAILEY, WHO WAS STILL PRETENDING TO BE Christopher Hamilton when he was with Baktash, had been busy all day. He'd gone to Geoffrey McNulty's house with Baktash, and they'd begun to pack up Geoffrey's things. The furniture and all the kitchen equipment in the house belonged to Baktash, although he was never at home to use any of it. Geoffrey wanted to take specific things from his bedroom with him to his new life. He'd made a list for Bailey — quite a few of his clothes, many books, most of the contents of his desk, some files from his filing cabinet, and the boxes of memorabilia he had stored in his closet. He wanted a couple of items that were in the medicine cabinet in the bathroom. Afif/Geoffrey had always traveled light. His wife had taken everything with her when they divorced — their furniture and household goods, and Geoffrey had rented furnished places ever since. When they were finished with the packing, there were just eight boxes for Bailey, aka Christopher Hamilton, to take from the house. Four of the boxes were full of books.

They had left some clothes hanging in the closet and folded in the dresser drawers, things that Geoffrey had told them he didn't want. Raggedy underwear, socks with holes in them, and shirts with frayed collars and those that didn't fit any more, were not packed to accompany Geoff to his new life. A few outdated prescriptions, the half-full bottles of OTC medications that could easily be replaced, and other miscellaneous things in the bathroom were left behind. Paid bills and other paperwork that Geoffrey had kept but wouldn't need any longer remained in the desk. Checkbooks for Geoffrey McNulty's bank accounts were ignored. Geoffrey would be transferring money out of his accounts, but he would no longer need the checks or anything else that had Geoffrey McNulty's name on it. Hamilton and Baktash left the filing cabinet half-empty. Baktash would burn the rest of the files after he'd buried Geoffrey. The filing cabinet belonged to Baktash.

If anyone chose to investigate Geoffrey McNulty's death, Bailey didn't want the man's room to look like he had packed up and moved out all of his stuff before he'd died. That would certainly be suspicious. Bailey wanted the room to look just the way it had always looked up until the moment Geoffrey was found dead. Bailey knew he wouldn't be able to return to the house to salvage any of Geoffrey's belongings after the body was discovered, so it all had to be done today.

Bailey carried the boxes of Geoffrey's things to the van he'd rented. The wheelchair they'd used to smuggle Afif into the Penmoor was already in the van. Bailey had taken it from the hotel room that morning. The wheelchair was an essential part of their plan to move the body, when and if they had one. Bailey was getting nervous. They needed a body today. But Baktash hadn't heard anything from the person he was counting on to supply it. Time was running out.

When Bailey checked his phone, he realized Gretchen had called and texted him several times. He knew he would have his you-know-what handed to him on a platter when he read those texts and listened to her voice mails. She had every right to be furious with him. He'd promised her he wouldn't do this again, and here he was, right back in the thick of it. For now, he told himself he needed to focus. Gretchen would be angry whenever he read her texts. He would read them all later and then beg her forgiveness. He would buy her a gorgeous piece of jewelry. He would buy her a new house. He would make it up to her somehow. He just couldn't talk to her right now, no matter what she was calling about. He knew she'd been under a lot of stress, and he had let her down. He felt terrible about it, he really did, but he still did not intend to call her.

Just as Bailey was getting into the van to drive away, Baktash came running down the back steps of his house. They'd parked the van at the rear so no one would wonder what was going on when Bailey carried a bunch of cardboard boxes out and put them in the van. Neither Christopher Hamilton nor Bailey was supposed to know Geoffrey McNulty or Baktash.

Baktash was clearly excited when he told Bailey that they finally had a body. It was a homeless man, Joey B., who had succumbed overnight to what his friends believed was almost certainly cirrhosis of the liver. The homeless died ignominious and lonely deaths from the diseases of neglect and addiction. Baktash had known this particular man was close to the end. He'd asked one of his connections to monitor Joey B.'s condition and make sure nobody reported his death to the authorities.

Baktash had given strict instructions about what to do when Joey B. died. Baktash was to be called immediately, day or night, and someone was to hide the body and watch over it until Baktash came to collect it. Baktash had spread a considerable amount of Cameron Richardson's money around, and Baktash knew it was the cash that had convinced his group of homeless friends that their participation in this questionable scheme was for a good cause. The plan was that, as soon as he got the word that the body was available, Baktash would call Christopher Hamilton who would bring his van to the pick-up point. Because Hamilton was already at the house, they would save time and could go at once to retrieve the dead homeless man.

Bailey had hoped he would have time to go back to the hotel and get some sleep before they had to deal with the body. He and Baktash would be up most of the night tonight, and Bailey was not a spring chicken. He couldn't pull all-nighters any longer like he had in his younger days. But he was pumped now that they had a body, especially when he'd been afraid they might not have one. He rallied his adrenalin and pushed himself to follow through with the plans they'd made, even without the hours of sleep he wanted so badly. He could do it.

Bailey and Baktash couldn't load Joey B. into the van until after dark. They drove to the place where Joey B.'s body was hidden, and Baktash checked to make sure that his people were taking care of everything per his instructions. He'd brought an oversized plastic bag and told them to put Joey B. inside. Baktash and Bailey would be back at nine that evening to pick up the corpse.

Christopher Hamilton and Baktash drove to a Greek diner. They ate hummus, stuffed grape leaves, and lamb kabobs. They ate several triangles of baklava and drank multiple cups of coffee. Baktash knew the cook, who sent them off with a paper bag of meat pies and a thermos of coffee. It was going to be a long night.

They returned to pick up Joey B. Neither Bailey, nor his alter ego Christopher Hamilton, was as comfortable as Baktash was with hijacking a dead body and using it to perpetrate a hoax. Bailey rationalized his actions. Joey B., if he had ever had a family, no longer had one. As a homeless person, there probably was no one who really cared about him. His body would have been buried in a pauper's grave without a headstone. Or he would have been cremated, and his ashes would have been scattered to the winds. No one would have mourned the solitary soul. As Geoffrey McNulty, Joey B. would have a funeral, a decent burial, and a headstone. His body would be treated with the respect and dignity of a man who had served the United States of America as a hero. It was a much better ending than Joey B. could ever have hoped for. Bailey told himself that he was not merely stealing the poor guy's body, he was doing the homeless man a favor.

Baktash and Bailey loaded Joey B. into the van without much trouble. The homeless man had been ill for a long time. He had wasted away and weighed less than ninety pounds when he died. Bailey was wearing Christopher Hamilton's black spandex jogging suit and the dark curly wig. He was not happy that Baktash's colleagues had seen his face, but he hoped his outfit, especially the wig, would be a sufficient disguise.

The two had debated where the best place was to put Joey B. into Geoffrey McNulty's clothes. They couldn't dress their corpse on the grounds of the Penmoor or in a public parking lot. Bailey wasn't that familiar with the Colorado Springs area, but Baktash knew a place where they wouldn't be seen and wouldn't be disturbed. They headed for the isolated spot where they would prepare Joey B.'s body to become the body of Geoffrey McNulty.

Bailey had packed a duffle bag that held an outfit of Geoffrey McNulty's clothes, including shoes, and his identification. They took Joey B. out of the plastic bag and put Geoffrey's clothes on him. Of course, the clothes didn't fit. Oddly enough, the shoes did fit. Geoffrey was not a heavy man, but he was taller and healthier than this poor wretch who was going to be buried in his place. Anyone who had known Geoffrey McNulty would not for one second believe he was this man dressed in Geoffrey's clothes.

They put Geoffrey's wallet with all of his identification in the pocket of the pants Joey B. wore. They put Geoffrey's cell phone in his jacket pocket. The jacket was the one Geoffrey been wearing when he'd been in the fight with the Russian man at the Air Force Academy. The jacket had been stuffed into a Walgreen's plastic bag and hadn't been thrown out with the rest of Geoffrey's bloody clothes. The jacket had plenty of blood on it. Joey B. was ready. The transformation was complete. Joey B. had become Geoffrey McNulty. Joey B.'s body would be found the next day, dressed in Geoffrey McNulty's clothes with McNulty's wallet, driver's license, credit cards, phone, and all the rest of it. They put the clothes Joey B. had been wearing when he died into the plastic bag. They would drop the bag in a dumpster on their way back to the Penmoor.

They wanted the corpse to show injuries similar to those the real Geoffrey McNulty had sustained in the fight he'd had with his attacker in the parking lot on the USAF Academy grounds. Baktash had brought along a crowbar and a knife. Bailey couldn't bring himself to watch, even though he knew it was all for a good cause. These ruthless efforts were intended to convince, not only law enforcement, but also whoever had hired the Russian who'd attacked Geoffrey, that the man had died from these previous injuries plus injuries from a fall. The post-mortem wounds wouldn't fool the county coroner, but maybe an autopsy wouldn't be necessary. The attack at the Air Force Academy had led to the group's involvement in saving Geoffrey's life. This complicated charade that Bailey was attempting to perpetrate at Seven Falls was part of that effort. The body was ready.

Driving Bailey's rental van, they headed for the Penmoor lot where the resort's landscaping vehicles were parked. Baktash frequently drove a landscaping van to and from his jobs around the grounds of the resort, and he had the keys to one of these vans. He told Bailey to park close to it so they could transfer the body. It was late enough that no one was around to ask Baktash what he was doing there at that hour of the night. No one does landscaping work after dark. The two men quickly lifted Joey B.'s body into the landscaping van. Bailey transferred the wheelchair, and Baktash climbed into the driver's seat.

Bailey's rental van did not have a parking sticker to allow him to park it in any of the Penmoor parking lots. He didn't want anybody at the Penmoor to know he had ever rented a van. Baktash, driving the Penmoor's landscaping van, followed Bailey to a shopping center where he felt he could safely leave the rental van. There was a restaurant, a bar, and a movie theatre in the shopping center. There was a twenty-four hour McDonald's at the edge of the parking lot. No one would find it strange that someone had left their van in the lot overnight. Bailey locked the rental van that had all of Geoffrey's worldly possessions inside and climbed into the passenger seat of the Penmoor's landscaping van.

It was a fifteen minute drive from the shopping center to Seven Falls. This famous scenic spot was located about one and one-half miles from the Penmoor's main hotel. It was a feast for the eyes in the daytime. The series of seven waterfalls was the only Colorado waterfall included on the National Geographic's list of international waterfalls. Visitors could access the falls and the 1858 Restaurant next to it by way of a special shuttle bus. The views were spectacular. This was a unique gem, seven distinct falls that flowed down the side of a 1,250-foot-wall box canyon. People made reservations weeks in advance to have lunch at the 1858 Restaurant. You could sit outside on the porch to eat in nice weather. The recent snow had made the site even more breathtakingly picturesque.

Bailey was feeling sorry that his friends were going to have a rude surprise awaiting them the next day when they arrived to view the falls and enjoy their lunch. He and Baktash had talked about the best place to leave the body. One option would have been to drive above the falls and drop the body down the canyon wall. This would have been a fall of more than 181 feet and would have done considerable damage to the corpse, but it would have required some kind of ATV to make the climb up the steep hiking trail.

They'd decided instead to use the elevator across the driveway from the restaurant to move the body up to the Eagle's Nest where they would drop it over the railing of the observation deck. They were hoping that the fall from the deck would inflict sufficient damage to the body so that an autopsy might not be required. If the corpse looked as if it had sustained enough bodily harm as a result of a long fall, the medical examiner might be tempted to sign off on the fall as the cause of death.

They drove up the narrow roadway that the shuttlebus usually took, past the Pillars of Hercules, Prospector's Gully, and the Seven Falls Shop. They parked as close as they could get to the tunnel entrance that led to the elevator. Baktash got the wheelchair from the back of the van, and together he and Bailey lifted Joey B.'s body into it. The night was dark as pitch, but they couldn't use a flashlight for fear of attracting undue attention. Baktash had even turned off the van's headlights as he'd made the steep drive up the mountain to the elevator access tunnel.

If any security guards or unlikely midnight hikers approached him about why he was at Seven Falls at night, Baktash had a cover story ready. They'd used the Penmoor landscaping van that had "Penmoor Resort" painted on the side, to help support Baktash's story. He was going to say, if anyody asked him, that he had been called out late at night to cut away a tree that had fallen across one of the access roads the shuttlebuses used. Baktash had a chain saw in the van and planned to say that his supervisor wanted the tree cleared from the road before early morning hikers were out on the trails. The shuttle buses began their runs to Seven Falls fairly early. The story would fool a member of the public, and it might even be believable to a security guard. Baktash hoped he wouldn't have to use his cover story. Because the Penmoor owned the Seven Falls property, if anyone saw them hanging around the area at night, the Penmoor's landscaping van would be less suspicious than a non-descript van. Penmoor landscaping vans belonged at Seven Falls.

They pushed Joey B., aka Geoffrey McNulty, in the wheelchair through the tunnel that led to the elevator shaft. It was cold and damp in the tunnel during the day because no sunlight ever reached this place, and it was bitterly cold in the tunnel tonight. Baktash had a key that unlocked the elevator. After the park was closed, the elevator was shut down and locked. The homeless love to take refuge in any and all elevators on cold nights. Bailey recognized that there was some irony somewhere, that Joey B. would take his final elevator ride on a lift that had been unlocked in the middle of the night, expressly for the purpose of giving this homeless man a ride to the top.

The wheelchair made things easy. They pushed Joey B. to the edge of the Eagles' Nest observation deck outside the Rock Hound's Shop. They made a thick solution with bottled water and some dried blood that Baktash had bought at a hunting store. They sprinkled the bloody concoction over the homeless man's face and body and lifted him out of the chair. It took both of them to tip him over the safety railing that encircled the deck. The blood was to attract wild animals to the corpse and tempt them to eat it. It was critical that several things be muddled about the cause and time of death.

A hungry family of bears or mountain lions would go a long way towards taking care of some of those difficulties. Work done by scavengers would help obscure what the face of the corpse really looked like. If the corpse remained intact for the autopsy, postmortem injuries would be revealed for what they were, and suicide would be ruled out as a cause of death. If enough of the body was disturbed and consumed, tissues would be destroyed, and wounds from the fall down the side of the mountain would be less likely to be determined to be postmortem.

On the other hand, enough of the remains had to be visible so that someone would see the body in the brush beneath the Eagle's Nest and recognize the shape as that of a person. Wild animals were needed to work on the body to confuse the coroner, but Bailey and Baktash hoped the hungry beasts wouldn't consume the corpse completely or carry it away someplace where it wouldn't be discovered. Bailey hoped that some poor tourist who was entirely unconnected to his group of friends would be the one to notice a human form lying half-way down the cliff and would raise the alarm.

They took the wheelchair back down to the tunnel, and Baktash locked up the elevator. No one would ever know about the after-dark trip the elevator had made to the observation post. Bailey hoisted the wheelchair back inside the landscaping van. Baktash drove Bailey to the shopping center where his rental van was parked. Bailey transferred the wheelchair to his van and followed Baktash to the Penmoor. Baktash returned the landscaping van to its designated parking space, and Bailey drove him home to the house he had shared with Geoffrey McNulty.

Baktash knew what he had to do when it came time to identify the body. Baktash would not see the man he knew as Christopher Hamilton after tonight's caper. They shook hands. If he ran into a problem he couldn't handle, Baktash could call Hamilton on the pre-paid cell phone. Once the funeral was over and Joey B. was in the ground, Baktash had orders to destroy the burner phone and get rid of the pieces. He was grateful to Geoffrey for paying off his mortgage. Bailey believed Baktash would follow through with his instructions if he possibly could. Bailey drove the rental van back to the shopping center where he parked it and locked it one more time. He called a taxi to pick him up at the all-night McDonald's and drive him back to the Penmoor West. It had been a long night.

Problems could arise if the El Paso County Medical Examiner thought there was something suspicious about the death of the man whose body was found below the observation deck at Seven Falls. If Baktash was convincing enough when he identified the body, or if the ME was particularly busy that week, the coroner might overlook whatever doubts he had about the death. If he did a thorough autopsy, he would certainly be confused by the postmortem knife wounds and by the fact that the man's actual cause of death had been cirrhosis of the liver. They all had their fingers crossed that things would not get to that point.

A second set of problems could arise, if whoever had ordered the hit on Geoffrey McNulty did not believe he was really dead. Unless the hit man or the man who was giving the orders was watching closely what happened at the coroner's office, they would know nothing about McNulty's death until it was reported in the newspaper. By the time the obituary notice appeared, Baktash would be certain that Joey B.s body was safely and securely in the grave marked with Geoffrey McNulty's headstone. That was the way it had been planned to happen. Whether or not it would actually happened that way, remained to be seen.

Chapter 28

WHEN GRETCHEN WOKE UP THE NEXT MORNING and saw Bailey asleep in the bed beside her, she was so happy to have him there, she forgot about most of the scolding she'd rehearsed. She hugged him and held on to him for a long time. She gave him a perfunctory account of what had happened to her in the spa the day before. She told him she would give him the details later, but she told him enough that he was scared to death and worried sick about her safety. He'd not had much sleep and was already anxious about whether or not the whole Afif/Geoffrey deception would go off as planned.

But he loved Gretchen dearly. She was his top priority, and everything else disappeared from his mind when she told him that someone had tried to kill her. He was shaken to his core. He vowed he would not let her out of his sight again while they were in Colorado. Gretchen knew he meant well, but she told herself not to be disappointed if he did let her out of his sight. She made a bet with herself about how long it would be until he disappeared again.

Gretchen decided she wanted to go on the Seven Falls excursion. She'd heard so much about the beauty of the setting, and she wanted to try to put her brush with death behind her and focus on something pleasant, something uplifting. The excursion to one of Colorado's most beautiful waterfalls would be a delightful change from murder. Bailey, who knew the trip to Seven Falls might not turn out to be as much fun as she thought it would be, tried to talk her out of going. He urged her to stay in bed for the day and take it easy. He would tell her all about it. Trying to confine Gretchen or tell her not to do something was the best way to motivate her. Bailey knew this, but he could never seem to help himself. She was now more determined than ever to go on the day's outing.

The group was tired from the traumatic events of the day before, and they had a late breakfast. Most were anticipating that the trip to Seven Falls would cheer them up. Matthew and Bailey knew differently. Richard suspected something was up with the trip to Seven Falls, but he'd been too preoccupied with Elizabeth and hadn't been paying attention to other things. Elizabeth would not be discharged from the hospital until the middle of the afternoon, and she urged Richard to make the trip to Seven Falls with the others. He could pick her up after lunch. Because Elizabeth wasn't making the trip to the falls, they didn't need the special van with the wheelchair lift.

The members of the group who usually dined on granola and yogurt threw healthy eating out the window today and opted for bacon, sausages, fried potatoes, waffles with whipped cream, pecan pancakes with Vermont maple syrup, and other things they would never normally eat. The comfort that food could provide was definitely on the menu this morning.

They gathered in the lounge at 10:30 and left the hotel to board the bus for Seven Falls. Their driver pointed out the sights along the short trip from the Penmoor. He made a special point of stopping and talking about the zip line. Everybody looked at Tyler, who was the one most likely to claim he loved extreme sports. Lilleth spoke up.

"I don't know why you're all looking at Tyler. He's not going on the zip line. I might go on it, but he is definitely not going."

The falls were phenomenal. Lots of photographs were taken. Some of the group chose to walk up many steps to the highest observation point. Others walked up to the Eagle's Nest. Most went through the tunnel and rode the elevator to the Rock Hound's Shop and deck. Matthew didn't have any idea where the body might be, or even if Bailey had been able to pull off their plan. He didn't want to know any more about the body than he had to know. He was jittery and hoped none of their group saw anything. Bailey knew exactly where the body had been tipped over the railing, but he didn't know where it had landed. He didn't go near the side of the deck where they'd thrown off poor Joey B., and he didn't look down at all. They oohed and ahhed at the beautiful scenery and the magnificent sights and thankfully descended from the Eagle's Nest without incident. There had been no sightings of any bodies.

They made their way up the hill and across the road to Restaurant 1858 for lunch. Originally their reservation had been to sit outside on the porch, but it was too cold today. They sat at a long table inside the charming and rustic log cabin. Several plates of French fried Vidalia onion rings with a dipping sauce were brought to the table. A few people considered ordering the Bison burger, but in the end most of those who wanted a burger could not resist the Angus burger topped with hickory smoked bacon and pimento cheese. Who in their right mind could resist that? The crispy Colorado Rocky Mountain red trout po' boy was also a favorite. Isabelle ordered the po'boy that came with a yummy jalapeno tartar sauce because she loved New Orleans cooking and loved po' boys. The restaurant advertised that they served Creole,

French, and Colorado-style specialties. It was a heavenly sandwich, but Isabelle was puzzled about why this log cabin restaurant, named for the year the Colorado gold rush began, served French and Creole food.

The group lingered over their lunch. Bailey was hoping they would hurry up and leave. He kept asking the waitress for the bill. Gretchen tried to get him to sit still and take it easy.

"I'm finally having some fun. I've been able to eat a nice lunch, and I'm enjoying a cup of coffee and relaxing here with my friends. Why do you have ants in your pants?"

"I'm tired and need to take a nap. We've kept this table tied up for hours, and I think it's time to leave." Everyone else, except Matthew, seemed to want to linger. The view from their table was unique, even inspirational. The air was crisp and cold. The recent snowstorm had enhanced the beauty of the scene. They had no deadlines. Most of the members of the group were content. Matthew was not content. He hadn't been able to eat his bowl of wild boar chili. As a rule, he didn't eat much, but he loved chili. He and Isabelle frequently split an appetizer or an entrée. Today they couldn't agree on what to order, so he'd ordered the chili. He pushed his chili around in the bowl with his spoon, too nervous to swallow. Bailey knew why Matthew was so anxious and realized that not everybody would make a good covert operative.

They finally paid the bill and left Restaurant 1858. With one more glance at the falls, they walked to the bench where the bus from the Penmoor would pick them up. The shuttle arrived and they were just getting ready to board when all of a sudden, a woman began to scream. Nobody could see where she was or tell where the screaming was coming from, but she continued screaming and didn't stop. J.D. was always ready to help when there was a crisis, but Bailey put a restraining hand on his arm when J.D. started to move towards the sound of the screaming. There were plenty of visitors who were viewing the falls, and several people rushed to the woman's aid.

Bailey knew exactly why the woman was screaming. Bailey had timed the drop of the body so that it would be discovered today. He'd hoped it would be discovered first thing in the morning, by some early hikers. But it hadn't been. He'd hoped the drama would be all over by the time the Camp Shoemaker crowd arrived to look at the scenery and have lunch. He'd hoped the staff at Restaurant 1858 would have all the details to recount to them. He'd hoped his friends would hear about the body, long after it had been discovered. It hadn't happened that way. Bailey had wanted to be on the scene at Seven Falls today to be sure the body was discovered by somebody. He also wanted to be sure that none of their group became involved when the remains of Joey B. were found.

J.D. gave Bailey a questioning look when he'd kept him from responding to the screaming. Now that Bailey was sure the body had been found, he wanted to be anywhere but at Seven Falls. His role in this part of the plot was finished. He really was worn out and wanted to go back to the hotel to go to sleep. But he knew this group was a curious bunch, and now they would want to stay until they'd found out what had happened. They'd almost made it onto the bus, and they'd almost been on their way back to the Penmoor.

Bailey took charge, crossed the road, and walked down the hill to consult with some of the people who had rushed to the scene. He came back and reported that he thought somebody had taken a bad fall. Apparently, the screaming woman had sounded the alarm that someone had fallen from the observation deck. It was none of their business. The shuttlebus was ready to leave.

Bailey urged his friends to go back to the hotel. "After everything that happened yesterday, none of us wants to see any more stuff like this. There will be ambulances and police and who knows what here in a few minutes. Let's skip the drama and go back to the hotel. We have all had enough excitement. This is not going to be a pretty scene. Let's get out while we can. I'm sure we will hear all about it later." Gretchen and Sidney especially did not want to be questioned by anyone from law enforcement. Even the most curious of the group agreed it would be best to leave. They boarded the bus, and soon they were safely back at the hotel. Only a few of them were wise to what had really happened that day at Seven Falls.

Matthew accompanied Richard to the hospital to pick up Elizabeth. Most of the group was settling in their rooms for naps. They had been scheduled to have dinner on Friday night at the very expensive five-star La Fleur Rouge restaurant. It was the Penmoor's most exclusive restaurant and would have been a grand meal. The chef was world-renowned. They didn't mind the high price, but nobody was up for caviar or spending several hours eating what they knew would be a luxurious prix fixe dinner. Maybe another time.

Considering everything that had happened, Olivia asked around, and almost everyone voted in favor of changing their reservations to the Penmoor's pub, the Silver Spur. It was casual and low-key, and because all the food at the resort was excellent, they knew the pub food would be, too. Olivia reserved a table for ten at six o'clock. The group was planning to meet in the Steele's suite at four for cocktails. Matthew was going to show two of his movie montages … at long last.

The group welcomed Matthew's movie presentation with gratitude. There had been too much excitement, and they were ready for some light-hearted and humorous movie clips. They all needed to laugh.

Elizabeth was thrilled to leave the hospital and delighted to be back at the hotel. She had not completely regained her strength and tired easily. She let Olivia know that only Richard would attend the movie showing, and neither of them would be joining the group for dinner. Elizabeth hated to miss anything, and Richard suffered from a chronic case of FOMO, fear of missing out. Tonight they were going to be sensible. They would order in-room dining and Elizabeth would go to bed early. Elizabeth's hospitalization had been just as difficult for Richard, maybe even more difficult. He would go to bed early, too.

Richard watched Matthew's movie montage presentation. He told the others that Elizabeth sent her best and would see them Saturday night. J.D. was anxious for the evening to end early. He had a long drive ahead of him — delivering Gregory Robicheaux to the ranch in Wyoming. J.D. had to eat at the hotel tonight and was thankful the group had voted to cancel the lengthy meal at La Fleur Rouge. He'd eaten there once before with Olivia and hated to miss the chance to dine there again. He knew it would be a terrific meal, but he didn't want dinner to drag on and on tonight. He needed to sign his check, leave the restaurant, and get on the road.

The truck from the RRD Trucking Company had arrived in Colorado Springs while the group was eating lunch at Seven Falls. J.D. had made a reservation at a motel for the truck driver who would stay overnight in town and drive the truck back to St. Louis on Saturday. J.D. took a taxi to the motel to talk to the driver and pick up the keys to the truck. J.D. was a generous boss, and he told the driver to take a taxi to a nice restaurant and have a steak dinner that night, compliments of the company. The driver would be reimbursed for any expenses he incurred while in Colorado.

Driving an empty truck to Colorado was somewhat out of the ordinary for the driver, but he knew J.D. used his trucks to make deliveries for charities and other worthy causes. The driver assumed he'd driven the truck to Colorado Springs so J.D. could use it for one of his projects. J.D. had even mentioned something briefly about a "Homeless Coalition." Tonight, that coalition would consist of J.D. and Gregory Robicheaux. Although J.D. didn't know it, they had Joey B., a former homeless man, to thank for Robicheaux's future safety and anonymity.

After J.D. picked up the truck, he and Bailey drove to the shopping center where Bailey had parked his van. They loaded Gregory Robicheaux's boxes into the RRD truck. Bailey was anxious to return the rental van and be rid of that piece of incriminating evidence. J.D. drove his company truck back to the hotel, and Bailey drove the van to Budget, hugely relieved he would never have to see it again. He would take a taxi back to the hotel.

J.D. had procured an overnight parking sticker for the truck. He couldn't give the truck to valet parking. After dinner that evening, J.D. and Gregory Robicheaux would drive the truck to Wyoming. No one could know. Picking just the right place to park the truck was tricky. J.D. wanted to be fairly close to the Penmoor West, so Gregory didn't have too far to walk. He could walk for short distances, but he got out of breath easily. He was still recovering. On the other hand, J.D. did not want to park his box truck too close to the upscale hotel's entrance. Most of the other vehicles in the parking lot were Mercedes and BMWs, high-end SUVs, and a few large and elaborate pick-up trucks. J.D.'s truck was a commercial vehicle. It did not fit in at the Penmoor. J.D. was hoping no one would notice that the parking space where his truck should have been parked was empty all night.

He drove around until he found just the right spot for the truck. He placed an order for sandwiches, bottles of water, and thermoses of coffee and hot tea from the Epicurean Café.

It was open late, and J.D. would pay cash when he picked up the order on his way out of the hotel later that night.

Now he had to try to relax and pretend to enjoy the movie montages and the dinner at the Silver Spur. He would enjoy these things, so it wasn't like he was really faking it. But, at the back of his mind, he could not help but think about the long trip he had ahead of him. He had to drive to Wyoming and back before breakfast on Saturday morning. Fortunately, Saturday was their free day. He and Olivia had built a free day into the schedule to give people a chance to rest and do things on their own. Some people were going to see the Charlie Chaplain Memorial. Some were going to the zoo. Some were resting. Several of the women had said they wanted to go shopping. J.D. would be sleeping. As soon as he'd signed the breakfast check, to establish his alibi, he would be collapsing in his bed.

The movie montages were a hit, and dinner at the Silver Spur had been the right choice. They got on the shuttlebus and arrived at the pub in a matter of minutes. Lots of Guinness on tap was ordered. Olivia ordered the French onion soup and declared it divine. Isabelle had the shrimp remoulade and wished Elizabeth had been there to enjoy it, too. They shared a love of New Orleans cuisine. Sidney ordered the Reuben and recommended the Creole shrimp and grits. The men all ordered fish and chips. Several of the group ordered dessert, and the mixed berry trifle won the prize because of the sweetness of the berries and the yummy vanilla custard. Gretchen wanted a bowl of the custard alone, just to eat with a spoon. Everyone seemed to be in a good mood tonight. Elizabeth was out of the hospital and reportedly doing fine. The traumas of the past few days had moved, if not really faded, into the background. At least everybody was trying really hard not to think about death and murder. None of those things had gone away, but the Camp Shoemaker group was determined to have fun tonight, in spite of everything.

J.D. finally signed his dinner check, and he and Olivia caught the next shuttle bus back to the Penmoor West. J.D. had told Olivia everything about what he was doing. She was nervous, but supported her husband in his efforts to save the man they'd rescued and who'd been recovering in one of the Ritters' hotel rooms. Even though the chances were remote that anyone would want J.D. in the middle of the night, Olivia would cover for him. He promised to call her every two hours while he was on the road. He'd bought two prepaid cell phones, one for himself to use on the road trip and one for Gregory to use until he had time to buy a better one and set up an account in his new name.

Gregory Robicheaux had spent all day transferring his money to untraceable accounts. Bailey had brought his laptop to the Penmoor along with the paperwork he needed to take care of his finances. Gregory had learned a great deal about computers as the chief supply officer at the Air Force Academy. He had become fascinated with the internet in his off-hours, and he knew how to hide his banking transactions. A couple of Geoffrey McNulty's bank accounts would continue to show small balances, but the bulk of his money would be gone. He'd paid off Baktash's mortgage and made it look as if it had been paid off in July, long before the Russians had come after him. Gregory transferred his money in such a way that he could access it later, but no one else would ever find it. He took care of all of his affairs so that no one would suspect he was not really dead. His long-term safety and security depended on the Russians believing that he'd died in Colorado Springs. Baktash would be sure the body was buried. The hope was that the Russians who had come after him would be convinced he was dead and would check him off their list.

He said goodbye to Matthew. His eyes were tearful as he thanked the doctor whose life he had saved so long ago and who had in turn saved his life just a few days earlier. Gregory promised to be in touch with Matthew after he'd established himself in a new place and in his new name. Matthew wondered if he really would ever make contact. They shook hands and Gregory put his arms around Matthew. "If it were not for you, I would not have a life."

Matthew answered, "Likewise."

J.D. and Gregory left the room and walked down the stairs. Gregory was winded from the five-story descent and waited in the stairwell while J.D. picked up his order from the café. They slipped out a side door of the hotel and made their way through the parking lot. Gregory was wearing a knitted cap that somewhat obscured his face, in case he got in the way of a security camera. But no one had shown the least bit of interest in the two men who mingled with the other guests streaming in and out of the Penmoor West on Friday night. They climbed into the truck and were on their way.

Chapter 29

When Sidney returned from dinner, she was stunned to see that her suite was completely overwhelmed with flowers. There were hundreds and hundreds of roses of all colors. She thought she even saw some blue roses. What? Who had ever seen blue roses? Vases and baskets of flowers crowded every possible table and desk and window sill. What in the world? There were two cases of champagne stacked by the door and two five-pound boxes of candy on the coffee table.

Sidney recognized the chocolate boxes. She knew the chocolatier. He was based in Los Angeles and only made chocolates for private clients. The chocolates were fantastic. Sidney pretty much ignored the forest of roses and the champagne and headed straight for the candy. They were her favorites. This kind benefactor had gifted her ten pounds of homemade, hand dipped caramels covered in the best dark chocolate you could ever dream about. Because she knew the chocolatier was from Los Angeles, Sidney knew who had sent them and the rest of the extravaganza that had exploded in her room. On the coffee table beside the candy, there was an envelope with a hand-written note inside. It was from Withers Singleton.

Had it been just yesterday that Sidney had saved Withers' life? It seemed to Sidney as if it had all happened during another century, even to a different person. Had Withers gone back to L.A.? There had certainly been a rapid and complete shutdown of information about what had occurred at the Penmoor spa. Sidney figured the Penmoor must have a great deal of experience dealing with famous people. She wondered if they had ever dealt with a triple murder attempt before … all in one day. She imagined yesterday had been a first, even for the Penmoor.

The note from Withers was effusive but sincere. She said she was sorry she'd not had a chance to properly introduce herself to Sidney and thank her in person. She said her security people had flown her immediately back to Los Angeles. The most secure of her several homes was there. Withers said she was still quite shaken and was under a doctor's care. She was taking tranquilizers but hoped to stop them soon. She would forever be grateful to Sidney for saving her life. She wanted to meet Sidney and Cameron and offered to fly them to Los Angeles for dinner. She said she was trying to figure out how to appropriately thank Sidney for what she had done. Apparently Withers' security people had missed the information that Cameron and Sidney had their own plane.

Sidney wrote a brief note back to Withers and thanked her for the flowers, the champagne, and especially the candy. She said all the right things in her note to Withers and reassured her that law enforcement and her own investigators felt the attack on Withers had been strictly a case of mistaken identity. She'd been in the wrong massage room, a room with somebody else's name on it. The bullets Withers had escaped also had somebody else's name on them. Withers had nothing to fear going forward. Sidney was gracious, as always, and she thought she would probably never hear anything from Withers Singleton again.

Cameron was flying out early the next morning to do the decoy run, in case the Russians were watching. Sidney hated it that Cameron was taking chances like this, but at the same time, she was proud of him for wanting to do his part. He assured her that the only dangerous time would be when he and Bailey loaded their dummy in the wheelchair onto the plane. Bailey would be dressed as a non-descript male nursing attendant. Cameron didn't want the pilot of the jet he had leased to know anything about what they were doing, so he and Bailey would load their "patient" into the plane themselves. As soon as they arrived in Little Rock, Cameron and Bailey would fly directly back to Colorado Springs.

J.D. and Gregory Robicheaux made good time on the road from Colorado Springs to the ranch south of Gillette, Wyoming. They took turns driving and sleeping. They drank all of the coffee and ate all of the sandwiches. They stopped only when they needed gas, and J.D. always paid cash. Robicheaux got out of the truck once to go to the bathroom. He put up the hood of his windbreaker, and no one ever saw his face. Occasionally, they even stayed within the speed limit. When they reached Edgerton, Wyoming, J.D. called a phone number, and he was given directions to the rendezvous point. They were ahead of schedule.

J.D. and Robicheaux were surprised that it was a woman driving the Tahoe that met them and picked up the man who was on his way to a new life. She was older but energetic and strong and helped J.D. load Robicheaux's boxes from the truck into the back of her SUV. Robicheaux thanked J.D. profusely, and J.D. told him goodbye and good luck. J.D., along with everyone else in the Camp Shoemaker group, had become invested in the man's continued safety. J.D. immediately turned his truck around and drove south. He filled his truck with gas again, bought more coffee, and drove back the way he'd come, heading for Colorado Springs and the comfortable bed that awaited him in his suite at the Penmoor West.

Meanwhile Bailey and Cameron got ready for their own performance. They did not really believe the Russian mob was watching them. They thought they'd smuggled Afif away from the parking lot at the Air Force Academy without anyone being suspicious. But, just in case, Cameron thought a decoy flight would be useful. He was not going to use his own plane or his own pilot. He'd hired a corporate jet and a pilot to use for the day.

Bailey had procured a life-size blow-up doll and some clothes in which to dress the doll. Bailey was good at disguises, and he thought his "doll" in a wheelchair was going to be pretty convincing, if no one looked too closely. Cameron had rented a car to drive the "three" of them to the airport. Bailey dressed the doll in the clothes and a wig he'd bought. Their rental car was parked in a lot outside the Penmoor West, and the "patient" was waiting for them in the car.

Early in the morning, so they wouldn't run in to any other hotel guests, Bailey pushed the empty wheelchair that Afif no longer needed, onto the elevator. Cameron drove the rental car from the parking lot and met him at a side door of the hotel. Successfully avoiding the curiosity of the bellmen at the hotel's front entrance, they loaded the wheelchair into the trunk of the car and headed for the airport.

Cameron drove the rental car directly onto the tarmac, close to the steps of the leased corporate jet. Cameron had arranged for a ramp to enable them to push the wheelchair onto the airplane. The ramp was in place. Bailey was dressed as a nursing attendant, just in case anyone was watching. The two men lifted their patient out of the car and into the wheelchair and pushed the wheelchair up the ramp.

Cameron had arranged for their car to be picked up by the rental company. This was standard procedure for people who flew private jets. They wanted to drive their rental cars as close as possible to their planes. One reason was to unload luggage from the car and load it onto the plane. Rental car companies routinely picked up cars from the tarmac at the private terminal. People who flew private paid an extra fee for their rental cars to be picked up from where they left them. Cameron had rented both the car and the jet with a credit card that belonged to a corporation with a name that could not be traced back to him. He felt secure that their decoy flight would not expose his real identity or Bailey's. Cameron conferred briefly with the pilot, and the jet took off for Little Rock.

Once on the plane, Bailey let the air out of the inflatable doll and stored it, with the clothes and the wig they'd used, in a duffle bag. He changed out of his nursing attendant's uniform. The uniform, the doll, and the wig might be useful in a future escapade. If the pilot came out of the cockpit to talk to them, he would find only two passengers, Bailey and Cameron. When they arrived in Little Rock, Cameron conferred with the pilot and told him the plane could return to Colorado Springs.

Bailey and Cameron would take a taxi from the airport back to the hotel. They would leave the borrowed wheelchair with a bellman at the front door of the hotel. Quite a few people borrowed wheelchairs from the concierge. The airplane was gone. The car was gone. The wheelchair would soon be gone. Afif was gone.

J.D. arrived back in Colorado Springs and went straight to the sunny breakfast room. It was nine o'clock in the morning, and no one else from the Camp Shoemaker group was there. J.D. ordered a big breakfast and made a point of chatting with the waitress who brought his food. He spilled part of a cup of coffee on the tablecloth. He left her a large cash tip because she had to clean up the coffee, and he apologized profusely. The waitress would definitely remember J.D. He signed the check to be billed to his room. His alibi was established. He had eaten dinner at the resort the night before, and he had eaten breakfast here this morning. No one would ever suspect that he hadn't been asleep all night in his room at the Penmoor West. No one would suspect that he had just driven all night and had covered more than seven hundred miles on the road.

He left the hotel and drove the RRD Company truck to the motel where his driver had spent the night. He left the keys with the driver and thanked him for driving the truck from St. Louis. J.D. hoped the driver would not be shocked if he happened to notice the number of miles the truck had been driven overnight. J.D. used his cell phone to call a taxi to take him back to the Penmoor. He knew he was walking like a robot now, counting the steps he had to take until he could rest. He made it to his suite where Olivia was still sound asleep. He sent a text to Matthew Ritter, collapsed on the bed, and slept until dinnertime. Mission accomplished. Afif and Gregory Robicheaux were safe.

Chapter 30

It had been Cameron's idea for the dinner tonight, and he was sitting at the head of the table and taking charge. He'd been in the air most of the day and had turned the menu and all of the details over to Sidney. She'd gone all out, happy to have something other than her brush with death to occupy her mind. She was still having flashbacks about what had happened at the spa, but she was relieved to have it behind her. Sidney had reserved a private dining room in the Penmoor West, and she'd had the staff take some of the flowers from her suite to decorate the table.

Sidney had ordered the seafood tower for twelve. It was terribly expensive, but it was magnificent. A meal in itself, the shrimp, crab claws, lobster, clams, and oysters of many varieties, arrived at the table looking like a work of art. Sauces of all colors and flavors added to the masterpiece. Cameron had told her to spare no expense. She'd ordered a soup, salad, and pasta course next. One could choose lobster bisque, Caesar salad, or angel hair with a garlicky butter sauce, or one could have all three. Mixed grill was the main course, and the group could choose from an enormous platter of sliced chateaubriand, grilled New York strip steaks, Colorado lamb chops, sautéed quail, and homemade pork sausages. Vegetables of every color and shape, and broiled tomatoes topped with sour cream, parmesan cheese, and just a touch of curry powder, were served family style. Desserts were from the menu, but Lilleth was the only one at the table who was not too stuffed to eat dessert. The others ordered dessert to go. It was an amazing feast, accompanied by champagne and carefully chosen red and white wines. Sidney was good at planning a party.

Cameron spoke. "I wanted you to be well-fed. I'm taking a chance that once we get started here, your brains will snap back into operating mode. I want to loosen your tongues and your inhibitions, but not to the extent that you are silly or comatose. This is a think tank. It is a well-fed and well-lubricated think tank, to be sure, but we have work to do. Look at this evening as my version of a Murder Mystery Dinner. The difference, aside from the fact that this food is much better than the food served at those dinners, is that nobody knows yet 'who done it.' None of the law enforcement people have been able to figure it out, but I think we can."

Cameron was on a roll and realized he loved having his own think tank, even if it was just a bunch of his old Camp Shoemaker buddies and their wives and girlfriends. "We have experts in many fields here tonight. We have two physicians, including one pathologist who has done countless autopsies and at one time worked for the Philadelphia Medical Examiner's Office. His mentor was one of the giants in the field of forensic pathology. We have a lawyer who is also a logistics genius and knows more than a little something about handguns. We have two psychologists. At least one of them has a photographic memory. Maybe both of them do. They will be invaluable in analyzing motivations and relationships. We have a man who won't tell us the truth about whether or not he actually flew the SR-71, but he will admit to knowing a lot about Russia.

He also has two, yes, two, degrees from Stanford University. He must have a few brain cells in that head of his to be able to achieve that. We have an engineer who has also been an operative for the Defense Intelligence Agency. He knows how to use disguises, and he loves to be on a secret mission. We have a member who works in HR and knows people. She has worked in corporate America, and she has worked abroad. She's a strategic thinker. We have a mathematician who used to work for the NSA and can identify any and all kinds of patterns. She knows politics, and she is an expert on Russia, China, and many other things. We have one of our own who has phenomenal skills in the areas of inductive ... or is it deductive ... reasoning? Maybe it's both. She used to work for a government agency that will remain unnamed. Her husband says she can read minds. Maybe she can. We have a former law enforcement profiler who is also the smartest women I know. She can read people. She's uncanny. She is brave. And she is never wrong. Then, we have me. I have some computer skills, but tonight I am the moderator of the panel."

"You are all aware of what we know about these three killers, these three men who entered the high-end Penmoor spa with the mission of murdering one or two or more women. The women were there to relax and rejuvenate. This made them vulnerable. One of these three men is dead. One is in custody, we hope for quite a long time. One is on the loose. Who were they after? And why? How did they find their victims? What happened at the spa that morning? Finally, we have an outlier, a crime that might have been perpetrated by an evil prankster or might have been attempted murder. Who pushed Richard, who in turn pushed Elizabeth, into the lake? We know almost nothing about who that person was. We are here tonight to sort it all out, to talk it through. You can call it group therapy if you want to. Each of you is invited to say anything you want to say. Elizabeth can even say that, although Richard's pushing her into the lake the other night was a mistake, she had always suspected there were times when he'd wanted to do it on purpose. That was meant to be a joke, although maybe it isn't, since nobody is laughing. Before I turn the evening's discussion over to you, I want to offer a toast to Tyler Merriman who jumped into a freezing lake and helped to save Elizabeth's life."

Everyone stood up and raised their glasses. Elizabeth shouted, "Bravo! Tyler!" She had tears in her eyes.

Gretchen spoke up first. "Although I hate to have to admit it, I believe that spa murderers #2 and #3 intended to kill me. My name was beside the door to the massage room. Almost no one knew that Withers was inside that room and I was not. Only a few people knew she'd requested that her room be changed. No one had changed the name plates beside the doors to accurately reflect who was in the rooms. Nobody ever intended to kill Withers. She wasn't supposed to be in the massage room that she was in. She was in the wrong place at the wrong time. Both of those men were after me. We don't have final confirmation on either one of their identities."

Gretchen continued. "I believe that murderer #2, the man who is dead, will be identified as the stalker who shot up his boss's house in Chicago and who threatened to come after me. The man's face was destroyed when he was shot, but when they find some DNA to compare to that of the corpse, I think they will find he is the former employee of my company who was fired from our Chicago office. I don't know how he found me. No one was supposed to know I was here. I didn't even tell my children where I was. Since he's dead, I guess we will never know how he tracked me down."

Gretchen continued. "I'm almost certain that the killer who is in custody, is a Russian assassin. This enters the realm of speculation, but he may have been someone I did business with a decade ago in Switzerland. Or, he may be an agent of that man. I believe he was sent by someone in the Russian government to kill me. I think he was sent to tidy up loose ends. My former boss, Arnold Sprungli, was targeted in this same clean-up operation. They took Arnold out with a long gun. They tried to take me out with one of their fancy secret pistols. The assassin was after me, and Withers got in the way. Sidney saved Withers. I was hiding under a massage table in an entirely different massage room when all of the shooting was going on. I do want to say that, if Sidney had not taken down the Russian, I might have been next." Gretchen had presented her view of what had happened in the spa, succinctly and clearly.

"What about the man who tried to smother you?" Cameron knew the answer but wanted Gretchen to verbalize it for the group.

"He wasn't after me at all. He said so. I fought him off when he attacked me. Once he saw my face, he apologized and said I wasn't Diane. Someone named Diane is the one in danger. I wish we could find her. I wish we could find him. He was the least professional of all. He came armed with a pillow. I could be at risk from him now, I guess. If he thinks about it, I have seen his ugly face … very up close and very personal." Gretchen said she was not afraid of this killer, but some in the group who had heard her analysis thought that maybe she should be.

Sidney spoke up. "I saw all three of these men. Two aren't players anymore, but the one who is missing was dressed as a massage therapist. He had on the official maroon uniform, issued to male employees of the Penmoor spa. We know he wasn't really a massage therapist. So, where did he get this outfit, his disguise? I kept telling the police and the FBI about the uniform, but they just wanted to know about his face. I didn't see his face close-up like Gretchen did. I think law enforcement needs to look at security footage of the employees' locker area. I think the man, who tried to smother Gretchen and who is after a woman named Diane, stole one of the massage therapists' uniforms from the male employees' locker room. I think security footage from there will show his face. A sketch is good, but a photo of his face is so much better. He's not a professional killer. He's an angry husband or ex-husband or a rejected boyfriend."

Lilleth agreed. "Sidney's correct, the murderer who is on the loose is an angry ex-husband or ex-boyfriend. There is something quite personal in his attack. This man has never killed before. If he were a professional and if he had been thinking like a killer, he would have gone ahead and murdered Gretchen. He should have killed her because, as Gretchen herself pointed out, she can identify him. This didn't occur to him. Instead of finishing the job of smothering someone who could put the finger on him, he apologized to her. He wants to kill Diane, for some reason we don't know about. He doesn't want to kill anyone else. He is the loose cannon, and nobody can find him. And nobody can find Diane, whoever she is. It is frustrating to know what this man looks like and to know the first or middle name of the woman he wants to kill, but not to be able to find either him or his potential victim."

Olivia spoke up. "I am having a hard time believing there would be three murderers on one hallway in one spa at exactly the same time. It is just too much of a coincidence for me. It belies credibility. And the killers are all unrelated? That just doesn't seem possible."

Lilleth wanted to respond to Olivia's doubts that such a coincidence could happen. "I've been thinking a great deal about all of this, and I've decided it isn't really that much of a coincidence. Let's take Gretchen's situation. If someone has been trying to get to her to kill her and if they have been watching her, the spa is the best and most obvious place to strike. It may be the only place they have a chance to get close to her. There has not been any other time that he could conveniently get near Gretchen. Think about it. She's in her room with the door locked at night when she is sleeping. Her husband is in there with her. This is not the ideal time to try to shoot somebody. When she isn't in her room during the day, she is surrounded by a crowd of friends. She's in the lobby surrounded by … us. She's on a tour bus full of people. She's in a restaurant, surrounded by other people. Everywhere she walks, she walks with a group. She is basically never alone. But, one or both gunmen could have hacked into the computer at the resort and discovered that she was going to the spa on Thursday. Even when she's at the spa, she is surrounded by other people most of the time. When she has her pedicure, her manicure, and her haircut, she is in a big open room, surrounded by a lot of people. None of these locations will work. The assassin has to strike when she is having her facial or when she is having her massage. The massage is the obvious choice. She is undressed. She is relaxed and lying on a massage table in a darkened room. At the end of the massage, the therapist always leaves the room for a few minutes so the client can rest. Many clients doze off to sleep after a relaxing massage. At that moment, Gretchen is not only vulnerable and possibly asleep, she is also alone. That is the perfect time to kill someone. It wasn't difficult for both gunmen who were after Gretchen to figure this out. There is no coincidence. She will be in the massage room for fifty or eighty minutes. At the end of the massage session is when and where I would strike if I were planning something like this."

Isabelle, who was also a psychologist, picked up Lilleth's argument. "Likewise, the man who was after Diane, probably followed the same line of reasoning. We don't know if Diane is surrounded by friends and untouchable the rest of the time. But once again, it makes sense that the man who attacked Gretchen by mistake planned to attack Diane when she was lying down, resting or sleeping on the massage table. It's a natural, a great place to kill someone. The only coincidence is that Gretchen and Diane scheduled massages at around the same time on the same day. But Diane, for whatever reason, cancelled or didn't show up. Or, and I think this is the even more likely scenario, the man who was planning to kill Diane made a mistake about when her appointment was supposed to be. He goofed and showed up on the wrong day. Maybe Gretchen looks a little bit like Diane. This man was not a professional. He was a bumbler. He bumbled into the wrong massage room, and he bumbled his attack on the wrong woman."

Isabelle continued. "It's difficult for me to believe that there are two men who wanted to kill Gretchen. It's difficult for me to believe that there is one man who wanted to kill Gretchen. That's the hard part for me. But, given that there are these two men who were bent on killing, it is not difficult to imagine that they would both choose to kill her while she is in the massage therapy room. That's the easiest place to carry out a hit. Lilleth is correct. No coincidence here."

Those in the group who had found the triple murderer situation hard to believe, now seemed more convinced as they better understood how the attacks had played out. The scenario became more believable to everybody, given the opinions of the psychologists. Even Gretchen, who'd also had a hard time believing two gunmen would both try to kill her at almost exactly the same moment, understood better why this might have happened the way it did.

Chapter 31

THE CONVERSATION HAD BEEN INTENSE. EVERYONE was quiet for a few minutes while they absorbed all the things their friends had shared. Cameron recognized that an interlude was necessary, to let everyone's minds take a rest, but he was anxious to continue with the discussions. "Does anybody know if the one with the Eurotrash boots, the man Gretchen thinks is a Russian government assassin, is talking? Is he in FBI custody, or is he in local custody?" Cameron was moving on to what might happen in the future.

J.D. had an answer for that. "Once they conclusively identify him as a foreign national, the FBI will take over from the locals. He will probably never be seen again. He will be made to disappear. Maybe his destination will be just down the road at the maximum security prison in Florence, Colorado. But the risk is huge that someone will kill him before he can talk. The Russians don't mess around. Whether he's mafia or government, if he was sent by Vladimir Putin, he won't last a week in any prison. If law enforcement can't get the guy to talk in the first few days, they can forget about it. He will be a dead man." J.D. had been a prosecutor before he'd founded his own trucking company. "If he's the same guy who killed

Sprungli, the Swiss will want him, but I'm almost certain he's not the same guy. The assassin in Switzerland used a long gun and killed Gretchen's former boss from a considerable distance away. The guy at the Penmoor used a handgun, and he was attempting to kill at close range. This one's an expert at using a prototype weapon. Assassins are rarely that skilled with both a long gun and a handgun. It is, of course, possible that one hit man could be accomplished at using both types of guns, but they usually hone their expertise on one type of gun or the other. I am guessing there were two assassins. I don't think the man who was sent to kill Gretchen is the same man who shot Sprungli."

J.D. paused. He was trying to decide if he wanted to continue. "I hate to say it, but I'm afraid Gretchen is still at risk from the Russians who are tying up loose ends. If the man in custody was sent by Putin, they didn't get her this time. The question is, will they try again? It might not be worth it to them. If Bad Vlad and his boys get some ugly publicity out of this, they might decide to leave Gretchen alone. She was Sprungli's assistant. She didn't work for the bank in Zurich for as many years as Sprungli worked there. She didn't have all the names and all the dirt on clients that he had. Maybe she's not as much of a threat as Sprungli was. Maybe the Russians will decide not to go after Gretchen again. I am concerned that, for political reasons, the FBI will decide to cover this up. There is a famous movie star involved. The Russians are being blamed for everything these days."

Tyler had known a lot about Russia when it was part of the Soviet Union, and everybody knew that Vladimir Putin now wanted to "put Humpty Dumpty back together again." Putin wanted the Soviet Union back. "In the old days, the Russian guy might eventually have been exchanged for one of our people that the Russians are holding. The rise of the

Russian mafia has changed all that." Tyler wouldn't say so, but his friends believed that back in the day he'd watched, from a vantage point high in the skies, a great deal of what had gone on in the Soviet Union. "If he'd been caught spying, he might have had a chance to return to Russia, but he's murdered someone on American soil. His lawyer could argue, if it ever went to court, that it was a case of self-defense. The other man in the massage room did have a gun. My best guess is that there will never be a lawyer or a trial. The fact that he's committed a violent crime changes the stakes. And, I don't believe Mr. Eurotrash Boots will live long enough to say anything about who hired him, even if he comes around and decides he wants to cut a deal. He may have a cyanide pill secreted in his tooth."

Richard wanted to talk about the other crime, the one that was very personal for him. But he had to add something to the discussion about the Russian mafia hit man. "As you know I had a brief conversation with the El Paso County coroner. J.D. shared with me, and I shared with the coroner some information about the way the suspected Russian chose to place his shots when he killed the pillow shooter, the gunman he found in Withers Singleton's massage room. We don't know, and probably never will know, the Russian's real name, but we know something about how this assassin was trained to kill."

Richard continued, "What I really want to know is who pushed me on the walkway bridge and caused me to push Elizabeth into the lake. Nobody knows anything about that man. We know a great deal about all these other guys, the Spa Killers, but hardly anybody got a glimpse of the guy at the lake. The witnesses say he wore all black with a black hoodie. There were no security cameras by the lake. I don't think he's ever going to be found, and I'm worried he will strike again. I don't know if he targeted us on purpose. Nobody else has been pushed into the lake. It could have been a random thing, but what kind of satisfaction would anyone get from pushing a disabled woman in a wheelchair into a lake?"

Isabelle had practiced clinical psychology for many years. "There are mean and evil people in the world. There are people who see a chance to do mischief or damage or hurt somebody, and they take it. I'm not saying I think this was a random act. I agree it's hard to believe that. But it is important to keep an open mind. It could be a sadistic and twisted jogger who saw a vulnerable couple and impulsively made a decision to hurt them. I think the jury is out on motive here. I hate to say it, but I don't think anyone is ever going to find this guy … unless he strikes again."

"Will he follow us home? Will he make another attempt, perhaps using a more lethal weapon than a push with his hands?"

"We don't know. It feels like an opportunistic crime to me, but I can't say that with one-hundred-percent certainty. I wish I had a better answer for you, Richard." Isabelle was correct in her analysis, and she knew her explanation had not been satisfying to anyone.

Elizabeth spoke up for the first time. "We will have to be on our guard. I hate to live like that, and I refuse to be afraid all the time. If he comes after me again, so be it. I'm not always in a wheelchair, but I am always armed with my cane. It can be an effective weapon."

Olivia had been quiet through the whole discussion. "Tell me some good news. I like good news."

"We are all still alive, and no one is hurt. That's good news to me." Elizabeth had been hurt more seriously than anyone else in the group had been, but she tried to be positive.

Tyler hesitated to bring up another item that wasn't good news, but he'd been sitting on his story for two days and couldn't wait any longer. "Cameron said we could talk about anything we wanted to talk about, and I've had something important I've wanted to say for two days. It's been heavy on my mind, but I haven't had the chance to mention it. I was going to bring it up the other night at cocktails before dinner, but that get-together was cancelled. Lilleth has been taking such good care of me. She won't let me do anything or go anywhere. This is my first opportunity, so I am bringing it up tonight. Art work from the Penmoor has been stolen."

Tyler looked around the table to see if he had their attention. His audience was listening with apprehension and disbelief. A robbery? How could there be something else going on? It wasn't possible. Tyler continued. "There have been a number of works stolen from the art collection at the Penmoor. I don't have details. I don't know what was stolen or when it happened. I think the theft has either just happened, within the past few days, or it has just been discovered. I listened in on a conversation that Dolly Wilder had with a colleague. It was the day she gave us our tour and was going to have lunch with us. She cancelled at the last minute. She was quite upset by the news she heard. I eavesdropped on as much of their conversation as I could. Dolly was so nice to us and gave us a wonderful tour of the art and architecture here. We're all crazy about her. I'd like to know if they've recovered the art or if they've found out who stole it."

Cameron was anxious to get in on this conversation. "I was going to keep my mouth shut and let you guys do the talking, but Tyler has brought up a subject I wasn't anticipating. This is news to me, and it's surprising. I probably shouldn't be telling you this, so I'm going to phrase what I say in a way that gives me deniability. I want to tell you about a new product that one of my companies has developed. It's a product that is evolving over time, as we come up with better and better iterations."

Everyone was wondering what in the world Cameron's inventions had to do with art theft, and now he was going to explain it to them in a round-about way. "One of my companies makes tracking chips. These are different from identification chips. Those of you with cats or dogs probably have had your vet put an identification chip under the skin of your pet's upper back. The identification chip technology has been around for a long time, and lots of companies make these devices. This way to find a pet's rightful owner has been popular and is relatively inexpensive. Reuniting a lost dog with its family has brought tremendous joy to hundreds of thousands of people. The identification chip is a passive device."

Cameron's audience was with him so far. "A somewhat more sophisticated application of the technology includes the LoJack which has been installed on most new cars for decades. You'll remember in Maine last year we were able to find Rita's stolen car because she had LoJack on her Neon. Law enforcement is usually involved in finding a car using LoJack. The police have access to a code they use to activate the LoJack mechanism in the car, which then begins to send out a signal. That's how they are able to locate stolen vehicles."

Cameron's audience understood. "You may have read about more sophisticated devices that can track vehicles, and even people, in real time. Movies and novels have given us a glimpse into this future world, that is, being able to see, on a phone or a computer screen, where someone or something is at all times. It certainly isn't science fiction, and it isn't even that costly any more. It is possible to see, on your watch or on your phone, where your child's backpack is at any given moment. This is all old news."

What was old news to Cameron was not necessarily old news to his friends. Matthew was a desert quail hunter, and he had hunting dogs. He could testify from personal experience about the GPS dog collar technology that allowed him to keep track of his dogs in the field. "I have a Garmin Pro 550 that has the capability to alert me that my dog is on point. It lets me know the dog's direction and how far away the dog is from me. It's a miraculous invention. It has relieved me of the constant worry that plagued me during the hunts of yesteryear, the fear that one of my dogs would run away and get lost. They occasionally did get lost, and it was sometimes many hours before we found them. Now my dogs are never lost. What a wonderful thing!"

The others were eager to hear what Cameron would have to say next. "The technology is there. What we have done is make the chips that can track an object or a person in real time, smaller, a lot smaller. It is now possible to make this kind of chip almost microscopic. Here I may be treading on dangerous ground, but consider all the possible applications of this technology."

"I want to go back just one step. If almost every dog in this country has an identification chip, I would imagine that most valuable works of art in this country also have these chips. Owners of expensive art, perhaps at the insistence of their insurance companies, would routinely implant their priceless paintings and sculptures with ID chips. The difference between dogs and art is that, with art work the chip must be miniscule. It has to be placed in the actual paint or in the actual clay or other sculpture medium. It can't just be on the back of the painting or on the frame. It's too easy for a thief to get rid of a device that's been slapped onto the back of a painting or onto its frame.

"I recently had the opportunity to visit the workshop of a valuable collection of art work." Camerson paused, looked at his audience, and gave them an exaggerated wink. "I noticed that technicians were using identification chips and inserting them directly into the paint on the surfaces of the paintings. They can't be seen if they are imbedded into the paint. If the art work is stolen and even if he knows about the chip, the thief won't be able to find it. If the stolen art work is recovered, a scanning device will instantly identify the legitimate owner of the painting. This is exactly like the scanning device in your veterinarian's office that can identify the rightful owner of a lost dog."

Tyler wanted to summarize what Cameron had been saying, to clarify for himself that he understood everything. "People who own valuable art are, or should be, using these microscopic identification chips." The theft of art work at the Penmoor had been Tyler's revelation, and it was obvious he'd been worried about it. He was relieved that he'd finally found a forum to reveal his news about the art thefts and that people were listening to him. "If a stolen piece of art work can be recovered and if it has had a microscopic identification chip inserted into the paint, ownership of the painting can be verified."

"You've got it." Cameron was always happy to have the chance to teach something to this group. They were smart and immediately caught on to what he was trying to explain. "What has not been available in a workable form, until just a few weeks ago, is the microscopic *tracking* chip. This is revolutionary technology and changes everything. The difficult part of this technology has been to develop a battery that is small enough to enable the chip to transmit its location. Neither the pet identification chip nor the art identification chip needs a battery. These are passive systems. Identification chips don't have to transmit anything. You take a lost dog to the vet and a scanner gives you the information you need. Likewise, a scanner reveals the ownership of a stolen work of art. The battery power is in the scanning device. The LoJack is a passive system until the car is stolen. Then law enforcement sends a signal to the LoJack and turns it on. At this point, the LoJack begins to transmit a signal, and it becomes an active system.

"The problem is, with an active system, a system that is able to transmit its location, you have to have a power source. If the power source is a battery, as it is in the case of the LoJack, that battery will run down over time. If the stolen car whose LoJack is transmitting its location isn't found within a certain time period, the LoJack's battery will die. Most active tracking devices, the ones that are put on cars and backpacks to keep track of these things in real time, have built-in batteries. But these batteries will eventually run out of juice. The use of these car tracking devices or GPS trackers is intended to be short-term. The device goes dead after a while and has to be replaced with a new one. Others are rechargeable. Matt has to plug his dog collar batteries into an electrical outlet at night so the collars can be recharged and are ready to transmit when he takes the dogs out the next day."

Matt nodded his agreement that this was what he had to remember to do every night. "It's worth it, believe me. I never forget to plug those batteries in to recharge them. It's too important to me not to lose my dogs."

Cameron resumed his lesson. "There is a kind of GPS tracker for a car that's hard-wired to the battery of the car. As long as the car's battery is working, this kind of tracking device has a power supply to send its signal. If you don't want someone to know you've hooked up a tracker to their car, it's a pain in the butt to install. It takes an expert and some time to hook up one of these trackers to the car's battery. But once it's been connected, the tracking chip works as long as the car's battery is working,."

Cameron continued. "Battery technology is taking off, and the longer-lasting and smaller a battery is, the better.

New chemical components are being developed all the time for use in cell phone batteries. But, as I am sure you are all aware, there have been problems. The lithium batteries in a certain company's cell phones caused fires, and that's just one example of the problems that have arisen while attempting to make batteries that are smaller and last longer.

"The new technology my company has developed includes a microscopic chip, an almost microscopic battery component, and efficient software for tracking on a cell phone, a computer, a tablet, or an Apple watch. This potent combination will enable those who own works of art, jewelry, or other valuable items, to keep track of where their valuables are at all times. If you have put your diamond necklace in a safety deposit box at the bank, you will have a program on your phone to alert you if that necklace moves even a fraction of an inch. Our new product has to do with miniaturizing the tracking chips, making the batteries very, very small, and being sure the battery is activated only when something moves or changes. The battery becomes active and the chip transmits only when the painting moves or the piece of jewelry moves. Think motion sensor; think about a light that comes on in your back yard when somebody walks toward your house or drives down your driveway. Think about the possibilities. You can chip your medication bottle to see if your teenage daughter's friend is stealing your Valium. Some people say it's too 'big brother,' but I happen to think it has tons of potential for keeping people honest."

"What does this have to do with the art that's been stolen from the Penmoor?" Tyler was holding Cameron accountable and urging him to get back to the subject at hand. "You've said that you are kind of letting the cat out of the bag by telling us that the Penmoor is already using the identification chips on its art work. If a stolen painting is recovered, ownership can be verified. But with art, isn't the main problem all about recovering the stolen art work? Everybody knows that stolen art is often never found, and is never seen again in public. Private collectors can choose to keep their masterpieces hidden away, especially if they have acquired that art work under questionable circumstances. Decades may go by before stolen art comes on the market or is recovered. This is not especially satisfying for museums and art collectors who have been the victims of art theft.

Cameron could barely wait to speak. "You have made my point exactly. The revolutionary and coming attraction is that miniaturization has made it possible to place *active* tracking devices in art work. I want to talk to the security people here at the Penmoor. I want them to try our new product design on their paintings. When a piece of art is stolen, we will be able to track exactly where that painting is, follow it, and recover it."

Cameron was in the technology business and worked with it every day of his life. It took the other members of the group, as smart as they were, a while to process everything Cameron had said and to grasp how it applied to the Penmoor art thefts.

"Do you think the Penmoor will be willing to let you put your experimental devices on their valuable paintings?" Tyler had keyed in on the next hurdle Cameron had to overcome.

"That's the big question, isn't it? I am going to try to get whoever is in charge of the Penmoor's art security division on the phone tonight and ask for a meeting with them first thing in the morning. We've been looking for a real world opportunity to try out our revolutionary system. We will offer it to the Penmoor for free, in return for the chance to see if it's going to work. I'm a pretty good salesman. I think I can convince them this is something that can work for the Penmoor and for my company."

Cameron had said he wasn't going to talk tonight, that he was just the moderator. But when he'd heard about the art thefts, he couldn't help himself. This had been Tyler's big news, but Cameron had taken that news and run with it. The new technology sounded to the others in the group like an incredibly exciting development ... if it worked. Cameron's adrenalin was pumping. He was ready to roll.

The others, who had not slept on a plane all day and who had not been to Panama for stem cell injections, were exhausted and ready to go to bed. There had been too many exciting events to occupy this group in the past few days. They'd needed a night off, but Tyler's revelations about the art thefts had thrust them into a whole new scenario that inevitably demanded their attention. They were going to bed for the night, but not one of them could wait to have an update from Cameron the next day.

Chapter 32

Sunday was the Penmoor's famous buffet brunch and the group's last day together before they scattered to the winds. But there was an unexpected Sunday morning surprise for those who had intended to fly home on Monday. They received emails or texts from their various airlines that, because of a massive winter storm that was on its way to Colorado, all Monday flights to and from both Denver and Colorado Springs, as well as to and from all other airports in Colorado and several surrounding states, had been cancelled. No flights would be allowed to fly into or out of the area for at least three days, possibly longer. Airlines would work with passengers to find seats on future flights, but it was going to be a gigantic mess. It might be a week before anyone could get a seat on a flight out of town. It often snowed at the Denver airport. It was the mile high city, and they were used to dealing with snow. Because all airlines had cancelled flights, the expectation was that the approaching snow storm was going to be an especially ferocious one.

Cameron and Sidney had their own plane and their own pilot, and under normal circumstances, they would have flown home on Sunday morning, a day early, ahead of the storm.

Because Cameron thought he had an opportunity to test his newest invention at the Penmoor, he was not going to let a little snow get in the way of progress. His only worry was, if the Penmoor agreed to adopt his technology on a trial basis, would he be able to get everything delivered to Colorado Springs in time, before the storm made transportation of any kind impossible?

The members of the group who had been told their flights were cancelled were concerned about where they were going to stay. They had reservations at the Penmoor only through Sunday night, and after that, they were stuck. Olivia, who had become friends with their concierge, took action. After a conference with Elle, Olivia told the group that, because of the impending storm, people who'd been expected to arrive at the Penmoor in the next several days, would not be arriving. The airline reservations of many of the resort's future guests had been cancelled, and these guests in turn had cancelled their room reservations.

Elle guaranteed all of the couples' rooms for another five days. They would not have to move to different rooms. In addition, the Penmoor was offering them a discounted deal. The hotel and its guests were captives of the weather. If guests decided they didn't want to pay the high price for a room at the Penmoor and went to a less expensive motel, the Penmoor would not be able to fill its rooms. Incoming guests were not coming in. The Penmoor hardly ever offered bargains, but they were offering the reunion group their existing rooms for half price. The Penmoor management knew their guests would continue to purchase meals and other resort services over the next several days. The resort could afford to offer them discounted rooms.

No one was happy about the inconvenience of having their flights cancelled, but the benefit was that their vacation was going to be extended — and at a bargain rate. Doctor's appointments and business meetings that had been scheduled in their home cities and towns had to be rescheduled. There were a number of disruptions to be dealt with.

As soon as the death of the stalker could be verified with certainty, Gretchen's boss would want her back on the job. For now, she thought her boss would be happy to have her out of the office for another few days. Gretchen found solace in her work. It was her tonic. She needed to get back.

Richard never liked for his plans to be turned upside down, but Elizabeth was delighted that she might be able to have a spa day after all. Cameron had work to do with the art security people at the Penmoor. He didn't intend to leave for several days anyway. J.D. could run his business from anywhere, and Bailey was connected to his clients as long as the Penmoor's WiFi was up and running. Matthew hadn't had a chance to show many of his movie montages, so he was happy to have more days added to the trip.

Isabelle was perhaps the most out of sorts about not being able to get back to her store. She had good help that covered for her when she was away, but she'd already been gone for more than a week. She had appointments that would have to be cancelled or rescheduled. Isabelle was a good sport. There was nothing she or anyone could do about the weather. If something critical came up with the store, she had a phone, and she could do Facetime or Zoom with an employee or a customer.

It was Tyler and Lilleth who were determined they could leave early on Monday morning and beat the snow storm to their home in Bayfield, Colorado. The others urged them not to tempt fate and try to outrun the storm. Lilleth had her dog in a kennel, and she wanted to get him out after having left him there for a week. Tyler had an appointment for an important medical procedure, and he didn't know if he would be able to reschedule. Tyler and Lilleth ignored the warnings from their friends, but they were listening to the Weather Channel in their room. Tyler kept checking his phone that had a weather app on it.

After the Camp Shoemaker friends had survived the initial shock that they would not be going home as planned and would be staying at the Penmoor for several more days, they settled in and began to think about where they could find washers and dryers to do their laundry. They needed clean clothes. Elle, the concierge, had it taken care of. All they had to do on this gorgeous sunny Sunday was put on their best outfits and find their way to the Penmoor's Lake Terrace Dining Room to enjoy the fabulous buffet brunch. It was such a warm day, and there was not a cloud in the sky. It was impossible to believe, as they looked out over the beautifully manicured green grass of the golf course and reveled in the downright summery-feeling of the resort on this brilliantly sunny day, that a storm was coming.

They drank champagne and mimosas that were included in the price of the brunch and put their worries of weather and murder and art theft and everything else aside. They attacked the stations of the brunch with gusto and enthusiasm. Every dish, without exception, was so artistically prepared and presented, it was almost a crime to disturb the perfectly arranged platters. Each serving piece had been thoughtfully chosen to show off the food it held. The garnishes had been selected to look exactly right with each culinary presentation. The buffet was a feast for the eyes as well as a feast for the body, not to mention the soul. Artists were at work in the Penmoor's kitchens.

Several of the group had omelets made to order. Gretchen and Richard opted for the eggs benedict. He enjoyed his so much, Richard went back a second time. Bailey loved lobster in all its forms, and the Penmoor served two varieties of miniature lobster rolls in tiny squared off hotdog buns. Cameron went for the sushi bar and the roast beef with au jus. The Penmoor had a sushi chef who made California rolls to order, and Sidney went back a couple of times. Matthew loved sweets but was usually strictly disciplined about indulging. Today he was so relieved that Afif was off his hands that he splurged and ordered Belgian waffles with berries and whipped cream. He couldn't even remember the last time he'd eaten whipped cream. It was so good. Isabelle chose seafood and all the dishes that sounded remotely like they might come from New Orleans … remoulade sauce, potatoes dauphinoise, grillades and grits, oysters Fitzpatrick. Olivia was a big fan of soup, and she had a bowl of each kind offered on the buffet table. She also enjoyed the smoked salmon crostini with capers, minced onions, dill, and sour cream. J.D. had been to the Penmoor brunch before, and he quickly piled his plate high with his usual favorites. Lilleth went mostly vegetarian, but the Chicken Kiev was so buttery, she had to return for another serving. Tyler wanted to try a little bit of everything, but he was full before he got half-way through the stations. Elizabeth keyed in on the rare roast beef with horseradish sauce, but the roasted leg of Colorado lamb won the day. The chef had made lamb gravy with just a touch of mint. Elizabeth decided to have a second helping of mashed potatoes with lamb gravy rather than eat dessert.

 Those who had saved room for dessert were not disappointed. Several tables in the Lake Terrace dining room were dedicated to every confection one could possibly imagine. Bailey took a photo of the fruit tarts. They were as colorful as any crown jewels. Chocolate desserts of every kind were the most popular, but the pecan pie was a close second. Everybody groaned. They swore they would never be able to eat again.

A few were determined to take an after-brunch walk around the grounds. They wanted to soak up the sun and talk about how ridiculous it was that a snow storm was predicted for the next day. It was not possible. Richard wanted to take a nap. J.D. tried to get a group together to play a round of golf on the gorgeous green course, but he couldn't find any takers. Cameron and Matthew had football games they absolutely could not miss. Sidney was a huge sports fan and wanted to watch the games with the guys. Tyler and Bailey decided to join them. Olivia, Isabelle, and Gretchen felt compelled to walk off some of the calories they'd just consumed.

Elizabeth wanted to sit in front of the fire in the lovely room at the end of the hall by the elevator at the Penmoor West. She'd passed by it many times, but had never had the chance to sit down and enjoy the space. The room had such pleasing proportions and was decorated in soothing colors that appealed to her senses. She had a new mystery novel she'd been too tired to read at night. She would sit in front of the fire on this Sunday afternoon and read to her heart's content. The sun was pouring in the room's many windows. She'd just had a delightful meal. She had survived a frightening near-death experience and was feeling fine ... and lucky. She was alive.

Richard was awakened from his nap by a call from Dr. Eliot Landers, the El Paso County Medical Examiner. Landers wanted to hear what Richard had to say about the five-shot assassination. The ME wasn't terribly forthcoming about why he wanted the information, and Richard didn't press him. Richard did, in the interests of full disclosure, tell Landers that the woman who had saved the life of the movie star, Withers Singleton, was a friend of his and the wife of someone he'd known since he was a child.

Richard told Eliot he knew about the shootings at the Penmoor spa. He said that their group of friends had not spoken about what they knew with anyone outside of their own circle. This was news to Landers. He seemed surprised that Richard Carpenter knew so much about what had happened at the spa, but he was grateful that the people who were closely involved with the crime were being discreet. The Penmoor resort had an important presence in Colorado Springs and in El Paso County. The resort was a significant driver of the local economy and a first-class operation in every way. Law enforcement respected their reputation and the privacy of what happened on the resort's property.

Richard was eager to share his knowledge of firearms with Eliot Landers. "I happen to know that the five-shot assassination is, as you might have guessed, actually a variation on and a combination of the double-tap and the Mozambique Drill. You are probably familiar with both of these. My understanding of the five-shot assassination is that it is used at close range and often in conditions where it is difficult to see the target. It is the opposite of the long-range, one-shot assassination done by a sniper with great precision and the use of a scope. The Mozambique Drill is sometimes called the triple tap. Two shots in rapid succession are fired into the body mass followed by the kill shot. Fired immediately after the first two body shots, the third shot, or kill shot, is sometimes directed at the head, at a spot somewhere between the eyebrows and the upper lip. When the triple tap is used as part of the five-shot assassination, the third shot is usually fired directly into the center of the neck, at the larynx, with the objective of instantly severing the spinal cord. The last two shots of the five-shot, the double-tap, are directed at the face ... between the eyes if perfectly placed.

"The large number of shots taken and their placement are intended to insure that the target dies instantly and has no chance to fire back. The two body shots of the Mozambique drill are intended to stop the target, immobilize him or her, and make it impossible for the target to get off a shot of his or her own. The third shot is the one meant to paralyze or kill. Following these three shots with a double-tap guarantees that the target will die immediately." Richard paused, but Landers had no questions. He was listening.

"Five rapid-fire shots targeted at very specific locations on the human body is a difficult kill. The series of precision shots requires a great deal of practice as well as a great deal of natural ability. Often used at close range with a silencer, it guarantees the target will die. It could almost be termed the overkill kill. Nothing is left to chance. It can destroy the face of the target, depending on the caliber of the ammunition that's used. Sometimes, this destruction of the face is important. Hardly anyone uses the five-shot, even government-trained commandoes. Because it is such a difficult shot, or really set of shots, not many assassins attempt it. I would guess your man who used it is Russian mafia or a member of some kind of secret Russian government killing squad. These organizations have been known to use the five-shot. The conditions inside one of the massage therapy rooms would have presented the sort of circumstances where the five-shot would guarantee a kill. Darkness, bad weather, smoke, ... or feathers, ... in the air ... these are the kinds of things that make it difficult to see the target. This is exactly the place where the five-shot would be used. But, as I said, not many assassins are skilled enough to use it effectively or even to try it. Because apparently someone did use it in the Penmoor shootings, I suspect he is a very special kind of assassin. That's all I know."

The ME had listened carefully to all of this information and was grateful to the retired pathologist. "What you've told me confirms several things we've suspected about our shooter. He's not talking, and I don't think he's going to talk. His

DNA shows he's Slavic, from Siberia. We think he is Russian mob, and we suspect he has some kind of government connections. My firearms expert believes the handgun he used is a Russian military prototype, not yet available to anyone, even the Russian military. Our shooter is certainly highly trained. What I don't understand is why this particular target was so important that whoever sent him to kill her sent such a skilled marksman. Was the target that valuable? It is almost as if this was a vendetta as much as it was an assassination attempt. That's just my interpretation of what I saw at the crime scene."

"He is an extraordinarily dangerous man. I hope there's not any talk of trading him for anybody, like our spies being held in Russian prisons, or anything like that. He's too dangerous to ever be allowed to have a gun in his hand again."

"Well, you know how politics works. It doesn't matter to some judges or politicians that these criminals are dangerous to the public in general or to some member of the public. If it serves a political purpose, they just let them out of jail."

"I hope that doesn't happen in this case. This man needs to be locked up for the rest of his life."

"I agree with you, but I'm just the guy who renders the final diagnosis. You understand, I know."

"Is he being held in a local jurisdiction, or is he in FBI custody?"

"I'm sure the feds will get him eventually, but right now he's with the local people." Landers paused. "I've done posts for the FBI in the past, and they trust my work. They wanted me to do this one, here, as soon as possible. I will sound like the super duper expert when I explain the five-shot to them. Thanks, Richard. I owe you."

"You will never find out the man's real name, I'm sure, but if you find out why he targeted Gretchen, will you please let me know. It's important."

"I will tell you whatever the FBI says I can tell you. Thanks again."

Dr. Eliot Landers hung up, and Richard went back to his nap. He would have to thank J.D. for giving him the scoop on the five-shot. Richard had known about the double-tap and about the Mozambique Drill, but all the rest of what he'd related to the El Paso County ME had been because of J.D.'s expertise.

Cameron had an appointment scheduled for Monday morning with the head of Penmoor security and the person who was in charge of security for their art collection. Because of the impending storm, Cameron had decided to go ahead and fly in the materials and the experts he would need to implement his new tracking application for the Penmoor's art. Cameron was always thinking three steps ahead of what he was actually doing, and if and when the Penmoor said they would like to try his revolutionary tracking system, he wanted to be certain he could deliver. This was one personality trait that had made him so successful.

Chapter 33

ELIZABETH HAD DOZED OFF READING HER MYSTERY novel on the comfortable couch in front of the fire. When she woke up and looked out the window, she was shocked to see that the sky had turned from light French blue to gloomy storm gray. She could feel the barometer dropping. Her limbs felt leaden, like the sky. She'd been reading for little more than an hour and had dozed off for just a few minutes. How quickly the Indian summer day had turned to overcast and threatening. If she hadn't been in front of a fire and had a throw over her legs, she night have shivered when she looked outside. It appeared as if that winter storm was on its way after all.

A man in a waiter's uniform approached her and asked if she was interested in having afternoon tea. He told her that a lovely cream tea was served in this lounge every day. Elizabeth had not yet had the chance to try the resort's afternoon tea, one of her favorite treats.

"You are my only customer this afternoon. We usually have a full house on Sundays, but with the storm .... " He shrugged his shoulders. "Our cream tea is quite lovely."

Elizabeth looked around and realized she was alone in the room. After the buffet brunch, she'd sworn she would never eat again, but she could not resist indulging in what she knew would be a wonderful experience. Everything at the Penmoor was first-class, and she was sure their afternoon tea would be a delight. "I know I will love it. Bring it on."

She ordered the Lapsang Souchong, a smoky dark grey tea, and it arrived with honey and sugar, heavy cream, and lemon. As she took her first sip of the heady brew, she noticed that a few snowflakes were beginning to fall. She worried that Tyler and Lilleth were still determined to drive home to Bayfield tomorrow. Or maybe they'd left early. Everyone else had decided to stay put for the duration.

A tiered silver tray of exquisite finger sandwiches arrived. All the classics Elizabeth loved were there — cucumber and cream cheese, curried chicken salad, minced ham with pickle, cheese and tomato, and watercress. The watercress were always her favorites, and the Penmoor's interpretation did not disappoint. The scones arrived next and were warm and dusted with sugar crystals. They were served with clotted cream, lemon curd, and apricot preserves. Elizabeth could eat only one. The waiter graciously wrapped the rest for her to enjoy for her breakfast the next morning. She had a microwave in her room. Then the pastries arrived, and she picked at those. Her waiter put those in a bakery box for Elizabeth to take with her. She had a third cup of tea to wash it all down.

She tried to read some more, but the fire and the food were taking her in the direction of another nap. Just as Elizabeth was about to drift off again, Olivia, Gretchen, and Isabelle hurried into the lounge through the outside door. They'd been caught in the snow and were stomping their feet and brushing off their clothes. They descended on Elizabeth and gathered their chairs around the fire. The waiter's eyes lit up. He could tell that these women, who had been walking in the snow and cold, needed a pick-me-up. He took their orders for tea, and the lounge seemed suddenly full with the laughter and voices of this lively group of older women. More sandwiches, scones, and pastries began to arrive. Olivia ordered a glass of white wine. It was a party.

After the football game ended, the sports fans made their way to the lounge to join the women. They ordered drinks and wine. Richard roused himself from his nap and sent a text to Elizabeth, wondering where she was. Bailey and J.D. turned up, and they had news. Tyler had panicked half-way through the first football game and decided he needed to get on the road if he was going to be ahead of the storm. Even though the snow was not expected to begin until the following day, he and Lilleth hurriedly packed their bags and set out on the road to drive to Bayfield.

There was no really good way to drive from Colorado Springs to Bayfield. I-25 was fine as far as it went, although it could be closed down at a moment's notice because of snow. One had to travel on the smaller road, Rt. 160 for the remainder of the trip. Cell phone service was spotty in many places along the route. Their friends had tried to dissuade Tyler and Lilleth from leaving the Penmoor just as a snow storm was threatening, but the two were determined to set out. Tyler had lived in Colorado long enough to know better, but they left anyway. Leaving so late in the day, they might be driving, not only in a snow storm, but in the dark.

Most of the group had decided to embrace their situation ... being snowbound. They knew the Penmoor would take good care of them. Most of them were retired and had no pressing agendas. Isabelle was in contact with her store, and Cameron was on the phone, managing the delivery of his software, hardware, and personnel. Gretchen was still incommunicado with her boss and staff. Those who had not enjoyed the afternoon tea were hungry and decided to have pizzas delivered to the Steele's suite. The movie aficionados in the group prevailed upon Matthew to show some movie montages. They put their worries of the past few days behind them. Maybe this extended vacation, an unexpected bonus thanks to the weather, would be the relaxing and carefree time they'd hoped to have at the Penmoor, the respite they'd not yet achieved.

Cameron's meeting with the Penmoor's security personnel the next day revealed more details about the art thefts. He learned that the thefts had not really been robberies, that works of art from the Penmoor's owner's collection of Western art had seemingly been "borrowed" for extended periods of time. Paintings were taken, and days or weeks later they were returned. The artwork had disappeared exclusively from the collection's workroom. No paintings had been stolen directly off the walls of the resort where they were on public view. Taking art from the hallways would have been too noticeable.

The "borrowing" of the art had been discovered by chance when the art department's bi-annual inventory had shown some pieces were missing. A few days later, one of the missing pieces turned up — back in the workroom. A few days after that, another missing piece reappeared. It was quite a mysterious theft that was not really a theft. Why would someone borrow a painting for a week or two and then return it?

Dolly Madison Wilder sat in on the meeting with Cameron and the Penmoor's security people. She knew Cameron from the tour she had given to his group of friends, and, of course, she knew all about the vetting he'd been put through by the security services of another of the Penmoor's high-profile guests. She could vouch for Cameron. The Penmoor had

Googled and researched Cameron and his various companies and knew he was indeed who he said he was.

Dolly Madison Wilder believed the art disappearances were an inside job. She thought someone who worked with the collection was responsible. She had initiated a review of everyone who had any contact at all with the paintings, including security staff, all docents, and the people who cleaned the underground workrooms and storage areas. Screening and checking of references and backgrounds was rigorously done for those who worked directly with the art on a daily basis. Those who restored, cleaned, catalogued, and hung the collection had been thoroughly investigated before they'd been hired. Likewise, security staff had been carefully vetted. Screening of cleaning people was not as strictly monitored, and there was frequent turnover in cleaning crews.

Chapter 34

ENID HARRISON HAD ALWAYS WANTED TO GO ON a really nice vacation, a trip to a luxurious, first-class resort where she would be indulged and waited on. She'd never had a really nice vacation. When she was a teenager, her family had twice driven to the Jersey Shore for the weekend. The vacation had been fun at the time, but the motel room where she'd slept on the floor with her siblings and the soggy subs they'd eaten for lunch and dinner could scarcely be called luxurious. She had finally arrived at the Penmoor Resort in Colorado Springs for a week of relaxation, and she was loving every minute of it. She had scheduled spa appointments and was eating in all the resort's restaurants. She even ordered steak from the menu.

Enid, formerly Diane, had grown up poor. She'd struggled to put herself through her local community college while she worked two part-time jobs. She'd been a fool to marry Gino Rimaldi, the good-looking, fast-talking lothario who just wanted to be a gigolo. He was slick and sneaky and could turn on the charm when he wanted to. He might have made a pretty good salesman, but he didn't want to work that hard. He always had some kind of a deal in the works, a deal that never amounted to anything. Diane worked hard to keep food on their table, pay the bills on time, and cover the rent on the condo Gino had insisted they live in but couldn't afford.

After five years, she finally decided she'd had enough of Gino and filed for divorce. After the divorce was final, she got rid of the expensive condo she had shared with Gino and moved to a smaller, more affordable apartment. She continued to work hard, and her life was much happier without her worthless husband. She was frugal and careful with her money. Her one indulgence was to buy a lottery ticket every week. She knew her chances of winning were miniscule, but when she bought the ticket, she had fun spending the fantasy money she pretended she might win. In her imagination, she planned what she would do with her lottery winnings. She set priorities about how she would spend the windfall. A nice house and a nice car always made the list, but the first thing she wanted, more than anything else, was that luxury vacation. In her entire life, no one had ever really taken care of Diane or waited on her. If she ever won anything in the lottery, she intended to first splurge on a week of being pampered.

Gino had not been happy when his wife divorced him. He hated having his ticket on the gravy train cancelled. At first he begged his wife not to dump him, and when he realized she was determined to go through with the divorce, he harassed her. When she started dating again, he followed her wherever she went and played dirty tricks on her. Then Diane bought her winning lottery ticket.

She won two million dollars. Diane was stunned and could scarcely believe her good luck. She was excited and a little bit frightened. She didn't want to waste any of the money, so she consulted a financial advisor to help her make the most of her newly-acquired riches. The financial advisor helped her invest the money and gave her sensible advice, but the one thing

Diane insisted on was to take a vacation at a luxury resort. She would have a suite, and she would fly first class to get there.

Before Diane had time to come to terms with her newfound wealth, her ex-husband Gino found out about the winning lottery ticket. He was aggressive in his pursuit of Diane and insisted that part of the money belonged to him. He was entirely wrong to believe that part of his former wife's winnings were his. The two had been legally divorced before Diane bought the lottery ticket. But Gino was a greedy scoundrel and engaged in serious convoluted thinking about how he had put up with Diane for five years while they struggled financially. Because he had been married to her when they were poor, his distorted reality led him to conclude that she owed him part of her lottery winnings now that she was rich. A lawyer told her Gino had no case, but he was relentless in stalking her, calling her, following her, and in general making a frightening nuisance of himself.

Diane called the police, but Gino had not actually done anything to her ... yet. Diane got a restraining order from a judge to keep Gino away from her, but he completely ignored the court order, a piece of paper he considered worthless. He became a little bit crazy as he began to live more and more inside the fantasy of his belief that he deserved half of Diane's new wealth.

Diane's lawyer felt Gino presented a significant threat to her. The restraining orders were not working, and Gino's behavior was escalating. Her lawyer advised Diane to legally change her name and relocate to a different part of the country. The lawyer helped Diane Rimaldi become Enid Harrison and move almost three thousand miles away from Allentown, Pennsylvania.

Gino went completely over the edge when Diane disappeared. The illusion of great wealth had led to Gino's deranged thinking. When Diane disappeared with the money,

Gino became terminally cruel and completely insane. He had convinced himself that he deserved what he considered his share of her lottery winnings. He made it his life's mission to hunt her down. He was determined to get the money, and he devoted himself full time to finding her. Diane had stolen from him what he truly believed was his. He convinced himself that she was hiding from him and living off his money. He had to find her. As he searched for his ex-wife, the idea of killing her and getting all the money began to overtake what little rationality he was able to cling to.

Gino had some minimal knowledge of computers. It took months, but he finally found the person he thought used to be Diane Rimaldi. She had changed her name to Enid Harrison and moved to Bend, Oregon. Gino bought a used camper to tow behind his ten-year-old car, and he was on his way to Bend. With the illusory promise of two million dollars in his future, he was careful as he planned how he was going to murder Enid Harrison. He watched her from afar and tracked her every move. He broke into her house. He discovered that she was planning a vacation to Colorado Springs. He decided her guard would be down while she was on holiday, and that was when and where he intended to strike.

He hacked into the computer at the Penmoor Resort and found that Enid had signed up to have spa services during her stay. Gino had worked as a janitor at a spa in Upstate New York for a few weeks and knew there would be an opportunity for him to get close to Enid while she was visiting the spa. She would not suspect that he was watching her or that he was anywhere near her on her vacation, let alone while she was spending time indulging herself in the resort's spa services. He made plans to go to Colorado Springs.

Gino drove his camper to Colorado. He arrived three days before Enid was scheduled to keep her spa appointments. He was good looking and could talk a good game, and he hung out in the Golf Club Pro Shop. The Penmoor resort's spa was located in the same building as the pro shop. Gino took the elevator up to the spa on several occasions, and on one of his secret trips to the employees' locker room, he stole the uniform of one of the male massage therapists. He double checked when Enid had scheduled her massage and what massage therapy room she was assigned to. He checked out the room ahead of time. He wore a uniform so no one would question whether or not he belonged in the spa area. He was ready to attack and kill.

Unfortunately for Gino, Enid changed her appointment time at the last minute. She decided she wanted a longer massage and also wanted to add a pedicure to her spa schedule. The eighty-minute massage and the added pedicure could only be accommodated on Wednesday rather than on Thursday. Enid had already completed her fabulous spa day by Thursday, when Gino came after her, ready to smother her with a pillow. Gino had always been at least a day late and more than a dollar short.

Gino stumbled into the massage therapy room where Gretchen was napping after her relaxing session with the masseuse. It was dark in the room, and Gino couldn't see very well. He believed his ex-wife was scheduled to be in this room and on this massage table at this specific time. He would smother her with the pillow he was carrying. While she was unconscious, he would strangle her, just to be sure she died. Somebody would find her dead. He would be long gone, and no one would ever know he'd been the one who'd killed her. An autopsy would reveal that she had been smothered and strangled. Gino had not figured out the details of how he was going to get his hands on Enid Harrison's money, but as his mental health had deteriorated, revenge and murder had become equally important motives for Gino. By the time he struck, he wanted to punish his ex as much as he wanted her money.

He knew he could overpower her, and he almost succeeded. The woman on the table put up a more powerful fight than Gino had expected from Diane. The woman he attacked fought hard and eventually pushed Gino away. As he stumbled back, away from the massage table, he stared at the woman he'd tried to smother. He was looking at a face he had never seen before. It was not Diane's face. It was not Enid's. He didn't understand how this could have happened. He had planned so carefully. How had he made this terrible mistake? He would have to rethink his plans. He mumbled an apology to the woman on the table and hurried out of the room and down the hall. He had to get away. Gino had completely lost his sanity by now, and he was no longer being as careful as he should have been.

Enid loved the Penmoor. It was everything she had imagined it would be. She enjoyed sleeping late, ordering a room service breakfast, and having a delightful tea every afternoon. She paid the high price for the Sunday brunch in the resort's Lake Terrace Dining Room and savored every indulgent bite of the extravagant meal.

She returned to her room in a food coma, intending to take a nap. Snow was predicted for later that day, and Enid could smell it in the air. She crawled between the sheets of her king-sized bed in her beautiful suite and fell asleep. She woke up when she heard something scratching at her door. She sat up in bed and listened. Someone was trying to break into her room. She picked up the phone and called security.

She had only begun to explain that she thought someone was attempting to get into her room when the door burst open.

Gino almost fell into the room. Enid recognized him immediately and was astonished to see her ex-husband. She could not imagine how he had ever followed her to the Penmoor. He looked odd. He looked crazed. Enid reached for the drawer in the table beside her bed. She knew she was in trouble. Gino was not here for a chat. He was not here on friendly terms.

Enid's lawyer had warned her that her ex-husband was exhibiting signs of insanity. No restraining orders or threats from law enforcement officials were going to deter him from coming after her. He was already angry with her for divorcing him, and he wanted her lottery winnings. He would not give up until he had taken her down. Once she realized how dangerous Gino had become, she'd agreed to change her name and relocate. Somehow, in spite of all the precautions she had taken, her nemesis had found her. He had tracked her to this idyllic vacation spot. If Enid had not been so frightened, she might have cried.

Her lawyer had recommended that Enid learn to protect herself. She advised Enid to study the martial arts and buy a gun. Enid took her lawyer's advice and began taking self-defense classes. She'd bought a gun, taken a gun safety class, and spent time every week practicing at the gun range in Bend. Enid had a concealed carry permit and always had her gun with her, either in her purse or in the table beside her bed at night.

She didn't want to shoot anyone, not even the pathetic Gino. But she would defend herself. She would have preferred to talk to Gino, but she could tell from the look in his eyes that he was beyond the point of talking. He was a man on a mission, a man determined to kill. Enid hoped to be able to keep him at gun point long enough for a security guard to show up. Even if the guard showed up in time, Enid wondered if he would be armed.

Gino grabbed a pillow from the bed and came towards Enid. "I will get you, Diane. You think you can run away with all your money and hide from me. You think you can keep me from getting my hands on your lottery winnings, but I have always been the boss of you. I am still the boss of you."

Enid had her gun ready, but she didn't want to use it. She scrambled off the opposite side of the bed, the side towards the balcony of the suite. Gino had her blocked from the rest of the room. She had nowhere else to go. She moved towards the French doors that opened onto her tiny balcony. Gino charged after her. She opened the doors even though she realized going out onto the balcony was a dangerous thing to do. Gino caught her in the open doorway, and they struggled. Enid was small and not particularly strong. Gino was getting the better of her. He held the pillow against her face. She pushed it aside and tried to get away from Gino's grasp. He continued to push her outside onto the balcony. He forced her towards the railing. She pushed back. The balcony was slippery because snow was falling. Gino shoved the pillow in her face one more time. It was either fire her gun or try to escape from Gino another way. But there was no other way. She was afraid she would go over the railing and made the fateful decision to shoot. She pulled the trigger, and feathers flew everywhere.

Enid thought she might have fainted briefly. When she finally opened her eyes and looked around, she was sitting on the balcony. Gino was nowhere to be found. Her small handgun was nowhere to be found. At that moment, two security guards rushed into her suite and ran out onto the balcony. Enid still did not see Gino. When she was able to stand up, the security guards were staring over the railing at the ground below. Enid looked down, and there he was. Gino lay motionless in a crumpled pile on top of what had been a neatly trimmed yew hedge. He was obviously quite dead. He had fallen seven stories. Enid sank to her knees. The guards helped her stand up and guided her to one of the chairs in the sitting area. This hotel room was now a crime scene.

It would be days before law enforcement sorted it out. Enid was interviewed many times by various officials. The Penmoor moved her to another suite on a lower floor. Enid Harrison was finally free of her ex-husband Gino Rimaldi. After it was all over, someone finally put things together and realized that Enid was the elusive "Diane" that the resort had been desperately searching for. They had wanted to find her so they could tell her that someone was after her and wanted to kill her, that her life was in danger. They'd not found Diane in time, but Enid was safe now. Word reached Gretchen MacDermott on Tuesday morning that spa killer #1 was finally dead.

Chapter 35

THE BODIES WERE PILING UP AT THE EL PASO County Coroner's Office. In addition to the usual crimes and unexplained fatalities that every community inevitably experiences, there were three additional bodies that had come from the Penmoor Resort, a place that rarely, if ever, had any suspicious deaths. There was an occasional heart attack or a rare accident. But this week, three corpses had arrived from the hotel and the grounds of the resort to complicate the autopsy schedule and put pressure on the county's ME.

In two cases, it was guests at the hotel who had provided information that led to the identification of two of the deceased. One of the women who had almost been a victim and who had been an excellent witness to what had become known as the "Triple Spa Killer" episode, had been able to identify one of the bodies. Although Gretchen MacDermott had never seen the man in person, she suspected that the dead gunman in the massage room, killer #2, was a former employee of her company, the disgruntled man who had been fired from his job and had been stalking her.

The investigators in Colorado Springs made some phone calls and rushed a DNA sample through the lab. They identified the man who had died from a series of gunshot wounds in one of the massage rooms at the Penmoor Resort's spa as the same man who had shot and nearly killed a woman in Chicago. The authorities in Chicago were delighted to have the news that this suspect, who had been on the run, had been eliminated as a future threat. Gretchen MacDermott wanted to know how he had been able to find her, when she had gone to such great lengths to keep her location a secret. She suspected that her phone had been the culprit, but because the former unhappy worker turned violent attacker was now dead, she would never know for sure.

A female guest at the Penmoor was able to identify the second body that had arrived in the morgue. The man who had fallen over the railing and ended up dead in the yew hedge underneath her balcony was the Penmoor guest's former husband, Gino Rimaldi. He had a gunshot wound to his abdomen, but it had been the fall from the seventh floor that had killed him. He had landed with such a tremendous impact when he'd hit the bushes, that branches from the base of the yew hedge were sticking up through his body. This death by yew hedge was a first for Eliot Landers, M.D.

The unusual part of the story about Gino Rimaldi was that he had also been in the Penmoor Resort's spa on the same day and at the same time as the man who had killed two pillows in Withers Singleton's massage room. The authorities did not think Gino had ever crossed paths with either the pillow killer or the man who'd shot the pillow killer. Gino had tried to smother Gretchen MacDermott because he'd mistaken her for his ex-wife, Diane Rimaldi. He was killer #1 from that terrible spa day, and now he too was dead.

Investigators were leaning towards calling Gino's official cause of death an accident. Law enforcement now knew the full story about how he had harassed his former wife because of their divorce and because he'd felt entitled to her lottery winnings. Nobody wanted to charge Enid, the former Diane, with anything. She had been through enough and deserved to enjoy her good luck and financial prosperity in peace. She had changed her name and moved all the way across the country to try to get away from bad boy Gino. Enid had bruises all over her body to prove there had been a struggle as she'd defended herself from her crazed ex. Even though Enid's gun was found on the ground underneath the yew hedge, no one could say for sure who had fired the gun in the struggle. Enid had a permit to carry a concealed weapon. There was no crime here, other than those crimes perpetrated by Gino Rimaldi. He had made more than one attempt to kill his ex-wife and steal her money.

Of the three killers who had entered the Penmoor spa on that fateful day, only the highly trained assassin with Slavic DNA remained a mystery. He had mostly recovered from the wounds that had been inflicted by the heavy lamp. He was out of the hospital and was staying strictly mute in the county jail. The FBI had been called in, but neither the feds nor the local law enforcement people had been able to get the man to talk. They kept him heavily guarded because they were aware that, if he was as they suspected, a Russian mobster or a shooter sent by Vladimir Putin, his days were numbered. Someone would be sent as soon as possible to take care of business and silence the five-shot killer once and forever.

Gretchen knew the man from Siberia had come to the Penmoor to kill her, not to kill Withers Singleton. Gretchen was alarmed that she was on the hit list of such a skilled assassin. She assumed the attempt on her life was linked in some way with the murder of her former boss, Arthur

Sprungli. Even though the man who had had come after her in Colorado was now in custody and would probably die before he could be brought to trial, Gretchen was terrified that someone else would be sent to finish the job this man had failed to accomplish.

Gretchen now knew the entire story of Enid Harrison, aka Diane Rimaldi. She'd met and had tea with Enid. Gretchen admired the woman for having had the courage to change her name and disappear, in an attempt to hide from a deranged former husband. Gretchen's life was such that she was not able to disappear. She could not enter any kind of witness protection program. She had a job she loved and was unwilling to give it up. She had a large and complicated family that she adored. Grandchildren were being born, and she was not about to miss being a hands-on grandmother. Her life wouldn't be worth living if she was not able to be around her loved ones.

Likewise, Bailey had a job that was important to him. He had built a reputation in commercial real estate and had many valued contacts around the world. Becoming other people and relocating to hide out from their current lives was completely out of the question for these two. But they were worried and were anxious to know more about the Russian man who had wanted to kill Gretchen.

Neither the FBI nor local law enforcement appeared to be interested in the motives of the mysterious Slav. They had him for the murder of the man who'd shot up the pillows. They also had him for the attempted murder of Withers Singleton. He had entered the room where Withers had just had a massage and pointed his gun at her. All levels of law enforcement were desperately trying to keep him alive. They were certain they knew who had sent him, but they could not touch either the Russian mafia or the Russian government. Motives for the murder and attempted murder didn't seem to interest them. Gretchen's dilemma, that someone else would be sent to finish her off, didn't seem to matter much to anybody but Gretchen and Bailey and their friends.

The third corpse, that arrived from the Penmoor and rested in the county morgue, had been identified as that of Geoffrey McNulty. His body had been found at Seven Falls, the popular tourist attraction on the grounds of the Penmoor Resort. Because McNulty's wallet and cell phone had been found with him when his body was discovered at the base of the observation tower at Seven Falls, there had been no reason to question the identity of the dead man. Because the body had been partially eaten by either bears or mountain lions, it was in terrible shape. The cause of death did not appear to be anything other than a fall from the observation platform. Because there was no indication that the man had died from any kind of foul play, the autopsy had been pushed to the bottom of the list. Dr. Eliot Landers had been preoccupied with the other two more puzzling cases. Given all the circumstances, the ME was leaning towards accident or suicide in the case of McNulty.

Because he was pressed for time, Landers was tempted to do a cursory postmortem on the body of Geoffrey McNulty. The coroner's office had notified McNulty's next of kin, a man whose first name was Baktash and whose last name was unpronounceable. Baktash was listed in McNulty's wallet as the person to notify in case of emergency. It turned out that Baktash was not actually a family member or any kin at all to McNulty, but was in reality his roommate, a man with whom he'd shared a house. Baktash had come to the morgue and identified what remained of the body as that of McNulty. The roommate had appeared appropriately shocked and upset when he'd made the identification. Baktash had almost fainted when he'd viewed the dead body. There was no reason for anyone to question that this corpse was Geoffrey McNulty.

The ME decided to do a postmortem on McNulty, and he ordered routine toxicology studies. Because of the backlog of bodies to autopsy, Landers did not order the more obscure tests he might request if an unattended death seemed to be suspicious. If the post turned up anything that was questionable, Landers would order more laboratory studies done at that time.

When he performed the autopsy, Landers was surprised to discover that McNulty had suffered from terminal liver disease. Wild animals had gone after the liver of the dead body. What the predatory animals had left of the man's liver was such that the Medical Examiner was able to determine that the man's death from cirrhosis would have been imminent. Knowing he was going to die soon, from a chronic medical condition, could be a reason he might have decided to take his own life and throw himself from the observation post at one of the most beautiful places in the state of Colorado. Suffering from terminal liver disease also might cause an incurably ill man to fall from an unsafe spot while he was enjoying some of the last moments of his life. Perhaps it had not been a willful suicide but rather a kind of sinking into death and giving up the fight against an illness that he knew would soon and inevitably take his life. McNulty's death was a low priority, compared to the other more dramatic and high profile deaths of the two men who had attempted to kill.

Eliot Landers didn't know anything about the life of Geoffrey McNulty. If he had known more about the man, he might have been suspicious of the advanced liver disease. If he had known about McNulty's service to his country, Landers might not have believed that this man had killed himself because he'd literally drunk himself to death.

Baktash had called the coroner's office a couple of times, asking when McNulty's body was going to be released for burial. As his closest friend and former roommate, Baktash insisted that he wanted to give Geoffrey McNulty a decent funeral. Landers decided, given all the circumstances surrounding the death, there was no reason not to release the body to Baktash.

Geoffrey McNulty would finally be laid to rest. A body would be buried, and McNulty would be at peace. If the Russians believed the former Soviet soldier was really dead, Gregory Robicheaux would be able to live out the rest of his days in Wyoming without fear that his former lives would come back to haunt him or that his former nemeses, the Russian mafia and the Russian government, were on his trail. It looked as if Afif, Geoffrey McNulty, and Gregory Robicheaux were turning out to be one incredibly lucky man.

Chapter 36

CAMERON RICHARDSON WAS AN EXTRAORDINARY salesman. He was brilliant with computer technology, hardware and software, and he could sell an ice maker to an Eskimo. He had explained to the Penmoor's security team in great detail how his innovative technology worked and how it could be used to keep track of the Penmoor's art. Because the paintings that had been stolen had all disappeared from the subterranean art workroom, Cameron suggested that his techs begin to "chip" the artwork that was in storage and being cleaned or repaired. None of the paintings that hung on the walls in the hallways and meeting rooms of the resort had ever gone missing while on public view. The public had access to these paintings at all times, and no one had stolen or borrowed any of them. The security people at the Penmoor agreed with Cameron that the art in the workroom was the place to start. Art was rotated from public display to the workroom for maintenance and repairs, so eventually all of the artwork would be chipped.

Dolly Madison Wilder's background screening had not turned up anything suspicious. All references had been rechecked and rechecked a second time, and everyone who had been hired to work in the Penmoor's art division had been cleared. It was a dead end and a mystery. Someone who worked at the Penmoor was stealing and then returning the artwork. Dolly and the security team were stumped. They hoped that whoever was taking the art had decided to cease and desist, but they didn't want to count on it.

In addition to placing tracking chips in the artwork, Cameron's technicians trained those who worked with the art on how to use his company's software. If a painting was scheduled to be moved, for whatever reason, the software made it possible for the tracking device to be disabled. By turning off the alarm feature when a painting was being transferred from one place to another or had work being done to it, a computer alert would not be sent. Only when an unauthorized movement of a work of art occurred would an electronic notification be transmitted that something had changed.

The mechanism was sensitive. If a mouse jumped onto the frame of a painting that was resting in its special rack, waiting to be cleaned, and the mouse jiggled the painting's frame just a fraction of an inch, an alarm would be sent. Sensitivity could be adjusted.

It took two days for Cameron's people to instruct the Penmoor's art staff how to chip all the artwork. The curators of the Penmoor's art collection, who worked in the subterranean facility of the resort's main building, were bright. Cameron had been impressed with how easily the staff had grasped the technique for imbedding the chips and how quickly they had mastered the software that tracked each piece of art.

Everyone was excited about how the revolutionary technology allowed the Penmoor's art department to instantly locate each piece of its extensive collection. The next step would be to put tracking chips into each of the paintings that hung on the walls and meeting rooms throughout the resort. Inventories were scrutinized to be sure that no art work was missed.

The staff had practiced how the new system would work. The staff tested the software by intentionally moving paintings around the resort, inside and outside. Everyone, including and perhaps especially Cameron, was delighted to find that the hardware and the software worked perfectly. The software continued to track a work of art that had been moved off-site over a radius of at least twenty-five miles from the underground workroom. Cameron's newest invention was a success. It worked as he had always envisioned it would.

After less than two days, the Penmoor art staff was excited with their new technology and felt prepared to leap on any attempt to remove another painting from the collection.

The bad news was, their inventories revealed that two paintings were currently still missing from the workroom. One of Dolly's personal favorites, *Long Jakes, The Rocky Mountain Man* had been taken down from its wall in the Penmoor Main because the frame was loose and needed to be reglued. The famous painting by Charles Deas had been transferred to the workroom, and the next day, it was gone.

The depiction of the lone hunter on his horse, traversing the Great Plains and Rocky Mountains, was an especially interesting painting because the artist who'd created it had been an ardent advocate for Native Americans and Native American art. Not as well-known as Russell or Remington, Deas had, with his paintings, established the mountain man, the fur trapper of the mid-19th century, as an iconic American character. Deas was a native of Philadelphia. He'd traveled west to find his subjects and spent time living among the Indian tribes, familiarizing himself with their manners and customs.

A man ahead of his time in terms of attempting to showcase American Indian art, Deas returned to New York City in 1848 and tried to rally support to open a gallery dedicated to the work of native Americans. Before he could accomplish this goal, he was declared legally insane. He was committed to New York's Bloomingdale Asylum and institutionalized for the remainder of his life. He felt passionately about native peoples but was denied the opportunity to display and recognize their creative accomplishments.

Another painting by a lesser-known Western artist was also missing. The two paintings had been removed from the workroom before Cameron's chipping process had begun. Everyone hoped that, in time, both works would be returned. Cameron's technicians fine-tuned the tracking software to the specific needs of the Penmoor art collection. The security staff and the art restoration staff were delighted that the collection would be protected in the future. Everyone was thrilled with the results of the project, and they tried not to be too angry or too sad about the theft of the two paintings that had been lost.

Chapter 37

TYLER AND LILLETH HAD LITERALLY BUNDLED their clothes into their suitcases and thrown their suitcases into the car. Lilleth was secretly wishing they were not driving out of town at the beginning of a terrible winter storm. Tyler was wishing the same thing. But neither one wanted to speak up and say to the other that they should reconsider. Their friends had begged them to stay, to delay their car trip home. Having been so determined to leave and having been so openly confident that they could beat the snow to Bayfield, it was difficult to back down and reverse course. They set out on their risky journey, and before they'd left the city limits of Colorado Springs, they knew it had been a mistake.

At least the small SUV they owned had four-wheel drive. Everybody who lived in Colorado had four-wheel drive. The snow, that had been predicted for Monday, had arrived early. Tyler and Lilleth drove through increasingly blinding snow and realized they were not escaping ahead of the storm but were driving directly into the middle of it. They did not make good time on the road. Lilleth finally spoke up and said out loud what she and Tyler were both thinking, "We should turn around and go back to Colorado Springs. This was a bad idea. We should never have left when we knew there was going to be a snow storm. This looks like it could be the storm of the century, and we might end up like the Donner Party."

Tyler cringed when she mentioned the ill-fated group of pioneers who had spent the winter of 1846-47 snowbound in the Sierra Nevada mountain range. The travelers had run out of food, and some very bad things had happened. "You could have gone all week without saying that." He knew Lilleth was right, but road conditions would make it difficult to turn his SUV around and head back to the resort. Visibility was zero. Tyler had been so adamant that they could brave the storm and make it home. "But I think you're right. As soon as I can find a place to turn around, we'll head back to the Penmoor. See if you can call them and reserve a room. It shouldn't be a problem. Plenty of rooms should be available, but it will be very late when we get there. We'll be exhausted, and I don't want to have to argue with a front desk clerk about whether or not we have a reservation."

Lilleth tried to call the Penmoor on her cell phone. Cell service was spotty in the mountains under the best of circumstances. Sometimes, it was possible to make a call, and sometimes it wasn't. Tonight her calls were not going through. She kept trying. As she concentrated on her phone, Tyler was concentrating on the road. Before he could find a safe place to turn the truck around, they hit an icy patch, went into a skid, and came to a stop in a ditch filled with snow. Both were wearing seat belts, so neither one was hurt when their SUV went off the road. Stuck in a snow drift, they definitely were not going anywhere. Tyler belonged to the AAA, but that did him no good at all in his current circumstances. If Lilleth couldn't get a signal on her phone to call the Penmoor, she would not be able to contact the AAA. Lilleth and Tyler were stranded in the middle of nowhere in the mountains of Colorado. The sun was going down. They were in trouble.

The couple had packed their leftovers from the room's mini-fridge. The portions in the resort's restaurants were generous, and Lilleth always had food left over which she brought back to the room. She'd thrown the leftovers into a plastic bag when they were frantically packing their things to leave the hotel. Thank goodness for the days-old servings of meat and desserts. The couple wouldn't starve as they sat in their stranded vehicle and waited for cell phone reception or for a highway patrolman to find them. Realizing they were going to have to spend the night in the truck, they debated the pros and cons of whether or not to leave the engine running or turn it off. They opted to turn it off, although the temperature was dipping lower by the minute. Lilleth and Tyler dug out their warmest clothes from the luggage and donned layers of socks, turtlenecks, and sweaters. It was going to be a long, cold night.

When they woke up the next morning, chilled and cranky, the truck was completely covered with snow. They'd survived the night and had not frozen to death. They couldn't see anything outside the windshield of their truck. Tyler tried to open the driver's side door and realized the snow was now so deep he could not get out of the car. He turned on the windshield wipers which couldn't move the frozen snow. They turned on the engine and set the heater to defrost. Finally, a small opening appeared in the snow that covered the windshield, and they tried to glimpse what was going on outside. They couldn't see a thing. It was a total whiteout.

They wondered if a helicopter flying overhead, should there ever happen to be one, would be able to make out that there was a car in the ditch, completely buried in the white stuff. They decided it would be impossible for anyone to see their gray vehicle covered with snow.

Lilleth dug in their duffle bags to try to find a piece of red clothing so they could mount a "help" flag on top of their car. Tyler climbed into the back of the SUV and freed a tool from the compartment that contained the spare tire. He tied the red shirt to it. He forced his way out of the driver's side door and precariously secured his flag to the roof of the vehicle. He had his fingers crossed that their flag would not be blown away or covered up with snow. Surely someone would be able to see the red shirt flapping in the wind and sooner or later would come to their aid.

Losing track of time and becoming a little desperate, Lilleth and Tyler finished every bite of food they could find. Their sleep the night before had not been restful, and both dozed off while bundled up with layers of clothes, waiting for help to come.

Lilleth woke to the sound of someone tapping. A face appeared beside the passenger door window. When she looked outside and saw the face pressed against the glass, she uttered a short scream of alarm. She had hoped the first face she saw outside her window would be wearing a uniform, the uniform of a Colorado State patrolman who had come to their rescue and would transport them to warmth and safety. But that hoped-for face was not the one Lilleth saw when she woke from her fitful nap. She saw a scary face grinning at her. The mouth on the face was missing most, if not all, of its teeth, and the hair on its head was sticking out in all directions from around the edges of a black knitted toboggan cap.

Lilleth's first inclination was to be afraid, but the toothless man or woman, it was difficult to tell which, kept smiling at her. Or at least she thought it or him or her was smiling at her. Was this the face of a drug dealer who had come to steal their money or to kill them? Or both? Or was the grinning face, as scary as it was, here to help them survive and get back to civilization.

Lilleth immediately woke Tyler who was also startled by the wild eyes of the man or woman at the window. He was shouting something at them, so Tyler opened his window and shouted back at the creature.

"Who are you? Are you here to help us?" Tyler asked the black toboggan.

"I seen yer red shirt flappin'. Then I seen youse stuck in the ditch. You need help, and I am here to help you."

"Who are you?"

"Don't matter who I am. I'm gonna save youse lives and get you to a safe place."

Lilleth didn't trust the eyes or the face, and she tugged at Tyler's arm as a warning. But Tyler was desperate at this point, and he didn't think they could avoid an interaction with this wild-eyed person. The voice was low and sounded more like a man's voice, so Tyler began to think of their potential rescuer as a "he."

"Do you have a snow plow or can you bring a tow truck? We may need a helicopter to come and get us out of this mess."

"No copter gonna be able to find you here, or land anywhere abouts, even if it could see you and your red flag. You gotta come with me. I have a place where you won't freeze to death."

Lillleth did not want to go anywhere with this guy. He gave off all the wrong vibes. She was a psychotherapist and knew people. Her instincts told her to avoid this person at all costs. But here she was, stuck in the middle of nowhere in the middle of a snow drift. She really had no choice other than to stay where she was and freeze to death. None of her options were good ones.

The man helped clear the snow away from the doors so they could climb out. Before she even got out of the Bronco, Lilleth could smell him. He was not a person who bathed frequently, if at all. Lilleth's stomach turned. She wanted to stay inside her own vehicle. Once they stood outside their truck with the snow up to their thighs, they could see that the toothless man was wearing cross country skis. The skis were ancient and in terrible condition, but the man didn't seem to mind. He moved easily, even expertly, through the snow, balancing with his poles. Tyler stared at the skis with undisguised envy. The man told them to follow him.

"Where are you taking us?" Lilleth spoke up for the first time.

"Someplace dry where you'll be out of the storm."

Lilleth felt sick to her stomach as she held on to Tyler's hand and climbed out of the ditch. They followed the man that Lilleth knew was up to no good. Every brain cell she had was screaming in protest as she tromped through the snow. Their progress was incredibly labored and slow. Snow was still pouring down from the sky, and the depth of the drifts made it almost nearly impossible to put one foot in front of another. It seemed as if they trudged on for hours. Lilleth could feel her body's core temperature going down with every step.

Finally they arrived at the entrance to a cave. Was this the safe and dry place their toothless benefactor had in mind? Tyler had heard about the caves in the mountains of southern Colorado, caves where those who sold marijuana kept their cash profits. Because of some discrepancies between the federal and state laws about the sale of marijuana, those who raised and sold weed were in some kind of a strange and tricky legal limbo, a place that had to do with the profits they made from their cannabis stores. They were allowed to pay their employees and their rent, but they could not take their profits.

Tyler hadn't paid much attention to the details of this legal conundrum, but he suspected he and Lilleth had just arrived right in the middle of some of that trouble.

"Cave's full a money. Can't use the cash I've made sellin' mah weed. Keepin' it here safe 'til the lawyers and the feds can get their asses sorted out. It's a mess. I cun pay my help, and I cun harvest my crops. But I can't use no profits I've made. Crazy. Goes against all the principles a private enterprise, far as I'm concerned. Course I don't pay it all no mind. I spend whatever I want to a my profits."

Lilleth was beyond trying to figure out what the man was talking about. She just wanted to lie down and rest. They collapsed on the floor when they got inside the cave and out of the storm. At least it was drier. Whether or not it was safe was yet to be determined.

Apparently, the man with no teeth lived here, at least some of the time. There was a small camp stove for warmth and some canisters of fuel. There was no electricity in the cave, and it was bitterly cold unless one stayed close to the camp stove. Lilleth was thirsty, and when she spied a case of bottled water, she reached out to take one from the carton of 36 small bottles. The man slapped her hand with one of his ski poles. It stung, and a welt began to swell where he had hit her. Lilleth felt even sicker. She knew they were in for terrible trouble now.

"Gonna have to buy the water off a me. Can't go takin' whatever you want from my place. I'm the boss here, and you gotta do what I tell ya. Nothin's free in this world, and you got a fancy car down there in the ditch. You gonna pay me every cent you've got on yous before I let you leave here."

Lilleth looked at Tyler who had been listening carefully to everything the crazy guy was saying. Tyler though he and Lilleth could take him down. Toothless would underestimate how strong and athletic Lilleth was. Toothless would see her as a woman, not as a force to be reckoned with. Tyler was old, and he was bent over with arthritis. But he was strong, and he was also athletic. They'd have to do it soon. Neither Tyler nor Lilleth was willing to spend the night in a cave with this dangerous looney. Lilleth saw a rope and a shovel in the corner of the cave. She also saw boxes and boxes of what she assumed was money. All the money in the world did them no good. The only thing that mattered now was getting out of here and finding help.

Lilleth signaled to Tyler that she was going for the shovel. She talked as she stood up and began to walk around the cave. "What do you mean we're going to have to pay to get a bottle of water? I thought you were a Good Samaritan and wanted to help save our lives." At the exact moment she said the word "lives," she picked up the shovel, and in one fluid movement, swung it at the toothless head. The crack was loud and sounded deadly. That couldn't be helped now. Lilleth kept swinging until Tyler was beside her with the rope. They secured their adversary, and Tyler stripped him of the skis attached to his feet.

Lilleth grabbed four bottles of water and threw them into her backpack. Tyler strapped the skis onto his boots. He was a ski instructor and loved to ski. He could ski anywhere, and he could ski on any kind of skis. As a young man, he'd learned on the long wooden skis that were almost impossible to turn, and everything else since then had been a piece of cake for this pro. Within two minutes they were ready to leave. Lilleth stood on the backs of the cross country skis that Tyler had secured to his feet, and they set off across the frozen snow. She held tightly to Tyler's waist. Lilleth had learned to cross country ski when she was a toddler and barely able to walk. She had stood behind her older brother and hung on to him for dear life as they'd sailed across the snow-covered fields of their family farm. She was also an expert skier, so staying on the skis and holding on to Tyler who held the poles was just another variation on the sport for both of them. They were on their way.

Tyler thought there was a house down the road. It would have been too far for them to walk to the house from their car in a snow storm, but he felt as if they could get there now that they had the skis. They were desperate to reach the house before it was completely dark.

In spite of their advanced skiing skills, it was a difficult trip. Tyler's sense of direction was almost flawless, but he had not remembered exactly where the house was located. They were in the middle of a storm, and his estimate was off. Eventually they found the cabin he'd been looking for. It was after midnight when they stumbled onto the porch and banged and banged on the front door. No one was home, but once they were inside, they thought the place showed signs of recent occupancy. Joy surged through Lilleth's heart when she saw the old-fashioned black telephone that was hard-wired to the wall. She lifted the heavy receiver and heard a dial tone. Nothing had ever sounded as sweet to her ears as the dial tone did that night. She put her fingers in the holes of the rotary dial and called 911. She almost cried when the voice on the other end of the land line said, "This is 911. What is your emergency?"

Chapter 38

LILLETH AND TYLER WERE TAKEN TO THE CLOSEST highway patrol barracks for questioning. They were cold and hungry and needed showers, but law enforcement demanded to know all about the man whose skis they'd borrowed. Lilleth and Tyler were placed in separate interview rooms, and they were more than a little annoyed that the state police seemed to regard them as would-be criminals. The couple saw themselves as the victims of a madman, a man who lived in a drug cave. What did these official people not understand about what had happened to them?

Because of the storm, no one was able to reach the cave where they said the toothless cross country skier had led them. It might be days before a way could be cleared to reach the cave that was full of drug money and contained the man Lilleth had attacked with a shovel. Would they be held until someone was able to investigate either the suspicious cave or the condition of the suspicious man they'd tied up and left for dead? What if he did die? What if he froze to death?

The fact that their car had gone off the road in the snow storm and ended up stuck in a ditch was obvious to all and verifiable. But that was the only part of their story that the state police seemed to believe. Everything that had happened after that sounded outlandish and suspicious, even to Lilleth and Tyler and even though they knew they were telling their true story. What if the man died because of the blows inflicted by a shovel? It was only their word that the man had threatened them. It was only their word that Lilleth's shovel defense was self-defense. Depending on when emergency crews could reach him, he might starve to death, all tied up with rope on the floor of a cave.

They were questioned about why they had gone with "the madman" in the first place? He was only one person, and they were two. Had they followed him to the cave under duress? They had not. Both Tyler and Lilleth admitted they'd been frightened and angry, as well as hungry and dehydrated, by the time they'd reached the cave full of money. Maybe they had been confused? The story about both of them being able to ski together on one pair of skis sounded preposterous to the law enforcement people. Tyler asked if he needed to call a lawyer. Tyler was losing his patience.

Lilleth finally decided to beg. She told the state policewoman who was questioning her that they had been foolish to begin their drive to Bayfield in the snow. She told her they'd just spent a week at the Penmoor resort with friends. She almost cried when she said how hungry she was. Most of the time, she tried to be healthy and eat a vegan diet, or at least a vegetarian diet. But right now, she would kill for an enormous greasy double cheeseburger and a large order of French fries. The officer who was questioning Lilleth took pity on her and said she would get the cheeseburger as soon as the roads opened up enough to reach a fast food place.

After hours of questioning, the law enforcement people decided Lilleth Dubois and Tyler Merriman were not criminals. But they insisted that "Toothless" and his cave full of money had to be found before the couple would be released. Lilleth fell asleep on three chairs pushed together. Tyler was too upset to sleep and stomped around the police barracks, making a lot of noise. His cell phone still would not work. He kept asking to use the land line telephone. He insisted that he was entitled to a phone call. The state police told him once again that he hadn't been arrested.

Finally, someone told Tyler he could use the phone. He called the Penmoor and asked for J.D.'s room. Besides the fact that Olivia and J.D.'s suite had become reunion central for the group, J.D. was a lawyer and had once been a prosecutor in Oklahoma. He would be able to tell his friends what to do. The phone rang and rang. Tyler was beside himself that no one picked up the phone. The call went to voice mail. Tyler left a long message for J.D. and hoped against hope that somebody would notice the blinking light on the phone beside the bed.

Two men covered with snow came through the front door of the police barracks. There was a lot of gesturing and talking among the few officers who were present. Tyler had lost one of his hearing aids in the events of the past couple of days, so he couldn't hear what the men were saying.

An officer approached Tyler to tell him what was going on. "Good news for you, Mr. Merriman. We have found your cave, and we have found your Mr. Toothless. I probably shouldn't tell you this, but your girlfriend has accomplished what we've been trying to do for years. She found and subdued a drug dealer, a very bad guy who has eluded us for a long time. We had begun to think he didn't really exist. He was like a ghost who came and went at will. We don't even know his real name, but we call him 'Mountain Man.' We think he lives in that cave where he took you. Anyway, thanks to Ms. Dubois, 'Mountain Man' is now in custody."

"So I take it he's still alive."

"Oh, yes, he's alive all right. And he's not going anywhere any time soon. Lucky for you he didn't die. Actually, if he had died, we would have been hard pressed about whether to charge Ms. Dubois with murder or give her a medal. This is one especially bad dude. In addition to major drug and money laundering transgressions, he has broken into countless houses, gas stations, liquor stores, grocery stores, and other places. He steals whatever he needs to live. We have your statements. You are Colorado residents, so we know where to find you. I doubt we will need to have you testify in court. We have this guy on video, and we have his fingerprints all over this part of the state." The state policeman paused. "I guess we owe you guys a debt of gratitude, really. I know you understand why we had to hold you."

Tyler was still angry about being detained like a criminal, but he was more relieved that they were free to go.

"We towed your car out of the ditch, and it's sitting right out front. The roads have been plowed back to Colorado Springs but not south and west of here. I suggest you go back to the Penmoor and spend more time with your friends. Wait until all the roads are cleared before you head out again for Bayfield."

Lilleth and Tyler could not get out of the police barracks fast enough. They'd already decided to return to the Penmoor. They could wait a few days to get Lilleth's dog from the doggie hotel. Tyler had already missed his doctor's appointment. He was hoping the doctor had realized that none of his patients would be able to keep their appointments in the middle of a snow storm. The procedure could be rescheduled. Tyler kept asking himself why he had been so stubborn.

With the roads cleared, it took less than two hours to reach Colorado Springs. All Lilleth wanted to think about was having a long, hot shower. Tyler was hungry. The cheeseburgers had been consumed hours earlier. They stopped for breakfast at a roadside diner, just outside Colorado Springs. Lilleth's cell phone was working now, and she talked to the concierge at the Penmoor West and to the owner of the luxury kennel where she'd left her dog. Tyler and Lilleth ordered an enormous amount of food at the diner and ate it all. Buttermilk pancakes and sausage, bacon and eggs, waffles, fried ham and hash browns ... all gone in minutes.

They were pulling into the parking lot of the Penmoor, which had thankfully been plowed, when Lilleth's phone rang. It was Olivia, and she wanted to know if Lilleth and Tyler were all right. She'd just listened to the message Tyler had left on their voice mail. Olivia was tremendously thankful to know they were no longer being held by the authorities. Everyone was relieved and delighted that Tyler and Lilleth were returning. Dinner reservations were being made at the Saloon for that evening.

The two bedraggled travelers could not wait to step into the shower and then collapse on the bed in their room at the Penmoor. They gathered their backpacks and duffle bags stuffed with dirty clothes. Surely they could find something that didn't need to be washed. Lilleth was in her own world as she walked toward cleanliness and rest. Tyler was lost in his thoughts.

Tyler had his eye on the man with a cane and watched him closely as he made his way across the parking lot. The man was headed in the direction of the Penmoor. Tyler thought he looked vaguely familiar. Hadn't they seen this man when they'd had their tour of the subterranean art facility with Dolly Wilder? He'd not been using a cane at the time. He'd had a mop in his hands, and Tyler had thought to himself that the guy was not a terribly efficient cleaner. The man who was pushing the mop around had seemed to be killing time to collect a paycheck rather than actually trying to scrub the floor. Tyler watched as the man came closer. Tyler was an athlete, and during his life, he had driven himself hard in several extreme sports. As a consequence, he'd sustained numerous injuries over the years, and he had occasionally been forced to temporarily use a cane. Tyler knew how to use a cane, and this man who didn't know how to use a mop, also didn't know how to use a cane. He didn't need a cane, and he was faking it. Why would anyone use a cane if they didn't need one? Using a cane was an annoyance. It was always in the way, always falling over wherever one propped it up.

Tyler turned to Lilleth, "Isn't that guy with the cane someone we saw at the underground art place … when we were with Dolly?"

Lilleth didn't remember the man, and she'd never used a cane. She was not suspicious. "I don't remember him."

"Something about this guy isn't right. I'm going to talk to him."

"Oh, Tyler, don't. I just want to get into our room and take a shower and go to sleep. Don't engage this guy. You aren't even sure he works at the Penmoor."

But Tyler was on a mission, and he headed straight for the suspicious cane user. He approached the man. "Excuse me. Don't you work at the Penmoor? In the art department?" The ordinary-looking fellow was startled at being accosted. He looked at Tyler with fear in his eyes and began to run. He hung on to his cane, the one he definitely didn't need. Tyler's knee was shot, so his running skills were challenged. But Lilleth's were not. She didn't know why Tyler wanted this man who didn't need a cane, but she took off after him. He'd not made it out of the parking lot before Lilleth had tackled him and was sitting on top of him.

"Now we've got him. What are you going to do with him?" Lilleth asked Tyler.

Tyler knew there was something fishy about the cane. He tried to take it from the man who lay on the pavement underneath Lilleth. The man held his cane in a death grip. This made Tyler more determined than ever to inspect the cane. It seemed to Tyler that this cane was thicker than most. Looking at the cane from every angle, Tyler saw that the tip of the cane looked odd. It slipped off more easily than it should when Tyler pulled on it. Then he realized what he was holding in his hands. The cane was indeed unusually thick, and it had a hollow space inside. There was something tightly rolled up in the cane's secret compartment. Tyler immediately knew what it was and told Lilleth to call 911. "We have an art thief here. After you've reached the police, call Dolly Wilder."

Tyler extracted the painting from the hollow space inside the cane. He spread it out over cane man's legs. He remembered the painting from the tour Dolly had given the group. It was by Charles Deas. The man with the cane must have been intending to return the painting. Tyler couldn't remember exactly what the painting was called, but he thought it was titled something like *Mountain Man*. He grinned at Lilleth. "It looks like you've caught yourself a couple of 'Mountain Men' in the past few days."

Lilleth looked at the painting but had not remembered its name. Slightly puzzled by Tyler's reference, she remained sitting on the art thief and swatted him with his cane whenever he moved. Lilleth was not a woman who put up with foolishness.

Dolly pulled on her boots, left the warmth of the Penmoor, and tromped through the snow. She arrived before the security people did. She laughed at the scene she found at the edge of the parking lot. When she saw the painting that had been rolled up inside the cane, she gasped. She threw her arms around Tyler, and then she threw her arms around Lilleth. The mystery had been solved, and the perpetrator had been caught. It was a happy day.

Chapter 39

The man who didn't know how use a cane to walk with but who had used it to smuggle art work in and out of the Penmoor resort, said his name was Machs Sobril. He pronounced his first name like "Max." He was willing to give his name, whether or not it was his real one. Otherwise, he wasn't talking. He had been part of the janitorial staff that worked in the underground art workshop at the Penmoor. Whenever his references had been reviewed, they had always checked out. Cleaning people were not vetted as rigorously as others who worked with the art, and Dolly Wilder understood that this was a weakness in the Penmoor's security system. She had spoken up about the issue and had asked for more security checks of the janitorial staff.

Machs had decided to reveal nothing about himself. A test of his DNA showed he was probably from Gibraltar, an unusual spot to call one's home. His references were from various parts of the United States. For a low-level, unskilled worker to have traveled around the country like Machs' references indicated he had, should have raised a red flag. When his references were investigated in depth, every one of them was found to be bogus.

The only thing law enforcement could find was a vague reference to a similar crime perpetrated at the Philadelphia Museum of Art a couple of years earlier. Calls to the museum in Pennsylvania yielded mostly confusion and "nobody really knows anything about this guy" answers. They said a man from Gibraltar who'd worked as a security guard had just disappeared one day. No museum likes to admit, let alone advertise, that they have had security breaches and art stolen. It was a puzzle. It would take days and weeks to sort things out, and the Penmoor accepted that they would never learn the whole story.

What they did know was that Machs was an art forger — a very, very good one. The police had gone to Machs' house and discovered the other missing painting that had disappeared from the Penmoor's collection. Machs was copying the art, and his copies were brilliantly done. He borrowed the originals and copied the art work. Then he returned the originals and probably sold the forgeries. Or, maybe it had happened the other way around. Maybe he had returned the copies and sold the originals. It seemed it was almost impossible to tell.

During the ensuing weeks, top Western art experts were called to Colorado Springs. They checked the age of the pigments and the canvases and all the rest of it. These specialists had a difficult time saying beyond a shadow of a doubt, even with the best technology available to them, which paintings were the originals and which ones were the copies. It was uncanny. They thought they had recovered the originals, but even the best of the best of the authenticators were not one-hundred-percent certain. Machs was a genius at the painting part of what he did. He was also very good at smuggling the art. He was not as adept at using a cane, and no one knew what he did with his forgeries ... if they were indeed forgeries. No one knew how long Machs Sobril had been in the art forgery business. No one knew where Machs Sobril had hidden his ill-gotten gains.

Because Machs' crimes were non-violent and he had not harmed anyone, except financially, a judge allowed him to post bail and stay in his home until the prosecutor brought formal charges and his trial was scheduled. This turned out to be a horrible mistake on the part of the judge, who had not viewed Machs as a flight risk. As soon as he was out of jail, Machs disappeared completely. It happened so quickly and with such a little bit of fuss, it seemed he must have done this before. Sobril was in the wind ... again.

The good news was that the Penmoor thought it had its masterpieces back. They were treated as such and chipped and added to the tracking data base. The Machs of the future would have a much more difficult time borrowing, or stealing, any art from the Penmoor collection. Cameron had succeeded in proving the value of his tracking device. This newest business venture would make him even more millions.

Dolly Madison Wilder had not rescued the Gilbert Stuart. And she had not rescued the Charles Deas. But this smart volunteer docent had persevered. Her star amateur art enthusiasts had delivered the art thief to her feet, and the art work had been recovered. That a foolish judge had allowed Machs to go free was terribly upsetting, but the Penmoor would never again be a victim of someone like Machs. They would know where each and every one of the pieces in their huge collection was at any hour of the day, 365 days of the year.

Dolly prevailed on the management of the Penmoor to comp three days' worth of rooms for each of the couples in the reunion group. They were delighted with this generous gift. They had grown fond of Dolly, and she'd agreed to have dinner with them at the Saloon that night. They would eat well and drink more of the Malbec, among other libations.

Dolly had become a friend for life. Cameron paid for dinner again. He was riding high. They would all be leaving Colorado Springs the day after tomorrow. It had been a wild gallop in the Colorado Mountains for this group of old friends.

Chapter 40

On their last day in Colorado Springs, someone from the FBI called Gretchen and asked if they could come to the Penmoor and speak with her about the incident at the spa. Gretchen was torn between wanting to find out everything that had happened on that terrible day and wanting to put it all behind her and forget it had ever happened. She agreed, of course, to talk to the FBI, but she dreaded what they would have to say to her.

One female special agent and one male special agent came to Gretchen's hotel room. The first thing they told her was that the killer, who had been taken down by Sidney Richardson, arrested, and incarcerated in the El Paso County jail, was dead. He had been murdered in his jail cell. The FBI pointed out that the death had not been unexpected. The Sheriff's department had done what they could to keep the man alive, hoping they could convince him to talk. But when the Russians were involved, someone was always sent to "take care of things." This meant making sure that whoever had been arrested was silenced and did not last long enough in custody to give the authorities any information. The still unnamed Slav had been assassinated by means of a homemade knife. His throat had been cut.

The FBI agents expressed their disappointment that they had not been able to successfully grill the man who was so accomplished with the five-shot kill. But they'd learned from past experience not to get their hopes up with felons who worked for the Russian government or for the Russian mob. The life expectancies of these men and women, once caught, were known to be extremely short.

The good news was that they had learned a few things from him before he died. A federal informant had been placed in the county jail cell with the mysterious prisoner. The informant was Russian-born and spoke fluent Russian. He was adept at getting his jail cell roommates to talk. The informant had said all the right things to the Siberian Slav and had never asked the shooter to reveal his name. This built trust with his cellmate, and the Slav in turn, had opened up and told the informant his story about why he had tried to kill Gretchen MacDermott.

As some of the investigators had suspected, the attempted murder had been about revenge. The unknown shooter in custody told the informant that his first cousin Alexi, another Russian of questionable reputation, had died in Bar Harbor, Maine the previous fall. The two cousins, in spite of the differences in their ages, had been close, closer than brothers.

In the old days, before the fall of the Soviet Union, thousands who lived in Siberia died each year because the brutal Communist regime chose not to allow its citizens to earn enough wages to keep themselves warm or feed themselves. The five-shot killer's parents and Alexi's family had died during one particularly devastating winter. The only two remaining members of their families were left to fend for themselves. Alexi was fifteen years older than his young cousin, and he raised and cared for the child who had been orphaned at age three. Alexi had been father, mother, and everything else to the boy. The boy would do anything for Alexi.

The previous year, Alexi had traveled to the United States to take out Gretchen MacDermott. Years earlier, when she'd worked for a Swiss Bank, Gretchen had seen Alexi's face. Even though Gretchen had not worked at the Zurich bank for more than a decade, anyone and everyone who had ever dealt with a certain right-hand-man of Russia's president and his money was being silenced. Those who knew the secrets about where the money had been hidden were now being eliminated one by one. Gretchen was on the list of those who were believed to know these secrets. She had to go.

Alexi was the link to Vladimir Putin. He had met and worked with Arnold Sprungli and with Gretchen to disperse huge amounts of Russian oil money to a variety of secret bank accounts around the world. At the time, the accounts and transactions had been as secure, anonymous, and cloaked in privacy as the safeguards of the day could guarantee. But computer technology had advanced in the ensuing ten years. Now that computer hacking had become a blood sport, those accounts, that had once been so obscured, could be traced back to the Russian president.

The money had originally belonged to the Russian government, that is, to the Russian people. Vast sums of oil revenue had been confiscated by the country's president and transferred to his private accounts. A number of Swiss banks had helped with these money transfers. What had been considered fool-proof security ten years earlier was now obsolete. Past secrets were now vulnerable because of advancing technology and improved access to all kinds of computerized information, including bank accounts. Security had not kept up with the ability of hackers to expose everything about everybody.

In an effort to hide the fact that he had stolen money from his people, the Russian president had decided to eliminate anyone who could possibly know where his massive fortunes were stashed.

Gretchen and Arnold Sprungli had personally dealt with Putin's man, Alexi. Gretchen remembered him, and although she'd never been certain of his real name, she had recognized Alexi in the parking lot of the Inastou Lodge a year earlier in Maine. Although Alexi was not primarily an assassin, he had been assigned to clean things up. Gretchen MacDermott was his target. Because he spoke good English, his controllers had agreed that Alexi might not stand out in Bar Harbor. He had followed her when she'd gone on her vacation to Maine. Alexi had mistakenly thought that killing the unsuspecting and unarmed Gretchen would be an easy hit. He was determined to strike while she was vulnerable, relaxing at a remote resort with her group of friends. He would shoot her, and no one would ever know who had been responsible for her murder.

Unfortunately, things had not worked out the way Alexi intended. He'd waited for Gretchen in the woods at the edge of the parking lot of the Inastou Lodge, ten miles outside the town of Bar Harbor. It was Alexi's bad luck that a young Russian woman, who had been trained as a Russian spy, happened to see him lurking in the woods near the Inastou and recognized him. Elena Petrovich knew Alexi was former KGB, and she thought he had come for her.

Elena was a post-Soviet Russian agent who'd been sent to the United States to gather information and cause trouble. When she fell in love with her university professor, Darryl Harcomb, she'd decided she wanted to work in academia and spend the rest of her life with Darryl. She'd naively told her Russian handlers that she was through being their spy. She just wanted to be left alone to be happy with Darryl. She had to have realized the Russians would not just let her walk away from them because she was in love.

Elena had recognized Alexi when he was prowling around the parking lot at the Inastou. She thought her time of reckoning had come, and she was determined to take Alexi out first, before he could kill her. Alexi and Elena had engaged in a loud and heated argument in the parking lot. They were seen and overheard by other guests at the Inastou. Trained in the martial arts, Elena was able to maneuver Alexi into the woods, and she attacked him there. In the ensuing skirmish, Alexi's gun had gone off several times, and he had died. He had come to Bar Harbor for Gretchen MacDermott, not for Elena Petrovich, but his own gun had killed him in a struggle with the wrong woman.

The five-shot killer was Alexi's younger cousin. Devoted to Alexi, the assassin was furious that his cousin had died pursuing Gretchen MacDermott. Although his controllers in Moscow had objected, the assassin had insisted on going after Gretchen. Putin's powers-that-be had told him she wasn't worth it. The Slav was one of their best, one of their most highly-trained killers. The Russians did not want to send him to the United States or waste him on someone as unimportant as Gretchen. Even if she talked, who would believe her?

It had been necessary to kill Sprungli because he really did know too much. Now that Sprungli had been eliminated, the Russians decided that Gretchen had been merely an underling at the Swiss bank. They had reassessed the situation and did not now believe it was necessary to kill Gretchen, Sprungli's assistant. They especially did not want Alexi's cousin to go after her. He was emotionally involved in the hit that had now been deemed unnecessary. It had become personal for Alexi's cousin. Loss of objectivity was the best way to screw up any mission.

But the Slav was determined to avenge his cousin, and he'd set out to kill the woman he felt was ultimately responsible for Alexi's death. It had been a disaster from beginning to end. The feather shooter, whoever that idiot had been, had reached what was supposed to have been Gretchen's massage room ahead of him. To compound the confusion, the room that had Gretchen's name posted outside the door had actually been occupied by someone other than Gretchen.

Another unknown woman had attacked the Slav with a lamp and almost killed him. He was one of the world's premier assassins. How was it possible that he'd been so badly hurt by a woman wielding a lamp? *That* was humiliating! He was arrested and was being held in the El Paso County Jail. Just like every human being who has a story to tell, the Slav was eager to talk about all of this with somebody. He knew he could not talk to the authorities. He would never tell them anything, but he decided he could trust and tell all to his fellow prisoner, a man from the Rodina.

The two FBI agents were happy to pass along the news to Gretchen that the man who had come after her to kill her at the Penmoor Resort's spa was dead. Because of what he had said to his cell mate, they did not think Gretchen was at risk from any further assassination attempts. The Russians had already lost two operatives trying to kill Gretchen. The FBI said they doubted the Russian government would waste another killer on her. Gretchen hoped they were right.

When Gretchen shared all of this information with her friends, she summed it up perfectly. "The man who tried to kill me, didn't really want to kill me at all. He wanted to kill his ex-wife. He found me by mistake. Likewise, the two men who were in Withers Singleton's massage room weren't really after Withers. The man who was in that room and shot the pillows, died there. The man who shot the pillow killer five times was downed by Sidney wielding the lamp. Neither one of those men were in that room to kill Withers. My name was on the door, and they were, in fact, both there to kill me."

An unexpected package arrived at the Carpenter's hotel room door the night before they checked out of the Penmoor. The box was large and wrapped like a gift with a wide blue satin ribbon. Elizabeth immediately knew what was inside, something she thought she would never see again. Richard couldn't wait for her to open the box. He had no idea what it could be.

She pushed the heavy gold tissue paper aside, and there, in all of it glory, was Elizabeth's leather coat. She took it out of the box and held it up in front of her. It looked and smelled like brand new leather. Somebody had done a rush job and had spent a great deal of money to clean up this old but much-loved garment. The lining had been replaced with beautiful silk fabric that looked like a Hermes scarf. The original lining had been torn in quite a few places, and even when it had been new, it had never been as nice as this replacement lining. Elizabeth guessed that Elle, their concierge, had been responsible for having the coat rehabilitated and returned to her. Elizabeth ran her hands across the soft leather, thankful to have her coat back.

The Camp Shoemaker group of friends had survived another reunion. They had triumphed over adversity and danger one more time. As they went their separate ways, some hoped that next year they might finally succeed in having a vacation that was relaxing and drama-free. Others wondered if they really wanted a get together without excitement. Would they be bored?

Epilogue

The snow had been cleared from the roads. Enough of it had disappeared from runways that planes had begun to fly again. It was time for the group of friends to bid each other goodbye until next year. Every year, when they disbursed, they wondered if they would all be alive and healthy enough to get together again. Their friendships sustained them, and with every year that passed, their memories, old and new, became more precious.

As they made plans to meet again in a year, none of them could know that a world-wide pandemic would ravage the United States and every other country in the world. They could not know that a terrible virus would send a plague into every city and town on earth as it found its way from an as-yet-unheard-of-place in China called Wuhan. They could not know that they, along with billions of others, would be quarantined inside their houses for weeks and months. They could not envision a world in which they would not be able to go to the beach or to a restaurant for a meal and would have to wear a mask to go to the grocery store.

No one had a crystal ball. They only knew that they loved each other and valued their time together. Each one of these elderly people was focused on maintaining his or her individual health and well-being, hoping to be able to make the trip the following year. Disaster lurked ... whether it was bats or pangolins or both ... or just a screw up in a Level 4 Laboratory in a far-away land. They said goodbye to their friends in October and hoped for the best.

WHEN DID I GROW OLD?

When did I grow old?
    It is now so still around me.
    When did all the noise turn to quiet?
    The cacophony of busyness that engulfed me
        for so many years, has subsided.

When did I grow old?
    Did it happen slowly as the years passed by?
    Did it happen as I filled my time with immediacy ...
        moving from one crisis to the next?
    Did it happen all of a sudden when I found I had to use
        a cane to get up and down the steps?

When did I grow old?
    Did I fill those years that passed with goodness and giving
        and love?
    Did I spend too many days in anger and hoping for retaliation
        for things in life that didn't go my way?
    Did I spend too many hours organizing and cleaning and
        worrying about my material possessions?
    How much time did I spend shopping? Sorting out
        my closet?

When did I grow old?
    Was it when I learned that I was deaf in one ear
        and there was no help for that?
    Was it when I realized there were so few days ahead
        and so many already gone?
    Was it when I accepted that I would die?

When did I grow old?
    Was it a gradual process as the hairs on my head
        one by one turned white?
    Or did it happen overnight? And what night was that?
    Was it when I became a grandmother?

When did I grow old?
    Did I spend this precious time I have been given
    To make a difference?
    To make the world a better place?

When did I grow old?
    Is it today when I know that however this life was spent,
        it cannot be respent?
    It was what it was ...
    Full of imperfections and mistakes and trying hard
        and often struggling and falling short
    And full of joy and good luck.

When did I grow old?
I just don't know.
Or, maybe I'm not old yet.

MTT 5-7-2014

Acknowledgments

Heartfelt thanks to my readers and editors. I couldn't have done this without you. Thank you to my amazingly talented artistic team that developed the memorable cover, the photographer who always makes me look good, and Open Heart Designs. Thank you to friends and fans who have encouraged me to continue writing.

About the Author

A *former actress and singer*, **Henrietta Alten West** *has lived all over the United States and has traveled all over the world. She writes poetry, songs (words and music), screenplays, historical fiction, spy thrillers, books for young people, and mysteries. She always wanted to be Nancy Drew but ended up being Carolyn Keene.*

More Books By
Henrietta Alten West

I Have A Photograph

*Book #1 in the
The Reunion
Chronicles Mysteries*

*Available online
everywhere books are sold.*

Released 2019, 277 pages
Hardcover ISBN: 9781953082947
Paperback ISBN: 9781953082930
ebook ISBN: 9781953082923

Coming Soon!
When Times Get Rough
Book #3 in the The Reunion Chronicles Mysteries